HEROES OF AN UNKNOWN WORLD

HEROES OF AN UNKNOWN WORLD

THE FINAL LIMINAL NOVEL

AYIZE
JAMA-EVERETT

Small Beer Press
Easthampton, MA

Heroes of an Unknown World copyright © 2022 by Ayize Jama-Everett (ayizejamaeverett.com).
All rights reserved.

Small Beer Press
150 Pleasant Street, #306
Easthampton, MA 01027
smallbeerpress.com
weightlessbooks.com
bookmoonbooks.com
info@smallbeerpress.com

Distributed to the trade by Consortium.

LCCN: 2022932119

First edition 1 2 3 4 5 6 7 8 9

Text set in Minion 12 pt.

This book was printed on 30% PCW recycled paper by the Versa Press, East Peoria, IL.
Cover illustration by David Brame.

For Auntie Shukuru,
I owe a debt I'll never be able to repay.

In Memory of Ibrahim Farajaje-Jones/Big Boops/El Nino,
There's not a day that goes by . . .

In memory of Andrew Vachss,
My recruiting officer into the only holy war worthy of the name.
Never has someone impacted my life so much with one
lunchtime conversation.

Part One

The wind is still. It only whispers nonsense then shouts. We live in motion, the Children of the Wind, the souls it doesn't need but has abundant access to. We are one, all the Children of Forever, forgotten and always remembering. You've seen us, forgotten us, called on us to keep your secrets, and banished us with the precious messages you wish to forget. Some of us, like me, were once like you; human, made of flesh and substance, not still but oh so slow moving. You may remember me, as I remember what your world once was. When you can see me, you call me A.C. I am a Child of the Wind. But now the wind is still.

Do you remember the Liminals? Taggert, the broken healer? His is the closest to a human tale, so his life you may remember. Servant to Nordeen, the petulant ghost of the Liminals, grandfather and assassin to the younger generation. It was Taggert who broke free of Nordeen to rescue his love, Yasmine, and her daughter, their daughter, Tamara, from a life of shadow work and death. He only partially succeeded. In Taggert's world, Yasmine died. But he saved Tamara from the breaker of bone and mind. For a moment, Taggert had peace.

Can you recall the Animal totem Liminal, Prentis? The adopted daughter of Taggert. For her, he defied time, space, and a God. To save the girl he even broke with the Liminal acolyte of the God of connections, Samantha, who brings the gift of vision to other worlds with the merest touch. He even managed to convince Mico to travel back in time with him to aid the girl.

From Mico L'overture, we all expected more. His God, the underground tuber that grew for a millennium before the first dinosaur egg was hatched—the one the desert dwellers tried to call Manna—chose L'overture as its vassal of connections in the world of flesh. His was the chance to steward a new age of connections between man, God, and beast. Mico's allies, formed in his time as the DJ Jah Puba—an adopted father Munji and the smuggler queen Fatima—were primed to form a trinity of connections with the body of the Manna Elohim. Instead, he allowed himself to be seduced by Taggert's call to friendship and family, and joined in the mission to save the lost Liminal, Prentis. In doing so, Mico left his timeline vulnerable.

All of creation has its opposite number, and the Liminals are no different. Cosmic tautologies that speak their existence from the maw of nothingness, the Alters wear the forms of beautiful humans to advance the most inhuman of agendas: the joining of all life with entropy. It is not their cause, it is their reason for existence. If they drew breath, entropy would exhale. In the hinterland of their time, Taggert and his Liminal brood, with Mico in tow, ended the semblance of life of their leader, Kothar. The timeline paid the cost, for no Alter ever took a straight line to decay.

From a rearguard stance, Kothar's spawn such as that kind reproduces—Rice Montague, found a way to take over the current time/space. He erased the old world that created Taggert and his circle of Liminals and re-created the norms of day, diminishing the power of the Manna and by extension Mico. He's chosen Baron, Taggert's brother, a warped version of Yasmine, Tamara's mother, and a thoroughly corrupted Samantha to be the figureheads of their global aesthetic reach. And somewhere in the shadows of this new world, Nordeen, who shows nothing, controls everything, and lives to pervert the good, lies in wait.

A confession. Taggert and his ilk I call friends. When they can remember me, they do so as an ally. I once loved a Liminal named

Chabi. I—We lost her to the manipulations of Rice and the Rat mother Alter, Poppy. Trained by the Alter Narayana, Chabi knew the Entropy of Bones, a martial technique that could end even the densely powerful corpuses of Alters. I could not save her body, only Chabi's soul. I bound it to a ship and let her sail the in-between worlds as thanks for saving what's left of my life.

It was this Child of the Wind who rescued Mico, Taggert, Prentis, and Tamara from being stuck in their own past. It was this Child of the Wind who brought them to the new present and sheltered them in an old theater in London. It was this Child of the Wind who refused to let their spirits die despite all that's been leveled against them. It is against my nature as a Child of the Wind, but entropy is the end of all movement and the winds must always be free. This Child of the Wind takes responsibility for the chaos his Liminal friends inflict on this impacted, infected, unknown world.

This Child of the Wind does not take responsibility for the actions of Mico L'overture. No more. I cautioned against the entropy blades he forged for Taggert, against the trip back in time that fractured the present reality, to his partnership with the so-called reformed Alter, Narayana. It is the nature of Children of the Wind to know but not be listened to; Cassandra was one of us. Even so, dealing with Mico is annoying as sin. From the safety and shelter I provided, Mico has convinced Taggert to accompany him to rescue a human mentor, the Rastafari Bingy man, from the prison of Portmore on the island of Jamaica. They've barely escaped with their lives but have also exposed their existence to the Alters. All for a human who doesn't even remember them. Mico continues to act as though he is in his reality and not a forgotten world. He will learn, as will all the Liminals, soon enough.

Got friends, yeah? Go across time and space for ya? Rescue you from a bloke make the devil look like a poser? No? Then my friends are better than yours. They're family, zene?

Course now the world's gone a bit to shite. Turns out I was a bit of a distraction, a way to get Tamara and Taggert, and more importantly, this DJ I know as Jah Puba but they call Mico, out of play so that these beautifully powerful shit-talking void-worshipping lunatics called Alters could, well, alter reality. Didn't think it could happen, never had that as a concept. But when we got back to the here and now, it was like the whole world took a Xanax. Everything is muted, slowed down, depressed. We are not home. Home's gone and this wet blanket of reality is all that's left.

"We're out!" Tamara tells me. Made a home of this abandoned movie theater in Brixton ever since we've been back. Can squat anywhere, I guess, as people aren't really feeling the cinema anymore. But when Tamara yells, instead of using her telepathy, usually means she's impatient. Gather my gear from the snack stand where I sleep and head over to the stage.

"Found them?" I'm asking. My rats make a way for me but I ask them to hide when I see Tamara. Tall, not a bit of fat on her, light brown skin covered in slick black pants and an ash-colored knee-length shirt, long red tanned hair braided back, and bandannas around her face and hands, know she's all about business. At her best, Tam tolerates my rats. Tag missing along with Jah Puba? Definitely not at her best.

"The Wind Boy did. Get on stage quick." Pulls me up with her telekinetic powers. Used to it. But damn, she really is nervous.

5

"Who?" Ask before the rats can remind me.

"Keep up, luv." She's kind as she turns her head gently toward her right. A blast of wind in my eyes and my memory/recognition gets triggered.

"Bastards couldn't just wait," The Wind Boy, A.C., snaps. "They went to bust out Bingy man!"

Animals hold the memory of this guy for me. A Child of the Wind, as they understand it. Is fully human, not a Liminal like Tam and me. But also more. The disciple of movement, of change, of flux. Anything that moves is owned and owed to A.C. He's the one that brought us back to this time. Been our guide to this grayed-out world. But while Tam is ready, he's seething.

"That means J.A.," Tam says as she ties my tangled hair back with a red strip of leather and so much love, have to kiss her cheeks.

"I'm gonna get sunburned." Tell her.

"Gonna get killed if we're not careful." A.C. moves closer to the front of the stage.

"Shush your face, Wind Boy," Tam turns on him slowly. "You've been catty since we jumped back." Around us this push and pull begins, a group of invisible bullies shoving. Lose my breath and find it again and again. Feeling of wind pushing against us. Felt this before, it is how A.C. moves us, how he moves through the world, every time, I swear every time, throws me off. So hard to see and stand. All I have to keep me from losing my mind is a hand in mine. Tamara. Feel her creeping in my mind, not smiling, not freaking out either. She's not losing it, no reason I should.

Cough hard twice, almost flinch, then fall . . . through invisible impossible space. The lizards, a field rat, and a house cat all reach out to say "Welcome to Jamaica." Ceiling replaced by sky as blue as it gets here with a hazy sun. Sea air replaces stale scent of rancid popcorn butter and the gift of earth under me feels more comfortable than the hard wood of the theater stage. We've arrived. Mostly.

"Fuck to shit!" Tam yells at A.C. If she couldn't levitate, fly really, she'd be off the cliff he tried to land us on. Gray as this world is, this land is gorgeous, the dolphins in the ocean say the same about their home. "What's up with your aim?"

"When I talk, do you listen?" A.C. scares me, talking from behind me on a patch of sea-fed grass. By-product of his power is that people always forget him. "The world is changed, the psychic positioning and focus points are all off. It's not just me that's fucked. It's the entire world."

"Whatever, mate." She comes down to us so gently, I can tell she's been practicing. Won't let the effort show. "You got a lock on the dynamic duo?"

"This is as close as I get." Almost apologizing.

"For the love of all . . ." Tam squirms. Taggert can take care of himself, hell, he taught the both of us how to do it. Back in time, in the American south, he went toe to toe with the king of the baddies, Kothar. Tag won, saved us all, but damn near killed himself in the doing. Tam's been mother lion over him ever since.

"It's a huge island!" she moans after reaching out with her telepathy. Scared of reaching out too forcefully. Last time she did, I was missing. Gave most of London panic attacks. That's a level of attention we don't want. "I can't . . . He's here but . . ."

"Oy!" tell them before they get too tense. "Seagulls half a mile away say they're at a prison."

Dunn's River Falls, Jamaica
Prentis

"What the hell is wrong with them?" Ask with my first gasp of fresh air in twenty minutes.

A.C. yells and the birds twist in the air. Ask me to get him to stop as soon as I come up from the ocean with six large red snappers too

7

slow to run from me and my dolphin friends just outside of Ochos Rios. World of man may be going to a gray sort of hell in this world, but the nature thrived in the absence of coordinated destruction. Coral reefs are rich and strong here, the fish know where to avoid the nets of the fishermen. In the deep, animals are happy and want me to stay. Got a job to do.

When I surface, I ping Tam. Like a Liminal game of telephone, Tam sees the grimace on my face as I come up from the sea and blasts A.C. with telepathy, telling him to shut it. Love her.

"They still at it?" I ask, throwing the fish at my girl.

"Bare twat! A.C. keeps coming at Tag I'll knock him back to the future, that's facts." She grabs half the fish with her hands, the other half with her mind. "Your fish buddies okay being dinner?"

"Cha." Laugh as we head up the cliffs to the Bingy man's shack of a house. "Told you before, just cause I can talk to the animals doesn't mean I talk to the ones I'm about to eat. Nature eats itself, remember."

Rescue of Tag and Puba was easy enough. Bingy in tow though not sure who we were, saw a jailbreak and couldn't resist. Broke Mico's heart to not be recognized. Get the sense there's more of that to come.

Walk up in silence, me half wet, her just taking in the mental stillness as a gift. Not as hot as it should be. Wind doesn't flow as smoothly as it has been. I smell the fish. They've missed essential algaes. Want to push something, No, I *can* push something in the snapper, do like Tag does, manipulate the bodies of the snapper. Make them redder. Not oriented that way, it's not my nature, it's barely in my talent, my liminality, but I'm tempted.

"You remember any of your time with Nordeen yet?" Name enrages me for a second. Stumble but I keep walking.

"Remember whipping his arse well enough."

"When he had you, he made you. . . . You put me and Tag up against giant Praying Mantises." Grin tells me she murdered them dead.

"Been chatted pon." Remind her.

8

"I've never seen you transform animals like that."

"Can't." Lie. Then, "Can. But it's not good for either one of us. Likely, animals don't last long and . . ."

"And what?"

"Takes them a while to trust me afterward. The species." Praying Mantis generates cycle every three years and technically transformed them in 1971 so I've been forgiven. But sharks are ancient and violent. Would barely tolerate me in the water now if we were in our world.

"We let you down . . ." Tam starts.

"Shut your face. You come for me when no one else would have known to. Even though it cost the world."

Dunn's River Falls, Jamaica
Prentis

"Seriously, mate, feel free to shut your trap for ten minutes. I swear it won't be the end of all things," my girl tells the Wind Boy as we pierce the wall of smoke he's been masking us in since the breakout. Small bluff next to a sheet metal roof, one-room hut. Fireplace outside serves as living room. Warm enough here. And the view of the ocean can't get better. Master magician A.C. is, when we can give a toss enough to remember him, A.C. is. Makes him being a right git somewhat tolerable. Tam throws the fish at A.C's feet.

"Too late for that," A.C. says as soon as he re-materializes, dodging the fish. Accuses Tag after, "I thought you were going to keep him in line?"

"I did. Best as I could." Tag don't so much apologize as mumble. Kneels to the fish with a fresh grown long and sharp pinky nail, Wolverine style. Fat slice up a fish's belly and red and gray guts come raining down. "Got to respect loyalty to one's clan."

"The stakes are too high to be playing favorites." Wind Boy right but the damage is done so Taggert focus on scaling the fish.

"It's not about favorites," Mico says, exiting the shack Bingy calls home. Mico is a fine man. Even in the humble dress of the now, gray cotton T-shirt and thin sweats, no belly but also no arm muscle on him either. But long and tall, light tan skin wrapped so tight to his face, can see his skull contours. And those eyes, swear they change colors but always a different color dark. Not pretty, stunning, boy is. "Bingy is necessary for whatever comes next."

"So you say Dread. But I nah known you by name or face." Bingy pushes past Mico, obviously perturbed but happy to be in what passes for sun. Bingy's Black, rooftop Black, tar-in-the-sun Black. With fat dreads. Bit anemic, more from this world than from him—like in the old world bet they were shiny and brilliant. Here, twelve bulgy twists fall from his pin head to halfway down his back, studded with silver strands throughout. Frail body, prisoner frail, but he have a big man vocal.

"No reason you should 'known' him," A.C. says, finally settling down a bit. "He doesn't exist in this reality, most of these fools don't."

"So ya spring man only to vex, man?" Rasta says.

"I can't use words . . ." Mico looks at me for a solution but I've got nothing. When his eyes plead toward A.C., we get a light show. Wind Boy pulls a large diamond-shaped crystal from under his jacket.

"I fucking do," Tam says accepting a silent marriage proposal.

"Not on my watch," Tag snaps. A.C. uses his wind power to keep the crystal floating then makes a small hole in his wall of mist so that a ray of sunlight hits the crystal. A light tan rainbow paints over all of us. Full master of mystic arts this one is.

"Bit sad, ennit?" Tam asks.

"Yeah, mate," I chime in. "Lot of bother for a lot of gray. Turn up the hue or something?"

"What ya talk, gal?" Bingy says, reaching out to touch the light. "Wot go on with the rainbow?"

"Looks normal to you," A.C. starts, closing the light portal. "That's because you are of this shift in the universe, a darker part of the spectrum. You've never seen the color, experienced the energy from the higher spectrum. Everything is closer to the end, the final cooling of the universe now. Even light."

The old Rasta skeptical. Even I hadn't fully seen what we were up against before now. Heat was cooler, what few stars, constellations I recognized from twinkled light blue, not a bright white among them. Kept seeing the enemy as the Alters, Nordeen, Taggert's brother. Failed to see how they already won.

"Can you show him the light of my soul?" Mico asks A.C. as the Wind Boy lets the crystal drop in his hand.

"He's right. He's got to see what he's fighting for." Tamara chat after taking a lung-filling toke of Bingy's home grown. Shoots daggers with her eyes at Taggert when he kills her ability to get high with his powers.

"You're going to have to sing." A.C. says floating the crystal back up.

"Oh, I know this one." I jump up and join in with Mico as he begins one of his low mystic chants. Common Jungle verse sampled a thousand times but he kills like the first call to prayer for the sinners of the universe.

"I've been saved by the most notorious. I got saved and his love is so glorious. I could have been one of the most devastating. I got saved and his love is everlasting . . ." He repeats it three times with Tam pulling back up duties before he takes a freestyle verse.

> *"Yes I hold me to truth*
> *It is the job of Bingy*
> *Nyabinghi in the mirror of the man, do you see me?*
>
> *Turn a babylon boy to a Zion i chief*
> *Yes I, I drink in his wisdom and water like tea. I say*
> *I would have been one of the most notorious . . ."*

A neat small light flows from Mico's chest. Not a steady ray but an oscillating beam that pulses in time to the music. A.C. floats the jewel to the light and a more radiant double rainbow shines, one you couldn't find in any other part of this creation. Even Tamara grins from ear to ear. Bingy does his best to hide tears.

"DJ Jah Puba with his laser light show!" Tam says, finally giving Mico a small measure of respect.

"In your time, all dem color dem like this?" the Rasta asks.

"Not all." Give a bid for the honest. "But potential is there."

"And I&I am part of this endeavor?" Rasta asks gently, touching the place on Mico's chest where the light had come from.

"From the time I was a child you were my guiding light, my path when I had none. My ally and my mentor. This light I shared would not shine nearly as bright if not for you." Mico finally gets to hug his homeboy. Taggert uses the compression of his lungs to squeeze bits of the manna smoke out of Mico's body and into Bingy's mouth.

"All right, Ras Mico. Share they exhalation." A bigger dose than either of them realizes, A.C. provides small draft to help channel the smoke from Mico's mouth to the old dread. Not a kiss but intimate as a shotgun toke gets.

"Selassie I, Jah Rastafari. Blessed be the fruits and flowers of the earth in all their portion, skin, stem, seed, and root. Praise Ras Mico and the council of the Gray Rainbow oppressors!" Say spirit breathed back into Bingy sounds simplistic. But Dread's strong vocal echoes through all the hills and valleys surrounding us. Posture he struggled to maintain now his default. Even his dreads look more serpentine.

"Great." A.C. chat, not meaning it as he sit next to the fish fry. "Now it's six against infinity."

Dunn's River Falls, Jamaica
Prentis

Moon come and the wind goes quiet. Still hidden from prying eyes, but a fire is good for heat and light. No need for the shelter of the little Rasta cabin. Shadow world heat warms flesh well enough. Just not soul. All are fed but one of the crew is still.

Know Taggert better than he knows himself. All trained, responsible like. Forgets the importance of instinct. Not I. Animals wouldn't let me forget the lesson of reflex. Know when Tag sees this Bingy bloke turned to a sense of normal that his next instinct will be his lost love, currently cuddled up with his brother. Samantha.

"So this the plan?" he says right on cue. "We go around gathering up allies then take the fight to the Alters?"

"Any of your allies know how to stop the universal entropic shift?" A.C. asks. "Cause if not, we'll be wasting our time."

"There's only one entity we know that could help on that score," Mico chimes, high on the return of his bestie.

"Your shit talking tuber god?" Tam snaps. "Last I checked the God of connections was disconnected from everything."

"I said I couldn't feel it," Mico chat back. "But I bet he can."

"Bingy ain't Liminal," A.C. says.

"Exactly. The Alters have gone out of their way to defend against Liminals, either by recruiting or destroying them. They've wiped all traces of true Manna vassals out of existence, but not humans . . ."

"Not yet," Bingy say.

"How's that?" Tag asks.

"If dis Alter as you say is the power, the Babylon power then I and I see their approach for the end of humanity. It's for why Babylon lock I man up."

"Translation? Someone? Anyone?" Tam asks.

"I speak of the Decimation."

Tag gives her the silent go-ahead and Tam does a quick search of everyone in Jamaica's mind for the word. Takes a lot to shake

13

Tamara. A lot. When she gasps, I come close.

"Doesn't make a lick of sense," she tries to say.

"Tell it to me," I say back, trooping up army ants around us for protection.

"It's exactly what it says. A decimation. Ten percent of the world's population to die. To reduce population explosion, to clear prisons, to ease water demands. They've made it sound . . . It's perverse, but they've made it sound rational."

"They're going to kill ten percent of the world?" I ask.

"No, pretty P. Ten percent to commit suicide. All the same day. The same time. You volunteer, you live like a king or queen on any island of your choice for this entire year. No rules apply to you, everything's free, the best medical care to make you as comfortable as possible if you're dying. The incarcerated get let go and get a free pass to do whatever if they're chosen by lottery. They're using the islands like party central, Babylon incarnate. . . ."

"To speak against this heresy is a imprisoning offense," Bingy man says, confirming what Tam knows to be true.

"That's . . ." Mico can't find the words.

"Who would agree to . . ." Tag starts.

"The overpopulated, spiritually morosely weakened collection of seven billion souls known as the human race," A.C. chimes in. Beginning to see the source of his irritation. "Remember, all their music is for shit, all their religious leaders are for hire. Their sciences are all oriented toward the depletion of more resources and their collective imagination is a static-filled cocoon, where the God of connections used to do its best work. Get it right, people. We are fighting against the entropy in all things."

Taggert gives Tam the ability to get high back. Soon as she's done with her massive toke, he takes one. See someone else in need.

"How long has it been for you?" ask the Wind Boy as he makes small whirlwinds by the outside ashes of the fire.

"What?"

"That you've known? That you've seen humanity giving up?"

"I move," tells me after a minute. "That's what the wind does. We keep moving. As things get still, less mobile, I'm talking thought and ideas as well as the material world, I feel it. It's . . . things have been slowing down for a while . . ."

"And with Liminals being hunted down to conversion or death and Mico gone, you've been riding solo with this info." Put an arm around him and call up four hill dogs, not yet a year old, to nuzzle beside him. Wind Man tries to wiggle free but who says no to a puppy pile-on? Dogs nudge him from his purposeful squat to his ass.

"You're not alone anymore," tell him. "It's easy to feel like you're separate when you're by yourself. But you've got crew now, Wind Boy. And that forgetting thing you do? Doesn't work on animals. They forget and remember every second of every day. They've seen the work you've done, fighting against the Alters and they like you, mate. So don't go getting morbid, yeah? We ain't done yet."

"How come he gets a puppy pile?" Tam crawls over how I taught her to join in dog play. Tell her about the fleas later.

Dunn's River Falls, Jamaica
Taggert

"She is the best of us." Mico echoes my words back to me at night as my girls, Bingy, and A.C. all chill around a built up fire with Prentis's stray dog posse surrounding them.

"Told you." I see his African arm and imagine the spirits living in it deciding whether or not to exit and attack me. I think about Prentis for a second; thrown away by question marks of parents, exploited by Alia, as mad and powerful a Liminal as I've ever killed. Taken in by men before I had any idea of how to protect her, kidnapped by my nightmare and thrown back in time to be the Alter's kennel girl. And yet here she stands, cheering up others. I almost miss Mico's whining.

"I don't know what to do," Mico confesses quietly. He turns his back to the crew to face the shack and hide the shame in his face. "Taggert, if I fuck up . . ."

"You can't," I say.

"Of course I can. If I fuck up . . ." Mico goes on like he hasn't heard me, so I put my hand on his chest, where his soul shined out.

"Get the 'I' out of it. If we fuck up . . ." I say slowly.

". . . Seven billion people die."

"No," I tell him. "If we do nothing seven billion die. We've already taken one of that number . . ."

"So as long as we save one person we're good? I don't like that math." He turns to look at his old mentor, smoking a massive weed chalice.

"Then change it," I tell him.

"I'm not a soldier, Taggert. I'm a singer. And with these numbers, this is about to turn into a war." Like I didn't know.

"Dude, we've been at war for a while now. So what are you saying?"

"That I trust you. That I need you to draw up the battle plans." He does that sincere eye lock thing that pisses me off.

"It's like you said, we find the manna . . ."

"And what about the Decimation?" Mico asks.

"Three months away. We've got time," I tell him.

"Maybe." Then Mico goes all sad puppy face. "If I hadn't convinced you to come with me for Bingy. Now the Alters know we're here. You really think we can avoid their forces and find the manna at the same time, in under three months?"

"We're going to need more allies and a strategy," I tell him after thinking on the practicals. "I don't even know what a global anti-suicide campaign look like."

"Music," Prentis says from the shadows. She's one of the few that can sneak up on me.

"That only worked on Bingy because . . ." Mico starts.

"Shut your face and listen to the girl," I tell him.

"Thanks, Da," she slips but I don't react. "A.C. said it. No music, real music with soul. Want to show the lunacy of suicide? Piss on Mico spiritual mucked whatnot. Be Jah Puba, the DJ that saved my life. Besides, not doing a team-up with you without getting a back-stage pass to a Jah Puba set."

"We even attempt to rent a space, Alters will be all over us . . ." Mico starts.

"Have to be underground about it then." Prentis grins. "Like every other one of your shows."

"Anything recorded since the Alters' ascension is, for lack of a better term, polluted."

"Record new music. Find the underground scene. Good stuff is out there, it's just not being recorded, marketed, and released. Fat tunes is always under," Prentis says seeing the glimmer of hope in his eye.

"No one said it would be easy," I tell him. "You wanted a general. Fine. You got one. First order, prep for a show in three months. We figure out the rest tomorrow. Go sleep."

Prentis cuddles up under my arm like one of her dogs as soon as Mico leaves. I've learned not to resist her. Besides, she's comforting, until she speaks, that is.

"Generals can't go off on solo missions," she says softly into my chest.

"I thought Tam was the mind reader."

"Target rich environment, Tag. Samantha's a fixed mark. She'll stay close to your brother, Baron. 'Member, you taught us to handle moving targets first?"

"Your mistake is in thinking anything we've done in the past has prepared us for this," I tell her, gaining a little distance.

"So toss what little effective knowledge we do have?" She stares incredulously through the dark of night, like I'm the fool. "Cha. Even you aren't that self-destructive, Taggert. And besides, us? Been

17

fighting the world since birth. Only difference is now it's fighting back. Itching for a fight with a fair chance of winning."

Dunn's River Falls, Jamaica
Taggert

We wake up with the sun and Biblical chants provided by the newly invigorated Bingy and Mico. I wolf down some old salt fish and mango juice Bingy has in his shack. I won't give my girls time to get hungry and complain about it. As I look at them from Bingy's doorway, rolling awake and alive, I promise myself one thing. Even if I lose, even if reality itself crumbles around us and entropy reigns, those two will be the last free beings on the planet to go down.

"Circle up, posse," I whistle once they're all fully conscious. We form up around the dead fire. "If we're going to do this, all of us are going to have to be smarter, sneakier, stronger than ever before. No random heroics, Mico. No off-the-radar missions, Tamara. As of now, we're all together or we're all screwed. Agreed?" They all nod their heads. "Okay, first off we need allies."

"Tag . . ."

"Shut it, Prentis. I'm talking about the smuggler chick."

"Fatima," Mico says slowly.

"Yeah, her and your former forever favorite Alter . . ."

"Narayana." An almost hate comes from A.C. "But why him?"

"If Alters are more powerful now stands to reasons Narayana is. If he still has any loyalty to Mico, he might be our most significant addition."

"I know a ghost ship captain that might have a problem with him on our squad," Tamara tells me.

"I'm counting on it. With any luck she'll link up soon enough."

"Wait, you know Chabi?" A.C. says, getting excited.

"Later," I tell him. "If we're gonna have a concert we're gonna need the smuggler chick on our side."

"Even in our reality Fatima has never jumped to my aid . . ." Mico starts.

"That's why I'm sending Bingy and Prentis."

"But for why?" Prentis asks, reaching out longingly for Tamara.

"Cause I don't know a body that can resist your charms," I tell her as I pat her head. "A.C, I don't know a smuggler alive, in this dimension or another, who hasn't said prayers to the four winds. You can locate her. And, Bingy, if anyone has a line on the manna, it's gonna be a smuggler operating under the radar of the Alters."

"So the rest of us are going after Alters?" A.C. asks.

"Nope. That's you and Mico. You guys are the heavy hitters anyway. Get Narayana on our side or get him gone. He knows too much about how you work, Mico."

"Real question is," my daughter asks, "where the hell are we going?"

"Figured you should get to know your uncle."

"I knew it," the animal girl shouts. "Taggert, you can't . . ."

"Can't live in fear?" I tell her. "I agree. Alters are dangling a giant 'Screw you, Taggert' carrot all across Eel Pie Island. Baron, the evil version of your mom, and what's left of your Samantha just all happen to be running the human level of the Alter program? I don't believe in small coincidences and there's nothing small about this signal. Springing Bingy let them know I'm alive. They'll be waiting for this play. Why make them wait?"

"King of the nonsense plan!" Prentis snaps at me. "Their world, their rules. Want to go to the heart of their power base to do what? Play chess?"

"You ever known my madness not to have a method in it?" I ask her. "Trust me like I trust you."

"Where's the meet-up?" Tam asks softly after some telepathic conversation with Prentis.

"There's a half-faced man on Pangkor Island. Light joss sticks at his temple and I'll come collect you," A.C. tells all assembled.

"For those of us not versed in mystical shit talk, wot now?" Tam asks. But it's too late. A rocket propelled grenade lands at our southernmost ridge overlooking the sea. Then it explodes. We scatter. Below us, scrambling quick, I feel forty heartbeats, thirty-seven human, scaling the craggy flintstone cliffs, with malicious intent. But my crew is not easily shaken.

Tam throws my body, along with her own, in a high arch over our assailants and into the ocean. I dodge automatic fire from the ground easy and watch as the rest of the crew disappears down into a fishing cove. Just as I'm about to grow gills that can handle salt water, A.C. appears with Tam and sucks us through water and space violently . . . back into the theater in Brixton. This world makes his transportation rocky where it was once smooth. But even for him, that was a rough jump.

"Warn a girl, will ya?" Tam begs, choking out salt water at the head of the stage. I ended up in an aisle actively controlling my gag reflex.

"No time. Fucking Alters are quick. Remember, they track all money spent. So use favors and debt as currency. Gotta grab the others."

"Go!" I manage to choke out before a vacuum of air replaces him.

"Fucking A . . ." my daughter starts.

Then the theater explodes.

Brixton
Taggert

Last time I was in an exploding structure it was a car—with Tamara's mother, her real mother. If I hadn't been blown out of that car, it would have been the end of me. But I heal quick. It was the end of Yasmine. At least in that reality.

In this one, our daughter is not only powerful but smart. So when the first explosion went off on the second floor of the building she immediately pulled me close to her position and made me boost her telekinetic abilities with my healing. She managed the tons of concrete, steel, and debris falling like a pro as she levitated in a lotus position with eyes closed. She created an impenetrable telekinetic bubble complete with oxygen for the two of us. Tam let the building collapse happen, protecting only what mattered to her. Wish I had been as smart at her age.

Rather than going out, after the bubble method, we went down. I bulked up to Juggernaut size and smashed on the already weakened floorboards until we found the sewers. Anyone looking at the demolished building would think it was just rubble settling.

"You good?" I ask my daughter as London sewage flows by our feet.

"I'd be better if I could reach out to Prentis," she tells me. "Oh, you meant the building? All good. Would have been easy if not for the A.C. trip right before."

"That's life." I smile at her, impressed. "Don't worry about Prentis. She's just as strong as you."

Tam catches the compliment but won't respond. Unconsciously, we make our way to the first waylay station we shared, an out-of-use Tube station both she and Prentis used to hide from traumatic lunacy. At least in our reality it was out of use.

"Fucking A," my girl moans as we approach the fully functioning Red line stop. "Is nothing sacred?"

"I think that's the point," I tell her, hugging the subway wall. "We've got to think this through. If Eel Pie Island is mission control for the Alters, you know they've tapped into every CCTV within a hundred miles."

"That's a lot of footage. Even in our dimension or whatever, London surveillance is heavy. So what? Change looks?" she asks.

"Still got that giant 'Fuck You Taggert' flag they're flying for me in sight?"

"You mean the trap we're walking right into at Eel Pie? Yeah. Oh, I see. You think they might have a way to peep your face changing skills," she acknowledges. "So what? I snag a wallet and we lay up at a hotel?"

"Remember the wind," I tell her. "All currency, commerce is the Alter's providence as well. Stolen cards or not. Any credit card swipe gives them insight into our behavior."

"Well, I've had enough of sleeping in sewers for one lifetime, Da. So tell me you've got a plan."

"Time to embrace our criminal nature," I tell her as I turn away from the light of the station and head back the way we came.

"Meaning what now?" she asks, following.

"Any system, capitalism, democracy, oligarchy, doesn't matter really—there will be people who resist it. Alters have a stronger hold than they did in our time, but it's not complete."

"How do you know?"

"The Decimation. They wouldn't need it if their control was total. Plus, we're here. If their grip was that tight, we'd be toast already."

"We almost were. How the hell did they find the theater?"

"Probably my fault for going off with Mico making big noise. Now we go quiet. Powers only when we need them and only in proper proportion."

"Still confused, Tag," Tamara tells me. "How are we going to challenge your brother, the Alters, and all the rest if we can't use our powers?"

"Simple, Love. We're going to take over the London criminal underground."

Dunn's River Falls, Jamaica
Prentis

Trust rats. Brown rats, woodrats, city rats, country rats. Doesn't matter. They are survivors. Heard them tell me to run the second before the bullets started flying.

Would have dodged them all easily if Tam hadn't been so bloody pigheaded. Forget her act, once Taggert said they were going to square off with her uncle, she shut down. Practically had to scream my thoughts into her head before she'd move. When the explosion hit, that's when she kicked back in, saving us all by deflecting the grenade. Called what venomous snakes I could to strike at the soldiers but by the time I looked around, half our numbers were either in the water or just plain gone.

"Prentis, come on!'" Mico shouts at me halfway to Bingy's house. But use a seagull's eyes and see the trajectory of another R.P.G.

"Get back!" I shout just before the tin shack goes up in flaming pieces of red hot metal that fly everywhere.

"Down the cove!" Bingy pushes roughly with his free hand. In his other he carries a well used black machete. Working with what he's got, but if those Alters get close, just as well with a toothpick.

Put our backs to the ocean I fished from last night, Mico, Bingy, and me. Want to be scared, to wonder where my pack is, but no time. Troops with heavy artillery have swarmed our den from last night. There's only one path to cove. They'll find it in a minute and come for us.

"Behind me, girl," Bingy says, almost pushing me into the warm sea.

"You're sweet," tell him as I circle around the dread. "But I'm better prepped for this scrap that you'll ever be." Bring flocks of seabirds to the beach, pool a crew of electric eels at our feet, and make my wild dog packs howl in the hills to make my point.

"You take the humans," Mico orders as the soldiers begin to descend to our location. He respects my gangster at least. "But leave the Alters to me."

"And for me?" Bingy asks.

"Pray to a god you've forgotten for aid." My pups, snakes, and dive bombing flocks take most of the weapons from the initial soldiers that make it to the beach. That's all I ask them for. When they die in my service, it's not fair. Want the soldiers to come into the water but they're cautious of the darting black bodies just below the surface. For the ones still with weapons, Mico is singing one of his songs only some can hear, and it's driving them to their knees. But this is unsustainable.

Just as a soldier's body, driven by something obviously inhuman, snatches a sparrow out of the sky in midair and clears the cove corridor we three are suddenly jerked back in the air. I tell my critter crew to scatter just before a massive wave, propelled more by wind than water current, smashes the cove.

"Cut it close why don't you, A.C.?" Mico says to the air as we continue to fall backward twelve feet in the sky.

"Who are you talking to?" I ask.

"Look to your right." About to after a quick survey of our rapidly shrinking former shore. Sparrow killer Alter still stands like a monument even after the twenty-foot wave, but right shoulder starts aching for real. Damn bullets. Would've dodged them all.

Khamilia, Morocco
Prentis

Wake up to multicolored scorpions stinging bullet wound as subtle maggots eat my dead flesh. Dryness in the throats of the dogs around, heat off falcon wings, swiftness of the snakes tell. In the heat of desert. Deep desert.

"How you feeling?" A.C. asks. Casual defense stance the snakes take says he's been around long enough for them to get accustomed.

"Okay. Water would be nice." He's made it extra cool with his wind. "Bingy and Mico? Wait. Where we at?"

"Khamilia. The last bit of proper city before the Moroccan desert goes big."

"Morocco?" Sit up from the bed, best bed ever really, and take in the room. Desert dogs know it's time to find shade so it's got to be near high noon, but room is completely dark. Beautiful tapestries block out heat and light coming from the windows.

"Relax . . ." He tries to come closer, but three cobras coil up from under the bed as my scorpions pick up the same cues from my emotional response.

"No. Tag says stay away from Morocco. Nordeen territory!"

"Hey!" A strong wind blows all my defenders through a window at the same time as he grabs me arms with his cool hands. "You took Nordeen out some seventy odd years ago remember? Low key Prentis, remember?"

"Sorry." Tell him when I feel fatigue of the falcons circling over heat. Summoned animal crew to stand guard in on instinct and beastie hype no good for low profile.

"Good girl," he says, offering a bowl of couscous with almonds and apricots in it. "Sorry I wasn't able to snag you guys quicker."

"'M not Tamara, brethren. Won't slam ten quid for not being twenty," laugh at him. "Speaking of, word from fam?"

"No, but that's good. Better we all stay unconnected. Harder to trace. You good to be mobile?"

Feel my shoulder. The bullet missed bone and went out clean. Lucky. If not for the scorpion stings, pain.

"No lifting my arm over me head and good. Wait up, who changed me?" Realize I'm wearing sleek two-layer silk baggy pants and a near unibra beaded top with a deep red off-the-shoulder blouse. Girly clothes. Not my clothes.

"Me, don't worry. I didn't take any liberties. I had two fucking coyotes growling at the doorway making sure. Come on outside. Me and Mico got to get moving soon. Narayana won't find himself."

"Narayana?" ask, following him down a flight of stairs into a narrow corridor of shops and hostels. Desert heat and sand blasted every building and person in this town. All the color of the sand, tan with hints of red and black. Pale skin stands out. They all study me, cautiously.

"Converted member of the opposing team. At least in our time/space. Given his nature he probably still remembers how things were."

"Don't sound too excited to find him."

"I trust him about as far as you could throw him with your bad arm. But Taggert's right. If the Alters' star is in ascension, then Narayana is an invaluable ally."

"Or enemy who clocks how Mico ponders."

"Taggert raises them smart," he says, genuinely impressed.

"The point of being any other way?" I smile.

Off the center of the town, this moaning so deep, takes a second to recognize the words. Winding paths floored with foot-pounded sand and rock all dead end into what passes for a town square. Women darker than Taggert sit in front of their houses rocking to the same sound. Men draped in those full-body tent clothes walk holding hands with guys in track suits and bad logo fashion. Even they bop a bit in their steps, excited by the music. A bit more color in this gray-tone sky now because of it.

The lyrics and the voices come at the same time as we head out of the oven heat and toward the music; Mico and Bingy man singing "The Show Must Go On" by Roots Manuva. Holding court in a tiny restaurant that has a large keyboard connected to speakers chained to wooden ceiling beams. Jah Puba holds down the keys, giving his crowd calling power to Bingy man on guitar. Old dread barely needs it. Desert nomads, tourists, and village berbers all sit wrapped, ignoring their midday meal.

"It's like the rainbow only with sound." A.C. answers my questioning gaze from the doorway of the establishment. "People can't help but be attracted to it. As soon as any of you express yourselves, you'll draw folks. So be careful. The bigger the crowd . . ."

"More likely the Alters will notice. Still, Jah Puba's show gonna kick ass!" Laughs at me and we go to sit in the back. Give our waitress a hug before we sit because even though she can't understand the words of the song, she's crying a little.

"Remember, no commerce. No cash or credit. Bank on trade or favor. Steal if you must, but as soon as you get into currency and coinage the Alters will be able to zero in on you . . ."

"And none of you will be close enough to help. Got it. How do you know the smuggler girl will come here?"

"See the old man at the side of the stage?" Dark sandy red beard. Light brown eyes smile as his belly shakes in time with the song. "That's her father. This is his joint. She doesn't go a month without checking on him . . ."

". . . according to Mico, the dude she can't stand."

"Taggert's plan," is all he has to say. "But I've given the winds her name. She'll have some turbulence issues soon until she heads this way."

"So me and Bingy have to convince a smuggler that's never met us to link up with a dude she's never met to fight against the shadow authority of this reality for no pay while you two walk into what is at best a hard conversion parable?"

"Taggert's plan," he repeats.

"Fucking Taggert."

Khamilia, Morocco
Prentis

Hate dreaming. Used to love it. 'D be a queen ant or a lioness with her pride. Now, all the white-hot pain of shark teeth and predatory mating of mantises. Nordeen took good sleep. Maybe that's why I made Munji cry.

Not on purpose. Been wonderful these past few days. Him and Bingy talk through broke accents like old friends. He brings pieces of fruit and baklava early in the mornings when I can't sleep and wander down into his forever open little restaurant/tea shop/curio display.

"Do you sing?" he asked after offering me a seat with an open hand and a generous smile.

"Want all your dishes broken? Cause one note from me, mate . . ." Laughed as I lied.

"So you and the Bingy man are not traveling musicians?" He didn't so much ask as insinuate.

"What he told you?"

"He only says that you will be here for a few days."

"Got you worried?"

"Concerned," he confessed. "You see how it can raise suspicion. Three near strangers, one from the UK, one Jamaican, one American, maybe? The way you speak, so simple and direct but also, as if you have a better way to communicate. Strangers in Khamilia, bright and beautiful as you both are . . ."

"Flatterer. Golden tongue like, surprised you're still single." Hid it quick, most wouldn't have noticed, don't see tears as much as smell them, feel them. More sleep maybe wouldn't have been so bleeding careless with words. Hate words.

"Sorry. So sorry. Please forgive. Didn't mean to bring up painful . . ."

"It's okay."

"It's not." Woke up every flea-bitten mutt in town with my panic. All coming to lick Munji's tears away. So calmed down. "I didn't mean to push . . ."

"I was not always single, you know?" he said, picking the filo flakes of the finger-shaped baklava out of his beard. "I had the most beautiful wife in the world. The strongest as well. She came from the desert, deep inside, beyond where even the Tuaregs can live. But she left her life there. Her family as well. For me."

"She look like?" asked as a group of lizards scampered around my toes.

"Deep red hair that went to her shoulder, only a bit taller than you. She could have been a dancer with those long fingers and muscle-wrapped arms. But she could never perform on a regular. A false word never left her thick lips. And if you tried to lie to her, eyes like polished ebony would stare down your soul."

Didn't want to fake a lie like "Did you have any children?" after a line like that. Just played with my toe friends Munji came back from putting on a hissy cassette tape. Still was better than all the radio shite.

"You know Gnawa?" he asked, sitting back down.

"Owes me ten quid," joke then shake my head no.

"Black mystic men. They work music and ritual power to summon djinn. You understand?"

"Like genies? Aladdin?"

"Yes, but they are real." It sounds like the blues in Arabic. Type of stuff that doesn't get recorded here, anywhere. Not my type of music. But Jah Puba could remix it, make it a banger. Munji says slowly, "They used to come to my wife for counsel."

"Counsel for what?"

"She wouldn't say. Only that when the time was right she would show our daughter the true nature of things and that if *she* wanted to tell me, Fatima could. But not her."

"Did your daughter learn?"

"My wife was killed by Saudis." My turn to cry. Not for what he said, but for the matter of fact, dead inside way he did it.

"Sorry."

"You are no Saudi and you didn't kill her. Don't apologize for the sins of others. Besides, she took four of them with her. Fatima was only eight years old. Not old enough to learn the true nature of things, I guess." He tried smiling and it made me laugh.

"There was a light in her that I saw in your friend Mico. That I see in Bingy and in you. Though yours seems a bit dimmer."

"Tough life I've lived," told him quick, scared about what he saw. "Want to see something cool?"

Called all the lizards under two inches long to the table. Munji was surprised but didn't freak out like most of the world would. So I pushed it.

"Circle the wagons, boys!" yelled as they all start running head to tail in a circle. "Aannnd, play dead!" All stopped and flip over on their backs. "Just playing! Back up!" All but one of them did.

"You might have killed one, I'm afraid," Munji said, softly taking the small desert salamander in his cracked and calloused hand.

"He's fine!" let him know. "Just stuck in his startle response. It's kind of a big deal for him, any of them really, to meet me."

"You are the queen of lizards?"

"Guess animal totem would be the correct term," said, puffed up.

"And you show me this why?"

"Because need you to trust me and Bingy. My life in your hands now. The leaders of the Decimation would pay good money for us. Probably exclude you and your daughter from the lottery, play your cards right . . ."

"Stop mentioning that damned lemming event in my establishment," did his best not to bark. "You and Bingy are against the Decimation?"

"Against every oppressive aspect of this morally fatigued world. Got the vague outlines of a plan. Wanna help?"

"Is it my help you want?" said smiling as his little salamander friend woke up and shook his tail. "Or my daughter's?"

Khamilia, Morocco
Prentis

"You're in my bed," Smuggler Princess tells me, small rifle held at her waist. Thin mosquito net between us won't count for squat if that trigger gets squeezed. Night now. Been waiting for her to show up for few days now.

"Super comfy." Raise up to my elbows. "Hope it's not a shooting offense. Your da said could crash here rather than the tourist trap he's got going in town."

"Who are you? For real now." Have to rely on the sound to track her. She's cocked her weapon. "And none of the vague nonsense you've been feeding my father."

"Tend to explain better when not being threatened." Swing my feet over the bed to sit up. "You look below before you put your finger on the trigger."

"Who the hell are you?" Credit, she doesn't move. Not an inch. Neither do three hundred scorpions, though they all want to.

"Friend to the animals. Friend to your father, and hopefully your friend as well."

"My friends don't talk to venomous creatures." Tam was right. She'd met Fatima before and said she was beautiful. Sand-complexioned like the whole village, but a red fire in her eyes that make you stare at her slightly oval face. Ever had a zit, her face doesn't remember. Even dressed like Safari Joe, in khaki's and a loose button-up, she hips got me thinking I could mess with girls. More beautiful than anyone in this dimension has a right to be, realize when I turn the lamp on.

"You've got friends?" joke, sending my tiny poison army back to the shadows. "Don't see anyone other than your father worth respect much less admiration. Man dem seems bland, lifeless, depressed even, yeah? Wonder if you were born in the right time and place, yeah? Bet that's why you're the smuggler queen, looking underground for what you can't find above, attracting all manner of attention from those drawn to your shine."

"Done acting like you know me?"

"Don't know you. Not at all. But know man who does. Misses you with a crazy passion. Willing to meet him, you might just help save the world."

Khamilia, Morocco
Prentis

Two days with this Fatima and can see why Mico fell so hard for her. Eight rogues of every creed that constantly surround her treat Fatima like a big sister. Fat deference to Munji, but it's clear he relies on her desperately for the feels. Gal has the weight of the world on her narrow brown shoulders but no flinch in her. Gal's competence that's sexy.

Half my words, half the relationship between Munji and Bingy, convinces Fatima to take squad serious. Call her Fatty to have a laugh and lose a little bit of credibility every time. Fuck it, though. Give her the only directions I have for the link-up, damn near lose the tip of my nose to her smuggler temper. Luckily she's seen more of the world than I have and knows her way around vague instructions.

"Pangkor Island is off the northeast shore of Malaysia. Don't know about any half-faced man," tells me with a cigarette hanging from her lip once we're flying in her Beechcraft Super King Air. Feel like a superstar, with the silver seats, and the fancy displays Fatty's looking at. Fuck if I know what all the dials do.

Munji sits in the co-pilot seat as Bingy rotates something in his hands over and over back in coach.

"That's a start." Smile at her from the cockpit door.

"You're lucky I've got business in KL or I would even be entertaining . . ."

"Ah, knock it off. Admit it, craving to see what your love from across dimensions looks like, yeah?"

"Sit down," Fatty grumbles, choosing fog banks over my mug.

"Fly low enough my birds can tell you about the weather . . ."

"I've been flying since I was seven without the aid of birds. Go! Sit!"

Hope she never gets into it with Tamara. Fatty didn't spring for the soundproofing model of her plane. Main cabin so loud, have to squeeze puppy pile close to Bingy to have conversation.

"What's that then?" ask about the thing in his hand.

"Dem a call dis Manna." Shows me a bag of pre-rolled joints at his feet. "Tell dem people dem it cause a schizophrenia, hydromania, chronic masturbation, and a host of other fuckery."

"Tam told me it was a conscious dick of a tuber weed. Left out the masturbation and the other other."

"Since Ras Mico liberate I sight, the world looks different, zene? Where the smoke that free I exist, I man feel, yah hear me?"

"Yeah, mate, hear you."

"So I say clearly, this whole bag of Manna joint, this bulkhead load Munji put on transport, less than half a pound of the Manna I and I know is on here. Put this on my beloved mother, yes I."

"Sure, man? Cause I see stuff as well. Same light coming from you coming from Fatima. She smokes the stuff so . . ."

"But na Munji." Shit, Rasta is right. "And Munji smoke more than his seed. Plus Fatima crew back in Morocco, dem a smoke a phat spliff an hour, but not a light between them all."

"Makes sense, I guess," confess, still confused. "Alters don't want the actual Manna getting to the public. It would start preaching against the Decimation and they'd lose power."

London, England
Taggert

Okay, I'll admit it, I didn't think I'd have to break out the entropy blades to run the London underground. But when what can only be described as a good luck Liminal tries to hit my third eye three times with three bullets, I'm thankful for them.

The Lucky Liminal breaks away from the Thames on Bankside heading toward Emerson Street and I continue my chase. You'd think after Tamara and I destroyed three of his four warehouses, this guy'd be coming for us. Instead we're in pursuit of the #1 THC amber glass supplier from Brighton to Brixton, a street tough everyone calls Pasha Maaco, in mid-evening traffic.

Fast as I am, this Pasha is lucky. I'm dodging cars on Aryes Street that swerve to miss him. I'm half an inch from Mr. Maaco as we round Marshalsea Road when a taxi's door opens into me. He dives over it, into the cab, pushing the driver to take him halfway across Little Dorrit Park before I can sit up. I feel for the cabbie's legs and make them slam on the brakes. Holding Pasha's body is like smelling for roses in a field of jasmine. It's doable but difficult. Besides, the resulting thud from the back seat is pleasurable enough.

Still, he's out the cab before I'm halfway down the crowded block. Smart and flexible, adapting to each new challenge with a quickness, I can understand why my brother chose him as a recruit. No way Pasha could've known I'd be waiting for him at, at his third supply fire of the week. But he barely caught sight of me in the crowd before he bolted. Only took aim when we were clear of civilians. Shows he's got a code. That's why I move hard on him through the norms, confident he won't shoot. Nope, again he rabbits. This time to some corporate buildings filled with cameras on Brough High Street. Smart son of a bitch.

"I need a power outage, girl," I think out hard to Tamara as I slam everyone around me with a case of temporary blindness. I liminal my legs up and jump five stories high then anchor myself with the entropy blades. I pull up hard on them for another three stories, then restore everyone's sight. People don't generally look up, but even if they did, it's almost nighttime and I blend in. Still feel like mini King Kong climbing this building looking for my Lucky Faye Raye. I ascend the same way to the twenty-second floor, then the lights in the building go dark. I think a thanks to my girl.

By the time the broken glass of my entry hits the ground, I'm already inside. Of course Pasha doesn't take an elevator like a normal person. He's running up flights of stairs, his lungs barely working under the strain. And with my impromptu King Kong impersonation, I'm only one flight above him. I charge the hallway connected to the stairway he's running up, aiming at the rose-scented Liminal like a horny fucking bee. Just as Mr. Maaco hits my floor I slam the door open with all my strength and knock him down a flight of stairs.

"I need a doctor!"

"Nah, you're fine." Okay, so I shattered a rib. I heal it so casually he doesn't even notice as I walk down the stairs. "In fact, you're quite lucky."

"I'm no snitch." He turns and runs as I get my first good look at him. Just shy of twenty-five, with a sharp chin, wide oval green eyes, and that complexion that only comes from some Middle Eastern and Caribbean UK miscegenation.

"That's why we picked you, ya daft idjit," Tam says, pushing him back upstairs with her telekinesis from the floor below. "Taggert, we've got five minutes max on the blackout. I've got a camera blind the whole way out but I'm not swearing on it."

"All good. We won't need that much time." Pasha pulls his piece on me, but at this range, even he can't resist my skills. I cramp up his deltoid.

"If he stops acting like a bitch," Tamara joins in.

"You're no fuzz," he tells us.

"Not as dumb as you look," Tam snaps back.

"Let me free then!"

"To do what?" I bark in the quiet dark stairway. "Keep pushing that amber glass at below market value, making that subsistence level profit just to keep you and yours out the bing? Jesus, man, in another life I took over the Kenyan Khat trade routes and got more pushback from them than we got from your crew."

"So you's the new kings? That's what this is?"

"This is the destruction of the throne," Tam says in his head, overdoing it as usual.

"What the hell are you?"

"Liminals." I flood him with oxytocin to make sure he can still hear us. "Same as you. Difference in abilities doesn't erase kinship."

"I can't . . ."

"Bet there isn't a gambling hall you haven't been kicked out of, no woman you've wanted you haven't gotten, or a bad spot you haven't been able to turn. You're a liminal. I can read it all over your body."

"If I'm so lucky, what am I doing braced between you two derelicts?"

"Your lucky day." Tam smiles. "What's your stance on the Decimation?"

"You lock me up to talk politics? All right, It's bloody idiotic, insane. Puts humans on the level of lemmings. I didn't join the lottery and my number wasn't called so that's the end of it."

"And suppose I told you the man you pay up to on Eel Pie Island is not only the chief organizer of the Decimation, but also an inhumanly large prick whose sole desire is to watch humanity crumble and falter?" Tam tells him with thought, making doubt of her sincerity impossible.

Plus my oxy rush makes us infinitely trustable. The poor Liminal doesn't stand a chance. Lucky for him we're on the side of the angels.

"I'd say what the fuck can I do about it?"

"Well," I start. "You can keep moving your weak-ass product, refusing to ever get rich . . ."

"Like a bitch," Tam adds.

"Or you can join with us, travel the world, meet some awesome people, get into some real gangsta shit. Or stay in London town . . ."

"Like a bitch . . ."

"Ignoring the wrong you know the Decimation is . . ."

"Like a bitch."

"See, you're bad but not that bad 'cause you're not able to beat the baddest. At least, not yet. And definitely not alone. But you're smart enough to gain allies, hence your low cash for weight drug game. Smart, favors are always worth more than cash. But you've got low-level hood rich favors."

"Meanwhile I've never heard of you," Pasha strikes back.

"And yet me and mine just shut down your whole operation in a matter of days." I smile. "It's simple, Mr. Maaco. I'm offering you a chance to stop fighting your conscience and stand against your boss and his allies, the prize being the entirety of the London drug trade. Say no and you return to your regularly scheduled life."

"Like a bitch."

London, North Peckham
Taggert

". . . But how are you going to stop people from killing themselves?" Pasha asks. "I don't understand."

"Keeps me up at night that does," Tamara snaps at him. We're at Pasha's flat. Honestly, it's three flats all on the top floor of North

Peckham Council estates. That most families would make themselves content in a space a third this size is a testament to the Alters' influence over this world. Pasha has knocked out walls that separated living rooms from kitchens, forming a shotgun-style living space with enough bedrooms and space for at least ten.

Outside, the neighborhood toughs look way rougher than they are. None of them with all their baby teeth out, half sleep on Pasha's floor most nights. They've got loyalty to him and weapons enough to make noise. If anyone comes we'll hear their death gurgles at least. And with five points of egress including the roof it's damn near impossible to turn away as a base of operations.

"Suicide is a permanent solution to a temporary problem," I tell him after showering off. "The Decimation is a solution to a problem that doesn't exist."

"Overpopulation is real." He's taken down some of the psycho punch. Couldn't be helped.

"So give contraception to every woman in the world free of charge with no man able to say shite about it," Tam starts. "Make vasectomies and tubal ligations free. Give tax breaks to people without kids. Mandate sex ed for everyone. I'd understand any of these steps, even forced universal sterilization, if that was really the concern."

"Some of those things have been tried . . ." he starts.

"In small test groups with inconclusive results," I tell him. "Yeah, I read the website as well. Doesn't make it right."

"Look, no one's being forced. Some people want to die."

"And I want to bounce you all over this flat like a piñata," Tam says, going into the bathroom. "Don't see me doing it now, do you?"

"Okay, what's she so mad at me for?"

"It's not you. It's me," I lie. "I told her to trust you. That's not a natural state for Tamara."

"But you trust me?" It's like he's looking at himself through my eyes for the first time.

"Well, not exactly trust you. Where I'm from, when, whatever, that part still confuses me—well Pasha, I killed you."

"Who?" He stands ready to fight until Tam gives him a splitting migraine from the bathroom.

"Relax," I tell them both. "See, you were an incredibly lucky child. Like a cruise liner with your whole family capsized and killed. But somehow you survived, super lucky. At the time I worked for a guy named Nordeen. Think AIDS with a sadistic smile. He wanted you for himself or dead. I knew you'd be better off dead so I made sure your foster father was too tired to get out of his garage after parking the car one night. He left the engine running and your four-year-old lungs got all the carbon monoxide they could handle. You just went to sleep."

"You killed kids?"

"And worse. And now I'm aiming at your boss and the Decimation. You getting a sense of how bad this shit is yet?"

"You know your brother has his claws deep in this dude's dome, yeah, Tag?" Tamara tells me telepathically.

"Figured as much. But Pasha isn't decided yet. He still might work with the side of the angels," I think back.

"Prentis keeps telling you we're no angels, Tag."

"Give it time. Give it time."

Eel Pie Island
Taggert

"Is there a reason why I shouldn't stab you in the heart now?" my brother asks, only slightly more than miffed as he sits at a staid elegant table in the middle of the restaurant, which itself is in the gravitational middle of the fifteen-story building made of black glass and cobalt-colored steel.

In my dimension Eel Pie Island is half artist commune, half dispossessed monument to an older time. Mico was rebuilding it, making a home for war children and Manna worshippers in the middle of the Thames. Seems like the Liminals of this world have turned it into a cenotaph to the dead-eyed stares of the Alters. Developments throughout the island are filled with sharp angles and tall ceilings; they want everything to cut you and listen as your screams echo throughout their buildings. Such intentionality in the architecture tells me they've been at this for a while and no one has protested. Even with no Alters, I felt their heartless cold as I force legs, feet and hands to give me entrance into the building. It was hard to keep the body still as I rode the elevator to the seventh floor, and keeping the pulse rate calm standing before Baron, Samantha, and Yasmine is all but impossible. This whole body is resisting it.

"Nope, If I were you, I'd take my head off right now. Only, you've been trying that since I walked across the threshold and it's not working." Seven floors up in an oblique-looking fifteen-story high rise, I'm finding it hard to navigate past the cowed waitstaff that avoid eye contact with my brother and his companions. These eyes are sharp enough to pick up the goose bumps on Yasmine's skin against the dress that's the orange of her hair in my world. Samantha's hair is still braided laying flat against her small back, her lips are forever pursed on that small oval head; she seems a closer approximation of her other dimensional self, save for the disdain and confusion that beam out her eyes when she looks at me. If any part of the woman who loved me in my time is in this simulacra cuddling up next to my sociopath of a brother, she'll see through my ruse. Then all a body has to do is survive.

No matter the dimension, Baron is smart as hell. Sharp, damn near transparent filaments, ultra flexible, thin and light try to push hard at the back of my head, floating like homicidal acupuncture needles. It's only Tam's TK's pushing back that keeps me alive. She's hidden, but I can tell my girl is sweating. Baron's lip is barely curling.

He's a taller, leaner, crueller version of me. It's only seeing him in this adult body, a body he'd never reached in my world, that I realize how much I still model my physique off of him. That almost throws my confidence and my focus.

"So should I aim at giving each of you heart attacks or can we just cut the threats and get to our issues?" I ask.

"Oh, really?" A tarted-out version of my Yasmine leans forward, showing as much of her breasts as that thin bright orange dress will allow. "I bet I could set your eyes on fire before you could bring yourself to break your lover's heart."

"Spell pickle," I tell her. Whatever this slag sitting in front of my face is, she's not my woman, not Tamara's mother. Despising power more than caring it meant our Yasmine held her fire and her seductive abilities at bay. "Seriously, take your time. I'll wait."

"Pill," she starts. "Ickeling. Carly. What the fuck?"

"Very specific type of aphasia. Think of it like a localized stroke. You can only speak because I'm not giving you a grand mal seizure. But I don't want you to spell, so I'm cutting the flow of oxygenated blood to that spelling parts of your brain. All of your heads. It's easy. If I can do that, you can be damn sure I can cut your powers off whenever I damn well please."

"There's something wrong with you," Samantha says.

"Yup. Trying to change the world with one well-placed assassination at a time." My chair gives with body weight as I shift this body back. It is an old ploy: when weak, play strong. I've used it half of my life now with varying degrees of success.

"No, I agree." My brother stops and stares deep into the eyes sitting across the table from him. "No way I would let a sibling have lived to be this flippant to my face."

"Oh, you didn't let me live in my time," I tell him honestly. "I let you live. Beat you to a pulp. When I was a child."

"I get it," he says, casually ordering dessert with the raised eyebrow and the finger flick of a despot at home. At no point does the pressure from his glass spikes of death weaken. "You're trying to intimidate me."

"No I'm not . . ."

"Shut up." He closes the lips I speak through with his powers instantly dropping all his filaments. "This is what you have to understand. Whatever version of me you beat in another dimension was a lightweight. I wasn't being hyperbolic; when my mother told me she was pregnant I crushed the embryo on instinct. As an afterthought. I joined the Navy and got combat experience with my powers years before the Alters found me and showed me what true power is."

"Do you know what they are?" I pull the lips open and mute the pain as I speak through bloody ridge wounds on the mouth. The trick costs me control over the oxygenated flow going to Samantha's head. Won't be long before she notices.

"The winning side," he says like I'm an idiot. "You understand that you're fighting against a fundamental law of nature, right? Things don't go from cold to hot on their own. That requires energy, a finite resource in this universe. Without it all things, all matter cools, slows, reduces to stillness. Why would you want to stop that?"

"It doesn't need any help! And aren't you supposed to be Mister Billy Badass? What, you only fight battles you're guaranteed to win?"

"Better than fighting battles you can't win," Yasmine chimes in.

"I've been beating odds like that my entire life."

"I don't understand you," she says after laughing at me. "This isn't your world. You know we want you dead, and you decide to come to our place of power. Why?"

"That's not him." Samantha sounds like she just figured out the crossword of the day. The shock causes my brother to stop eating his meal.

"I knew you'd get it first," I tell my other former lover. "I only vaguely look like this. But I shaped your boy Pasha to look like me. Good idea on the infiltration through a covert, by the way. But me and mine can call a traitor out from twenty paces."

"How are you speaking?" Yasmine asks, more annoyed than anything.

"Obviously he has a telepath with him." First time I saw that look in Baron's eye he threw me out a second-story window with his power. I was nine years old.

"Your niece actually," I tell him. Then to Yasmine: "And your daughter for lack of a better version of you. I'm here for three reasons. First, to return your little turncoat." I let Tamara terrorize Pasha's brain as I release my modifications and let his agony show while his legs and shoulder condense back to their normal size, his hand and feet muscles contract, and his melanin count dissipates. I know how much that last part stings. We let him writhe but still control his mouth.

"Reason number two was to let Samantha know that if any part of her soul, the real her, the part that screamed across time and space to tell us not to come back is in that body, we came back for her. She knows how to reach out to me if she's in there."

"And the third reason?" Yasmine does her best dragon impression, juggling fire in her mouth.

"Well, to kill you, of course." They never expect me, or the Pasha Maaco shaped me to turn away from Liminal abilities in favor of a grenade. So that's the last thing I do before giving up Pasha's animus and corpus entirely.

I come back to my body in the inappropriately flashy orange two-door Lotus Tamara said we had to steal. I usually don't dissociate so fully from my body, but it's not every day I not only morph but "drive" another's body. Tam's eyes refocus in the driver's seat about ten seconds after the explosion halfway across the Thames and seven stories up.

"They all survived," she laments.

"You thought it would be easy?"

"Wot's with tarted up Ma?"

"That slag couldn't hold a candle to your mother."

"Think Samantha heard you?" It's sweet of her to ask, but she pulls into traffic right after ambulance sirens start streaming toward the island, so I don't bother answering.

Pangkor Island, Strait of Malacca
A.C.

Leave it to Narayana to be in the last place I look but the first I told everyone to meet. Pangkor Island, like all islands, has at least two sides. Asian and Indian tourists are served by dark-skinned Tamils that look like Narayana's cousins on one side. But for the other side, past the dump, slightly inland from the native Malay villages, the remains of an old Chinese temple of a forgotten deity serves as a place of power for the drowned Alter.

Most people think Narayana is the Alter of piracy. But it's far deeper than that, literally. Alters are formed from the gross inchoate material of the great nothing, first experiences of a violation that defies comprehension.

When early humanity first observed the ebbs and tides of the ocean, they followed what receding waters they could trying to find the "source" of the sea only to run back to the safety of the shore when quickly advancing waters began to caress first their toes, then feet, and then ankles.

But sometimes those who stayed at the fortress of the shore watched as their friends and family disappeared into the horizon, never to return. At some point, one of those coast-dwelling orphans got careless and chased the receding ocean past seaweed, refuse, and assorted primordial crustacean, only to come face-to-face with the hidden terror of the ocean. That was the birth of the first Narayana.

So it doesn't surprise me to find him in rapt conversation with Rice Montague, new de facto head of the Alters. Rice is in the costume of his human camouflage, tan suit with a billowing shite shirt. His black trainers, the only hint of malice he'll offer, unless you study those dead green eyes, notice how his bright blond hair stays permanently still, or realize you can cut coconuts against his seemingly perfect high cheekbones. Mico's disbelief shouldn't shock me but I'm tired from popping all over this misaligned ley-lined world. Thank the south wind I shut him up before I materialize us fully.

"Seriously? We're going to have this conversation again?" I tell him on a gust of wind designated only for our ears. No Alter, human or Liminal, can see or hear us now, unless I declare it necessary. Or they are really powerful. "Listen and maybe learn something."

"I've taken over the aesthetic space of the human race, old Master. On the other side of this island I have teenage girls in hijab with pierced nipples and clit rings. They mix their henna leaf with the root for lickable abortions." Rice laughs, almost like a human. I've faced him before. With Chabi. Wish I had shot true then.

"I have an army of deformed children from the Kahrizak Polygon drooling ready to impose my will. In India, I have people scalping girls so they can sell their hair to American Blacks. These women walk around with dried bits of human scalp on their own. I've got one eighth of the male population believing it's a father's job to teach his children how to have sex. I mean literally. I've got the rich in Western Africa believing homeless children are possessed by demons that can only be exorcised through bloodletting. The mortalities are in the thousands. There's not a papistry, ministry, sangha, or sect that doesn't bow down to us, whether they know it or not. I've got Muslims collecting interest on loans, with the heretical dividends paying out to us. Once the Decimation is complete we won't even have to hide behind corporate and religious constructions. This is all my free labor . . ."

"The crippled rat kings no longer on your side?" Narayana, voice like a drunk shadow, asks. Not caring about the answer. His small carriage, pin pricks of eyes that you can never tell are open or closed, the way his skin held to his bones, as though there was no muscle between them, all of this I have to remember is a choice for him. A physique made of absence and not form.

"The Poppies? They are still with me, as are all the others . . ."

"Then you don't need me." The Indian-looking Alter turns his back on Rice as he offends every sensibility I have by lighting joss sticks and sticking them before black-faced Chinese icons riding tigers.

"You're right." His monotone rises but Rice stays still in the middle of the temple, still as the statues Narayana bows before. "I don't need you. But this is an offer based on your legend. You are of the same generation as my sire, Kothar. The old powers."

"So was Salmovar. What good did that do him against the Liminals?"

"He was unprepared for the Liminal he faced." Rice does something disturbing. He smiles. "Please don't concern yourself about your time away from us, or your previous . . . associations. You are the bastion of the hidden treasure. It's your right to bury yourself as you see fit. What . . . oddities you find in the darkness, in whatever form, are of course yours to play with. There is a risk we all run in doing our duties. What's important is that you fulfilled your role. The Liminal Chabi died."

"In my day, we did not hide behind our words," Narayana says not getting up from his prostration despite the fact that his fetid attempt at prayer literally causes the icon to break before him. Alters are not meant to be reverent.

"It's said the breaker of the male Rat King's bones and the crippler of Salmovar might be one in the same. A female Alter with martial skills that could only have been taught by a djinn. In your away time, you trained with a djinn, didn't you?"

In the past, I've grown bored in the seconds between a puma's decision to strike and its muscle twitch. With the very djinn Rice is speaking of, the one Narayana and I both trained with, I saw Narayana outrun a diving falcon. But I can't clock how quickly Narayana stood, turned, and faced the younger Alter. If they fight, I don't know what side we should be on: Narayana's or none at all.

"Is this how you took your sire's place? Hiding all meaning in half-placed words until he had no choice but to return to the ever present dark for a sense of comprehension and rest?" Narayana snaps. "Make yourself plain, Rice, or leave my island."

"I don't care about the Poppies. I'll give you both their hearts as a gift. But with you at my side we can take not only the aesthetics of this world but the physicality as well."

"To what end?" Narayana says, distancing himself from Rice and looking out to the troubled ocean currents his still rage causes.

"The only cause worthy of our kind. The return to the great stillness, the end of all things."

"This sounds more like desperation."

"It's the tipping point. The human spirit is all but broken. I've commodified the root god that gave you and Kothar so much trouble. It's treated like a narcotic and not a divinity, so its power is muted." If Mico keeps reacting I'll put him in another dimension until these two are done. I shoot him a look to let him know. "Another gift to you should you desire. But there are still Liminals out there from this time and others. My victory against them is assured. But with you by my side, it would be quicker."

"Someone so sure of their victory shouldn't be in such a rush. We are formed from divisive material. Collaborations among our kind are rarely effective. I say no. Ask again and see me lose what poise I've maintained thus far."

Absolute stillness—the lack of breath, pulse, eye movement, of all biological reaction—is an indication that an Alter is summoning their cold power. They instantly become impossible to move, infernally rooted. Rice takes on these attributes for a good minute. I see the micro preparations Narayana makes in stance to handle whatever angle of attack Rice may decide to take. I have to shoot Mico a look to silence his growing tension. I still don't know whether joining in the fight is better than hoping they both ice each other. I'm fortunate I don't have to make the decision.

Like he just got out of the shower, Rice shakes himself off and walks down the long gray stone stairs that lead to the temple proper. None of us expect him to just crawl into his powder white Aston Martin and drive off, but we don't expect his booming voice either. No one on the island could expect it to be so loud. Even half manifested, living on the wind, it's loud enough to deafen.

"It would be folly to mistake exuberance with panic, drowned one. And remember, the closer our kind come to our creator, the stronger our abilities become." With that he goes to one knee and bows his head. Where his knee makes contact with the ground, the very spirit of the earth objects to his supplication and splits in two.

What noise his mouth made is no comparison to the sound of the earth separating. His lips part and so does the ground. His tongue flickers and grotesque shards of land shoot up from long crusted over soil; he exhales and ancient methane and stygian vapors hiss forward from long trapped pockets of gas beneath the island, beneath the ocean. The three-foot-deep crack widens and yawns as it expands outward toward the temple itself knocking out its very foundations. Rice is on his feet and walking toward his Aston as the unstable nature of the land does what he himself would not do directly and topples the small temple. Narayana tolerates the tons of falling stone and broken roof collapsing as most would the slamming of a door, proving once again Alters are notoriously resilient and a pain to murder. This was no killing blow from Rice. Just an Alter version of a tantrum.

"Now?" Mico asks me once we see Narayana crawling up from the rubble, shoving collapsed pylons away from himself in irritation, but unharmed.

"Not yet. All we know is he's not allied with Rice. Doesn't mean he'll link up with us. Besides, I want to test his jaw."

I go full physical before Mico has a chance to say anything. He's got the savior curse; he thinks he can save everyone. Even a soulless being like Narayana. I grew up around this Alter. I know how he thinks, what he smells like when he lies, and what an authentic fight with him feels like. I let Mico down once before and the world suffered for it. I won't let that happen again.

"Never thought I'd see the day the Terror of the Deep was humbled by a Scion of Montague," I tell Narayana, letting him hear my feet meet stone rubble. He shakes broken masonry and multi-colored roof tiles off like a child would toss blankets off on a warm summer night.

"What do I care what you think of me, Wind Boy?" Rather than look at me, the Alter chooses to survey the rubble from where he fell. Those not from this island would see a small dark-skinned Indian man in all black tossing one ton ancient mortar as though they were pebbles.

"This you care about? Some forgotten Chinese temple at the ass end of nowhere?" I send a strong gust across his feet to kick every kind of debris and bring dust to his eyes. Narayana barely blinks. "You let the whole world go to shit!"

"I let?" He turns from me and picks up a nine-foot molten red pylon like it was nothing and replaces it where it fell. "You attribute powers to me I don't claim. To face Rice and his allies without reasonable offense would give my enemies all the clearance necessary to destroy me."

"Oh. 'Cause for a second I thought you were scared." He doesn't even bother to look in my direction for that comment, continuing focusing on clearing rubble. "What happened to your fight?"

"Fight for who? Mico left to chase after the time lost Liminal and his god was never convinced of my conversion. Alongside who? You? You gallivanted off into the ether soon after my savior. No Liminal or human can tolerate my company for too long. Fight for what? Mico's center couldn't hold without him. The Liminal Baron's network took the place of all his good works and replaced them with abominations, Teratomas, the dead voice singers . . . I told him this would happen!"

"What about Chabi?" Birds deviate flight plans to avoid the cone of stillness he projects as I say her name. "Isn't she worth fighting for?"

"She died." Black bullet hole eyes lock on me. "Years ago."

"I know. I was there. What? You thought you could bury a Liminal trained by an Alter and my blood-cursed gear in the mystery of way back when?" I slip my hands close to my holstered accursed six-shooters, praying for the speed to draw if he moves on me. "I found them all while I was *gallivanting.*"

Time doesn't flow in one direction for me. It is the whirlwind I ride. On one trip I found his mentee, Chabi, and I fell a bit for her. I gave her what I could to stand against the Alter, but in the end I was the tool they used to capture her. I would have gladly given my life for her, but she ended up feeling the same way.

"Did you kill her?" I feel the rotation of the earth stop. I could get iced off a misunderstanding here.

"I fought by her side."

"Against who?"

"The Alter you were just having tea with!"

Had he moved, altered the pathway of a single atom between us, I would have felt it and drawn my weapons. Instead it was his very stillness that reached out and grabbed me by the physical and spiritual throat. Alters do know how to stop things, like my ability to breathe.

"So you sat in your blustery pocket dimension and watched as the entity that killed my daughter destroyed my temple and did nothing?" I think he asked while grabbing my floating rib through cloth and skin. He started yanking at it. As I was blacking out, I couldn't be sure what he was saying, but I know. "And *you* sit in judgment of me, A.C.? Me?"

"Don't act like you didn't know!" I budge his offending wrist left while swinging my legs up and kicking right. Whatever approximates pain registers in his face and forces that cold grip to loosen. I gain distance and flip over broken stone as I draw both six-shooters. "Or that you cared for that girl at all!"

"I gave her everything!" He's so casually deadly I don't know if he means to kick broken wall and ceiling bits at me at Mach 3. Wind carries me aloft on instinct and I twist my body to avoid the fist-sized fragments that spray everywhere when the stones break apart. "I protected her. Showed her how to protect herself. I loved her!"

"You are an Alter!" I let five shots fly from four feet in the air, another seven from the ground. The first three land and hurt, but barely stop him. They force Narayana to gain cover behind a half-propped-up wall. "Your love is a curse. Your protective sigil on her back gained the attraction of Rice and his clique. But that wasn't the worst of it, you idiot!"

The infernal quaking behind the stone relief confuses the hell out of me. It didn't feel like a summoning, a gathering of power, but rather a release. But whatever energies Narayana was letting out weren't being directed at me. So with guns drawn I advance on him.

"When I found Chabi she was half broken, half muted, spiritually I mean," I say. "And Rice hadn't laid a hand on her. She could take on a thousand men, a hundred Alters, and not flinch. But the one thing that broke her in two was that you left her." As I rounded the corner I saw the energy release, an improbable and I thought impossible occurrence. Narayana, ancient Terror of the Deep, weeping in rubble. I've cried like this before, lost and broken, impotent and without hope. But I always thought that was the place where Alters got their power from. Now, suddenly, I felt like a bully with weapons in my hand and this soulless thing in a human body weeping at my feet.

"Enough," Mico says behind me with a honeyed soft voice. "There's been enough hurt."

"My God . . ." Narayana scrambles to Mico's feet like a servant of old and I brace for the consequences of his supplication, but nothing shakes or breaks. This may not be Mico's world, but his subtle power remains strong.

"We can't keep treating each other like this," he tells us both as his hands almost lift Narayana to his feet. "If we're going to pull this world together, we need to put each other together."

"You died . . ."

"No, it just felt like it," Mico tells Narayana.

"Actually you did," I tell them both. "In all other possible realities but the one I pulled you from, you died, Mico."

"I witnessed your fall in every one of them," Narayana confirms for me. "Don't listen to the Wind Boy, I didn't just give up. But one by one, I saw your life wiped out in every corner of existence." And then a skeptical glance toward me.

"Thank your daughter," Mico tells Narayana. "You told me to call her name if I got in trouble. She found me, gave me and Taggert the time to figure out how to survive what should have been an impossible journey."

"You saw Chabi?" Again, tears that burn through stone fall from his face.

"Dead," I tell him. Despite a cold stare from Mico, I continue. "And pissed. I don't know where you found a ship made of Ashvattha wood but she'd spent enough time on it that it could contain her spirit. I gave her the option of moving on or being bound to the ship. Her rage at you kept her in the astral plane with a promise that she'd find you and break you in two."

"If we're going to save this world, this reality, and by extension all realities, I'll need her help and yours." Mico brings us back to task. "You have no reason to trust, and I have no right to ask, Narayana, but I'm asking. Will you rejoin my cause?"

Pangkor Island, Strait of Malacca
Taggert

It takes us about a day of being on Pangkor Island before we find A.C. Tam has just about lost her mind searching for a guy with half a face when A.C. barrels past us in a four-by-four Chevy Blazer.

"He didn't even recognize us," Tam shouts right before she guns her scooter after him. I'm dodging fat bugs on suicide missions to keep up with her. The sea competes with the mini roar of the scooters for noise. I imagine diving in it to get rid of the heat stench I can't escape.

"Means we're hiding right," I tell her as I struggle to keep up on my scooter. We end up tailing him around a quarter of the island to an air strip so tiny we'd have driven by it and never noticed if A.C. hadn't jerked his ride so harshly into the dense thicket.

"You guys didn't buy those scooters, did you?" The first words out of his mouth. But his actions tell more. He's using strong winds to clear debris from the abandoned runway.

"With ten grand in Manna bucks," Tam mocks him. "Who's coming in?"

"You do run a tight ship," A.C. tells me just as a familiar body calls out from the horizon of the setting sun.

"About time." Tam grins as she feels Prentis's thoughts. But she loses the smile quickly. "Something's wrong."

"I saw Fatima land a DC-9 on desert sand like it was nothing," I tell A.C. "So why is she off target now?"

"Shit," A.C. says, flying high in the air. "Phoenix Stillborns."

"English, you twat!" Tam screams.

"You can't see them? Fuck. They're spirit entities . . . Alters, shit, looks like Alters found a pair of Phoenix eggs and, well, scrambled them. The result is confused air- and fire-born spirits that try to kill and rebirth everything in their path for eternity."

"And they're attacking Prentis?" Tam asks, pissed already in her voice, levitating to his height.

53

A.C. shoves a small blast of wind in my eyes and I can see them, giant gray peacocks with ashen plumage dive-bombing at the plane a quarter of their size. The only reason our folks in the plane are still alive is Fatima's skill behind the stick. But with no weapons, it's all she can do to stay in the air as the Phoenixes bear down on her plane's wings with their talons.

Pangkor Island, Strait of Malacca
Prentis

"Cockpit!" bark at Bingy. Faring better than the plane. No way Fatty's gonna be able to keep in the air with this much weight thrashing around.

"You first!" Bless him for being protective. Useless sentiment but happy not to die alone.

"Like I'd let that happen," hear in my head. Bless my lunatic bestie. "Now get in the cockpit and tell everyone to strap in."

I do, along with Bingy. Of course Fatima has something to say.

"Move your fat ass out of my way so I can steer." Turn to tell her it's only as fat as her mouth when I see out the pilot's vantage. Plane-sized massive peacock/hawk gray creatures circle us releasing a spray of gray mist from their wings.

"What the fuck are those?" ask.

"What ya see, girl?" Bingy asks me. Look around and can tell. No one else can see the birds.

"Who gives a shit?" Fatty barks. "We just took on a thousand extra pounds on a wing and lost seven-eighths of fuel. Everybody grab parachutes."

Know this feeling. When something material is moved by something mental. Tamara. Like a lightning strike in the middle of the ocean. Never seen her try to move anything as big as a plane.

"I see dem," Bingy says just as the cockpit door begins to warp. It's the depressurization of the cabin. But in front, A.C. is using his wind to push against the dark birds. Their ruffled feathers and screams combined are nothing to the sound of metal ripping from itself.

"He's going to tear us apart!" Munji finally loses his jovial demeanor. Grabs his ahimsa, begins whispering a song.

"This ain't him," tell them all. That's when the cockpit flies eighty feet away from the rest of the plane. We spin and fall. Fall and spin. Whipping in uneven downward spirals, frets of stripped away metal loosed from its home whistling in the wind for a high-pitch-deceleration death song.

Fatima is the first one out of the nose of the plane and spinning in the air, her chair not properly bolted in. Grab for her but get my hand slapped back into the hull of the broken plane. Even over the rushing air as we plummet, hear Munji wails. Blinking hard, see him reaching for his own seat belt. No need to live if his daughter is dead.

"Don't you fucking dare!" all hear in our minds right before the cockpit stops spinning and starts controlled descent. Tamara, like I've never seen her. Not hovering but flying over the island. Not that far above it or the ocean. Can see the splashdown of bits of the plane's wing, deep blue enveloping what once was after the briefest splash of white. My girl using her power to slow our landing, making sure we aren't the victims of splashdown. The strain—when younger—would have killed her. Now, black-red streaks of blood flowing from her nose and ears. Not like that will stop her. See invisible fingers plucking us all, Bingy first from the remnants of the cockpit. Don't dare risk peering over the shrapnel edge of our dingy to see where she's dropping us. Besides Munji's crying is too distracting.

"Fatima!" he moans.

"Silly man!" shout over the raging winds. "Think Mico would be anywhere near your daughter and let her come to harm?"

Pangkor Island, Strait of Malacca
Taggert

It's less that we spring into action and more that we just react. Fuck if I know how to stop deformed Phoenix babies or anything about getting on a crashing plane in midair. But I'm good for support. So when Tam and A.C. take off in the air, I beef up my leg strength and lung capacity and bolt to the nearest harbor. Three minutes later I'm piloting a mid-sized fishing boat toward the plane impact trajectory. That's when the agonizing sound of metal ripping in two makes the ocean water vibrate.

It takes all my nonexistent piloting abilities to avoid the larger part of the falling plane. Then I realize A.C. is helping out where he can with strong gusts designed to either launch pieces in front or behind me. I take a second to give a thankful look up and see Tam holding the nose of the plane from falling. I feel her neurons firing off like firecrackers, pruning more now than they ever have before. If it wasn't for the manipulations I made on her to be able to travel through time, she'd be bleeding out of her eye sockets right now.

I move the fishing boat as close to her as possible before Mico shoots off the island like a cannon. I zero in my pupils to see where he's aiming. The unconscious Fatima falling loosely is almost as surprising as Mico in full African spirit armor gear.

"Let Jah be praised and the wicked men scatter!" Bingy proclaims as soon as Tam drops him telekinetically on the deck.

"Come inside!" I tell him from the captain's nest. "It's raining plane and cosmic fuckery."

But he waits until Munji gets delivered. The old Arab is so distressed I cut the engine and abandon my post to check on him out on deck.

"Calm yourself, Munji." I flood his body with endorphins, but he can't stay in that mode.

"Who are you?" he asks in Arabic.

"A friend. You've got a few of them." Mico flies in so low and fast he almost overshoots the deck. In his arms he cradles an unconscious Fatima. Munji is on her in a second. I can empathize.

Tam descends with Prentis in hand but barely has enough energy to push the nose of the Beechcraft plane from our fishing boat. We all get splashed. Only Tamara stops bleeding once it's down.

"Heal her!" Mico, or rather African spirit possessed Mico, says as he gets in the way of me going to my daughter. I didn't even call the Entropy Blades to my hands, but they were ready.

"In a minute!" I tell him.

"Now!" When the African spirits envelope him, they speak in a tortured chorus that threatens to add more misery to its baritone. I shift my grip on the entropy blades and prepare to swing

"Stop, you two!" A.C. tells us as he lands. "Or you'll miss something pretty cool."

"Shouldn't you be up there fighting the demon chickens?" Prentis barks.

"Nah. I just ruffled their feathers. I'm not the one they should be worried about."

Imminent death, proximity to many magical mystery men, or I don't know what, but while I couldn't see the Black Phoenixes before, the malice-heavy beasts came through with perfect clarity as the giant emaciated peacocks, flecked with all manner of gray and black plumage, began to dive towards us. Later A.C. would tell me they formed from the stillbirths of binary stars and the pain of miscarrying mothers of all species. All I could tell at the time was that they were going to feed on us.

"You gonna do something?" I demand of Mico and A.C. at the same time.

"No need," A.C. tells me just as an eighty-foot plume of ocean shaped like a hand reaches up and grabs both birds between its fingers. Their fight against the grip is as piercing and dramatic as it is fruitless. Their screams are like dog whistles on the soul, and for a quick moment their eyes flare like nuclear explosions in reverse, shimmering white hot then blue and finally cold red against the fractured shades between black and death that their feathers are. Sixty-foot wingspans and beaks tough enough to tear a plane in two turned out to be nothing compared to the will of the drowned Alter. In a second, that water hand turns to a fist and descends back into the ocean proper with its victims in tow, then, screaming and flapping the whole while, causing waves and whirlpools that turn our fishing boat every which way and encroach onto the roads well past the coastal highway of the island. And riding the middle finger knuckle, all the way down, Narayana.

Pangkor Island, Strait of Malacca
Prentis

"We're are grossly unprepared," A.C. tells us after we regroup on the shore at a three-star hotel.

"You've got two fathers in here with injured daughters." Tag's voice made it clear. "Say something useful."

Narayana had a resort on lock on the trendy part of the island run by Sri Lankan immigrants as dark as him. All of them well fit, on the timid side. Least with the humans. Macaques, they're downright brutal. Sometimes have to be that way with monkeys, otherwise they'll disrespect and take your kit. Only understand naked aggression and threats. That's that hooting and screaming they do all the time, brutality and posturing. Thought Narayana was like that. But he's not. He's worse.

Locals didn't know why they let him do whatever he wanted, but they did. Told them the resort was free and open to all of us, it almost made sense that their tiny wall-less central office became our meeting place. The most brightly colored building in the resort complex, even if that is only a light sepia. Sloped roof made of woven palm leaves rustled whenever the wind hit, sound like rain was just starting, always. Cliff bats raiding for insects by the outdoor pool just by the door made me feel protected from the invisible inevitable hate from without. Narayana, though, kept feeling like the hate from within.

"We didn't know the Alters' influence went so far as calling mythical beasts. That means they have hold on at least some of the concept Zoo. So I checked. They've got the Peripatetic Shadow Babe, the Boundless Pption and its infinite spawn. The Teratoma Terrors are all gone from their flesh cage. They've even got the Angels."

"I thought they were the servants of the one true god?" Mico asks.

"They think so as well. In the old tongues, Angel just means messenger. So does demon, by the way. They're the messengers of the Dominance of this reality, The Alters. Don't worry, they're just flaming, neutered winged Concepts of Death." A.C. almost smiles.

"Concepts?" Taggert starts. "They have concepts on their side?"

"Another thing." The Rasta speaks. "Fatima, girl, yah. She know Manna."

"Of course." Munji spins in his chair. "We supply a quarter of the European market."

"You're talking about Manna for real?" Mico picks up on his friend's inclination before the others. Nod to agree.

"Thought you said she didn't know Mico and that none of all the past had been?" ask A.C. It's only what everyone is thinking. Shrugs his shoulders then starts thinking for real.

"Bingy, you sure?" Tag persists.

"It a same feeling as what Mico breathe in my lung." The Rasta nods.

"But nothing from Munji?" The Dread shakes his head, no.

"I am confused. What's wrong with my daughter?" Munji looks so scared that both A.C. and Mico go to give him a supportive hand.

"Nothing is wrong with her," A.C. said. "In fact she may point the way to the Manna."

"Someone want to walk me through this?" finally ask. Feel stupid in this room of heavy road men. But Taggert feels me, stays close, and somehow brave enough to ask for what I don't know.

"There are places even I can't see," A.C. starts. "Places I don't know how to get to, where the wind keeps secrets even from its children. When I first met Mico, he was brand spanking new in his skill and just on the edge of one of those places, about five hundred miles northwest of Majane, in the middle of the Sahara."

"I don't know where the Manna first found me," Mico confesses.

"That was probably by design," A.C. says. "What I'm saying is maybe your girlie, the love of your life, maybe she's your compass back to the true manna."

"I'm no one's fucking true love compass." Words fall effortlessly from her mouth as Fatty beelines toward her father. Mico almost tries to hug her but even he can't ignore the woman unbuckling a thigh-holstered rifle.

Munji and Fatty twitter in a tongue meant to exclude the rest. She won't let her father stand, instead kneeling next to him as he pets her head. Type of good parenting everyone else feels uncomfortable around. We've never had it. Sad sacks us. A.C. walks over to me and Tag as we all turn our backs to give a little privacy.

"In terms of mythical beasts," the Wind Boy starts, and I know where he's headed. "Your girl here can handle that, right? If she could manage Robert Johnson's Hellhounds . . ."

"That was Nordeen's doing," Tag tells him. I'm grateful and ashamed at the same time.

"I get it," A.C. pushes. "Your powers can take you to uncomfortable places but . . ."

"You don't get shit." Tag puts "Dad voice" on. "Not unless you've been in that sociopath's grip. Prentis will put in what she can. Right now that doesn't include unicorns, hellhounds, or burnt phoenix eggs . . ."

"Sorry . . ." start but Taggert bumps me and I shut up. A.C. says something about one hand being tied behind our backs then circles out to talk to Mico and Narayana. Last thing Tag wants to hear is another apology so give him more bad news.

"Tam's awake."

"Figured."

"Think she's pissed at you."

"Which one of you pricks owes me a new plane?" Seeing Fatima command the attention of every man in the room, with just the power of her voice, reminds me that Tam and I are still just girls.

"Sounds like she's not the only one." What does Tag do whenever a woman is pissed? Leaves the room.

Pangkor Island, Strait of Malacca
Taggert

Disconnected as I am from this world, I barely notice the thrall Narayana has the people of this island under. He's the number one head chief of all he surveys, which is expected and common to their understanding. But it's only when I step in the room we've set up for Tam to convalesce that I realize how far that dominion goes. We came in wet, bleeding, and battered, and somehow secured a glass-tiled, air-conditioned, three-bedroom suite two flights above where the grubbiest monkey can reach. With the thick green curtains drawn one could almost forget the chaos outside. But then I'd have to deal with the drama within. Everything I do is for this girl, and she still finds reasons to give me shit. Even as I try to heal her wounds.

"I'm keeping these scars." It hurts to look at them. High-velocity heated metal instantly cauterized slices out of my daughter's face just below her left eyebrow and above her right cheekbone. Three inches either way and she'd have lost her right eye.

"Fashion statement," I say, trying to avoid the bait.

"Reminder for you that I can handle myself." She sits up in her king-sized resort bed as I sit on it. I can smell less of the baking drapes and know the sun is beginning to set.

"I let you handle . . ."

"You didn't let me do shit. I tore a plane in two and plucked everyone out of it like raisins off a danish while you were driving a boat. And when it came to healing time, rather than going to the one person I missed, you almost go to blows with Mico over healing this!" She points to her face. "You can't be that bloke."

"The kind that looks to his daughter's safety first?"

"I'm not your daughter!" She realizes how much it hurts. That doesn't stop her. "I'm your soldier. One of your best, get me? I dunked one Alter in the ocean and liquidated the bones of another. And don't act like dragging me to London was a decision based on common sense. You know it would have been better to have one of these mystic spazzes with you in case an Alter had been there. You took me 'cause you wanted to take care of me. Same way you're softballing Prentis. Yeah, I'm psychically ear hustling. That's not the point."

"What is your point?"

"You're scared!"

"I can't lose you!" I shout. "Fuck the planet, girl. Really. Fuck reality. Fuck Mico and A.C. and all their lunacy. I'll help as much as I can without losing you or Prentis."

"Then we've already lost," she tells me like I'm an idiot child. "You know, back when we first met the Manna and it called you selfish? I jumped to your defense, yeah? But thinking, Tag, you don't get to keep us safe while the world goes to shit just because you've had a rough go of it and don't feel like losing any more people you love. That's just not fair. The only way we're winning this is if you get over yourself and start acting like the dyed-in-the-wool asshole Taggert of the Nordeen days."

Part of me wants to smack the shit out of her. The part that knows she's right. Instead, I get up to leave the room.

"You ever wonder why they set up that table in London just for you?" She's not done, so I stop.

"How do you mean?"

"Don't act daft. Your brother, both your lovers just happen to be the Alter's main tool for controlling the Manna? What'd you say about coincidence?"

"Best found up a unicorn's ass." I try to smile. "But given what took the plane down . . ."

"There's reason in it is all I'm saying," she interrupts, putting her feet on the ground for the first time in hours. "Maybe it's because they're trying to hit us at our weak spot. And maybe we're weakest when it comes to you and family."

Pangkor Island, Strait of Malacca
Prentis

Fair play, expecting Mico to make an ass of himself, proper like. Got popcorn ready and everything. Expect him to go straight for Fatima, make a big romantic show of it all. Instead, caters to Munji like a young elephant to an elder about to leave the herd. Soon as he starts joining in their private hill language bird talk, see Fatima get confused and even more protective of her father. Wanted to laugh at the DJ, but this scenario is just sad to see.

First time I feel like one of the heavy hitters is A.C. and Narayana chat up outside the office by the forty-foot pool. Update them on what Tam's been through in London and an instant later, all strategy.

"My island is secure," Scary Alter says.

"If sounding scary was all there was to it, I'd agree," A.C. answers back. "But your waters were just attacked by twin Phoenix . . . phoenii . . . what do you call multiple Phoenixes?"

"Call them drowned because I dealt with them."

"There's no need for a watch?" Ask "For no other reason than to give you a chance to get water fist of doom prepared? Was in the plane overhead getting torn apart by ginormous death birds and the like while you was deciding which finger to use."

"Set your animals to a perimeter guard if you must." Shadows could grin, Narayana would be doing that toward me. "The humans under my protection on the island will alert me if there is any activity worthy of our attention."

A sharp angle jawed dark-skinned Indian woman in a drab sari runs up to the Alter and bows deeply before rattling off something so quickly it sounds like a made up language. Just as quickly, she leaves. Narayana walks slowly in the same direction, inviting us to follow.

"So. Mico and Fatima . . ." ask A.C. as we make our way toward the beach across the road.

"If she's related to the clan I think she is, then their relationship isn't just about lust and disgust. It's also about the Manna," he says in time with the current. "So. You and no mystical critters?"

"What does the Manna have to do with why they would like or hate each other?" Thoroughly ignoring his question. He's doing the same to me as we angle through the competing fish restaurant fronts with pictures of brightly colored species they've never had. But behind both stalls is the beach, warm and wide. Sturdy long wooden table sits flush in the sand surrounded by the perfect number of seats for everyone in our crew, complete with silverware and settings for a feast. Not too long ago, could count my mates on two fingers. Now, need two hands.

"Mico is a convert to the faith of the Manna." A.C. sits and opens one of the beers in a black metal tray at the center of the table. "I think Fatima might have been born into the religion."

"You think she's Bint al-nas?" Narayana says, shooing away a girl with short hair, a rareness here.

"For the non-Arab speaker then?"

"A daughter of the desert," A.C. says while Narayana's people light torches all around the table to confront the oncoming dark. "And not her Narayana, but her mother. Even in my circles Prentis, the Bint al-nas are a rumor. A people out of space and time, protected and raised suckling at the teat of the Manna."

"Like a whole tribe of Micos." Narayana laughs and the torch closest to him goes out.

"More like insurance policy," Shadow man say.

"The prevailing theory," A.C. says kindly, so I don't feel so stupid, "is that they exist to keep an eye on the Manna's champion. Should he decide to go rogue the Bint al-nas would come for him."

"But mate did go off script when he came for me, right? Or what about now? Where are they, now that the Manna is getting bought and sold like dimestore smoke?"

"Don't know. Just a theory." The Wind Boy takes a swig from a light blue bottle on the table, then returns it. Seems disappointed it's just water.

"Weak ass theory," tell him.

"Weak as your control over the mythic beast," the Shadow man croaks.

"Oh, you're in on this now?"

"Every creature that flies hears your thoughts as law." Narayana's voice gets colder than the breeze off the ocean. "Yet you didn't even try to command the Black Phoenix."

"Bad luck with all that, get me?"

"The deviant Liminal tore you from your family and time and used you to control hellhounds and ghost sharks fat off African slaves." I nod. "So what?"

"Fuck off!"

"Make me, child. And before you go sacrificing this hornbill and that rabid monkey to my distraction, know that the only creatures that could hope to delay me from ripping your throat out are lying submerged in this bay."

Too scared to leave the table. Like when I first met Taggert. Just from the way he spoke, the way he walked, how he used his powers, I was outclassed. Taking all I have to keep about fifty monkeys nearby to not surround me.

"How Chabi survived your teachings I'll never know." A.C. tosses a beer, something physical to get me out of my head. Tam told me about Chabi, a ghost girl on a ghost ship forever sailing the spectral seas. A Liminal raised by an Alter, Narayana. A daughter looking to kill her father. A.C.'s words are enough to silence the Shadow.

"Kid, hate that it's true, but he does have a point," Wind Boy tells me, blowing my bottle top into his hand from across the table. "Alters have been into you for a while. Maybe they know something about your skills you don't?"

"Know how many praying mantises there are in the world? Trillions. How about hounds? Millions. Sharks? You get the species together, hundreds of thousands. I used to be best friends with all of them. More than friends. They all would have died for me in a second. Nordeen fucked that up for me. Now they're terrified of me. Trillions of beings that thought of me as their best friend now living in fear that I might call them up for service."

"I'm sorry . . ." A.C. starts.

"Damn right you are. Got no bloody idea what it feels like. So fuck off, both of you. Neither one of you has ever had a lick of harmony in your miserable lives. I can tell. That's why you hold Mico so tight. 'Cause he's the only idjit on the planet thick enough to call you two friends. Multiply the feeling of losing him by a species and you'll get what I'm dealing with."

"Nothing you've said argues against this truth," Narayana says. "If one of my kind is aiming for your life, your only defense are creatures you are too afraid to call upon."

"How's eats?" Tam hid her approach from me and the monkeys side to prove she's okay. An old trick of ours, one Tag taught. Hug her so hard she knows something's wrong. But won't have her fighting my battles.

"Service is slow. The company, a bit repetitive."

"How are you standing, Liminal?" Narayana takes a swig from a naked bottle of something. Can smell it from the other side of the table.

"It'll take more than a crashing Cessna to knock me down." Still, she sits with a thud.

"That was a Beechcraft Super King Air." Despite being flung from a plane, even walking with a slight limp and her father's cane, the smuggler queen is still hot as sin. Think it's her voice. She limps through the same sheet metal buildings we emerged from with Munji behind her. Instinctively, Tam stands to face her.

"You the one that tore apart my plane?" Fatty asks, a nose hair away from Tamara.

"Yup." Tam waits until I nudge her to speak again. "Was either that or watch all aboard meet a watery grave."

"That's what the guy inside, Mico said. I don't trust him." They lock eyes for a while. "But you don't flinch. Don't make excuses. And most importantly, you saved my father's life."

"So we're good?"

"Good as we're going get around here." Fatima shakes Tam's hand with the only hand that could reach her rifle. A display of trust indeed. "Once we're free and clear of this menagerie of mystics and lunatics, I'll pour from a proper bottle for you and light you a real smoke."

"Yay friends!" A.C. speaks and the pirate princess almost draws on him until she remembers who he is.

"You're not invited!" Tam snaps and sits. Fatima and Munji do the same next to her. As if on cue, ten dark-skinned Indians all bring out huge fishes, each prepared a different way; some fried whole, some grilled and chopped, some boiled then pickled, I think. Two are wrapped in banana leaf. Plus, french fries, salad, and rice.

"For an agent of entropy, you sure throw a good spread," Tag says, walking from beach jungle shadows behind Narayana with Mico by his side. Can tell by their faces they've been plotting.

"I leave such arrangements to my lesser." The Alter stands with his bottle. "But this bottle. Listen all. This bottle was lost in these waters five hundred years ago by a group of Portuguese sailors headed for Borneo. For five centuries, the dark tides and the pressure have cultivated this rum into something far better than the original. Some of you remember, some don't. I do. We were something before. A group, myself, least among you. But we've been lost, scattered. Alone, in the dark . . .

"But we've returned," Mico says. Behind me I feel Bingy walking slowly to Mico's side. "Coming back to the surface, stronger, and richer. The dark didn't blind us, the tides haven't broken us, and the pressure has only made us tighter. We will be more than we have been. A more potent potion than this world has ever tasted."

Got to admit, when that bottle came around, it was a good swig.

Pangkor Island, Strait of Malacca
Taggert

I fall asleep listing our enemies as Mico and Prentis practice singing every song they've ever heard. While Tam brags about hearing a live Bob Marley jam session to the assembled, I'm lying on a bed in a ground level suite organizing our threats: The top is easy, The Alters. Specifically, the ones that hate us, Rice, for the slaughter of his father, and the Rat twins for insult and injury. After them come my personal oppressors, my brother, and my lovers aided by what stray Liminals like Pasha Macco they can muster. According to A.C. we've got mythic beasts to handle and, of course, angels. I have to ignore that here are only eight of us to get some much-needed rest.

But more than anything, it's Tam's voice banging around in my head that keeps sleep at bay. I never asked for leadership, let alone fatherhood. And it's not that I've never imagined I was good at it. But if I send those girls into battle with the chaos assembled against us then why didn't I just keep Tam's head under the toilet seat when I first met her? I didn't get sung through the fabric of space and time to save Prentis just so she could end up a smear on an Alter's heel. Bad enough I'm letting Samantha down. Samantha. I don't care what happened in London, she heard me, she saw me, I know it. And I can't shake the idea that she has something to do with the Decimation. My last few moments of consciousness are served by Prentis and Tam doing a duet of Valerie June's "Working Woman's Blues."

I wake to the sharp point of a blade resting gently on my clavicle. Pasha Macco smiles as I wake, as my senses clear. I must have been tired to let him get murder close without sensing him. Either that, or he's luckier than I realized.

"You know you sleep with your eyes open?" he whispers. Good, he's covert. This isn't all out war just yet. I'm not dead just yet.

"A useful trick." I try to tap my power, not to move him, just to keep him still.

"Hey!" he says sharply. "Try that again and I'll drop this blade in your gullet."

"No you won't."

"Is bluffing your entire tactic? Is that literally all you've got? I've got a blade at your throat, old man. All your allies are dead drunk and passed out. I win. Just admit it."

"If you were still working for my brother I'd be dead already." I piece together slowly as I push the blade off my throat. "You're not here for murder. So stop wasting time and tell me what you want."

"Why'd you let me live?" He's a boy, I see now as he rolls off of me and sheathes his blade in his sleeve. "Not that I wanted you to kill me. But like you said, in your time, you slaughtered me. Your brother, he definitely would've killed me. Almost did after you played me like the last finger-banged puppet with a thumb up his arse."

"I'm trying to be a better man than I was," I tell him at the same time I mind scream at Tamara to wake up and get the others to secure the island. "Besides, I already got what I wanted from you. And there was an off chance this would happen."

"What?"

"You'd see the light and come work on the winning side."

"Ha! I've seen your crew. Pirates, broke psychos, and fringe Liminals. You've no idea what you're up against."

"And neither does my brother. Neither do the Alters or they wouldn't have sent you alone to handle me."

"You don't get it, Taggert. I didn't expect to find you and your crew here. And believe me, I didn't come alone."

"Terror Tomas!" A.C. says, literally blowing down my door just as I reach my jacket and the entropy blades.

"What now?" I ask.

"Random assemblages of teeth, flesh, hair, and skin, formed to look like not men inhabited by spirits that hate humanity!" I can barely understand him, he's going so fast. I see his sword drawn and bloody. "And who the hell is that?"

"Pasha Maaco. He's with us now," I say, opening the sliding glass window.

"I never said that!"

"Yeah, but you think Tamara's cute and you'll do what you can to get close to her. Now come on!" I bark.

"I never said that either!" But he follows.

Outside, chaos is birthing itself. Rolling, rocking, and limping human shaped cancer cells with sharp deformed teeth on their feet, where cheeks should be, at what approximates stomachs, at the end of fingers, at their necks, everywhere but where teeth should be, amble with deceptive speed at anybody standing, taking them down and devouring them. Sprigs of coarse red, black, and blond hair sprout all along their pink bloated and splotched bodies as well, as if to better approximate that which they could never be mistaken as human. When two roll attack one of Narayana's servants, I move quickly with my blades.

"Don't be an idiot!" I hear Pasha say under the murder pulse of the blades. I dive on one of the giant boiled pustules, careful to avoid a set of teeth while pushing the human out of bite range with my foot. I land, twist, and hurl one terror whatever into its oncoming friend. And they get bigger. Two feet, sixteen sets of teeth, and broader shoulders. The one merges into the other.

"What the shit?" I ask, backing up and taking them in.

"They're Terror Tomas!" A.C. says.

"That means nothing to me!"

"They're blind, deaf, and dumb self-replicating, joining organic murder bots." Pasha steps in. "They don't feel pain, they're infinitely divisible."

A single bullet breaks the cries of the Terror Toma's victims all around the island and interrupts even the malformed screams of pleasure from the ambling disease monsters. The shot comes from behind us and buries itself between what would have been the eyes of the creature. It stops moving instantly and falls backward, dead. A.C. blows on his six-shooter like he's in a damn Western.

"Got any more of those?" Pasha asks, lighting a cigarette trying to cover the adrenaline rush pulsing in him.

"One, but they only work for me."

"Well, you better get to moving cause I came with about fifty of them." Pasha says.

"Who are you again?" A.C. asks, leveling his six-shooter at Pasha's head.

"A Lucky Liminal," I interrupt. "And we're gonna need all the luck we can get. So he lives for now. Come on." I take off in the direction of Tamara's focused rage.

At the foot of Tamara's building one of the man-sized cancer cells falls with a large splat in front of us. I barely have time to dodge it before Pasha is complaining again with that South London accent. I can barely hear him. I'm looking up at the war with Tamara, hovering at balcony height fending off her attackers as a troop of white-handed gibbons clear a running strip for Prentis to dive from.

"You can't kill them like normal creatures!" Pasha shouts.

As I'm looking up, Tam telekinetically catches Prentis in mid leap and descends safely. I feel the recently splattered Terror Toma's cellular reconfiguration with my Liminal power. It's composed of infernal stem cells capable of taking on any function necessary to keep an infinitely divisible organism going. Its only function, to masticate organic matter enough to infect it with itself. With A.C. letting off kill shots at whatever Terror Tomas try to rain down on us, I focus my Liminal power on the dozen or so smaller creatures.

Nordeen asked me once if I knew how my power worked; if I reminded flesh of its original form and modified it, or if I imposed my will upon that eternal primal material. Right now I'm choosing the latter. Nothing in these creatures was ever human, so I unleash my most inhuman side on it, my Liminal aspect. I infect the smaller creatures made of mouth, aggression, and flesh with an inescapable desire to devour the closest flesh, its own. In a second I convert the ankle-sized infectious balls into cannibals.

"Fucking gross that is!" Prentis yells as Tamara drops her.

"What is he doing here?" Tam demands as she launches Pasha in the air without a hint of telekinetic control over his ascent.

"Working for us now, and I don't have time for your shit now, girl. We need to center around Bingy and the other humans and find Narayana. Now!"

"I can't find Narayana, but Munji and Fatima are just on the other side of the road. She didn't want to sleep near us," Tam says.

I'm moving before she can finish speaking with A.C. and Prentis on my tail. I have to avoid minor horrors of innocents being slaughtered to protect the ones that truly matter, the ones that can end all of this. I try to cast a general cannibalistic sense to all the Terror Tomas on the island, but their physiology, chemistry—it's all so disgustingly foreign and malevolent I could just as easily increase their hunger without proper attention. I content myself with knowing Tam catches Pasha and he's no worse for wear.

A.C. shoots a cyclone through the road to clear it of the Terror Tomas as soon as we hear shooting from the beachside hotel, around the bend of the road. I feel Munji's left arm swinging hard, Fatima's well worn trigger finger cramping, and I know they've been holding their own for a while. At the front lobby four workers lay writhing in pain and transformation, bit by the Terror Tomas. I give what compassion I can quickly, and turn their skulls into brain daggers. Prentis kicks down the door to the main suite, where Munji and his daughter were resting to see twenty of the infected cutting our people off from the window they were trying to escape out of.

Somehow, without eyes or ears, the uglies know to avoid A.C's bullets. Half their number come for us, while the others stay on the task of trying to devour Fatima and her dad. I infect two with the strong desire to eat each other, but the other eight get by me and are contending with a pack of gibbons riding stray dogs Prentis called up while A.C. tries to get off clean shots. I'm just about to pull my entropy blades again when I hear a sound that vibrates my skin. A second later the back wall to the room falls away from the rest of the building with a whirring sound. Even the deaf, dumb, and blind Terror Tomas can't help but notice Mico standing on the beach. Pissed.

I expect words, even sounds. But what comes from Mico is pure emotion. Insult, anger, frustration, and rage in a vibration. I cut off the hearing of my allies to spare us at least some of his fury. The Terror Tomas get a new experience just before they descend into a puddle of oozing putrescence. Agony.

"Are you okay?" I turn Fatima's hearing back on just as he runs to her, laying hands on her despite her raised gun.

"What did you do?" She can barely think straight. Neither can I.

"He sang them the song of flesh in reverse," A.C. tells us, entering the room proper and examining the puddles. "They're gone for good."

"Then you've got bigger problems than them." From the other side of the beach Pasha comes running with my girl by his side.

"Who dis man them?" Bingy asks, coming from the shadows, machete in hand. When the drama hit, he'd been with Mico from the look of things.

"Convert to the cause, far as I can tell." Tam does her best to back my play when it comes to Pasha. "I'd listen to him."

"They aren't here for you. The Terror Tomas. They're here to bug an Alter named Narayana . . ."

"I am here." Don't ask where he came from. I couldn't tell. But Pasha turned to see Narayana standing behind him and almost had a heart attack.

"Umm . . . Sir, will you allow me to speak or . . ."

"Get to it!" I snap.

"Okay! Rice told Baron to get me to escort the Terror Tomas to this island. So long as one cell of them is alive, it will get back to Rice and report everything it knows. They are here to annoy Narayana. But they don't know shit about you guys."

"So what?" Fatima asks casually.

"So if even one of those globules gets back to Rice, he'll know not only that we've linked up with Narayana but also that we have entropy weapons and skill enough to manage his little annoyance," I tell them all.

"So we wipe them all out," Prentis says, still not getting it.

"Cut one cell of them down another two takes it place." A.C. does the explaining for me. "Maybe we can get Mico on a loudspeaker system?"

"They're over the entire island," Mico tells us. "That's what took me and Bingy so long to get here. And they learn from each other. Cut one down, another will learn to avoid that blade."

"So what then?" Tam asks. "There's like twenty thousand people on this island, Tag." She knows what I'm thinking even if she doesn't want to admit it.

"Can you sink it?" I turn to face Narayana.

"Taggert . . ." Mico starts.

"You got a better idea? 'Cause I'm all ears. We're outgunned and outnumbered. The only thing we've got is the element of surprise. That goes out the window if one of these terror balls of shit and piss get back to the Alters."

"These people are under my protection," Narayana says slowly.

"So was Chabi. You let her go because it served a greater good. Same concept, bigger scale." I'm not disrespecting him. We've both done the unspeakable in our time. "So can you do it? Take the whole island down completely and keep everything on the island drowned?"

"An earlier aspect of myself sank Lemuria. I can sink this island."

"Okay. We've got twenty minutes to save as many people as you can. Tam, send out the psychic alarm. Push who you can to boats. Fatima and Munji, you're on plane transport. Prentis, you, Pasha, and Bingy are protection for them. You are our way off this island, stand firm. A.C., Mico, Tam and I are on clean-up. You see one of these Terror shits, destroy it."

"You don't understand," Pasha says. "There are hundreds scattered across the island by now. You'll never be able to save everybody from them. And how can you evacuate an island in twenty minutes?"

"We can't," Tam says, pulling away as everyone breaks for their duties. "It's called cutting your losses."

I did my best. Used all of my focus, rage, and skill on every molecule of Terror Toma I could find. Tam did her duty right, not only strongly motivating folks to get off the island but keeping all of our players appraised every minute while taking out a few dozen of the walking cancer cells herself. It didn't matter. It was a losing fight and we all knew it.

"If we weren't here," Mico asked Narayana after whistling a pack of five-foot cancer bloody beasts back toward the jungle hills, away from a fleeing family of fifteen, "what would you have done?"

"To show my lack of care." I hear the confession before Narayana finishes. His stare alone reduces the mass and height of a pack of Terror Tomas that have teeth for fingers and mouths for eyes. "I would have immediately slayed the ones they'd infected then sent them and the remaining beasts back to Eel Pie Island in a wreck of a ship. I would have made sure the ship, the trade routes, and individuals, every part of the journey was owned by Rice and his associates so that the infection would be returned in kind." When he's done his stared-down Terror Tomas are small enough to crush beneath his foot. And so he did.

"They're amassing by the dock." A.C. flies in on a tight gust of wind to tell us, his guns still smoking.

"How many more boats are there to fill?" Mico asks.

"Forty, maybe more. It's chaos down there, even with Tamara . . ." he starts.

"Get me to her," I tell A.C. "Mico, get to the damn plane, tell them to take off. Narayana, soon as you see that last boat, drag this whole place to the bottom of the sea." As one of A.C's upward gusts sends me into the sky with him I think to my daughter, "I'm coming."

I have A.C. drop me at the ship side of the pier while Tam works the dock. I don't know how she's differentiating the beasts from the folks but she's doing a good job of only knocking critters into the ocean with her telekinetic ability. Still, some slip by her and continue to chase the humans to the waiting jetties. These are fishing ships and ferries these poor people are rushing into. Woken in the middle of the night, they'll do their best with what meager supplies they've managed to collect before they're forced into refugee status. Their world was pale and colorless before, but the world was theirs. I'm taking even that from them. I am the birth of true Chaos for these people. And I hate myself for it.

I pull the entropy blades, double my arm and leg strength, dilate my pupils to take in more night light, and get some super-charged lung efficiency going just before I look over my shoulder to see A.C.

with his sword drawn prepping for the oncoming slicing fest. The Terror Tomas shake and bend the three-feet-wide plastic planks under them.

"What are you still doing here?"

"Backing you up!" he barks.

"I'm fine. Mico's the linchpin. Make sure he gets to the damn plane." And then, before he can protest. "Besides, I need this."

A.C. gives me a gust at a cluster of Terror Toma's and is gone. I run, leaning forward, running almost parallel to the dock. My face and blades are at human knee level, it's where half the wharf Terror Tomas have biting mouths. I dive over a crowd of humans chased by the beasts, slash, roll, and turn. I'm a deadly bowling ball. I take out five cancer-celled chasers, letting the human get the distance needed to hit the boats. Ten more creatures emerge from the dock, another four climb up from the ocean, all with attention for me. I click the blades together. "Bring it."

One tries to distract me coming in front as three of them try to rush me from behind. For some reason I'm feeling the capoeira so I throw a meia lua de compasso kick at the one in front and use the force of my kick to turn around and cut at the approximate heads of the beasts behind. I stop all cellular movement in the third one and watch what could be surprise flow like a wave on its tumor face before it dies.

Twelve more, the size of linebackers, take up the dock as they run toward me, neglecting the humans. Perfect, just what I wanted. Hungry as the blades are, I'm more in need of venting. I feel for the calcium deposits in each of their "mouths" and yank them out with my Liminal ability. The front two stumble as they had shark-sized teeth on their feet, but the others keep running over their fallen friends. Doesn't matter. I use those sharp teeth against them, sending them flying through all of their bodies, cutting them up into pieces so small they can fit into a baby's mouth.

With all that focus I almost miss the four that climb up behind me, almost. I tumble forward just as a mouth-equipped hand lunges for my head. The next time it comes I parry with one hand and slice at the shoulder with the entropy blade. I take the arm by the wrist and beat the one grabbing at my right in the side with it, letting my weight shift so the other two on my right miss their murder attempt. I make the mistake of stabbing one of the grabbers in the top of the head—no brain—and have to leap and front flip over both of them to avoid the attack from the one-armed beast. I'm about to do the teeth thing again when I realize all the boats have taken off. Tam's caught up in her bloodlust and people are still coming, but it's pointless. They're going down with the island.

"Tell them to go be with their loved ones, girl," I think to Tam as I beef up the outer cellular membranes of the walking cancers.

"I can hold out. I'm fine!" There is exhaustion in her thoughts.

"You did good," I tell her, causing methane production to ramp up in all the Terror Toma's digestive tracts near us. Even they know something nuts is about to happen. "Just no more point in it."

She walks toward me after pushing all the humans out of one side of the building and bringing down the roof of the dock on the heads of the beasts back at the bay. I'd feel better if she reacted to the strain of using her power, the surgery writ large of killing walking cancer cells, even if she shook against the vibrations on the pier as a result of the crash. But Tam's in that place, feeling what warriors drenched in blood for too long experience. Of course I see her plane scar first. But other than that, she's crimson from the beasts, their plasma congealing and trying to form new mouths and teeth to bite with. Her hair's a mess.

"But there's fifty people waiting not half a mile up the coast. We could . . . Okay, just the kids. Tag, we gotta . . ." I generate ridges on the teeth of all the Terror Tomas so they create a large static charge when they grind their molars in hate. The charge, plus the ethanol and the methane, turns them into walking flesh bombs. All around us Terror Tomas go up with flashes and explosions. Before the last one blows the wooden deck is already on fire.

"Why didn't you do that in the first damn place?" she shouts more at the situation than me.

"It's a trick, not a solution," I tell her, pointing to the surface of the water where burnt clumps of Terror Toma are already starting to congeal to form crisper versions of themselves. "Now let's go."

She can say I'm not her father as much as she wants. Push comes to shove, she knows when to follow my lead and do what I say. She's pissed the whole time she levitates us to the airstrip where Fatima has fired up a larger than normal island-hopping plane. We're the last to get in.

We reach altitude just in time to not be sucked down by whatever Alter-inspired vacuum Nordeen generates below the island. It takes him slightly more time than the burnt-out birds, but it's still less than two minutes. The entire island, seven miles around and ancient, crumbles and disappears into a silent sea. I try to block out the sounds of innocence crying, like I've done my entire life. I want to do the same for Tam, but she's psychic. Her brain will carry those telepathic cries forever.

Addis Ababa, Ethiopia
Prentis

No one really said much until we got to Ethiopia. Could feel the sadness all around us. From Mico especially. If he started singing that would be the end of all things and we knew it. His death wails would sink us. Bingy man did his best to comfort his friend, sitting close to him, respondent like a pup to his needs. Munji and Fatima were still trying to figure out how to get away from all of us while flying. Tam did her best to sleep in my lap, but she wiped tears on my pants while no one was looking and I knew her pain was psychic and physical at the same time. Badass all she wants to everyone else, I feel her pain. Always looks like she can do everything. Really, she can endure everything. Always pays for it later in pain and fatigue.

Didn't want anyone to know what I felt when the island went down. How every lizard, rodent, mammal, and insect called out to me for help as unnatural gravity sucked them to the ocean floor. Taggert and A.C. sat across from each other, each sharpening their blades. Tag wouldn't admit a hint of guilt in his casual wide-leg posture, pushed back against his chair with his foot up. Bet he liminaled his pulse rate to super chill levels. Didn't stop A.C. from noticing.

"I ever tell you how I got this sword?" the Wind Boy asks.

"Would I remember?" Tag says.

"Funny. Old friend of mine, not the least bit a warrior, but born into this Paladin caste of Bedouin. Farji, his name was. Cool cat. Into books, booze, and women. Anyway, his dad, chief warrior of his clan, calls him up one day, says the ancient spiritual enemy of their people 'The Flayer' might be in Farji hometown of NYC and that he should 'handle it.'"

"What's a flayer?"

"Demon that gets off taking meat and flesh from bone and spirit from form," says like everyone knows before continuing. "Yeah, so my man has no practical fighting skills and can barely use the armor or sword his Mom sent him to 'help.' So he calls on me. Man, you think those Terror Tomas were hard? This thing was smart, fast, could leap into bodies, and had the most sadistic killing impulse I've ever witnessed. We were outclassed."

"So what did you do?"

"Not about what I did, but what he did. Farji was one of those renaissance autodidacts. He'd seen the binding sigils that imprisoned the Flayer in the first place in a book a few years earlier. Dude knew that if he didn't get a handle on this beast it would flay all of the five boroughs. So he put the binding spells on himself then offered his body to the demon."

——

Takes longer than it should to realize the unspoken. That immediately after the Flayer was bounded to Farji, A.C. used that sword on him. Taggert nods long before me.

"His mom made the sword from the tooth of the last known three-toed dragon."

"Dragons don't exist," Taggert says with no authority.

"Not anymore!" A.C. laughs. "But they used to plague the dreams of dinosaurs, let me tell you! Point is he did what he had to do, and made the ultimate sacrifice for the greater good. This weight on your soul, you can bear it. I've no doubt of that. But when it feels too heavy, like you should just go on a rampage, you remember those people on Pangkor Island. It'll keep you focused on what you've already sacrificed and what you're willing to do in order to return the world to its former glory. Whenever I lose it, or get close to it, I just look at this sword. Keeps me grounded in more ways than one."

Fatima put us down in Addis Ababa using smuggler connections. See how real the Decimation is, for the first time. We're used to going into back doors and side entrances. There are none in this airport. It's all soldiers and guns. Petrified quiet dominates every civilian, and some snarling rage is wrestling to get out of every green-uniformed assault rifle–holding soldier.

Tam uses her power to help us blend in, but what is it to blend in to a type of hate and fear that makes mass suicide make sense? Don't need to be able to read the words on the billboards all around as we exit the airport to know they are of two options: follow the rules or sign up for the Decimation. The follow-the-rules billboards are light and show beaches and people drinking, dancing, and smiling. The Decimation ones usually show a soldier pointing a gun at someone. When we get into cars with tinted windows, happy to close my eyes and rest my head on Tag's shoulder.

Needed to refuel and figure what would happen next. As soon as she settled us, the Smuggler girl cut out with her dad. Given their freaked out expressions, not sure we'll see them again. Tag sent Pasha to keep an eye on them, and to keep him out of Tamara's hair. Just when was about to ask where Narayana was, he showed up at the front door of the five-story smuggler house, beleaguered but still standing and smelling like the sea.

House is beautiful on the inside, all marbled floors, cold iron-casted fixtures, and the like. Like a mini castle. Outside looks like it was used for cannon target practice. Get the sense Fatima likes it like that. Still not sure how Narayana tracked us.

"Your clan tail you?" A.C. asks, appearing by my side with his hand on his sword.

"Shush your face!" I snap at his rudeness and make a way for the thing that's made me aquaphobic. "Can't you see he's ailing?"

Know his looks can kill and so it's fortunate that Narayana glares away from me as he walks into the main living room and sits at an ancient wooden table that's been sanded impossibly smooth . . . His presence alone causes everyone left in the house, Tag, Tam, Mico, and Bingy, to leave whatever rooms they were chilling in to see him. It's only when everyone arrives that he speaks.

"I shadowed what is left of the Nile to find you," Narayana offers by way of explanation.

"He's the drowned Alter. Without water, nothing to drown, he's weaker . . ." A.C. offers.

"Enough strength to take you . . ."

"I'm just glad you made it to a landlocked country." Mico cuts the hostility between them, placing his hand on Narayana's shoulder. It's a foreign and dangerous thing, seeing an Alter being touched. Like a baby's hand in an alligator's mouth.

"But why this country, my lord?"

"What's wrong with Ethiopia?" Mico asks.

"The Derg is nothing more than a puppet for the Alter presence on the planet, my lord," Narayana says, sitting slowly.

"The who now?" Tam asks.

"Derg, the Committee," Bingy pipes in. "Dem a infernal policing body cause a genocide in the land of the first civilization, zene?"

"In our time, the Derg fell before you were born, kid," Tag tells Tam offhandedly. But then he starts thinking. "But if they're still in power now . . ."

"Coincidence?" ask with a grin.

"Unicorn's ass ain't big enough for this coincidence." He smiles lightly.

"I-man nah see it." Bingy asks, "What coincidence?"

"Samantha is Ethiopian. More than that, she reps Ethiopia to the fullest," Tam says, stretching her neck out, getting ready for a fight. "Plus, she's the one who reached out across time to tell us not to come back. Meaning she's got some cross reality communication skills. Her . . . One of her Liminal abilities is the ability to influence folks. She make people do damn near anything . . ."

"Like convince folks to commit suicide," I add.

"She'd never do . . ." Mico starts, then thinks better of it. "She's not powerful enough to convince ten percent of humanity . . ."

"Okay, not just her," A.C. agrees. "But add the sway of that Alter Rice and their control over media, science, all of it, I see what the girls are saying. Samantha could be the linchpin to this whole Decimation plan."

"None of this matters," Tam says, plopping herself down at the same table as Narayana. "We did a straight run at her and the other Liminals and got ash and aggravation for our troubles."

"Yeah, cause you Liminals have the greatest of luck going straight ahead at stuff." A.C. grins and for a second we could almost believe we're all having fun. "There might be a way, if she is still connected to this land, if the Derg's influence is intimately connected to her . . ."

". . . if she's not defended by Angels . . ." Tam snarks.

"Well, that's a real possibility," A.C. says

"I was joking!"

"Cut it. The both of you," Taggert tells the whole table. "Tam, you're right. This is just a theory right now. While we're waiting for our pilot, take Prentis out and confirm it or debunk. I don't care either way but be sneaky about it. Without Alter support, the Derg wiped out a generation of their own people in our timeline. A.C. you got a way to liberate Samantha's mind?"

"It'll require some Danakil salt, a Gu'ez bible, gold from . . ."

"Whatever. Get your cauldron of crap together, but don't try to execute until you get the final word from me. Whatever your results, everyone back here in five hours. If you ain't gigging, get to sleeping. We're all gonna be needed soon."

Just as Tam and I are out the door, I see Mico follow Tag to the side, and I'm thankful we're leaving.

Addis Ababa, Ethiopia
Prentis

The monkeys told me to stay away from the carrion dogs that fed off the barely buried mounds of corpses that surrounded the city. Dogs have similar things to say about the vultures. When the animals of a city talk shit about each other, a rough place.

Tam was getting more from the humans. Wore it on her face as we strolled Bole Road, dodging packs of uniformed boys patrolling for weakness. She'd seen the face of the Decimation before in London. Closest I've been to the protracted suffering of the world was a tiny outpost in Morocco. Hadn't seen the billboards asking, "Is your life worth the planet?" Mix of envy and fear those marked for the Decimation evoked, with their free rein to do whatever they wanted in the meantime, had escaped me. Whatever was good and right in people was hiding in the corners hoping not to be noticed. When my girl started flinching at overheard thoughts, it was time to find a place to sit and be quiet. Hailed a cab and asked for the nicest hotel in town. Dragged us to the Naga Suites.

The gated hotel high on a hill overlooking Addis proper reeked of Alter funk—no animals save seriously twisted snakes would get near it, but this was their land and Taggert has always taught us the best place to hide was in plain sight. Cash flashes so gaudy they made the Russian rich look downright classy. Yellow gold sculptures of slaves worshipping at the feet of the favored dictator of the moment serving as centerpiece fountains, the bloodred hue of the uniforms too tight to allow for regular movement in all the staff. Endless security checks for those without military credentials. Enough to make a girl lose hope. We went to the lobby, cloaked in Tam's psychic miasma as top Derg generals, and ordered two large snifters of brandy.

"How the fuck are we supposed to figure out if Tag's side piece is running the show?" Tam finally says after her second pour disappears down her throat. She reclines down the plush red leather thrones we sit on across from each other.

"Yeah, cause that's what's bugging you." Smile and wait, trying not to notice how frightened everyone is of us.

"He told that . . . thing . . . Narayana . . . to sink the island knowing there were still people on it," she thinks to me rather than speaking.

"That was the plan, remember?" I say slowly.

"Yeah, but you didn't see his eyes when he said it. Taggert just . . . It was like he was swatting a fly away. He just said it and forgot about it, almost right away."

"Weren't you the one telling him he had to get hard, to make the hard choices?"

"Didn't mean I wanted to see him do it." All I can do is listen. "I know what it will take, at least I think I know what it will take to win this. I know who Tag will have to be. But what if we lose him, Prentis?"

"Eh?"

"You can only forget so much. You can only act like things aren't affecting you for so long before they don't. The day Taggert drops an island without thinking about it, with his own power, on that day he's not our . . ."

"Dad, you dumb git," tell her. "You've got a problem saying it. I don't. Never had a father before so for me he's as close as I get. Calm your shite concerns and think on this. When we met I tried to kill him. You did the same. Whipped both our asses but then came out the other side and knitted us together, big fat Liminal fam. Went through space and time for me . . ."

"I did too." She laughs a little with her mind.

"Appreciated. Tolerated every disrespectful snip and snipe you've ever thrown at him not forsaking his duty to us. Faced all anyone could ask and more. For us. Ain't losing him, ya daft cow. Ever. That simple. Our job is to make his current troubles easier, get me? Got enough doubt to fill a pit. Last thing he needs is second guessing."

"So what?" she asks using her voice, letting her illusion of an old bald-headed, fat-nosed Derg official shine through for my eyes to make her point. "We just play good soldier with no questions? Suppose he's fucking up?"

"About you realize that as hard-core as you are, you don't know everything? Taught us everything he knows, yeah? Not everything to be known. Let him take on the hard choices and you manage the heroics."

"It's not fair!" tells me, posh accent coming through a Derg old wrinkled black man face. "You know how much he's been through. This goes bad, it's all on him . . ."

"Think Tag's going to share the weight with you? Not on his worst day. Think I wouldn't lift this burden from all of you in the first place? Think I'm worth all of this drama? You guys and Mico hadn't gone back in time . . ."

"Stop it . . ." Tam tells.

"All got guilt, experiences, whatever we've got to deal with. Can't carry another's weight. No matter how much we love. Best is, yeah, stand by each other until the lights go out."

She wants to reach out and hold my hand, but that image wouldn't work with her illusion, so instead Tam does something weird in me head to make me feel warm and supported.

"Tag was right about one thing," Tam tells.

"What?"

"You are the best of us." Tam shares the feeling of her love.

"Shut it. Get on task. Flash Samantha's face in people's minds, see if there's a recognition?"

"Not here. This place feels like Alter central."

The stank of the Suites begins to get to us as we start leaving. Realize the warm feeling in the back of my head didn't come from Tam but from outside. Not a sound but vibration, three-tone impossible harmony. Bone level deep. The way Mico sings but with less practice. At first, impossible to parse out from the darkness of the African night; it's cold as we leave the hotel. But then the cars of nearby birds. Coming from the hills above the hotel closer to the treeline. Don't bother telling Tamara, just start running.

Feels good, moving like this. Hunting, tracking. Following something concrete. A job to be done that doesn't pull energies and entities I'm barely clear on. Not controlled by evil shits or pernicious nonhumans out to destroy my kind. Dad wants info. With my sister, I can get it.

Bound through the campus of the state-sponsored university, Tam ghosting us past the eyes of the Derg soldiers. What would they do to a white girl running breakneck speed in murder gear through their streets? Get the animals to triangulate the sound and make a path. Past closed shops, mini shanty towns, and weathered churches, we run, quiet, in the shadows. Settle on a tin blue-doored shack with four broken cement walls hidden deep within a worker's slum.

"That was fun," Tam tells by way of asking for an explanation.

"Don't hear it?" The sound makes me salivate, the hair on my neck stand up.

"Kind of . . ." Make her ghost us again as I push the door open casually, like the wind could have done it. Walk in silently and observe the healing. Three Ethiopian women and one young man stand around an older woman sitting in a chair. Each of the people standing, family by the look, hold small copper bowls they roll padded wooden mallets around. Like the trick with a wineglass around the rim. Same kind of vibration only more resonant, with four people doing it at the same time. Only the woman in the middle sat without playing a thing, just listening with her eyes closed, hands open, and mouth closed.

"Wot . . ." start thinking to Tam.

"A healing ceremony. Lady in the middle has some shingles or some such. My question is how'd you hear it from the hotel?" she thinks back quick.

"Let me finish a thought. Wot the hell is a singing bowl healing ceremony doing in the middle of Ethiopia?"

"How do you mean?"

"It's an Asian thing. Used to know these guys when I was on the street that would do them for like everything, colds, herpes, any illness. It's from like Vietnam and Nepal and places like that."

"Shit, you saw it in London streets so . . ."

"In our time, get me?" tell her. "Thought things were dismal here? How do healing arts travel over waters and cultures?"

"Good point," finally admits. See eyes go white for a minute and know Tam's focusing. Young boy almost loses his bowl circling trick for a second but gets back on it. Tam plunging deep in his head. But she's smooth. Comes back to her body without making him lose his beat again.

"Oh, you're gonna love this. Turns out he had a dream. Him, his mom, aunt, and his grand. They don't even know this woman. But they all had a dream that this ceremony would heal this woman. His mother had a dream about where to find the bowls, his aunt had a dream about how to afford them, and his aunt dreamed about the tone needed to play to heal. And they all had the dream on the same night."

"A lot of dreaming."

"All the same night. Covert message dreaming. None of them would have known what it was all for alone. And all for this woman? Who is she?"

"She's a fighter. Poisoned a head Derg official, the one in charge of Decimation selection. Got away with it but started getting sick soon after. Everyone thinks dark powers, aka Alters, might have something to do with it. She's an underground hero. But that's not the best part. Guess who they were dreaming of, the one who gave them the healing ceremony?"

"Mico?"

"Close. Tag's side piece."

"He was right. Samantha's not totally turned."

"Well, trust she's not fully on our side either . . ." Tamara stops, tenses, almost loses our illusion.

"What?"

"Outside. Someone I can't read clearly."

Check in with a non-carrion dog outside who identifies a human with a weapon but no more. Nod to my girl and we angle outside quietly and invisible to not interrupt the healing ceremony. Only when we've totally exited the shack that the woman with a short rifle leveled at our guts walks out of the shadows.

"Fucking A, Fatty!" shout at her. "What the hell are you doing here?"

"Better question, why are you at my contact's house?" she barks back.

"Coincidence?" Tam smiles.

"Like hell. Looks like we're not as dead in the water as we thought."

Addis Ababa, Ethiopia
Taggert

I let Bingy stand watch over Narayana after I confirm the Alter has completely drowned every bit of those cancer beasts forever. Mico follows me without request to the master bedroom. It's the only place in the first floor with a door that closes. I pull a small chair from a small desk and sit across the room. Mico does his stepping on air type movements and climbs on the desk, sitting calm and patient. He knows I'm working through stuff.

"What's troubling you?" the singer asks.

"What isn't?"

"Okay, what isn't troubling you?" Relentless, he is.

"My bowels." I'm the only one that laughs. "I'm the wrong general for this war."

"You're the only one we've got." Mico feels bad saying it. Doesn't stop him, though.

"Then we're screwed," I tell him.

"Unless you get better quick." Mico says it like it's a real option.

"Getting better means I get harder. It means more people might die . . ." I start.

"You just told Narayana to sink an island. It's not people you're worried about. It's your people," he says.

"I just sent Prentis and Tam into the Derg night of Addis on a fact finding mission," I say.

"You know they can take on anything short of a multi-Alter attack by themselves. And you're only a psychic shout away should anything happen." He looks at me like I'm a moron. "There was a time when our cells were linked in harmony, Taggert, remember? It'll take a little more to fool me."

"Okay, I've got a plan, or the vague outlines of one at least, but best case scenario, folks we both care about are put in a box they might not get out of. Plus you and me will be incommunicado," I say.

"Okay." Asshole says like I told him I want cheese on my burger. "That's it? Okay?"

"I'm not Tamara. I'm not going to hoot and holler every time you try to make a decision. My trust in you is absolute. If your best thinking for the planet, for creation, leads you to these decisions, then that's the play I'll back." Mico exhales slowly.

"Why?" I ask.

"What?"

"Why in the name of all that's sacred and holy would you charge me with all of creation? Like you said, you've seen me on a cellular level. You know what I am, what I've been, what I've been shaped into. I barely trust myself with those two girls. You are relying on me to take care of the fucking world. Are you insane?" I ask him as he closes his eyes softly.

He smiles at me like a priest who hasn't forgotten the goal of his mission. Then he sticks out his hand and makes a beckoning motion. If Mico thinks I'm giving him a hug right now, he's lost it.

"May I hold one of your entropy blades?" Every time I think my control over the damn things is absolute I run into one of these situations. It should be an easy thing to loose one of the kerambit shaped weapons from my sleeve and toss it over to him. Instead it feels like igniting my own marrow. I get up and place it in his hand rather than toss it for fear of causing semi-intentional harm. He waits until I've sat back down across the room before he opens the blade. It sings a song I thought only I could hear until I see Mico's head shift slightly. It's a bit of a violation to have the intimacy between me and the blade to be aurally violated, but I stand it without a word. I've suffered worse.

"When Samantha proposed to have these blades made for you A.C. was firmly against it," he says slowly, playing with the tip of the blade as though it could stop drawing his blood once it started.

"I remember. He didn't think I could control them."

"Samantha, our Samantha, your Samantha, she had faith in you. She told me the days of purity are done; that our champions could no longer fight against the darkness but that they had to learn to integrate it. To incorporate the divine darkness of creation with the light of existence to combat the absence that is Entropy. She told me these blades were an outward representation of your ability to utilize the dark within, and that as long as you had control over those blades there was no one more trustworthy than you. The time for white knights is as done as is the time for those obsessed with the darkness. Those that can maturely manage the gray, that can parse the dark within from the Dark from without, they are what's needed most. The very traits you fear make you wrong for this position, make you most excellently prepared for it."

"And why the hell should I trust you?" I feel the question come more from the blade resting in his hand than from my own sentiment. Still, my voice asks it. "Wasn't it that very trusting nature of yours, that desire to help and heal everyone, to leave not one Liminal behind, that caused the world to be in the state it's in now? I know I asked for it. But knowing what I know now of you, I don't know if I would have done the same."

I don't jump when Mico leaves the desk. He crosses the room calmly and offers the knife back to me, folded in the flat of his palm. I'm a junkie looking at a needle as I try not to snatch it from his hand.

"When the reckoning comes for my sins, you will not find me cowering. Can you say the same, healer?"

"What's that old line? There ain't no devil, that's just God when he's drunk. Yeah, well, your God doesn't even have a mouth to get sloshed with and still treats me like it's favorite redheaded stepchild to beat. I'm not tripping on reckoning and sin. And you can drop the priestly voice. Cellular closeness goes both ways. I feel your full-on panic whenever Fatima looks at you. What's that about?"

"We were a team once. Munji, Fatima, and me." Mico makes sure not to look me in the eye as he speaks.

"Running hash out of France?" I asks, the warmth of the blade fortifying me.

"That was just the work." He takes the chair from the desk and moves it closer to me, putting his feet up on the bed. "At the same time Nordeen was making you into . . . While you two were doing your business, they were growing into my family."

"Built-in father and lover sort of situation?" I ask, trying not to sound flippant.

"Yup. Provided to me by, at the time, some unknown force," Mico says.

"So why did you leave?" I ask.

"I wanted to find that unknown force. Deep in the desert, outside of Majane . . ." His voice goes pale, longing like.

"In Morocco?" I ask.

"The same. I heard a sound, a calling . . ."

"And that's all you've ever needed," I snap.

"Consider it my first meal. My first acknowledgment that I needed subsistence even. I couldn't figure it out but I had to leave, immediately. I got out of bed with Fatima, my Fatima from then, and went into the desert, alone. No food, no water, no supplies."

"What did you find?" I feel like I should know the answer.

"I don't know. To this day. A year and a half later I emerged, fully integrated with the Manna, as though it had been part of my psyche from day one. In many ways it had been guiding my every step. But that desert step was one that it kept hidden from me."

"But it's not guiding you anymore, the Manna, I mean. We took care of that." It still hurts him to admit it. "So maybe that proscription against you remembering is gone. A.C. talked about the Desert daughters, the Bint al-nas. That ring a bell for you?"

"No. And I know what you're thinking. I'm not letting Tamara smash around in my brain for answers."

"You have no idea what I'm thinking. If the Manna didn't want you to know something, it sure as hell wouldn't allow a Liminal to get at it," I tell him standing, looking out the window at the slowly rising moon. "The only way we're surviving, let alone winning this war, is if you make up with your God. That means we retrace your steps."

"But even if we do find the Manna in the desert, what makes you think it would help? I betrayed it, remember?" He pulls his legs from the bed, like having both under him will make him more secure.

"I'll perform my apologies," I tell him, hitting the door. "But this is all on you. I'll hedge the bets best I can, but if you don't get right with your God, we're all screwed."

Addis Ababa, Ethiopia
Taggert

"You pay my hospitality back by sending your children to tail me, Taggert?" Fatima starts yelling at me with her mare's leg rifle slung over her shoulder as soon as she walks in the door. I expected her to be calmer after Munji and Pasha came back an hour earlier, all buddy buddy. But when the girls walk in a second after the smuggler princess, I can see things have, as usual, gone off the rails.

"That wasn't their task," I tell her, not bothering to get up from the hot veggie stew Bingy made for us all. "Ladies?"

Once the motormouth tag team catch us all up, I stop eating. "A.C. was right. Samantha is fighting back," Prentis says with a smile stealing my bowl of grub as they both cross the room and sit next to me. Of course, Fatima stays standing.

"Or trying at least," Mico says, coming in from the kitchen, curious as to the ruckus.

"I don't know who this dream woman is and I don't care," Fatima hisses, advancing on me from the doorway, still not putting that gun down. "What gives you the right to follow me? You're in my safe house, understand? I cough wrong and Derg forces flood this place."

"Probably burn half of your network if you did," I guessed by the quickening of her father's heart rate when she threatened. "Sorry I hurt your feelings, but I've got bigger concerns."

"Fuck feelings, you arrogant shit," she tells me as she cocks her weapon. Only her father reacts like I'm in danger. Only her father hasn't seen me in action. "I've got people that rely on my discretion here. When I go to one of my contacts and I find your junior girls' brigade playing Nancy Drew, you put them all at risk. That puts my reputation at risk. That I can't have."

"Fatima, your point has been made," her father, sitting at the table, tries to caution her.

"Sorry, El Ab," she says as quickly as she can without cutting him off. "But I don't think I have, because this shithead is still acting like I'm a joke to him."

"More like he knows that peashooter isn't going to do much against him." A.C. appears at the doorway smelling of salt and old warped magic with one of his six-shooters in hand. To Fatima's credit she doesn't turn to face him. Instead she raises her weapon at me quickly.

"Yet and still, Lady," Tam says quietly, "best to get that gun off my daddy." When Fatima doesn't move, I risk speaking again.

"I sent Pasha after you to see how good you were. He's a disposable tool I'm still not sure I trust . . ."

"Hey!" Pasha starts.

"Shut it. He was a test. If you killed him it would mean you were ruthless, smart, and cunning. In that order. But your dad converted him, distracted him while you angled free to link up with your folk. That means you're smart first, cunning second, and now with the gun at my gut, I'll give you ruthless. That's useful. This drama isn't. As for your network, I'll be honest. If it was necessary, I'd drown them like we dropped Pankour."

"Son of a bitch!" I can feel her trying to squeeze her finger. She'll give herself a stroke pulling against the muscle death I've given her trigger finger. But she's smart, quick. She tosses her gun to the other hand. I'm out of my seat, holding the barrel of her short rifle down at the ground before she can blink.

"I'm not trying to win a city, an island, or even a continent. The stake is the planet. The entire world. It's all or nothing. That's what's on the line. You get that, you understand what I'm willing to sacrifice."

"It's not your call to make!" she shouts in my face.

"You don't know how much I wish that wasn't true," I confess.

"Get your hands off of her." The words hit like a bass drum, and I know it's Mico.

"Keep trying to eye-fuck me, boy, best you put a condom on," I say after deciding to not to beat his ass in public. Fatima finally realizes how pointless her rifle is when I hand it back to her and sit down. With the assembled looking at me, once again, I give it to them all.

"We grab Samantha now, Alters know we're in town and can start gunning for us proper. Not even paying attention, they've had us scraping with all manner of vile bodies. The shadows are our only advantage. A.C, your 'Free Samantha' plan time sensitive?"

"Not really but . . ."

"Then we sit on it," I cut him off. "Unaffiliated allies are the priority. No offense to the assembled, but we need more firepower than what this room can muster. And we need it quick . . ."

"And quiet," Prentis chimes in. "Not like Samantha. Folks the Alters wouldn't notice were joining against them."

"Exactly." I settle my eyes on Narayana until the drowned demon of death looks back. "If I set you after your daughter, think you can bring her back without killing her again?"

"That's uncalled for," Mico chimes in, having sat back at the table.

"Wouldn't go that far . . ." Tam says. "But that's not to say Chabi won't murder the hell out of him on sight."

"That's why you're going with him. You too, A.C. You've all got good history with Chabi. Bring her into the fold. Pasha, you're with them as well."

"Why me? I don't even know the woman," the Londoner whines.

"She's a ghost Liminal trained by Mister Drowned Death over there to liquidate the bones of Alters." Prentis can't resist smirking as she says it.

"So they'll need all the luck they can get to find her and stay safe," I tell him.

"I'm not going anywhere with you and your psycho crew," Fatima tells me unbidden, sitting close to her father, her stubby rifle still in her hands.

"Not even to find your mother's people?" I say. Munji stands. Mico and Fatima tense, and I imagine how much of a threat they could be if they ever worked together. So I open my arms wide to signify I've got no weapons, that I don't want to hurt the old man, then stand.

"Make yourself plain, Taggert," Munji says, fully understanding his power in the situation.

"I hold no truck with coincidence. The Manna doesn't either. That God engineered its prophet, Mico, to near perfection. Everything about him, how he ate, what he thought, what he listened to. Even who he loved."

"I don't love him!" Fatima says with disdain, recklessly pointing her gun at Mico.

"But he loves you, don't you, Mico?" Everyone feels the troubadour's resentment of me in his silence. "See? Now look, I've got two former lovers in this time. I've seen them both. WIth one, Tamara's mother, it's just not the same. There's no way to describe it. She looks the same, sounds the same, shit. But that ain't her. Know how I know? No love! The other is Samantha, the one reaching out to Fatima's connects, trying to foment a revolution of dreams by dreamers. She's also an earlier convert to the Manna than Mico. She's the real deal. Know how I know? My heart is breaking that I can't prioritize her rescue. Real love. The common factor to both women, the Manna."

"This Manna. Maybe in your world, it was a God. Here, in this place it is nothing more than a drug, a narcotic . . ." Munji starts.

"Yeah, but where I'm from it's not just a God. A living sentient pain in the ass God that makes plans within plans. It's got a clique of folks hidden from space and time. If they're half as powerful as Mico, we could have a fighting chance against the Alters. Even against whatever assorted freaks they have at their disposal. The Manna is millions of years old. It plays a long game, and I think it coordinated Mico's love for your daughter . . ."

"Why?" Mico says a little too loudly. "Why would the Manna make me love someone who obviously doesn't love me back?"

"To lead you back home," A.C. chimes in so that I'm not taking all the heat for this plan. "If her mother was Bint al-nas, a daughter of the desert, then so is she. We go back to where you disappeared in the desert and follow Fatima's instinct, we might find the rest of the Manna's people."

"Or might end up wandering the desert looking for nothing," Prentis mocks.

"And you think, out there, somewhere in the Eastern Sahara, we will find my wife?" Munji asks with promise.

"No," I tell him honestly. "I think she is gone. But I think we'll find her people, her tribe."

"Fuck you." Fatima tells me honestly and sincerely as she leads her stunned father back to his seat. With heavy steps in soft-heeled boots she stomps over to Mico. He stands braced against the kitchen doorway looking tired and sad, a far cry from the prophetic pose he hit me with not two hours earlier.

"So you love me?" Fatima threatens.

"I . . . in my time, the Fatima I met . . ." She waits for him to finish. We all do. "I would have died for her."

"And now? What you feel for the woman standing in front of you, speaking in your face right now?" Her accent and her annoyance slips.

"I only know that when I see you in danger every part of me screams to help you. It takes all of my power and focus not to touch your face, to not hold your hand. I have a hunger for you that is painful to not address. The world is melting down around us and all I can think about is what I'd have to do to make you rely on me, trust in me."

"I already have a father . . ." she starts, trying to cover how much he's affecting her.

"I know. And I love him as well. For his kindness, his intelligence, but mostly because he made you, kept you safe and healthy in this Jahiliyyah . . ."

"You speak of love but it sounds like nothing more than a desire to protect and stay close . . ." Fatima says, trying to dismiss him.

"What the fuck do you want? Flowers and chocolates?" Pasha chimes in, trying not to wipe a tear from his eye. "He's a bloke. That's how we show we give a fuck . . ."

"Shut it." Tam telekinetically pulls the Lucky boy's chair out from under him so he falls. "Though he does have a point. These mystic types, they aren't great with the words. Men of action, they are. The more they do, the more you know they care."

"Any part of this plan require me to like you, Taggert?" Fatima asks me while still staring at Mico like he stole something.

"Just fly half this crew to Morocco and get lost with us in the desert," I tell her.

"Good. 'Cause you're an ass." She says it like no one could ever debate the fact. Then to the rest of the posse, "Wheels up in three hours. Stay indoors until then. I fucking mean it!"

Most everyone empties from the living room, securing what bedrooms they can. Everyone takes bowls of the chili Bingy made. We're all sleep deprived and starving. Wish my girls would do as the others. But I don't think they know how to leave me alone.

"It's never easy, is it?" Tam asks me after everyone but her and Prentis leave.

"Wrong type of life for easy," I say calmly.

Addis Ababa, Ethiopia
Taggert

"Are you going to make me your puppet again?" Can't tell if Pasha is genuinely nervous about it or not. He's got that sincere effort face on, trying to show that he's not overwhelmed by everything going on. Still, he almost jumped when I called him into the kitchen for a private chat.

"In a manner of speaking," I tell him, calm, then pull one of the entropy blades. I've seen him fight enough to know his defensive stance; legs slightly bent, torso perpendicular to the person or threat. One hand hidden, the other hand low. Makes him look like a fencer. He doesn't know what to do when I toss the blade in his direction but won't let it just fall. Instead, he loses his form and cradles the blade from its falling arc onto the counter.

"You're giving up?"

"I can't spell those words," I tell him. Pasha's eyes are still on me, not the blade. That's good. Means he's not called to it the way he could be. For him, it can just be a weapon. "I'm sending you out as Tamara's bodyguard."

"Like she needs one . . ." He laughs.

"That's my daughter." I give him the tone drop. "Anything happens to her, slit your throat before I get to you."

"Wait, hold on . . ." Pasha protests. "First off she is literally one of the most powerful Liminals I've ever heard of, let alone seen. She's bodyguarding all of us most of the time. What the hell am I supposed to add to her skill set?"

"It's not a competition, little man. You're a complement. Tam gets focused, myopic. She needs someone to help her check the angles, to peek under the bed, to watch her six . . ."

"You're using me as the distraction again, aren't you?" I think he's authentically offended now. "You're sending me with her in case she needs a sacrificial lamb, aren't you?"

"Do the sacrificed get the knife?" I ask, indicating the knife with my eyes. He picks it up off the counter cautiously. "Proper respect is due to that blade. Its twin is screaming in my mind right now, saying they should be together. You hear anything?"

"It's heavier than I thought it would be." The boy moves elegantly but basically, letting the sharp edge cut through air alone. It's like he didn't hear my question. "It smells like . . . blood?"

"Can't wash that off. That's what it smells like when drawn. Practice with it and it'll be in your hand before you realize you need it."

"Practice how?" Finally he makes eye contact with me.

"The way you practice with all things. Give it space and time. Better to draw it when no one else is around. But if you call it, expect the blade to guide your hand to where it can do the most damage." I lose his eyes as he goes back to working the blade. It improves his form, his range, his ability to kill. It's an intoxicating feeling for him. I don't need him drunk. "Put it away."

I know the effort it can take to fold the blade back into its collapsed cradle. When Pasha does it, the sheen over his eyes disappears. His breathing returns to normal. But now he's pissed.

"You give the most fucked up gifts," he says.

"Least you know you're not cannon fodder," I say with a smile.

"This is better?" But then he thinks for a second. "Tam's blind spot is the mystic stuff. The Alter knowledge and all that." When I nod, he continues. "So the blades are to cut the magic stuff while she's handling the rest."

"Doesn't hurt that you're pretty lucky as well. You're just a good penny I'm giving to my kid, not keeping it for myself."

"You got a blade. I got a blade." He's smiling. "That make me your protégé now? You going to train me in the deadly arts of being a salty old man?"

"Much as I hate to reiterate myself, if anything happens to Tamara Bridgecombe, slit your throat before I get to you. That would be your best option."

Part Two

How broken can saviors be? How disassembled can the models for future growth be and still be followed? No one worthy of the title sane could call Taggert and his crew heroes, and yet look at them. They have nothing, know no one, and can do very little, but they're standing against the Decimation storm risking all. Even if they win, they've already lost. But they don't stop trying.

Listen closely and I will tell you one of the oldest lies. There are different gods. They number one and many. They are different from each other and gain power in the recognition of human devotees. Which was the lie? Sometimes, even I can't remember.

Manna Elohim, the food of the gods, is itself a god. Possibly the first, for it feeds all the other gods, as well as humans, when it so desires. But it is ancient and crafty. It knows it's enemies, the Alters, so well, its techniques sometime mirror theirs. The Manna has an agenda. It doesn't like to lose. In that, the Liminals and the Manna have something in common.

Even the wind doesn't know all of the Manna's tricks. But we hear stories; of the Children of the desert, hidden by the Manna from all, jumping through time and space, protected and fierce.

Of a Liminal silent girl trained to break the bones of Alters. Of this story, the wind knows a bit more. I was the one who fixed her soul to a ship made of the world tree wood when she fell after rescuing me from the hands of Alters years ago, in another reality. It's only now that I begin to see my role in the plans of the Manna. It takes an old god to be able to trick a Child of the Wind into doing its bidding. But if it's true, then the Manna is far crueler than any of the pantheons of old were to their devotees.

Eastern Sahara, Morocco
Prentis

Desert is boring. Or maybe I'm mad because Taggert's in the other Land Rover with Bingy and Munji. Stuck with the love lost duo of Mico and Fatty in the lead ride. Supposed to be the ones guided by voices but it feels like just driving around the massive barren end of fuck all trying to find potholes engineered for my ass. Sardined in next to the camping gear while the noonday sun makes an insulated oven of the car gives a well baked meat pie feeling. Shite, it's fucking hot.

"The desert always this hot?"

"Are you serious girl?" Fatty asks, after cursing in her home language.

"She's taking the piss," Mico tells her shotgun side. Then really nice to me: "It gets very cold at night, though."

"Yeah, the lizards have told me. Just makin' polite."

Better that than acknowledging the sum of Taggert's thought equals wander around the desert until Fatty recognizes a place she's never been or Mico recounts a zone he's forgotten about for the past twenty odd years.

"Best show ever," demand and Mico picks it up immediately.

"Spinning or in the crowd?" Mico asks.

"Start with spinning and if there's still time after . . ." tell him.

"Marseilles. About three years before I met Taggert. A.C. had just helped me take down my first mystic threat, the imprisonment demon . . ." Again with that way-off voice.

"Doesn't sound so tough," tell him.

"It was the demon of imprisonment!" he protests. "The defeated spirit of everyone and thing that gets locked up."

"The show?" Tosser. Can fuck with him all day.

"Anyway, we decided to celebrate. Bingy arranged one of those super yachts to dock in the middle of the pier. I started on there with eight monitors rocking classic Rai vocals over Wu-Tang samples for like an hour straight. Once the boat was full, we took off from port and I was doing breakbeat and dubstep oldies versus this collection of Lomax prison recordings. I sped up some classic Trojan ragga tunes and beefed them up with some original samples from this group of Javanese gamelan woman singers I'd found . . ."

"Please shut up." Fatty sighs hard but plaintive like. A genuine request.

"What your problem?" Mico snaps back. "No one is even talking to you."

"You say it, I see it," she tell him. "Literally. I can see you on a ship behind turntables. Makes driving difficult. It's not really your fault. I think you just get excited and radiate it out psychic sonically."

"I know." It takes a second for both of us to recover from that calm confirmation. "It's why crowds are attracted to my music, to me. What? You didn't think I knew that?"

"So why don't you reign it in?" Fatty jumps back in. "Some of us are trying to drive."

"Across a barren desert." Laugh. "Afraid a stray tumbleweed is going to get you?" At least that gets a laugh from her. "It's always been like that? Hear something and everyone around you see it?"

"You don't see it, really. You feel it," he corrects. "And to varying degrees, yes. It's a more concrete form of empathy, but we all have it to some degree. The Manna just made me more aware of it, better able to manipulate it."

Quiet for a while, even Mico does his best to keep the sonic empathy in check. I feel Mico and Fatima, feeling around for this distant god, around each other even. Reach out to a hawk overhead and borrow her eyes to survey our land. Aside from a few desert hares scurrying at the bird's shadow, there is only us. The silence, almost a stillness, broaches the peaceful.

"So do you pray to your god?" Fatima asks suddenly. Doesn't take her eyes off the road, but pops a joint in her mouth from out of nowhere.

"There doesn't seem much point these days," he confesses. "I used to not have the need. I used to have private conversations with the Manna. Now I'm like everyone else, howling in the wind and taking random reaction as response. I have to learn how to speak the divine language again."

"'re roaming the wastelands trying to find your ancient spirit," tell him after taking a hit. "Hail Mary, or hail Manna thrown to the sky might not be the worst idea ever."

"Girl's got a point," Fatty says with a bit of lightness in her voice

"I'm an idiot," Mico blurts. "Stop the car."

He jumps out quick and runs over to Taggert in the other Rover. They've pulled up short behind us, ready for a fight. Take the opportunity to change out of the clothes been wearing since Ethiopia. Hell with modesty, try to put on some Daisy Dukes I found in the safe house. Fatty comes around the front of the car and stops me.

"Little pale thing, unless you want skin cancer tomorrow I suggest you cover those legs up now." The hash and tobacco joint Fatty lights smells divine.

"Too fucking hot out here for pants!" tell her. ". . . the hell do you do it?"

"Feel them." She calls me over with her hand to touch her light tan pants. They feel like cool sand on the beach. Her top is the same, almost like it's absorbing heat and transforming it into cool.

"How's that then?"

"Two layers. One linen, the other silk. Old-school Chinese trick. Keeps you cool out here," Fatty says.

"Same thing you were wearing back in Addis, though. Wha? You always dress for the desert?"

"Yes."

"Why?" Like I asked her to take her O levels. She'd never thought of it before, just always outfitted herself like she'd be in the middle of the Sahara. Take the joint from her mouth for another quick puff. "Does me no good unless you've got another pair."

From the back driver's side, she pulls a pair of pants like hers and some heavy but flexible shades. Oakley' have nothing on these things. Change quick and she gives me the once-over.

"Righteous," she says after a long drag. "Now wrap your head up, or you'll lose water. I'll make a Bedouin out of you yet." See Fatty scoping out Tag and Mico at the other Rover. Everyone's out of their rides and it looks like we're setting up camp just off the road. She bristles at Mico laughing with her father.

"Still don't trust them?"

"In my position, would you?"

"Can't imagine like that." Tell her honest as I wrap hair behind a light blue scarf. "Tag calls me daughter even though I tried my level best to kill him when we first met. Hadn't even met Mico before he sang a hole in reality to rescue me from . . ."

"From what, girl?" Fatima asks me, coming close, helping me shake off the funk that blocks my soul whenever I think of the dark times with Nordeen.

"Flawed as they are, those are two good men in a bad world doing what they can to make it better."

"So why can't I stand the crooner? I see him and all I feel is anger." It's new for Fatima to ask questions of anyone.

"No clue." Flip my head back up, feeling ten degrees cooler all over my body. "But feelings are fleeting."

Together, like for the first time together, we walk. She's still the woman, taller, more confident than maybe I'll ever be, but she's looking at me like I've got some purpose. Borrow some of her swagger as we make our way across the road over to the makeshift camp ground. Munji, Bingy, and Mico are unloading one of the medium-sized tents from the back of their Land Rover. Fatty disconnects from me in a second and takes a two-foot-long tent pole from her dad's hand while I speak with mine.

"We're getting more eyes," Tag tells me before I can ask. Doing his own version of yoga, expanding and decreasing his muscles in seconds, lightening his skin pigmentation then returning it to normal half a second later, and other internal shit no one else would notice but me and Tamara.

"If you start growing eyes in the back of your neck you're gonna make me hurl," tell him, warning all snakes to get out of the way of the tent.

"Fat lot of good that would do. Mico has the souls of all the people that died during the slave trade in the Atlantic chilling in his right arm," Taggert says.

"What now?" Tells me the story of how they made it across the Atlantic and back in time, of Chabi and her ghost ship and the spirit sharks. How the souls of drowned Africans—and their rage—got a home made for them thanks to Tag's Liminals, Tam's psychics, and Mico's . . . Miconess. Guess they can shield him, coat him, like Iron Man armor. Only Black man armor? Of souls? I'd seen him encased in the weird shimmering blackness before when they first liberated me from Nordeen's grasp, but there was no way for me to trust my senses then. Wasn't sure what I was seeing when Mico saved Fatima from the plane. The whole time Tag's going on explaining in the naked sun, only got one thought.

"Wasteman Mico has all this going on in his right arm and doesn't think to call on these spirit things before now?" Look to find him, to kick his arse.

"He did. That's how he was able to grab Fatima out of the sky before she suffered too much damage. They aren't at his beck and call. Usually they only come out when there's some major drama coming his way," Tag tells.

"We put him in the sun and wait for him to turn into jerky? Don't rate him, Fam." He laughs and I done my job.

"Better that than the reality," Tag says.

"Wha?"

"Bastard has to sing to them." Shyte.

Eastern Sahara, Morocco
Prentis

Half an hour into singing solo and three caravans making their way across the desert came to pay tribute and join in Mico's song. An hour after the last of the collected ninety-nine singers and musicians joined up, their women and children finished erecting a giant circus tent around the makeshift band. African spirits started flowing from Mico. Desert man them showed no signs of stress. Acted blessed, they did.

Stayed in the animal skin smelling circus flaps for as long as I could. Between complex polyrhythms, the heat from the bodies, and the makeshift fires, and the overly sweet tea I need a break. 'Sides, not even singing.

Catch Tag and Prentis surveying the eastern sky for the oncoming storm just as a half moon begins to rise. The long tan wrap is uneven, clinging to my arms and back like it's form fitted. Fatty lights a beng just as I exit.

"Five hours too much for you?" the smuggler queen 'terrogates me, handing Tag a joint.

"Wasted on Grand," says, grabbing it from the old man's fingers.

"You're supposed to be standing guard," Tag tells me . . . I takes a massive drag.

"Only because I refused to tell anyone in there whether I was on my period." Mico's literal power is the ability to draw people to him, but doesn't know better than to interrogate a girl about her rag. Sacred space rules be damned.

"Say one more thing about 'their culture' and I swear, fam, even you will have problems dealing with the amount of scorpion stings you get tonight. And I am on watch. Duck."

Say it slow but Taggert catches my left iris zoom on something behind him. He responds to the cornea and hit the sand with a quickness. Mico's pitch black human spirits swoops down behind me and flies into the tent.

"Don't care what you say," say taking another hit. "Those things freak me out."

"You ain't missing anything in there," Da says calmly, switching joint out for water from his thermos. "And yeah, I wouldn't mind being able to feel them."

"That's what bugs you two?" Fatima almost laughs. "Not the asinine plan of sending lost spirits out to find a place their magician can't find?"

About to call fair play for her when we all hear her father Munji yell in frustration. Fatima moves against the rising wind faster than a normal human can. Her stress is infectious. Tag and I follow her around the back end of the tent and down a small dune to wear the caravaners tie their camels. Munji and a few other men and women doing their best to put down a camel uprising.

"Baba?" Almost cute the way Fatima says it. Munji is struggling for control over a dark sandy camel whose only weapons are its swinging head and voluminous spit. Bare skills, Fatima leg -holsters her small rifle. But we both stand at the perimeter of the makeshift pen trying to figure out how to intercede.

"I don't know, beloved. All at once they rose up in rebellion. Ballack Ballack!" Munji shouts back to his daughter. The last part he directed to the camel, to move before another camel backed into his face.

"Hold up," Tag tells her just before she enters the dust-up. Points to me. Didn't stop at the perimeter the way Fatima and Tag did but did slow down. Tag knows my trance look. Nearly not human.

Tamara can't read my mind when I link into a collective ether of a species. In this state, think and feel animal.

Transformation is never complete. Psychically, don't become an animal, only an expression of their royalty. Tag's been on the receiving end of the animal fury designed to protect their queen, their regent . . . their God.

Not surprised when the camels chill when I enter the flat ground of their pen. They turn to beg a pet from my hands. Liminal in me stirs and I make sound like a wet, out of tune saxophone. Language the camels understand. Telling them to chill. But they get bookey. Gently as a camel can, they nudge all other humans and put me in the middle of a dromedary circle.

"What's that now?" Fatty asks Taggert.

"Protection . . ." he starts, but as the camels move back in unison, so does Taggert, with a guiding hand given to the smuggler princess as well. From above, swirl of cold, blue, black, and movement crashes into a few inches below the sand. Even with fast grown reticulating lenses, Taggert can only tell there's a scrabble of limbs and claws. Half the herdswomen run as the sand grows cold and whispered screams of rage issue forth from light-tossed granules. Hopefully, Fatima knows what's going on, but she's debating how to get around the miasma in front of us to get close to her father. Get Munji on a camel before the mist, smoke, and cold can roll toward him.

Legs blacker than the shadow of midnight kick at a toothy mouth and rhino-like chest, and the two elements of the chaos separate. One of Mico's African spirits, sleek, near silent, perfectly proportioned. Scrapping partner is as ghosty, but paler blue and less fully formed. Seems more animal turned human, with hooves for back legs, a rolled armored chest, human arms, and a face even a baboon mother would put down for being too toothy. African ghost is made of . . . whatever the fuck ghosts are made of. Substance of this thing is a near arctic cold that freezes everything it "touches." Camels hate it. Can't stall the stampede.

"The fuck . . . ?" I ask.

"Djinn!" Munji shouts from a foaming mouth single humped. "Blue djinn. The Tuareg speak of them."

"Djinn, like fucking Aladdin?" shouts over the rising cold winds. "Meant to be funny and animated and shit, yeah?"

"These are the outcast of the original djinn! Creatures of Fire and smoke turned to the cold and mist."

Guess the djinn didn't like to be named, because in a millisecond it's shifted its focus from Mico's African to Munji. Fatima's mare's leg rifle let off four shots before it leapt but the bullets flew right through it. Still the African spirit was faster, wrapping up one of the djinn's legs and dragging it back to the ground through a fatally frozen camel.

Fatima wastes no time reloading and circling over to the renewed battle. Makes sense; the djinn tried to kill her father. I'd do the same. But as she fires her .357—with dense slugs—all she's doing is sending frozen chunks of sand into the air. Cursing in Arabic but I can barely hear it over her repeated shots.

"Back up," Taggert tells her after she reloads. She's smart and circles away from the scrap, doing her best to avoid the rapidly freezing sand. Tag whistles to the African spirit, now stuck beneath the djinn's snapping teeth and makes a rabbit kick motions with his fingers. It catches Tag's meaning and kicks the beast off just as it did before. Only now Taggert stands between the djinn and the ghost.

"You picked the wrong side," my badman tells djinn calmly. "Sure you don't want to . . ." Attacks before he can finish offer, so he dodges its swipe and makes an "X" across its prominent chest with the entropy blade before it can recover. Its scream is ice breaking against glass, its breath, frozen spittle aimed like daggers at his face. But before they can touch Tag, fade into droplets. From the time they dropped from the sky to its end was only two minutes but still Taggert gets grief.

"Why didn't you do that in the first place?" Fatima says, helping her father off the camel.

"Might want to keep that gun at the ready," tell her as she watches the African spirit pantomiming at me. Wild gestures and gyrations but without a mouth.

"What's it on about?" Fatima demands.

"Can't tell," Taggert says.

"Don't be daft!" shout, aiming my camel posse toward the tent. "What's the only thing that gets those things worked up? Mico!"

Reach the rise just in time to see Bingy man swinging a machete through the air at a Gnawa man, one of the singers, as they nearly fall out the tent into the rising cold wind. Don't bother to ask where the Jamaican got a machete from, if he's swinging it's because Mico needs it. African spirits are returning into the circus-sized tent, though not in the same numbers they left in, and Taggert's about to join them after causing blindness and muscle death in the neck of Bingy's opponent. But the tent takes flight on its own, spokes and all. Exposed, Mico's craft and combat make a joke of all previous warfare. Man's entire tack is to get close enough to anyone attacking to whisper in their ears. Can't hear what he says but as soon as he mumbles in that moment of awkward intimacy, the person passes out. Through it all, Taggert stays still, scanning their bodies.

"Were they on their periods?" ask, not bothering to get off my camel.

"Maybe they just didn't like his singing," Fatima says, securing three more guns from the fallen thirty or so musicians and singers now sleeping at our feet. I can't care.

"What ya see, healer man?" Dread asks Taggert. Looking out across the dunes, past an old oasis and into the coming cold storm. He's using his Liminal sight.

"Poppy." All he whispers. Last time Taggert met with her, the Alter almost killed him. Took Tamara to rescue him. Poppy laid the foundation for Kothar to infect my soul. Poppy. Pale, pajamaed, problem of an Alter.

See her, skin cold and dead like the moon, eyes, frozen pale blue, impossibly thin, wearing bedtime clothes, and the shimmering cold bodies of thousands of blue djinn towards the horizon. But that's not the worst of it. She sees us. From miles away, she sees me and blows Taggert a kiss. A signal to her djinn. They scrabble across the sand and the sky, freezing what air and land they touch with homicidal glee.

"We've got to go!" Taggert shouts, almost yanking me off the camel.

"Wait, what?" shout back at him. Instantly, I'm surrounded by suspicious camels. "We just won."

"No, he's right." Mico says, looking off to the ridge I was staring at. Already the air is colder. "That was a scouting party we were lucky to catch. Poppy is one of the worst of them."

"We can't fight?" ask Taggert as I consent to get off the camel's back.

"Take a look at Mico," Tag tells me. "He's been singing for four hours straight. Plus he's sent the majority of his African ghost task force to parts unknown. Numbers we're facing right now, my blades can only do so much." He hesitates to tell me the rest.

"Truth is we're going to need every second we can get to maintain this lead on the oncoming storm," says, dragging into a jeep.

"Piss off, Tag, there's got to be a better way," say, leaning out of the back passenger seat, finally getting what he's asking of me.

"I'm ready to hear it," Rest of our crew load in quickly. Either we find the forgotten spot now or we fall going against an Alter and her djinn. No need for supplies, we pile into one ride. "This cold ain't a natural wind, darling. It catches up with us we're left dead bleeding in the mud and the rest of the world with us."

"Seriously, piss off." But I do it.

The camels make their cry and charge into the cold wind in front of us. Tag won't look in the rearview mirror to see me crying; he just revs the engine. Mico rides shotgun. Bingy, Munji, and Fatima cram in the back and he kicks the jeep into gear.

"Camels will buy us some time but I need a direction," Tag tells Mico.

"Most of the spirits I sent east haven't come back," Mico confesses.

"Fucking thin thread of hope that is," Fatima barks.

"It's all we've go,." Taggert says, cranking the wheel and heading east.

Eastern Sahara, Morocco?
Prentis

Swear down, can't tell if it's day or night, if I'm going forward or backward. Can't allow for this ringing going off in my head, a beat with extra echo, a thousand hummingbirds using their wing strokes to speak. To shout, really. I can even hear Taggert above it all with his calm voice panic in full swing, but I'm barely responsive. After the camels—they were so brave, they ran to slaughter just to protect me—this damn banging song been plaguing me.

"She's as gone as he is!" Fatima says, shaking my shoulders, trying to get me to respond. Can't hear my own voice. In the front seat, I see Mico doubled over and rocking, but in time to what I'm hearing. So I try it as well.

Movement stops. At least inside movement. We're in a Land Rover I remember, because I slide off the seat and into the well of the back seat. But there's moves outside of the car. Peak wind rocking the ride. A storm. A big one. Severe and fast moving. But on beat.

"Can't you hear it?" Mico shouts.

"Who the hell can't?" I shout back.

"Everybody else in the damn car," Fatima tells me, trying to pick me up from the well. But I'm rigid, hands clasped around my ears, for all the good it does.

"Is this the blue djinn attacking?" Munji asks.

"No!" Mico shouts with more confidence than I could muster. "It's a sound, it's like a music, like singing, but louder than anything I've ever heard before. You can't . . . I can't believe you can't . . ."

Hear Taggert swear, the opening of the car, a mad desperate howl in the air, trillions of grains of sands threatening to shred the paintjob of the Land Rover, but all of it is still quieter than the sound in my head Mico called music. The car rocks and I think we're driving again but then realize we bounced. Air got under the car. All four tires were off the ground for a second. No word a lie, I'm shook.

"Taggert!"

"I'm here kid." It's his body I can hear and feel, crawled to the back seat. In his lap now, being cradled like a fucking baby. Hate it. Need it.

"You can't hear it?" I beg.

"No. But Mico just went to it. We've got to go towards the noise, the sound, you're the only one that can hear it. Can you lead us?"

"Waitaminute . . ." I hear the Jamaican protest.

"We stay here any longer and it's death by sandstorm or blue djinn," Taggert shouts back.

"You want to walk into a sandstorm?" Fatima says, and I can hear how offensive the concept is to her desert knowledge.

"Mico just did it." Da tell them.

"Tag, this hurts." Cry a little bit.

"Don't worry, it's just the life we live," he tries to joke with me. "Come on, girl, you're stronger than noise. Rise up. The world is counting on you." And just like that, I open my eyes.

To the east, the cold infecting the air, the oncoming blue djinn almost howl. Try not to think about the camels. To the south, just behind the nearest dune, there's a whirlwind—but it's not just made of sand and wind, it's also sound. Hear it. Only now, it sound like music. Impossibly loud, like someone yelling in my ears. Between that and the djinn Alter combo, I'm going for the sound. Taggert's done me the kindness of letting me walk, but part of me still wishes I was in his lap. Feel him at my shoulder. Not the others. Can't hear for shit. Everything is upside down. Taggert shouts. Lost someone. Fatty, I think. Should feel my feet against the sand, but everything is upside down. Taggert ain't behind me anymore, but he's still reaching out with his power. He's panicking, trying to hold on to me. But he can't. I'm flying. No control and deaf. What do you call it when you're flying, being spun around? Spun, like the whirlwind. Holy shit, we've been taken up in the air by a whirlwind.

Heart of the Whirlwind
Taggert

I wake up hard to a harmonious camel heartbeat. There's a confusingly familiar scent I haven't taken in for a while, and never this strong, that surrounds everything—like the perfume on a lover you've forgotten. It's just under the deep throat tickle I get around sun-baked hide.

The combination of a whistle, bark, and polysyllabic tongue roll issues forth like a question from the heartbeat body. I sit up from a plank four feet off the ground covered in wool woven blankets. Across the hide tent, bathed in the orange light of animal skins, is a palm oil red skinned woman. Six feet four with not the rumor of fat anywhere near her. Bronze jewelry grips her arms with the same casual tension her blue and gold skirt holds her hips. No bedouin tribe I've ever encountered is so casual with its women's dress.

"I don't understand a word you're saying," I tell her, finding my legs, my lungs, and my muscles once again. In that order. The giantess issues forth more gibberish, though I swear I can make out proper syllables in the whistles—as I attempt to scan her the way I did myself.

"Cha-Na!" She stands with a well-oiled knife in her hand before my psychic sensory organ can do much more than sense her. She's no Liminal, but she is sensitive.

"Okay, my bad." I put my arms up to show apology but still the big one advances, slowly, with that huge echoing heartbeat of her joining her words, and even her steps, with a bizarre rhythmic intention. I'm so distracted by the meter of it, I almost miss the nine-inch blade in her hand tapping her own pearly whites.

"Cha!" the camel-hearted says before trying to do the same with my teeth.

"Ease up."

"Cha!" she barks repeating the blade action.

"Cha! Cha!" I say.

"Cha!" she says again, this time touching her chest with the flatness of the blade.

"You feel it? Your Cha-Na? Okay, I can respect that . . ."

"Cha!" She taps her chest, clearly as tired of our game as me. But this matters to her. On a whim, I steady my heart rate, give it the same meter as hers, then repeat her bark. This time . . . there's a different feeling. A comprehension.

"Na," she says calmly, and I hear a change in her throat and her heart rate. But more, her blood pressure, even, I swear, her smell. I match them all.

"Na," I say it and know it means now.

"Cha na!" Camel heart almost smiles, sheathing her blade.

"Stop now," I say her words but I know what they mean. Somehow I know.

"Listen and watch, Liminal," she says slowly, giving me enough time to repeat her whistles, grunts, and tongue rolls. It's only by saying her words that I begin to understand them. "You will take our language in with less time and practice than you think provided you focus on observing and not interacting. Yes?"

"Yes." She makes it easy for me to agree with her.

"Good. You are safe as are your companions. For now. But you are also known to us. He who wrecks time and space for family. That is not our way."

"Who are we?" I hazard speaking entirely phonetically, knowing I'm attaching the right words to concepts, but it's impossible to guess at diction and proper pronunciation. The camel heart sits back down, smiling at her ability to school me, no doubt.

"We are the Children of the Desert and the Manna is our mother."

The Lost Ocean
A.C.

"Where the hell did you find a boat made of the Yggdrasil wood in the first place?" It finally occurred to me to ask Narayana after we began the search in earnest for Chabi. An all ash wood forty-five foot ship that reeked of smoke and the deep sea was rare enough that I should've said something. But it was only after I noticed the runes carved in the masthead, the bunks below, and the crow's nest that I sensed the ancient power was in the wood itself.

"It was sunken," was all he would say to me from the captain's deck. Not that I'm fond of Alters in the first place, but Narayana's cold quiet has always made me hate him more. So I distance myself.

The deck of the yacht is mostly empty save for a few strapped down barrels of food and clean water. It's clean, well polished, and stocked. No telling where Narayana procured it, but it was obviously meant for some luxurious coast-hugging getaway nine centuries ago and not some mid-ocean ghost trek. I want to go talk to Tamara, hiding/looking out high in the foremast. But she doesn't remember me. No one does.

Tamara recognizes me the moment she sees me, but she can't remember. She wouldn't remember that I was the one to point out her parents' car on the bridge the day it blew up, that I warned her away from Alia, the psycho responsible for the explosion, or even the push to tell her mother about her powers. I was there for all of it, trying to help, an insistent nag at her back. It's not her fault. Taggert, Prentis, even Mico can't recall all the ways I've been there for him. It's the price that I pay for all the other things I can do. But the Alters. They recognize me and more.

On deck, I see the Lucky Liminal playing with one of Taggert's entropy blades, going through some martial arts forms, holding the knife with no common sense on how to use it properly. Taggert never should have had them in the first place, but now he's handing off one of the deadliest tools on the planet to the most recent convert to the cause. It was a demonstration of control in himself and faith in Pasha I don't see is earned, but whatever. Time to learn.

I appear behind him. The skinny boy turns quick off of instinct to slice so I nerve strike his wrist with two fingers to get him to open his hand then fold the blade back in on itself with the butt of my sword. "You understand that blade can cut through anything, air, flesh, stone, spirit, right?"

"You know it's not a good idea to sneak up on me, brov, right?" He only says it after the recognition comes to his eyes. "I could've got a lucky slice off."

"That wouldn't have been lucky at all," I tell him, pulling my sword, ignoring its cries for his blood. "Not for you at least."

"What's this then?" he asks, taking a defensive step back.

"Let's call it training," I offer, taking as slow an overhead strike as I can. As expected he catches my blade in the curve of his own but then jumps back six feet at the sense of shock he feels.

"Fuck to Christ! What is that? Feels like a demon just shit my soul, get me?"

"What happens when two entropy weapons cross," I tell him as I ask a gust of wind to push me toward him, sword point at his throat. He leaps high over me. Not high enough to avoid my blade if I arch with him, but it's a good move.

"End it, fam!" he yells at me. The blade is still in his hand, but he's crouched with it behind him, his other hand extended forward.

"On one condition. Tell me why the hell Taggert would trust you with one of his blades?" I sheathe my sword slowly.

"He said I'd need it more than him." The wind carries his truth and I smile.

"True that." Then I shoot at the kid with one of my revolvers. I aim for his closest shoulder. The kid's instinct is pure and righteous. He slices the bullet out of the air with the blade, only a millimeter before impact. I holster my weapon before he gets pissed enough to attack me. "Good job, goofball."

"You're bait, blood!" Tamara barely controls her descent from watch and lands with a thud between us. "What gives? Trying to . . ."

"Relax. I'm just testing your boyfriend's jaw. Not to worry, the blades don't seem to have any control over him and he's got access to their abilities."

"He's not my boyfriend. Can you two kill the noise?"

"Someone's touchy. You worried about your fam?" I ask.

"And the fact that we've been wandering the deep blue for two days now with nothing to show for it," she tells us both, looking overboard.

"Been meaning to ask," Pasha asks, still cautious of me. "How are we supposed to know where this chick is?"

"She's not for us to find." I sigh.

"How's that now?" Now Tamara's on me. This gets tedious after a while.

"There are rules to follow if you want to find a ghost. Whoever lost her has to find her." It takes them a second but they both look up to the captain's cabin in unison.

"Is it now?" the Brit boy howls at me. "We're relying on him?"

"Calm yourself," Tam tells him. "Wasn't too long ago you were working for him and his kind."

"Nah, I'm bricking it." I'm forgotten as usual as Pasha turns to face Tamara. "I've never been face-to-face with one of the Alters before man him that drives this death boat. They are the terror of the world. Baron, my old boss, barely talks to them directly. They destroy and corrupt the way we breathe, unconsciously, without effort . . ."

"I broke all the bones of an Alter," she says so calmly the girl has to be believed.

"But . . . doesn't matter. Look, it's like that woman you found in Addis. She went for the Derg guy, right? And as a result she got some random disease that was probably going to kill her. That's the way the Alters work, asymmetrical attacks from the shadows. You never know what they're going to do, how they're going to come at you," Pasha says.

"But he's not coming at us, we're flowing in his wake," Tam tells him.

"And what do you think lies behind him, sunshine and puppies?" Pasha asks.

"It's true as far as it goes," I interrupt. Pasha starts at my voice but Tamara has gotten more practice at remembering me. "This isn't going to be a smooth and easy ride, but the closer we stay to Narayana, the safer we will be relatively . . ."

"Until we actually meet up with Chabi," Tam starts, practicing some old familiar katas that I've only seen Chabi practice. "After that, the question will be how to keep her from taking Narayana apart."

"Another option, yeah?" Pasha offers. "Big man T said this knife can cut through anything, especially those things that aren't supposed to exist. Sounds like it was made to take on Alters. I could sneak up behind him, take him out. Bet we can find this chick on our own . . ."

"She is no bird," Narayana says, standing behind Pasha. The small Liminal doesn't bother turning around. "She is a consummate killing ghost. The puff of wind might be able to locate her but I'm the only one who can bring her back to shore. And as for sneaking up on me, best you secure your own six before you scout another's."

I cry laughing alongside Tamara as Pasha scampers off to change his underwear. Narayana tries to dead-eye the both of us to stop the laughing, but the mean mug just makes us laugh harder. He gives up on us and makes his way back to the captain's seat.

"So, Wind Boy," Tamara asks, still practicing her lethal yoga. "Why are you here? And don't give me that loyalty to Mico noise. Every time someone mentions Chabi's name you get all fluttery."

"You met her," I state. I could just be silent, she'd forget she asked the question, or forget that there was someone there to answer, but sitting on the deck looking at her move, she looks so similar to Chabi I find myself grabbing for a moment, a chance, ironically enough, a memory.

"Yup. Saved our asses. We were going to be chum for some ancient ghost sharks. But Mico called her name and she came to rescue us. Guided us through the mist of time to the U.S.," she says casually. Like it happens all the time.

"She mention me?" I asked.

"Nope. Had a message for Narayana, though. Said to tell him she's coming for him."

"I taught her that move," I tell her when I see Tamara's right arm curve overhead to form a perfect overhead neck strike. It sounds more prideful than I mean to, so I add a bit more of the truth. "I also turned her into a ghost."

"How's that now?" Tamara stops her kata but gets in a defensive position, like I'm a threat.

"I didn't kill her. That was Rice and your favorite person, Poppy. At least, they're responsible. But rather than let her spirit fly away I bound it to the ship Narayana gifted her with. Like this one, it was made of wood from a world tree. It holds special properties, like the ability to retain a spirit. I made a few promises to a few deities I swore never to talk to again and . . ."

"Why? Why not let her die?" she asks as she starts her kata again.

"How cold is your heart, girl?"

"How cold is yours?" the psychic fires back. "There's nothing that radiates off her but vengeance and deadly intent. I don't know what kind of life she lived, but I get the sense she was a fuller being before. I saw my mother, this dimension's version of her. And trust, when it's time for her to go down I'd rather pull that trigger to put her out of her suffering than allow her to continue to live like that."

It's hard to be seen, to be remembered. I let the wind begin to pull me into the periphery of her consciousness, but the damn Liminal is strong. She won't let me go.

"Answer the question, A.C. Why did you do it?" she demands this time.

"She saw me. Really saw me. I made my bargains, got my skills in exchange, so I can't complain too loud. But I'm not going to lie. Sometimes, it's hard not to be known. To be forgotten. Constantly. But when Chabi spoke to me, when she saw me, it made me feel more alive than any fight, any weapon, any journey I've ever been on. Plus, she came back for me. The Alters were torturing me, were going to kill me if it took stilling the winds of the planet. But she came back for me, took them all on, and almost won. I owe her."

"Rubbish," she tells me calmly. "Paying the debt would have meant you gave her a proper burial or you go after Rice and his crew. Your sad ass linked her to that boat on the off chance that you could find a way to save her. Find a way to bring her back to life, maybe."

I want to protest, but how can I? The girl smirks and begins to hover over me, taking flight back to the crow's nest. She sucks her teeth before she leaves.

"Mystic dipshits every one of you. You'll fight every demon in creation except the one in your heart. We find her, you better tell her how you feel or I will."

The Lost Ocean
A.C.

Not a lot sneaks up on me. I do the sneaking. I'm good at it. But when the Mansai's double sails appear out of a deep fog bank off our starboard side, even I'm surprised. Last time I saw it was in dock in Sausalito, California. In another world. It didn't look so ethereal then, so thin. It's almost translucent now, shimmering with the waves of the ocean. Makes sense, it's a ghost ship. Most people think of large pirate ships when they think of ghost ships, not a two-person caravel looking ship rigged with a motor. And that's how she's managed to go unseen.

"I don't see anyone on it." The Lucky Liminal, bless his dumb ass, says, shading his eyes from the haze of light from the mist as he looks on stupefied.

"'Cuz she's a ghost and that's a ghost ship, ya git," Tamara says bored. Her eyes are locked in the right place. At the only one who can make this bass awkwards plan work. Narayana descends from the captain's deck, taking his shirt off as he does.

"What are the rules of your enchantment?" Narayana asks me solemnly when he gets to us.

"I bound her spirit to the life of the ashvattha wood in the boat," I tell him. "Combined with her blood and her training she is in supreme control of everything that happens on and around that ship. If we're seeing her, that's because she wants to be seen."

"She wants to see you all right," Tamara tells the Alter. "If for nothing else than to break you into pieces." I swear I see a smile make an appearance on Narayana's lips.

"So we just hang back here and you two work it out?" Pasha almost begs.

"You wish. Only successful end to this fuckery is if we come back with both of them," Tam tells him.

"But you just said this ghost wants to kill him?"

"What, you thought this would be easy?" And with that Tamara uses her telekinesis to throw the Liminal over to the Mansai like a sack of potatoes.

"Wot?" she asks with that fake South London accent when I stare at her. "That's what he here for, right? To take shots we don't want to, right?"

"When the combat starts," Narayana tells us, "don't try to help. Either of us. This is between master and student."

"D'uh." I let Tamara's comment stand both of us.

"Well, she didn't throw him back over," I say after a full five minutes. "Might as well get it on."

Tamara lifts the three of us in far gentler a fashion than she'd done with Pasha and glides us toward the ship of the only woman I've ever been close to loving.

You with him? Chabi's words echo in our minds, an innate skill as far from telepathy as grunting is from writing a thesis. She looks the same, two braided ponytails hang half the length of her back, come together at her waist, small bits of something sharp and deadly throughout. Her olive complexion dulled by death, but her pointed chin and high cheekbones giving her that Mongol royalty look that pulls me, every time. She looks the same, only dead.

Death never looked so good. Mistaking Chabi's casual neck stretching, loose fitting T-shirt and black gi pants, and calm tone as nonthreatening is a mistake only Pasha would make, so I make sure to take his wind from him before he can respond. Narayana does his part and takes a few steps away from us.

"Only in that we brought him here," Tamara says, even keel, acknowledging the menace implied by the dead girl's eye lock on Narayana. "Way we see it, you two have some things to work out."

Indeed.

Chabi gives me a quick look and for a second I want to say something, but what? Last time we saw each other I gave her the option of dying for real or being bound to this ship. Now the next time she sees me I'm traveling with her chief tormentor/teacher and two other Liminals. Not sure I have the words yet for her. But she's got some words for us all.

I've developed an aversion to entropy weapons on my ship. She indicates with dead eyes my sword and guns as well as Pasha. *Keep them sheathed or you'll catch the same wrath as this one.* She points to Narayana, who's developing his own cone of dead silence around him.

"Have you finished covering your excuses?" Narayana's voice stills every creak and moan of the ship. "You've sent word that you wanted to see me. Here I am."

You left me!

"I trained you."

You cursed me!

"I protected you with my mark."

You doomed me.

"I gave you a fighting chance. It's not my fault you lost."

If Narayana were at all human his throat would have been crushed by the elbow Chabi crashes into it. A normal human would double over or grab at his throat. Narayana barely flinches, but Chabi doesn't wait for his reaction. She already launches a knee into his groin, then twists as she returns her knee to land another elbow to the back of Narayana's head. That one he feels, so in the split second it takes Chabi to regain her footing he shoves her ribs and pushes her back across the deck.

"I spend years training you for that? No wonder you died."

Pasha is faster than me and gets to the side of the boat to move out of the combatant's way. Fat lot of good it does any of us. Chabi calls forth the chi of her ship using the type of kata only a dead Liminal trained by an Alter can. The deck begins to vibrate and glow a hazel and green mist. It seeps past our feet and encircles Chabi.

Where's the accent, old man? Was every part of you a lie? She demands, sounding, feeling more substantial than before.

"The only lie between us was your commitment. I gave you everything, and you repay me by dying? You could have been great. Now you are nothing but a ghost."

At first I think she's moving so fast that we can see multiple images of her attacking Narayana, but as he dodges and moves, I realize that she's attacking not just physically but psychically. The images push no wind, but Narayana reacts to them. Just as he's catching on—he tries to grab one and his hand moves through her—Chabi joins the fray in true, surrounded by her ghostly ship light. This time when she strikes, a low kick to the middle of his femur and a straight strike to his solar plexus using three fingers like a hook, Narayana is shaken.

"Did she just hurt an Alter?" Pasha asks.

"Expect more than hurt," Tamara says, levitating over to us as Narayana straightens from his one-knee resting position.

"Okay, but if he's wounded why is he smiling? It's never a good sign when an Alter smiles." Pasha's fear is palpable.

On the offensive, Narayana is confined by the human form. He doesn't run toward Chabi, he wills his body in the exact position he's in, one knee on the deck holding his stomach, to just under where she's standing. Then he stands with a fist raised. The blow is an explosion that gives lift to her entire body. She flies up, only to hit the main mast before gravity calls her back. But it's her ship, so by the time Chabi lands, she's aware again and the mast is already healed.

Die, old man, Chabi tells him, again summoning the eldritch energy around her by literally snatching it from the air directly in front of her and pulling it close to her body.

"You did that for me." Narayana's upper body rotates almost separately from his lower extremities. While Chabi grabs energy, Narayana generates his dark mists and stray gray strands of power by swinging his arms with blinding speed. It's not possible for a human to move that fast, but then again Narayana is what death fears. His circular rotation of his arms combined with the winding of his waist would be comical if I hadn't seen it before. The djinn we trained with taught us to utilize their essential natures in combat. But the nature of the Alter is death and ash, so instead the djinn taught Narayana his nature, the art of fire. I saw the master djinn do this move once, the Ark of Fire he called it, to wipe out a pack of 200 hellhounds.

All air turns to fire. It starts over our heads and descends to scalp-scalding levels. Tamara doesn't move but Pasha starts ducking.

"Spazz man me yeah, but I'm just wondering, do we have a plan B?" he asks.

"Sackless, I swear," is all Tamara will say, her eyes focused hard on the fight. Like a breaking wave, Narayana steps forward and bends his wrists without ceasing his spinning. The fire above coalesces into a column that arcs at his hands. He sends the full blast of heat and flame at Chabi.

I tried not to flinch, to take comfort in what I knew to be true. She was dead already so living flame could do little to her. But to see her engulfed in fire—I almost intervene. If it wasn't for Tamara's smirk at my impulse, I probably would have.

Still, Narayana's not an idiot. He wouldn't just send a firestorm at Chabi. So when I see Chabi's own dark eldritch energies dissipating, I realize that the Alter put some of his native entropic force along with the flame. Chabi realizes as well and refuses to stay still. The more flame he pours at her, the closer she stomps toward him, re-upping her own energies from the hull of the ship. Leave it to her to walk into the flames. Narayana refuses to back down with his flame game, even when Chabi is eye-to-eye with him.

The headbutt was the least expected move she could have made. Stopped the flames, though. Before Narayana can stumble back, Chabi drives both her thumbs into his solar plexus. Alters are not flesh—they are made of something denser and inexplicably less substantial—so when she begins to peel him open like a ripe orange, I get concerned.

"Last time I saw something like that happen," Tamara says, finally showing an ounce of human concern, "the Alter turned into a human-shaped black hole and almost sucked us all into it."

"See, when you say things like that, you make me think I made the wrong choice teaming up with you," the Lucky Liminal whines.

Let's see if you have a heart in there, Chabi hisses as she pulls at Narayana's chest like a helpless crab. The drowned Liminal swims his arms out from his body, breaking her grip, then uses that same force to circle behind her head and drive her face into a upward knee thrust. Even from our distance we hear the thud. Not sure if Chabi can lose teeth in this form, but if she could, it would have been from that shot.

"It seems death was a better instructor than I was." Narayana refuses to let himself sound weakened, but that move had to hurt. "Still, I find you wanting."

They'll find you in seven different seas by the time I'm done with you, Chabi tells him. But then a look of concern comes over her. Over us all, actually. At first I thought it was just her turning the Mansai in a circle, but as the speed increases and the waters get choppier, as she gets more concerned I get frightened for real.

Stop now! every creak and snap in the boat say in unison with her voice.

"What the hell?" Pasha demands, trying to find something stable to hold on to.

"She is the ship!" Tamara tells him, trying to telekinetically anchor herself and Pasha to the deck. "If Narayana can't take her out hand to hand, he's going to take out the ship."

"We're on rassclot ship!" Pasha says, like we could forget. "How the hell is he going to do that?"

"Remember Pangkor Island?" I ask him as I take off in the air for a bird's-eye view. My suspicion was right. Below the Manasi a forty-foot column of water pushes skyward. And from the spout a palm and fingers are forming. Narayana has gone too far. I fly back to the ship with my sword drawn ready to join in Chabi's attack, but she's already standing in front of the Alter loose limbed, brimming with chthonic fury. What catches my eye more is the tear that wells in hers.

Damn it Narayana, stop!

"Make me," he tells her. Only for a second, she hesitates.

Her form is perfect and fluid, almost instinctual. As unconscious as skipping. In a cascade of motion, Chabi strikes at least fifty times in fifteen seconds. Like we heard Narayana's knee on Chabi's head, we hear every bone the Alter has break. Furious, elegant, and deadly.

"What the fuck was that?" Pasha asks, holding on to rigging and trying to get as close to the deck as possible.

"It's called the Entropy of Bones. He taught her that trick," I say, watching Narayana fall to the deck onto broken kneecaps. I feel Tamara decelerate our fall to the ocean as the giant water spout crumples as the Alter does.

Chabi walks over to the fallen Narayana. Her pitiless posture tells me she's prepping for the killing stroke. I join her and see that she's even broken his cheekbones and teeth as he looks up and tries to smile.

"Good girl." I can barely make out through the broken Alter's cracked teeth. She turns from the both of us. She just won a battle against her mentor. I won't ask her to fight back tears as well.

The Lost Ocean
A.C.

"Off G.P., he's murked, yeah? She's gonna kill him, fam?" Pasha looks to Tamara for answers, but she stays ignoring him, focusing all her telepathic ability toward the weeping ghost at the captain's wheel.

"You won't get anything from her . . ." I tell Tamara, once again surprising her doomed suitor.

"Already have, Wind Boy," Tamara isn't bothering to look in my direction. "She's so alone. It kills her to think that she can't take Narayana out because then she'll be even less connected to the world she came from. Ending him means taking out the biggest part of herself."

"Taggert have a plan for this?" Pasha asks and then is again ignored.

"The healer is not the only one with a sense of strategy," we hear through broken teeth at the deck. The grinding together of Alter bones sounds like deep bass dolphin rape. These creatures were not meant to heal. Yet through centuries on the planet, Narayana has found a way to violate every mystic convention and pact ever established. I shouldn't be surprised that he knows how to knit together that which shouldn't exist in the first place.

"No offense, sport," Tam says, finally shifting her gaze from Chabi to the mess on the ground. "But looks like your last plan didn't turn out so well."

"I pull my victories from below," is all his voice will huff out. Narayana somehow shuffles to bracc his back against the side of the ship. Once he catches his breath, the Alter locks eyes with me and says, "And it's where I bury them as well."

"What do you have hidden in this ocean?" I say, beginning to understand his madness, his infernal plotting.

"Nothing that I would tell you of." Narayana rests his head against the hull of the ship as the thunderous knitting and mending of arcane bonelike structures elongate and strengthen his abused neck.

I fly to Chabi, eager to speak, then near shamed into silence by her silent fury. Whatever damage she sustained in the fight has nothing to do with pain she's experiencing now. I send a small gust across her eyes to get her attention.

I see you, Wind Boy. And I see who you're standing with.

"It would be the worst mistake of my life if I ever gave you the impression that I was not 110 percent team Chabi." My honesty takes her back, but like most warriors, she doesn't let anger go easily.

You brought him to my deck.

"You told Tamara you wanted to square off against him."

I'm a fucking ghost! I didn't think it would actually happen.

"But it did. And you won. Now why don't you collect your reward?"

I kill him and so what? I want Rice. I want Poppy. I want all the others responsible for killing me.

"One step at a time," Tamara says, levitating up to the captain's deck. "But I think A.C. might be on to something. You just spared Narayana's life. He owes you."

"What could he give me that he hasn't already taken . . ." The thought finally hits her. This is the world we live in, where the rules of life and death can be negotiated with, and sometimes refuted.

She jumps like a puma from the small captain's chair to the main deck. Even downed and broken, Chabi is smart enough to know Narayana is a threat and approaches him in a circular path. Only when she's close enough to tear his throat out does she speak.

I beat you.

"I can't deny that."

I can end you.

"If that is your will, I could not stop you."

I will spare you if you can give me something worth your life.

"My life is worth nothing. I am formed of ash and dust . . ."

Damn it, old man . . .

"All I can give you is a body."

What good is a dead body . . .

"Who said it was dead?"

The Lost Ocean
A.C

"Where the fuck did you find a clone?" Tamara asks as she uses her telekinesis to lift a perfect duplicate Chabi-sized popsicle out of the ocean and onto the deck. Encased in a half a ton of green and brown ice, a perfect duplicate of Chabi sits, immobile.

"I would never use traffic in such low trickery." Still limping, Narayana drags himself over to the ice-encased version of his adopted daughter. She's dressed . . . like a civilian. Pleated skirt, slightly stylish pumps, and a white button-up. She, it, whatever it was, wasn't even dressed for the deep sea, yet somehow she found her final rest in Narayana's undersea hell. I'm about to ask how, when my Chabi, the real ghost Chabi, clears all obstacles in her path and braces the Alter against the mini iceberg.

Who is she? Don't know how she expects Narayana to answer with her heel secured against his throat, but somehow he does.

"Across all space and time, you are unique. But that doesn't mean there aren't other physical versions of you . . ."

"What does that mean?" Pasha asks.

"The time and space we're in right now isn't our Chabi's native land," I chime in. "Things drift and out of the Lost Ocean. Narayana is one of the few creatures that can pilot these waters, much less secret something in its depths."

"So . . ." Tam asks. "So Narayana killed this reality's Chabi?"

"More secured her body the second after her soul left her body. And now you have a corpus to inhabit," the old Indian says, barely able to push Chabi off his neck. He gained no new strength, but Chabi's eyes well up at the sight of herself, only quiet and innocent, still, in the flesh. Through the ice I can tell the body has no martial arts training. The mystical tattoo/brand Narayana put on my Chabi's back long ago as protection is nowhere to be seen. This girl is pure.

"Can you do it, wind child?" Narayana turns to me. "Can you push her spirit in that body?"

Her name was Chabi, my ghost girl storms, deep fire in her eyes. *She loved dubstep, Hazel Dickens, and her mother. She had friends, people who gave a shit about her. And you killed her. Just like you did me.*

"Yes," Narayana says and we all brace for combat to recommence. Instead Chabi goes as still as death and glares at Narayana. For his part, he tries to look away, tries to move, even to snarl, but the eye lock refuses to let him go. Defeated without a blow being thrown, he speaks through recently split lips.

"I am an Alter. You don't know what that means. I am aware of the impending destruction of absolutely everything, and I crave it. Instinctively, I commit myself to the obliteration of all that would stand in the way of intergalactic silence. To call my draw to the still and quiet of nothing a desire is to radically underestimate it; it is the reason every cell in this physical form exists. My kind, we're aware of every element of our own existence as it is anathema that we should even rub against gross matter in the first place. So unlike your kind, we do not fracture into multiversal eternal reflection of self with every causal shift to reality."

"Fuck is he saying?" Pasha asks Tam.

"There's no multiple versions of him scattered through reality like Chabi and the rest of us, yeah? Now keep up," Tamara snaps at him.

"I have seen every version of you that has ever existed," Narayana continues while Chabi keeps her glare consistent. "And I tell you this again, child, so you hear me. Across the universes, none as you are. And so for you, to walk with land under your feet, yes, I ended a lesser version of you to make room for your spirit."

Why? Why not just leave the both of us alone? The psychic shout would have crippled all of us had Tam not shielded us on instinct.

"I was created to kill you. All versions of you. In all but one case, I fulfilled my duty. In that one case, I taught you how to kill my kind, myself. I couldn't stop your death, but I will resurrect you . . ."

Why? she shouts and all wildlife, all minds and spirits near us, go silent.

"Because . . ." I see the Alter's legs shake and gust Tam and Pasha upward just as Narayana goes to his knees in front of the ice-reserved Chabi. As he does, it cracks open under the force of Alter piety. "Because I love you."

The Lost Ocean
A.C.

I brokered with ancient and obnoxious powers to link Chabi's spirit to the Mansai. But those powers are dead now, thanks to the Alters. I can liberate her spirit from the ship; that's the easy part. Navigating these Letheian waters without her and only a damaged Alter for a compass will be harder. Even the skies above seem poised to shower us with disapproval.

"If she's just a spirit," Pasha asks, pointing at Chabi, "how come she can kick and punch and stuff?"

"Training," I tell him as Tamara focuses on preparing the body trapped in the ice. "What Narayana put her though made her spirit strong enough to impact the material plane."

"Bare dread to see her with a body," the London boy says.

"As well you should be," I tell him. "Okay, soon as she's prepped I'm going to need you hold her body."

"What's that, then?"

"You're lucky and we're going to need all the luck we can get."

"How's this work now? Like downloading on your computer?" Pasha asks.

"Yeah, a spiritual transfer is just like that." He flinches at my sarcasm. I pull my sword and Pasha reaches for his entropy blade.

"Relax, it's not meant for you. This time. The sword will cut her connection to the ship. Tamara will help guide her spirit to the new body and Narayana is going to stand watch in case his cousins or any other nasty buggers decide they want to come by and snatch her spirit."

"That's a possibility?" Pasha asks.

"It's like Narayana said, her's is a unique spirit. It may attract unwanted attention," I tell him.

"There's nothing left in here," Tamara tells Chabi as the psychic scans the body before her.

Swear to me, Chabi's psyche whispers.

"My word, girl. But you've got another minute max before the body starts breaking down in earnest." Tamara steps back, giving herself room to work.

"Get over there," I tell the Lucky Liminal.

"Does anyone else think this is a bad idea?" he asks. It's too late. With three strikes I break the ice encasing the Chabi body. A little wind pushes the uneven pieces apart. Pasha has enough sense to get to it, lifting the body up with his arms under her shoulder pits.

Yes, Chabi says, walking toward me. *But sometimes a bad idea is the only chance you have.*

I draw the old ruins on the deck with the tip of my entropy sword in the form of a circle. Narayana knows but the others can't see the effect of them; each nick on the deck is carved into Chabi's soul. She is the ship. She doesn't react to being cut. Instead she takes her place instinctively in the center of the circle. The sea goes silent. We haven't discussed what comes next but she sees I haven't sheathed my blade.

I'm beginning to think you like killing me . . . She doesn't look up.

"Chabi . . ."

It's a joke, Wind Boy. Relax. Can't a girl get a final ha ha in?

"Wish it didn't have to be me," I tell her.

Glad it's you. She smiles.

"Enough of this sentimentality," the Alter barks.

Nobody is asking your damn opinion about a fucking thing, old man! Chabi shouts back. To emphasize her point, she takes my free hand softly in hers and give it a squeeze. Then, in my ear she asks, *One true cut, okay A.C.?*

Three steps in front of me is the perfect distance. All I have to do is separate my legs for balance. I raise my left shoulder up and back until the hilt of the sword is eye level. With my right hand I secure the lower half of the hilt, trying not to let the sweat threaten my grip. I lock my eyes on my target. If I do this right, only the outermost four inches of my blade will go through her neck. Once I've marked the point of impact, I don't look away. Now it's a point, a contextless place to execute a strike that I've performed a thousand times without thinking. If I connect it to Chabi, I'll falter.

"Ready," I lie.

"Don't fuck up, Pasha!" Tamara tells him. "Go!" she tells me, and for a second all the nerves of the Chabi body are activated by Tamara's telepathy. They're open and receptive. It's my turn. I twist, extend the blade, then pull back in one quick motion. Where a body-shaped shroud should have fallen, an unmoored formless and vulnerable spirit begins to dissipate.

I call on the spirit wind and push all of Chabi's pneuma into the nose and mouth of the Chabi body. Tamara psychically anchors what she can and crudely but powerfully shoves the soul into the body.

"It doesn't want to stay!" Tamara tells me as the body breathlessly convulses.

"No spirit does!" I sheath the entropy blade and call all four winds to my aid. Six hand mudras I haven't used in a decade come to me quick as I fix the winds against the body.

"What the hell?" Pasha asks as he's bombarded by the same winds.

"She's got to link to the body!" I try to explain. "But her soul, it's not used to this reality. It's trying to run. Just hold on."

"I can't breathe!" he shouts.

"Then suffocate!" Tamara says, her eyes streaming blood as she fights to orient Chabi's consciousness. "But hold on and shut up! I'm concentrating."

The Liminal boy thinks it's me pulling Chabi's body into the air, but I'm the one keeping it down. Me and Tamara. To his credit, even fifteen feet in the air, he wraps his arms and legs around her waist, absorbing what punishments my winds can't save Chabi from as she rams against the main mast. She's wearing Pasha like a backpack.

I think we've lost this exorcism in reverse when Tamara stops bleeding. I'm about to invoke the Drunk Buddha's hidden mudra and say to hell with the consequences when Tamara and Chabi's body speak with one voice.

"Wake up."

Instantly, the soul bucking stops. Tamara falls over, but she's conscious. As soon as I disperse the winds, Chabi strikes nerve centers in Pasha's right arm and left leg, making his backpack hold impossible to maintain. As I attend him, Chabi, the full Chabi, slides to Tamara's side.

"Hey, little badass," Chabi says with unpracticed vocal cords.

"Just getting the job done." Tamara wipes the blood off her face, not bothering to rise too high off the deck.

"How?" I ask. "I thought . . ."

"Taggart's first rule," Tamara says with that pride she always gets when mentioning her father. "Work twice as smart as you work hard. Me and you were doing all the heavy lifting. Didn't think to wake up the chief scrapper herself. Once I did, Chabi anchored herself."

"But why attack me?" Pasha asks, nursing his numb thigh.

"Instinct." Chabi smiles.

"Brilliant. Wait, where's the Alter?" I ask.

Narayana comes crashing down through the deck like a comet with something vaguely human shape and on fire. Had Chabi's spirit still been connected to the Mansai, it would have a hole in it. The others scramble to the cavity while my eyes go to the sky.

"Is he conscious?" Pasha asks.

"Old man, you still kicking?" Chabi questions.

"Is that . . . fuck, that's an angel, isn't it?" Tamara asks, following my gaze sunward.

"Yup," I tell them, watching a herd of screaming six-winged fiery angels forming a cyclone of trouble high above the Mansai. "Yup, that's a fucking angel."

The Lost Ocean
A.C.

"But I don't want to fight angels." I'm beginning to get Pasha's humor now. We're the only two standing, Tam only recently stopped bleeding from her entire face, Narayana brought down an angel at the cost of his consciousness, and Chabi is doing her best newborn fawn impression trying to stand.

"Like we've got a choice," I laugh.

"I'm up." Chabi stumbles as the boy and I pull our blades. Taggert's isn't as powerful out of his hands, but it can still slice angelic flesh well enough.

"The hell you are," I tell Chabi. "Go below deck, wake up Narayana."

"Oh, you must have me confused for someone who takes orders." She laughs then takes a good look at the circling above. They've wings on top of wings, all made of fire. No robes or strategically placed sashes, these are the naked and neutered eight-feet-tall angels of the Old Testament. Thirty of them if there's one. The messengers of old, designed to kill Egyptian babies, smite cities with a single flick of their wings, and torment the sinner. "What are they waiting on?"

"Looks like Narayana took down the biggest one first. Archangels aren't being used to being handled, touched even. No doubt they're a bit confused as to why it hasn't swooped back up with Raj's head on a platter," I say.

The heat increases tenfold, like the sun is coming closer. One bright fire-winged angel arcs out from the formation above and swoops down at us. The furnace heat I was prepared for—meeting it with a cyclone blast—but the noise nearly throws me off. I keep my position but shift my sword blade down as the angel targets me. When it's heat becomes nearly unbearable, I step toward it at an angle, arching up with the sword. I shift and for a brief second I imagine it's bulky body racing toward me. Almost too late, I launch my sword. From the skyward facing position, I twist hard and extend my arms fully. The left side wings of the bastard, all three of them, fall on deck. The angel rolls, twists, flops, and crashes astern as I redirect my wrists into small wind spells to put out the deck fires caused by the wings. Before I can move in for the kill, Pasha has already done the job.

"I just wanted it to shut up," he says, pulling the entropy blade from the angelic throat. "What the fuck was that screaming?"

"In another reality it would be shouting 'Holy Holy Holy is the Lord of host; the whole earth is full of glory' constantly. But here all they can manage is the screaming and the noise," I tell him.

"Thanks for the theology lesson," the kid says as I cut the angel's head off and toss it into the ocean. He jumps back witnessing the amount of steam that rises.

"There's another twenty plus of the hairless ball-less wonders up there," Chabi says, gazing with new eyes.

"Will someone please try and wake up Narayana?" I shout.

"On it." Tam half crawls, half hauls herself through the hole in the deck.

"If they all attack at once . . ." Pasha realizes.

"We're dead without Narayana," I tell him.

"We might be dead with him," Chabi says with a casual awe as she flexes her fighting muscles in the new body for the first time.

What was once an overhead circling that kept up the ship in its eye now centers on Chabi. I step closer to her. She wants to tell me to stop being so protective but this fight is still beyond her, so instead she nods, eyes forever looking skyward.

"It didn't have no man meat." Pasha giggles.

"Who are you again?" Chabi asks.

"What does an angel need genitals for?" I ask. He hunches then flips Taggert's entropy blade downward, similar to the way I'm carrying my sword. "They are holders of the universal message. Keep your blade hidden, boy. Better they don't know what hell you can bring."

"You can fly, right? Why not just go up there and . . ." he asks.

"Against twenty plus?" Chabi snaps at him. "Seriously, I'm asking, who the fuck are you?"

Not that we could hear his reply. Losing two of their number, the angels decide long range might be better. They scream, shout the chaos of their universe down at us. The deck and mast shake and break. This is no mere sonic attack. I realize too late that their circling created an amplification effect that can be directed at us. I try to weaponize my wind. We're on our knees. I can't stand, let alone fight for the noise. And they're getting louder. I can't even form a basic mudhra. But then I hear her. Chabi.

"Shut up," she shouts with voice and spirit. It hits us all. Pasha and I can't speak but neither can the angels. It takes her a second to realize what she's done, but when Chabi stands and touches her throat, I know she gets it.

"I can talk," she tells me, lifting me up.

"New body, new vocal cords," I tell her after pantomiming a whisper of a spell to allow those on the boat to speak. Pasha bangs on the deck to get her attention.

"What?" she asks.

"Why didn't you do that from the beginning?" Pasha throws up his hands in frustration.

"Like I knew I could stop that shrieking whenever I wanted," she says, ignoring his annoyance.

"Look out!" Silently, another angel swoops low with malice aforethought toward Chabi parallel to the deck. She wraps the angel's head in a lock with her arms, then her legs around his body before anyone else can move. I think he'll take off with her, burn her with his wings, until she arches her back and squeezes. Instantly the oversized bird flips over, its back and wings slamming into the deck. Chabi liberates her arm and lands ten spirit breaking blows to its face before it can react.

"Jaysis," the Luck boy murmurs.

"Pasha, meet Chabi," I tell him.

"The flamy wing things, blow them out!" the rookie starts shouting.

"Let them burn," dead-leaves-in-the-wind voiced Narayana climbs from the smoke of the belowdeck, a broken flaming angel wing protruding from his thigh. "The lower deck is already incinerated."

"Fuck happened to you?" I ask just as Tamara levitates up behind him.

"Smacking him wasn't working." She smiles behind bloody teeth and red-stained cheeks. "So I broke off some angel wing and poked him with it. Woke him right up."

"Leave this ship," Narayana tells us all. But to Chabi, "Call them down once you have. They must comply."

Tam is thankful for the lift over to Narayana's ship. I keep all of us low so the angels don't get tempted to swarm us; they're already in a panic, mute and down three members. When Chabi speaks, it looks like an intolerable light is about to engulf the old Alter. But to those who feel the space between what is and what will be, Narayana radiates an ancient ecliptic dark.

A giant water hand rises up and snatches the Mansai like a thief grabbing a gold chain. In under a minute, even the glow from the angelic wings are snuffed. Despite herself, Chabi looks over the bow and waits until Narayana re-emerges, angel free.

"Hope nobody minds me taking a breather," I say, sitting down.

"Hope nobody minds me shitting my pants," Pasha says. I think he's serious.

"Don't strain your bloomers just yet, Luck," Tam says. "Chabi just gave us a shot at winning. For a decent chance, we're gonna need more allies. You and me are on recruiting duties."

Heart of the Whirlwind
Taggert

It's the rainbow coalition of the desert populace in this encampment. Tuareg, Shawi, Yemeni Maquil, Sanhaja, Oulad Delim, Beni Hassaan, tribes you'd never expect to see together. But then there's more. I feel and see a body type I haven't encountered since my trek from Somalia to . . . Nordeen.

From a group of little girls I catch the skin tone and bone structure of the San people. They have some of the oldest genes on the planet, most other genetic variations taking place off of their baselines. But they're a sub-Saharan group. So what are they doing in the Maghreb? I feel an al-Bu-Isa family, a nomadic tribe out of Oran, then distinctly Semitic folk straight out of the Sinai if I know anything, and Latinos, like from Latin America? Where the hell am I?

And of course, who is sitting in the middle of everyone having a great time after literally being taken up by a whirlwind?

"Tag!" Prentis runs to hug me. She's bird-chirping in the native tongue of these people like she was born to it before I can finish scanning her for injuries. I can't be bothered to repeat her every word right now. But even when I think the words, I understand the language a bit better.

"Slow it down and give me some English, please."

"I was saying three quarters of your plans are usually crap, but this one, we did it! We found the people of the desert." Her glow could make me forget we're in the middle of a war.

"Yeah, but which one?" I ask her, trying to walk away from the camel-hearted woman behind me. She's huge, skin the same color of the sand in the morning, wrapped tight in flexible leathers, and with a flat, large spear tied to her hip. Like most of the women here, Fatima included, she wears what looks like a battle corset, all black, loose-fitting, utility belt sort of thing.

"All." It sounds like she's mocking me with the truth, so I turn to face her. She doesn't flinch. It might be because I only come up to her mango-sized breast. "All deserts are the same."

"Who is she?" I ask once she gets some distance. There's something about her lopsided cowboy stride that makes me think of Fatima.

"Chief. Near as I can tell," Prentis says, leading me to a small wooden stool with bowls covered against the sand. "Close as they have one anyway. Everyone seems to do as they please here."

"So we're not prisoners?" I ask.

"I mean where do you want to run?" She points out the vast desert in all directions as I shove nuts and some roasted grubs in my mouth by the handful.

"Our crew accounted for?"

"Everybody, except Jah Puba." She waits for a reaction. Then "He didn't know what he was . . ."

"Getting tired of that excuse with him. Mico is forever guided by voices no one else can hear and somehow he always lands on his feet while the rest of us scramble for sure footing."

All around, chiming in on our conversation, tonal clicks and hums echo from the desert folk. They don't look our way, just click and hum in a polyphonic unity, like a bunch of old black church ladies agreeing about what their pastor is saying without using a fully articulated word. It freaks me out more when I see Prentis doing it.

"It's like saying you agree," she says by way of explanation.

"How long have I been out that you've had time to go native?" I say, downing some lightly spiced water out of an earthen container. Communal tables filled with food and clothes sit outside of every house. Offerings, not displays of wealth.

"A day? Maybe two? Time is weird here. And let's not get too comfortable speaking of Jah Puba's alter ego, yeah? They seem to have a special hate for him." Prentis guides me through the maze of tents and yurts, the family housing of the Bint al-nas. Maybe ninety structures, all easily portable, though different designs.

The whole thing, the language, the way everyone walks, talks, damn near breathes together, I've seen an imperfect version of this before. This is what Mico was aiming for on Eel Pie Island, in our time. He'd collected the disenfranchised and war orphans he could find and offered them community, home. Bingy was one. Samantha, another. I take a small bowl filled with a rabbit stew and some sand-baked taguella from a hut big enough to house six people and start sopping it up for real just before three warbling Tinariwen women start howling at me as a short Berber guy starts picking at a guitar in that methodical way they do. All four of them vibrate in unison. It feels almost invasive as thoughts of Samantha start coming up, a mix of longing, regret, and doom. If these folks aren't telepathic, it's still too fucking close.

"Ease up, Da," Prentis tells me when I drop the bowl and prep to kick in heads. "It's just their way. They don't know why you're feeling whatever it is you're feeling, they're just sensitive."

"And too fucking musical if you ask me." From a tall red tent, Fatima emerges as if from the desert born. Deep orange and light beige fabric wrap her waist downward, and her top is bound by the same black mesh corset Prentis and the camel heart wear, but I guess not even the desert customs would separate her from the ash gray pilot's jacket or her favorite mare's leg rifle. "Good to see someone else who hasn't drunk the punch." She makes a point to say, in English, giving me daps like a jail comrade.

Half joking, she tells me, "Your girl has been useless."

"Hmm, useless got you and your dad found, clothed, fed, and rested," Prentis protested.

"How's the old man?" I ask.

"Sleeping." She motions to the tent. "Bingy?"

"Damn near wifeyed up," Prentis tell us, pointing to a fairly distant yurt. There's bodies in there I don't want to feel.

"Jah Puba?" I ask them both.

"Fuck him!" Fatima almost shouts. "Fucker ran off into a damn whirlwind. Far as I'm concerned he should be swept out to the four winds!"

"So neither of you heard the music?" Prentis asks.

"I could hear a choir of angels singing all is forgiven, come to the light, and I still wouldn't lead you astray like that," I tell her calm, easy so I don't get the weird communal emotional echo chamber. She brings her hand to my face to touch it, and I smell salt, root vegetable, dried blood from meat, and something else . . . a common element in all of it. A connection.

"Manna." Before I finish the second syllable, every tent, yurt, and nearby hovel erupts in its version of praise singing throat gurgling so hard Fatima almost chambers her rifles. "It's in everything here. The food, the dirt, the people."

"No one's smoking it," Fatima tells me. "At least not that I've smelled."

"A.C. would be real useful right now," Prentis complains.

"Who?" Fatima asks.

"The wind guy . . . Oh fuck it." She gives up.

I make a resonance hall out of my throat and use my diaphragm and lungs to pump the bass then shout, "Mico L'overture!"

"Damn it, Tag!" is all Prentis has time to say before every sunsheltered multi-culti villager exits their domicile with spear, rifle, knife, or gun giving that same clicking hissing sound. My girl and Fatima get my back and face outward ready to take whoever comes.

Down the main throughway, the camel heart walks toward us, pissed, with a short iron spear in hand. I feel Prentis about to speak up, but I nudge her for quiet. To my right, I see Fatima with her gun already drawn at waist level and I can sense a disappointed Bingy man releasing his coital excitement to rush to our aid. I feel for the one entropy blade I have left, secreted by my thigh. I don't want to draw it but I will.

"Not yet a full day awake and already you're causing disruption, broken healer. Is chaos in your blood?" the camel heart sings to me.

"Mico L'overture. He's a pain in the ass, but he's my personal hemorrhoid. Tell me where he is."

Something deep within her smiles as she gets low and with her spear in one hand, drags it across the foot-pounded sand and sings "No."

The calm of her heartbeat is scarier than her Grace Jones–type smile, but I can't flinch. I pull the entropy blade and loosen up my arms and legs for a stabbing and cutting match. The tribe of many colors starts whistling and chanting as camel heart tries to circle and find an angle on me. I counter her movements, looking for a weakness in her game and finding none. Instead, I catch something behind her shadow, a black shade moving fast waist-level in the noon sun. Across the landscape, behind the houses, it's not a shadow, it's one of Mico's African spirits. But in zooming in on that, I miss the camel heart changing her grip on her spear. A quick step to the right and she's in perfect position to stab into my neck. I fake surprise when she attacks, jabbing upward. I callus my hand quickly and slap the razor-sharp blade to the spear and dive over her entirely. She turns but I'm already beating feet toward the shadow's trail. In a second she's on my tail but I've been running from women my whole life. She'll never catch me.

The shadow makes a right, a left, and is away from all semblance of living quarters in seconds. If it knows that me and half the tribe are following, it doesn't seem to care. I chase it hard across open desert for a while before I remember I'm running on empty. My body will start giving out soon if I keep this pace in the sun for too long. I catch a break after half a mile of soft sand running, the sound of the almost music Prentis was talking about. More than that, I see it. It's a whirlwind. An active, stable whirlwind from an angle I never thought I'd see. A few feet in front of me, there are winds that can lift a car, tear the skin off a body with a few grains of sand. But here, my hair is barely moving. We are inside the eye of a hurricane. I can see the arc of it, from horizon to horizon. A wall of moving, active wind. And kneeling at the wall of wind, damn near catatonic, surrounded by hundreds of African spirits, Mico.

Heart of the Whirlwind
Prentis

Taggert can't leave Mico's side, like another African spirit; they all shimmer and shake surrounding Mico's back, jet black tentacles quivering in fear. Mico stares into the wall of wind, of movement— the thing that keeps these people from the rest of the world, which they call Mother—and he cries, constantly. Not so much cries, as that would indicate some sound. Tears run down his face. Best shot at saving the world has been catatonic for six hours.

Chieftess, think her name is Othica, stopped chasing Taggert after he found Mico in this sorry state. Mico has thrown their "Mother" off course and almost revealed them to the savage and molested world we were just in. Death or worse the punishment until they saw Mico here strung out to dry. They's vexed about what happens next. "Same same," I want to tell them. All Taggert can say is that Mico is fit, physical like. So we sit in the middle of the desert waiting for Mico to get his shit together. Dead boring, the desert.

Hospitality of the desert folk can only be held at bay for so long. First water, then food. When day goes to evening, a fire and a form of friendship from the main village, a good seven miles from this wall of . . . Blue night begins to fall, Munji and Bingy get ridden out on horseback by well fit women only slightly less stunner than Fatty. Fatty rides on her own noble desert horse, bareback, not a half second behind her father. It's an Asian wild horse. Not sure why it's in the middle of an African desert.

The jockeys could all be Fatty's cousins. Feel like a frump, but now isn't the time to be self-conscious. With the two grandpas on the scene, Taggert relents and takes his eyes off the failed prophet to warm himself by the fire. Give him some lamb stew villagers brought in a wooden bowl. Othica waits until he's eaten a few bites before she sings/speaks.

"We are Bint al-nas," says in English but almost like she's in a musical.

"Daughters of the desert," Tag translates. "Guess the men in your village don't mind being clumped together with you."

"They prefer it, wounded healer Taggert." Tag doesn't flinch. "Now you will sit, we will talk, and together we will decide whether we fight or . . ."

Tag sits where she points with her spear, an area next to the fire with a red woven mat large enough for two. Sit by his side and feel his Liminal sight over my body, scanning me for injuries, his check-in, letting me know he's okay.

"What did you do to him?" Tag asks Othica as she sits across the fire with the two Fatima doppelgängers at her back. They each have one of the short spears at the ready. Call a few cobras up from their burrows, tell them to chill in striking distance of the girls. Snakes grow long out here. Tag lesson: Never to threaten, just prepare.

"To Mico? Nothing. Better to ask what he did to himself. Or what he'll do to us. Again," Chieftess claps back.

"You know him?"

"He was almost one of us, the best of us. But left as a heretic, a polluter of our most sacred rituals. We shouldn't have been surprised when we found ourselves taken off course by him . . ."

"Where are we?" He asks the question that's been bugging me since I first opened my eyes.

"El-nas. The desert."

"Yes, but which one?"

"All." Othica spreads her arms to indicate her "Mother" and smiles. "Deep in all desert is the providence of the storm. In your way, in your time, you see many wind storms, sandstorms. That is not our truth. Ours is the knowledge of the one storm that ever existed, that calls its children to protect them."

"Protect you from what?" ask more to distract myself from the Fatima duos near-constant low level hum chorus of their leader's words than for the sake of knowledge.

"Famine, slavery, oppression, genocide, border disputes, religious persecutions, Alters." Waits for a second then adds, "Crazy Liminals people reworking reality to their benefit."

"How?" Taggert asks, not taking the bait. "How do you stay protected?"

"One part you've heard," Othica says calmly, offering us large chunks of warm brown bread. "Our god does not speak. She sings. Our gift is the song. Song can do so much. It can break bones, start fires, save souls—"

"Cut a hole in space and time," Tag interrupts. "Yeah, I did it with Mico back there."

I have to whisper the word the hotness twins shout in unison before I understand it—traitor—but once I do I'm on them quickly. As they grab for their spears I'm about to order my snakes to strike. But Tag makes my arm numb, a sign to relax, just as Othica whistles slightly with her teeth, letting her girls know to do the same.

"To move through reality as you have is an honor reserved only for the Bint al-nas. And never without the aid of the Manna," Othica tells slowly and nods toward the bread. Looking closely, can see small white flecks in it.

"Don't eat anything here," Tag tells me quickly, then to Othica. "It's got to be a choice to join the Manna. That was the rule before."

"The rule applies." Othica laughs at him. "Manna is in everything we eat and drink. But you still must be called . . ."

"Wait, eat and drink?" Tag protests. "But not smoke?"

"What?"

"You don't smoke the Manna?"

"Sacrilege," Othica says it in her home language.

Takes a second but once Tag starts, it's such a strange sound coming from him that I'm genuinely worried until I'm sure it is his laughter.

"So DJ Jah Puba wanders out into the desert to find a mystical band of time-jumping nomads and the first thing he does is smoke your god? Fucking genius!" He can barely get the words out.

"Tag, you okay?"

"Time of my life, kid," tells me, still cracking up. Then he calls over his shoulder to the catatonic Mico, "You deserve every bit you get, you dumbass."

"He cannot hear you." Voice that comes from Othica is like a million people whispering all at once. It's not her. Can tell right away. The Fatima twins instantly bow. Tag sighs, exhausted, before he turns. Once he does, Othica's body stands. "We should speak, healer."

"Oh, now the Manna wants to talk to me," he says, standing to brush the loose sand off of him.

"In this world, you've yet to earn our conversation," the chorus from Othica's mouth says.

"Not sure I'll survive it," Tag says.

"Luckily, the universe hinges on such concerns." The noble diss is more elegant than Othica would've ever managed. Finally put it together as they walk off into the night as Mico's African spirits spin around in the air, somewhere between elated and panicked.

"Wait, that's the Manna? That's your god? In Othica?" I ask the Fatima twins.

"I can be in many places at once." The same voice comes from the lips of the one on the right. The Fatima girl on the left backs up slowly. "What kind of god would I be if I couldn't?"

"Fair point." All I can think to say.

"Can we speak Prentis, she who is loved by the animal world?"

Heart of the Whirlwind
Taggert

"Don't expect me to bow down or kiss the ring. I'm comfortable leaving it at mistakes were made," I tell the god in its warrior's body as we wander loose sand, surrounded by another aspect of its power, the circle of wind. We've cleared a fair distance from the camp where Prentis and the god's children wait.

"Your audacity never ceases to amaze." It laughs. Genuinely laughs at me. "You sit on the border of a land only you and yours have the power to wreck and the extent of your remorse is 'Mistakes were made.'"

"Like you didn't know it was going to happen."

"Tell me what you think you know."

"It's like they all said. A.C, Narayana, and them when we first launched through the cosmic muck and mire. You could have stopped it whenever you wanted. There's no way my crew could stand up to you and the Alters at the same time. The only reason we're still alive is because you wanted us here, now, as depleted and spent as we are. I'm just waiting on the why of it."

"I will answer your query. But first mine. Have you learned anything from your most recent journeys to personal hells and back? Are you the same selfish father I spoke with on Eel Pie Island? Willing to loose chaos on the world, and your life for the sake of two small heartbeats?"

"I'll destroy every vassal you have, you threaten my girls again." I stop walking, but the Manna in Othica keeps pace, keeps talking in that restrained shout of a voice. It's only when it starts speaking again that I make up the distance.

"Would you like to hear a god's confession, Taggert? I did not realize the damage Nordeen had done to you until just now. Are you so covetous of security, of your label as protector, that once achieved, all other potential titles, 'world savior,' 'paladin,' fall away?"

"Is it my fault I don't trust the only god I've ever met? I've seen the way you discard your holy warriors . . ."

"Mine are never discarded."

"Oh, so Mico's fit making and overabundance of tears are what now? Samantha screaming across the abyss? I heard it but somehow you missed it? Yeah, that makes sense."

"All of these pains could easily have been avoided had you kissed the ring, as you put it. I have only ever offered you protection from your mistakes and guidance away from further turmoil. But it was you who chose to reject my aid in your battle against Nordeen; it was you that seduced my vassal away from my cause with the romance of heroics, and made him forget his duty. These were your choices . . ."

"What the hell else was I supposed to do? Your offer of help came through Samantha when I barely knew her . . ."

"You knew her well enough to sleep with, to petition her for aid against your dark father, Nordeen."

"Don't call him that! And what would you have had me do about Prentis? Just surrender her to the Alters?"

"That was an option."

"You think that, then you don't know me at all, fungus."

"Another option was to have faith that I had a plan," it says, totally ignoring my insult.

"You denied me help before I even asked when it came to her."

"Yes, and I planned for the contingency of Prentis's abduction before her oldest ancestor descended a baobab tree. That contingency did not require your intervention, healer."

"Why didn't you tell me?"

"Because you didn't ask, and it seems beyond your ability to follow my lead or trust my design."

"You could have forced me to . . . If you knew your way was better . . ."

"Is that the type of god you desire, Taggert? Shall I control your every step, your every breath?"

"Seems like you already are," I snap tell it.

"Believe in this, if not me—your choices, your mistakes and fortunes are all earned by your own efforts. But I will not be held hostage by them, nor will I allow this world to be. I adjust my plans and fortuity based on the decisions of you and your fellow Liminals. Had you left Prentis among the enemy, they would have cultivated their own destruction by increasing her skill. At the proper time, her love for you and yours would have pulled her back to your side, our side. The girl would have been perfectly placed as a . . ."

"Hidden time bomb," I say, finally getting the long game. "But how long would she have had to endure Nordeen and the Alters?"

"A rough tutelage, to be sure, but better one Liminal suffer than we lose the light and color of the world, no?"

"Not that Liminal. I can't accept that logic," I tell it my truth.

"The way forward, towards survival, to stopping the suicidal impulse Alters have placed on the planet will require such acceptance as you are want to give."

"And if I can't follow your lead?"

"I am the god of connections, Taggert. And my world is in peril. What do you think I won't do to see my will done?"

"See, every now and then it sounds like you're threatening me," I tell it, wondering what my entropy blade would stab if I struck Othica's body.

"The only thing I'm threatening is your false sense of control over all aspects of your reality. To answer your earlier question: I wanted all assembled parties to have respite. I want you to meet those raised under my tutelage; they are the blueprint I have for the world. As I am speaking to you now, I'm also offering Prentis the same options I present to you. However you respond, however she responds, I will continue to do what is best for the planet and reality. This is an ancient war, Taggert, you and yours are engaged in only the latest skirmish."

"You understand that even if I work for you, with you, I'll never like you."

"If I had a heart, I'm sure it would break with such knowledge." It laughs gently. "But why, Liminal? What offense have I given?" it asks as we crest a dune. To the south of us, farther than I thought possible in the time we've walked, I see the lights of the Bint al-nas camp.

"Maybe I'm an agnostic at heart. You're not human, not Liminal, not Alter. That I know. But a god? I don't even know what that means. I don't like anything running my life and the lives of my family."

"You are a child in your understanding of such things," it tells me without judgment. "Call it nature, science, religion, or chance. Every cell in your body, every atom in the universe is impacted by forces outside itself. That which impacts us all is the Holy Monad, the sacred oneness, a felt divinity none—even you—could resist."

"You give me a pamphlet for an easy journey to other planets, I'm quitting this whole scene."

"I can take you to other planes of existence," it tells me, unaware of my joke. "I can show you colors you don't have words for, planets with no physical equivalents in this reality. I could teach you to intoxicate yourself and the world with divine elixirs. But you can barely accept my divinity, so I fear my lessons would be wasted. Sadly, I am as close to the Holy Monad as you are likely to get."

"If you're such a godly badass, then how come the Alters are winning the war?"

"Some would say because I give my foot soldiers too much freedom. Would you agree?"

"Fuck you," I say, scared. But I say it anyway. It knows I'm terrified but just looks disappointed in me. "Okay, fuck it, so long as I can hate you, I'm in. But again, you hurt the girls . . ."

"And what?" it asks, genuinely confused.

"I'll find a way. Let's just leave it at that."

"Fine." It takes Othica's body down off the crest and back across the dunes we just crossed. "Your plans, such as they are, are in accord with my design, with one modification. Rest, speak with the children, eat. But as soon as you're done here, liberate Samantha. She has been among the enemy for too long."

Heart of the Whirlwind
Prentis

After my conversation with the Bint al-nas/Manna connection—weird beyond belief—I went to find Mico. It/she, whatever told me he was okay, but he'd been a sight. But true enough, in his massive tent, all the black spirits were in his arm again. Conscious and not bawling like a baby, about to lose his mind. Caught him up on the events of the night, as many as I was willing to share. Began to sound like his old self.

"I am forgiven," says with that shy smile inside the mountain goat hide tent. Smells like the sweetest tobacco ever. "By the Manna at least."

"All clean then, right?" I ask. "Got your weird Vaseline powers back?"

"Vassal. And yes, I am once again the servant of the Manna in the world of flesh."

"Yes! Tam and them get the ghost ship captain or whatever and we've got a shot at this thing, right?"

"A shot, yes."

"Christ, fam!" I snap, throwing myself on a thigh level couch/bed. It's proper, though could use more cushion. "If it's all good, why the mean mug?"

"The Manna showed me what I missed. It explained itself to me, the first Liminal it's inclined to explain itself to in thousands of years." Stops looking for whatever he was searching for and climbs on another high-off-the-ground couch. "Did I ever tell you the first Manna reached out to me?"

"Brov, we've had all of five minutes together." I laugh at him.

"True." Gets a smile. Singer rolls on his back and looks to the highest point in the tan colored roof. "It was a dream. I was a kid. Right after my mom died . . ."

"Condolences," say off reflex. Then for real. "Can I ask how?"

"She decided the light of the world was too bright to see by. Even her spirit tried to squint a little, to offer her some solace from the intensity our world could bring." Silence. Then, "The gray world we just left might have suited her more."

"Shite, that bad?"

"She was hurt a lot. But she never hurt me. She did her best. I'm always thankful for that."

"Lucky," say putting too much on it.

"Who are your parents, Prentis?" he asks.

"An abuser and a man too weak to protect his daughter." Smile through it. "But we're talking about you and the tuber god, yeah?"

"Yes." He lets it go. "I was in a foster home. Dreaming. The Manna came to me in the form of my mother on a beach. I was walking alongside of her and she asked if I wanted to see my life, like all of it, what would happen? I said yes. There was something about the sand, though. I was only seven. I hadn't felt desert sand yet, but that's what was tripped me up. It was desert sand, fine and pervasive on a beach, that clotted my toes."

"You know the difference in sand grains?"

"Oh yes!" he says affectionately. "While I was obsessing over that, the Manna, my momma . . ."

"Your Manna momma."

"Yes, it tells me I'm missing everything. It told me to look up. The entire sky was a projector and every event that ever happened in my life was displayed on it with my eyes."

"Piss off."

"I swear," Tells me and rolls on his belly to look at me. Suddenly, I'm vulnerable just by looking at him. "I saw Fatima and Munji. I saw

159

Eel Pie Island and the Alters. I saw Tamara and I saw Taggert. I saw the Manna and the Bint al-nas."

"Should've been telling us that was gonna be happening from jump!" tell him throwing a pillow in his face, "instead of having us run around like lunatics."

"Oh, I forgot all of it." Mico laughed, catching the pillows and using it to prop his head up. "Soon as I woke up."

"Fat lot of good that did then. And no offense, mate, but you forget this place, forget this dream, try some ginkgo or some such."

"The forgetfulness was designed by the Manna," he says.

"For what?"

"Don't get me wrong, it gave me clues, hints about which way to turn in a crossroads. Like déjà vu. But do you really want a seven-year-old to bear the burden of an entire life? I didn't even remember all of it until Manna reached out once we arrived here. That's why I was crying."

"Ask you a question, Jah Puba?"

"Go for it." He laughs at his old name.

"In that whole dream, you see me?"

"No." A shock to him. So much so that he sits up. Searching his memories and my face at the same time for an answer. About to tell him what the Manna told me when Fatty walks in.

"Rested?" We both nod.

"Good. Cuz the tribe out here wants answers or blood. Maybe both."

Heart of the Whirlwind
Prentis

"First one a step up, first one a chop down!" Not sure where Bingy got the machete. Not that it'll do much good against the assembled faithful. Children, more than I've seen before, run under foot, laughing, chatting, play fighting with short blunt replicas of the palm leaf–shaped four-foot daggers their parents and older siblings all walk around with. In the center of the makeshift town, they all sing and argue at the same time. Even their disputes are in harmony.

Fatima keeps her distance from Mico while machete-wielding Bingy and Munji play it close. Shite, I know it's serious deadly out in this hot sun, but they all sound so pretty as they fight. I heard these singers one time, religious music, but from the Baltics. Women all chanted or maybe it was just speaking, all together but then like two or three would chant in counterpoint, like a shouting contest with these other women.

The desert folk, mostly women, split into three separate singing groups in the center of town. Not like there's a stage or something, like town hall with everyone agreeing and making points, and disagreeing and applauding, all in tempo. The largest group is doing a dirge for Mico. The second biggest is cataloging his failures as a community member, and the smallest is letting loose with a whistle of a plea for clemency. Occasionally, a singer will go from one group to another, but the numbers are pretty stable.

The second largest group starts stomping in unison as soon as they see Mico. All they need are feathers and a big drum and they'd sound like an Indian powwow. They've even got that crying singing thing down, one person lists the offenses and then thirty people repeat it, on beat, louder. If they could drown out the whistlers of hope they would, but sonic respect or clan code of conduct doesn't allow for it.

"This a concert or a trial?" manage to shout to Fatty.

"Bit of both," she warns. "Careful, girl. This lot could come for Mico any second."

"Real question is where you'll be," I tell her.

"Mico, I speak for the people." This boy has eyes that sparkle like black diamonds. Maybe two years older than me and mad buff but only in his legs. Tan and red cloth drapes his arms; he's hiding his spear as he steps forward.

"I didna sing it but ya hear what I say, boy!" Bingy steps up with the machete.

"Easy, Bingy," Mico says, calm but cautious. "He's speaking for his people, not fighting for them."

"You left us." Sounds prettier when star eyes sings it. More tragic as well. "That does not happen here. You took Manna/Mother and transmuted her. That is not done ever. But most of all, you forgot about us." Everyone, even the children, click and snap with fingers and lips about that one.

The accused bends low, placing his right hand flat against the earth, it being the most sacred object in reach. The three sections all quiet their chants to hear him. That trademark tenor I used to hear on pirate weblinks chants in their language, not defiant but sure. Jah Puba, not Mico, speaks.

"When I left, it was because the Manna told me to go. When I smoked, it was because the Manna told me to smoke. And when I forgot, it was to protect you all." The Whistlers get louder. "So that my enemies would not become yours, I asked the mother to purge all thoughts of the family from me."

"But we are warriors . . ." star eyes tells him.

"These enemies destroy planets," Jah Puba sings patiently. Then he points to me.

"Ask to hear this one's song and you can hear the damage done. Already they've drawn the color from the outside world and they're on their way to global suicide. Secreted here, the tribe remains safe. Even from me."

"Where did you find our sister?" Star eyes gesturing to Fatty.

"She found me." Mico laughs. "Without knowing it, she showed me the values of the tribe: strength, compassion, unity." Then to Fatima he does that sheepish smile. "These are your mother's people."

"Gathered that," Fatty says, her hand drifting toward her mini rifle.

"You don't get it. Everything here, the Manna, the song, the wall of wind, these are all your birthright. You can stay here. Your father as well." Sad sack can't read Fatima to save his life. This life ain't hers.

"She will not stay." Othica sings from across the houses and yurts and the like, from the other side of the village. That's how loud her voice can get. And she's not even shouting. Impressive as that is, more excited about seeing Taggert striding alongside her. Means they've come to a peace. And maybe even the outline of a suitable plan.

"This is my sister's daughter," Othica says when she's close enough to touch Fatty's head. I expect the mini rifle or at least a flinch from the smuggler; instead she melts under the larger woman's rough but familiar touch. "Like her mother before her she is a warrior. And there is war to be made upon the Children of the Absence."

"No." Mico starts out stupid and almost gets a volley of spears in his chest for that one note, song, word . . .

"Yes," Taggert says in plain old English. "Had a chat with your root god. You're a cog in a machine, Mico. Maybe a bigger gear than most, but trust you can't see the full plan on this one. Me neither. But your god let me know the Bint al-nas on our side turns this into an actual fight."

"Warriors born," Othica sings over Taggert to her people. "You are called to battle the outside world. Will you stand to be counted? Will you raise your voices and your spears?"

It's a steady but slow rising "LATLTALATLTA" that breaks in waves over us all. Only the women sing, I'm realizing. The men bang spears together.

"Da fuck is up wit ya men folk?" give in and ask. "Not a one of them fit to stand and fight?"

"Who would take care of the children?" pretty eyes sings back at me, dead serious.

"Men are called to the mother," Othica explains to me as the singing gets louder. "But only Bint al-nas, daughters of the desert, are born here. We carry the blood, the spirit of the mother within us."

"Taggert, are you sure?" Mico asks as the voices get even louder.

"We've been in this spot upwards of three days and I still can't tell where and when the sun rises and sets. I can't tell you what time it is right now. So no, I'm not sure. Not sure how much time has passed in the world either. You want to pull the war master title off me?" Even over the chanting everyone can hear Taggert offering his resignation.

"No."

"War requires soldiers. The Bint al-nas stay ready," the women howl in confirmation. "And from what I saw walking up, they wouldn't follow you if you paid them. So relax and let me deal with this part. Your job is to get us in touch with Tam and the rest."

Hear the mistake before Mico realizes he's making it. Stress, fights, discombobulation of it all has been building in Tag. Times like this it's best to give him space, feed him, and let him sleep or if you can, make him laugh. Worst thing is to push him.

"It's not your call to make . . ." The singer grabs Taggert's shoulder as he turns. Every fighter in the mix sees the setup: Mico off balance and overreaching, Taggert fueled by fury but relaxed enough to react, in one fluid motion wraps Mico's left arm with his right and pulls Mico forward, stopping that falling motion with well-placed knee to the stomach. Da takes that leg and places it behind Mico prepping him for a trip while at the same time trapping the singer's throat with a light chop from his left hand. Wanted to be a wanker about it, Tag could've kept the singer's arm trapped ensuring a break, but Tag lets him go. When the entropy blade comes out, see it wasn't mere compassion that got a hold of Tag. Bint al-nas all crowd in, not sure which side to take, but ready for combat. Call five king cobras, ten feet long each, to stand guard against Bingy and, surprisingly, Fatty. All the singing stops.

"Call the snakes off, girl, before he kills Mico!" Fatima shouts, trying to get by my vipers.

"Tag wanted any of you dead all he'd have to do is think about it, get me?" tell them. "Back off and let nature take its course."

"This is my best," Taggert hisses in Mico's ear as the curved point of the kerambit almost scrapes the singer's iris. "This is the best I can do. You keep pushing. You run off into a whirlwind, convince me to send my daughter off to secure the aid of a ghost, tell me to lead an army to war against a force of nature. I do it. And I'll keep doing it. But if you don't find a way to get me in touch with my girl soon, I will end you. Consequences be damned . . ."

Tag stands, surveys all the reactions to him. Bint al-nas more concerned with the entropy blade than anything. Fatima and Bingy rush to Mico, not yet standing. Othica nods in understanding. To him. And to me. Tag looks at me and sees the cobras, still standing at attention by my side, he speaks.

"Got my back?" He smiles.

"Your front too." Smile as he touches my cheek. He marches back to the tent Othica first woke him in and I trail behind, cobras in tow like two puppies.

"Nothing getting done until I talk to my other kid!" Taggert shouts over his shoulder.

The Lost Ocean
A.C.

"Where the hell are we?" Tamara asks me, looking over the bow toward the setting sun. Underneath us, sorrow, time, and mournful songs of desolation manifest as multicolored waves of muted starlight and cold ocean water.

"Somewhere between the fallen hubris of Atlantis and the remains of Lemuria satellite city," I tell her honestly. Still, I'm braced for her hit on my arm.

"English, Wind Boy. Last time I saw sea like this it was all ghost sharks, angry slave spirits, and time travel," she confesses. "Not sure I've got it in me for another one of those trips."

"Fear not, fair maiden." I turn to look at her. This journey, this life, have taken their toll. Not in her looks, but in her eyes. Give her combat and she'll smash all comers. But give her a second of reprieve and it's all she can do not to collapse. "One of the benefits of traveling with the wind is being under its protection."

"How's your girl?" she asks, smirking gently.

"Resting. Being recently re-bodied or re-souled takes it out of a person. She's below deck. Narayana is standing guard against angels or whatever may come for her outside her door."

"Still don't get that whole relationship," she remarks but settles down to the deck and pulls out a joint from her sleeve.

"You're one to talk. What's up with you and your puppy?" I ask, sitting across from her on a sedan of wind.

"The lucky one? He's not mine. Shit, is he still manning the wheel?"

"You know this ship sails the aperion of the middle worlds on its own, right? It would take a power greater than his to actually pilot this ship."

"Yeah, but he feels important with that big wheel in his hands, so where's the harm?" She laughs a bit. I can't help but join. Tamara levitates the joint to me and I take a hit before she speaks again. "I can't feel my crew out there."

"We are in between time and space, Miss Bridgecombe. 'Out there' is literally all of time and space. I'd be deathly afraid of you if you could feel them with mere telepathy."

"I know," she confesses, taking the joint back from the wind gust I send to her. "Just saying it wasn't too long ago that I freaked out because I couldn't feel Prentis. Now, I just take this lunatic shit for granted. So tell me, Wind Boy, it ever get less bizarre?"

"I ever tell you how I got these guns?" I ask.

"Tips from your stripping days?" she smirks.

"Ha! Okay, so I learn the whole wind thing from a djinn, genie, right? Good guy. The best, really. He tells me that if I want to take it to the next level I've got to clear my bloodline. Says the sins of the father not being passed down to the son is a unfulfilled project of the prophet from Judea and that if I want access to the ancient power, I've got to pay the old blood debt."

"Okay." She leans forward, tossing the joint my way again, fascinated. "So what did your granddad do, molest a sheep or something?"

"Wish that was it. I'd swear off lamb in a second," I tell her, grabbing the smoke. "No, few generations back, I have a buffalo soldier ancestor. Free black men who joined the U.S. army and tasked to clear Native people off their lands. He was one of the first. Young, dumb, and eager to prove himself. He was the first black man to shoot a Comanche, like a dumbass."

"So what, you have to do a sweat lodge or something?"

"Sheeit, I wish it was that easy. First I had to find his six-shooters. No easy tasks, some one hundred years after the deal was done. Then I had to find the bloodline of that Comanche. A real shit show of a woman named Spits with Bears. Had to go to her house in New Mexico, and come to her door butt naked . . ."

"Stop it . . ."

"It gets better. And in Shoshoni, their original dialect, I had to offer the guns and my services for a period of two years."

"That's how the Comanche do it?"

"Nope, that's how whatever African tribe I'm descended from do it apparently. Spits with Bears didn't know whether to kick my ass or 5150 me."

"Which did she decide?"

"Neither, once she saw I was connected to the wind. Had me clean her house, though. Break a few of her sons out of jail, heal some who could be healed, punish some who deserved it. Far as penance goes, trust it could've gone a lot worse. In the end, we reached an accord. I'd be the last of the bloodline, and the curse would stay limited to the guns." I unholster one for her and side-toss it her way. Smart girl catches it with the telekinesis, not her hands.

"You can hold it. They aren't like your dad's weapons. They only talk to me." Cautiously she lets the pistol fall into her hand. For someone who has never used a gun, she's smooth with it, instinctively breaking the Colt's hold on the barrel and checking for bullets. "I squeeze and they hit and keep on hitting."

"And you didn't think to use them on those angels?" she asks.

"Every life I take with these add to the weight of the weapons for me. Not sure if I could handle the weight of an angel soul."

"Fair enough. But sounds like the point of your whole story is that this shit stays bizarre." She tosses the Colt back at me, joint sticking out of her mouth like a lazy tooth.

"Pretty much." I laugh. "Best you can hope for is to get some cool toys out of the deal." I holster the piece and mouth the silent prayer I promised Spits with Bears I'd do whenever I drew. "The toys help you deal with the weirdness of it."

"Fam helps me deal," she tells me honestly.

"Guess we should check in with our squad then, huh?"

"Outside of everything, remember?" She makes a movement with her hand to indicate our strange winds, and I step off my wind to begin the portal mudra while calling the right djinn spell to mind to reach out to lost friends.

"For you it's family, for me, kid, it's cool toys and tricks." I exhale over my portal mudra hands and use that charged wind to create a full-length mirror-sized vortex directly before Tamara. She stands, ready for a fight, before she realizes what I'm doing.

"I can't see anything in there," Tamara tells me as I try to remember the syntax of a language only meant to be spoken by those who have fire in their throats.

"Get some of the temporal waters in there, that should make a reflective surface." Before I'm done Tamara pulls a stream of water from the ocean below and throws it into the wind vortex in front of her. In a second, I can see myself in it clear enough to realize I need a shave. It's a true mirror.

"Who is that?" she asks as I stop my gesticulating and walk over to her.

"That's you, kid," I tell her. She has to look at me to see I'm not joking.

"Looks like someone beat the shit out of me," she says.

"That would be this life."

"Fook." I've seen people break at the true reflection of themselves. It's a weird concept. All mirrors of glass and metal, all cameras, no matter how well calibrated, always distort and limit the vision. With the ancient words and timeless materials this mirror has no choice but to reflect the authentic person that sits before it. Kings fall when they realize they've been little boys their whole lives. Refined beauty queens crumble looking at the corruption of their souls. But Tamara, she just realizes how many blows she's taken. Still, the kid doesn't stop.

"Thought you were going to show me my fam," she says.

"Call to them." She barely whispers Taggert's name before the waves of the mirror turn from serene to choppy. A brilliant red-and-white flash of light issues from the portal and then it's nothing but desert. Like a camera on a swing, the image shifts and radically bounces until it comes across Taggert and Prentis standing in the middle of the desert with twin tall Fatima doubles holding spears in desert gear behind them.

"Hey, love," Prentis says with tears in her eyes as soon as she sees Tamara.

"Hey fam," Tamara says back, almost whispering. "Looks like you two have been busy."

"You okay?" Taggert can barely get it out. It's killing him to be able to see her, hear her, but not touch his daughter.

"Yeah, Dad. All good. Mission accomplished." She smiles a bit.

"No problems?" he asks.

"I mean angels on our tail but we'll all be mission ready in an hour or so, I'd think." We both laugh at the ridiculousness of the statement.

"Who's that with you?" Prentis asks.

"Keep up, love. A.C." And I give her a gust of wind from my side of the mirror to hers to remind her.

"Oh yeah. Hey, Wind Boy. All right?"

"Can't complain too loud, beastie babe." Then to Taggert, "Okay, what's next?"

"The Manna wants Samantha back now. It says she's the linchpin for global mind control. Problem is, either one of us steps out of our comfort circle, the entire world will be on us. One of the Poppy twins came for us in the desert. They can track us now. And time is running out."

"Tracking and taking are two different things," Tam reminds us all. It's disconcerting, looking at Prentis and Taggert sweating in the desert as we sway with the ocean swell. "We need distractions. If we can't be nowhere then we should be everywhere."

"Do we have the numbers?" I ask. "Even with the Bint al-nas over there, good job by the way, not sure if we can distract all the Alters long enough for me and Taggert to get Samantha free."

"True," Prentis says. "So let's give them what they want. Let them find us at a spot that's easiest for us to get out of. Then we scatter after they focus all their attention on us. Regroup after Whatshisname and Taggert bring this Samantha chick back into the fold."

"And what are the rest of you supposed to do while we're recouping her?" Taggert asks.

"Probably best I get Mico away from you for a while." Prentis smirks. "Figure we can set up the concert of the century."

"I've got an idea that neither of you will like," Tamara says. "So I'll be taking Pasha with me to execute. We should be able to stay off the Alters' radar. We can send Narayana and Chabi your way, Prentis, so long as you can get to an island. Don't think many will be trying to fuck with those two, no matter what."

"All well and good, folks, but we need a where in the concrete world to meet up. We can't keep hiding," Taggert reminds us.

"Gili Air." Narayana's dead voice almost scares me out of my concentration, coming from behind them. Even some of the Bint al-nas point their spears toward the mystical mirror upon hearing his voice.

"What is with you and Indonesia, man?" I ask him.

"Those islands are mine. My control is still inviolate there. Rice and his cohort have assembled one of their Decimation leagues on the adjacent Gili Trawangan," he says more to Taggert than to anyone else. "I can protect those lands better than I did Pangkor. More importantly, I can mask the presence of anyone on the islands. This, I swear."

"Okay," Taggert tells everyone but looks at Tamara. "Two-island divide this time. Mico and Prentis will lead the Bint al-nas to meet up with Narayana and Chabi on Gili Air. Everybody else, we're gonna take a slice out of Eel Pie Island."

Part Three

How do you tell the beginning of a thing? Or the end of it? Are there essential characteristics or is it just a feeling, a scent in the wind?

These damn Liminals and their plans. It's hard to tell if they are starting something new, a liberation? Or just hastening the ends. Here, more than ever before, my efforts are shown.

As the Manna did its more personal work—a strange notion for the God of Connections—with the healing of one vassal, the preparing of its children for the toxic world of the Decimation, and the intentionally vague handling of the totem, I did what work I could to rectify the damage done by powers larger than myself. I confess to my courage being spurred on more by Taggert's scion than from the man himself. Tamara was the one who elected to wander the gray roads with nothing more than a little luck by her side. And against demons birthed from her personal hells.

Never let it be said I was an enemy of Taggert. But friend? Was I ever his friend? Can you befriend someone who risks forgetting you whenever they blink? Better to just acknowledge him for what he is, War Master, General, Murderous Savant, Ally. And between him and the Alters, what choice would you have made? But let it also never be said that what I did, I did for him.

Samantha. There were worlds in which she was the Queen of the Horn, the Cushite Priestess that could not be stopped. In her own time, she survived the Liminal Shadow's touch, the corruption named Nordeen. She came out the other side to provide succor to Taggert and his brood before they knew they needed it. Off her word, I helped form the two Liminal blades that call Taggert their home. Her words screamed across the Abyss, warning us of the Alters' progress. It is for her that we would risk all. Samantha, pinnacle of the Liminals.

But first, the Nadir. Baron. Taggert's brother. For that attack, I had to drop Liminals from the sky.

This child does this type of lunacy just to get a reaction, I swear. Why teleport to Eel Pie Island Terra Firma when you can teleport two miles above and have a semi-controlled descent? I let her have what fun she can, but still . . .

"I'm getting sick of not flying," I think to Tamara.

"Not yet," she thinks back. "If I can feel them, they can feel us," she tells me. Still, she's looking down, wind fighting against his entire body, staring through the night clouds from this new angle as though she can see the whole world from this vantage and doesn't like what she sees. Moonless, cloudy night won't stop her from peeping everybody on the island. Can't see her, but I know she's biting his lips as the upward air pressure threatens to separate her upper and lower jaw. Bless Tamara for always scanning and thinking.

"You're prepped for this. They aren't," I think to her. "Wait."

Don't have to read Tam's mind to know she hates this plan, even though it's hers. Have to admit, not too fond of having the Wind Boy teleport me miles above Evil Central and letting gravity pull us into the worst family reunion ever. But talk about the element of surprise. Can't get much better than this.

"Prentis?" I think to Tam.

"Focus," she shout-thinks back. Then, "With Mico and them."

"She's good?" Tam tries to look up and that fouls her spin, sending her body off to almost over the water instead of the land. But Tamara lets her telekinetics anchor her back to my body. Still falling.

"Get ready." Her voice finally breaking the dead stare with the glowing tip of the church tower spire at the heart of Eel Pie Island.

"'Bout time." I smile.

175

"I make the noise. You make the mission," she reminds me.

"Come on, let me make a little noise." I throw my idea in her head. It appeals to his juvenile superhero tendencies.

Tam transfers some of the velocity from our descent and directs it at the windows in the tower of pain they're building. All of the glass flakes arch outward violently. At the same time, I mess with the equilibrium of every norm on the island. They all vomit everywhere.

"We're here." She tries to sound creepy in my head. I'm one step ahead of her, using my legs to push away from her body.

"They know," I think back just as one of her fireballs gets between us.

"Signal the boys!" I shout then point myself like a missile to the ground as I beef up my limbs. "I got this."

Still, she gives him a bit of help as I land an overhead flip on the ground that would make a world-class gymnast jealous. I'm standing against my brother. Alone. I look up just to see another set of high heat lasers aiming right toward my girl, the Lucky Liminal, and the Wind Boy. I've got my own problems.

Eel Pie Island
Taggert.

"Did you think anyone can arrive on this island without me knowing?" Baron's sneer reaches across the night and threatens me as soon as I land not too far from the shore. A troop of Shadows, most vaguely human looking, support his position.

"What part of falling from the sky makes you believe I've got stealth on the mind?" I ask after slicing the ten near-invisible murder spikes he hurls at me.

"It's a cheap distraction meant to keep me from your compatriots on the other side of the island." He must have used his telepathy; in an instant his shadow version of Samantha and some shifty hum-monculoids retreat into the shadows. "None of you will survive the night."

"As much of an ass as my Baron was, at least he was his own man. Not a puppet." I feel soil, rock, pebble, and grit reach up from the ground and secure my feet. The squeeze is so hard I have to bulk up my ankles just so they aren't crushed. Baron's doing. He walks closer to me, casually.

"You're too calm, Taggert, thinking you can get out of this. And I know it's you now. Not Pasha, no decoy. You are mine now. And in a second, Tamara and whoever she's with will be mine as well," Baron says, like he's bored.

"If I'm going to be saved, it won't be because of anything I do. At least, not directly."

"Wha . . ." That's when it hits. It was a chance but well guessed one. I bet that as soon as I started making the norms nauseous Baron would cut them out of his psychic feed. If he was anything like Tamara, he'd have strong psychic blocks. But one thing he couldn't block is pleasure. So while he threatened torture I flipped the script on the norms and flooded their brains with serotonin and oxytocin. More than any of them have ever felt. Sure, he could filter out one or two, but an entire island of permanent orgasm-level happy people? No psychic can filter that out for too long, unprepared. When the dirt loosens, I beef up my leg and send my foot into his dental.

"Feel the love, Baron!" I drop a dense elbow to the back of his head. Tough son of a bitch only goes down a few inches. He's not out.

"Fuck what the Alters say, I'm killing you slow myself." He points to me, and out of the shadows five Terror Tomas speed wobble their way toward me.

I run.

Eel Pie Island
Taggert

I'm thick but I learn. I didn't have time to practice on Pangkor but I studied the Terror Tomas, cancers fit to flesh. Cancer isn't scary because it kills. It's scary because it never dies. Back on the island, I thought the entropy blades would save me. Then I thought to take them apart with their own body parts. But that damn root god has me thinking in new ways. I didn't run away because I was scared of them, or Baron. I'm experimenting.

These blown out and abandoned homes I'm using for cover used to house Mico's followers, like Bingy man. They were bright and filled with hope, even though none of the supplicants had more than a few dollars in their bank accounts. What I wouldn't give for their hippy shit as opposed to this lunacy. I hide in the barn loft of the woman, who, in my world, formed the Liminal blades. I never caught her name, never really said thank you, I was so concerned with finding Prentis.

I stay quiet and still above the doorway as I feel a Terror Toma enter the doorway, stumbling in its shambling movements. I open my Liminal sight. I've been running from feeling these beasties, running from cancer. That never works. You can only fight it, and if you're lucky, heal it. The simple lesson I keep forgetting. Don't hurt, heal.

I give myself fully to the Terror Toma. It's less a single entity and more a collection of sores on top of tumors, bound by puss, ligaments, and bone. Dense calcium-rich bone infected with cavities. It grows teeth never used for eating. But at each tooth outcropping, a jawlike hinge exists, on its hip, its feet, the back of its arms. I'm an idiot for not figuring this out earlier.

I trigger major changes in the cytokine levels in the small tumor that represents the lower part of the creature's face. Once the osteoprotegerin levels get low enough, incisors start growing where molars should be and vice versa, but that part doesn't matter. On instinct, like a shark, the jawline starts ripping the new fleshy lips apart. I push myself one more time and clear an esophageal opening and connect two thin membranes of sinew curved over the arches of a church made of mutated detritus. I give it the form. It provides the scream all on its own. The Terra Toma screams.

The vibration alone is enough bring its pack mates running. The thing shakes the foundations of the barn with its voice. Good, it can hear itself. That startles it beyond belief. I'd start crying if the sound weren't so pathetic as it tries to communicate, to actually speak with its compatriots. I'd do the same work on the rest of them, my own taxed system be damned, if it wasn't for the body I feel coming.

"What the hell happened to you?" Baron asks the blubbering mass as it begins to speak its reality of hurt and pain.

"BALSrhg! Groagha!" it tries.

"Fuck it." Baron uses his telekinesis to explode the beast into a million parts. He throws up a TK shield for himself so none of the wasted talking tumor gets on him. "Don't really care."

In all my years with Tamara, and all the years before, I've never seen a telekinetic be so thoroughly brutal with their powers. That plus the deep work I did on the Terror Toma takes it out of me. I fall/sit. And Baron hears.

"You in here, little man?" He doesn't bother to answer. Instead, he dismantles the entire barn. Planks separate from nails that hold them together, glues are stretched beyond their limits, anchors are uprooted, but without a hint of heat or fire. It's a fulmination on every level, caused by Baron's mind. I'm thrown first up then outward. I'm still catching my breath at the banks of the Thames some fifteen meters away when he comes walking calmly down the bank, his pack of Terror Tomas still surrounding him.

"Look at that, now we've both blown up buildings the other was sitting in."

Eel Pie Island
Taggert

"Here ends the tale of the dumbass that ran like a rat across my dimension in its twilight claiming some kinship to me," Baron says, holding me up in the air with his telekinesis. Every time I get a clear moment to think, he shakes me like a drunk teen mom with an unwanted baby. The sadist loves watching me squirm.

"You're an idiot," I tell him. He crashes me into the ground but it feels like there's a giant foot that presses me into the soil.

"You don't know how to die well, do you?" It's a bully's trick. Taunting the defeated.

"I won't be the one dying today," I manage to tell him. Even so, the light is beginning to fade from my vision.

"I built this island, these people, this clan, up from nothing, Taggert. This is my locus of power. You came to my house thinking you could flash, bang, and win the day. You picked a fight with the wrong powers, boy. And now you and yours will die for it."

I feel the pressure on my head and neck increase. I let the Liminal spirit inside of me fight back, knowing full well it will lose on its own and focus my waning power on the Terror Tomas. I give them the boost they need. Once the right metabolites begin the cellular generation, I turn Baron's intestines to the perfect home for lactic acid. In under a minute he's cramping and losing his focus. This ash-infested air has never tasted so sweet.

"That was childish," Baron says, already recovering. The pain is still in him, but he's focusing past it. It's all I can do to stand. "And pointless."

"Tell them that." I point to the Terror Tomas. Their pink fleshy arms and necks all gyrate in pain-coordinated movements as the same mutation that I put on the first one takes hold of them.

"What did you do?" he asks.

"You think I get tired enough to have you get the jump on me off some mere body trickery? I was working on that bad boy in the barn on a genetic level," I brag.

180

"So it can speak. So what?" Still no fear in Baron.

"So I gave cancer a voice. And you killed it. Ever hear of cellular memory?" I ask Baron as he turns to hear the raging from his former army turning against him.

"First them, then you!" The head of one of the Terror Tomas is torn fifty feet in the air, dropping bits of matter across the island as it spirals up. Each bit grows to fetus size before it hits the ground. The vocal cords get stronger with each iteration. The cancer scream is getting louder. The psychic link between the Terror Tomas increases their rage. Baron tears into each Terror Toma like he doesn't realize they clone themselves.

"Did I mention I also sped up their rate of reproduction?" I tell him, slipping off down the beach. "Trust me, they're hard to kill. And they all hate you. Have fun, Big Bro."

Eel Pie Island
Taggert

The gust of wind in front of me makes me palm my entropy blade. Brittle rock and sand to my left go mute where, even in this pitch-black night, I should be seeing a body. I pump adrenaline and glutamate in my heart, readying my muscles for a fight.

"Wind Boy, that better be you." I sink my weight back onto my hind foot, holding my blade low and ready.

"Glad you can remember me," he says, coming out of the shadow of trees.

"Better you than the alternative," I tell him, scanning his trail for tails as he does the same for mine.

"Baron is still alive and kicking, I hear." He listens with organs I don't have.

"Not for lack of trying on my part," I say. "My girl okay?" Before he can answer, the assembled construction of black glass and steel that was Baron's half-constructed tower screams, quakes, then falls with a chaos that has become my family crest. From the other half of the island, the high-pitched scream sounds like it's right in my ear. I can't imagine what those on the mainland are hearing.

"Tamara delivered Samantha right to me. But Yasmine is dead." He knows how it'll hit me. It's not my Yasmine. I know that. Still . . .

"How?"

"The Lucky, with one of your blades."

"Tam?"

"Almost bit it going toe to toe with her Not Mom. She had the same look on her face you have on yours." The Wind Boy blows cold. "Luckily . . . Heh, Pasha was there. Stabbed the heat witch in the back while she was distracted with Tamara."

"Where are they?"

"She said she had a plan. Better you didn't know, she said . . ."

"Da hell?" I start.

"Said she'd let you know when there was something to let you know." I ignore him and try to scan the island for her body. Nothing.

"What is it with this island anyway? Mico had his base here. Now Baron in this dimension . . ."

"Ley lines, man," A.C. starts. "You want to control the planet you control the Ley Lines. The dragon's head . . ."

"Come on. Make it plain."

"You want to control the aesthetic, the moral center of the world-wide population? You have to control the Ley Lines. Eel Pie is a nexus point for about five different lines."

"So why aren't we sieging this spot?" I ask.

"This is the last locus for the west, what you think of as Europe. But all the other concentration points are already co-opted. We might win this battle, but trust we'd lose the war." I'm tempted to scan hard for Tamara, just to make sure she's okay. But that's the act of a father, not a general. She's earned my trust. Now, I have to give it completely. "You ready?"

"You got Samantha?" He takes me into the air.

"Thanks to your girl. Tam's good, you know?" I try not to smile.

"Better than me. How confident are you in this spell?"

"Disregarding the fact that the Alters have corrupted the messages of Islam, Judaism, Christianity, Buddhism, and every other religion you've ever heard of, I'd say I'm pretty confident."

"Really? So your spell requires pulling on other religions?"

"Older powers, really. You know why science gained dominance in your dimension, in most? Because it's easier. Reason and logic rely on the same thing happening again and again. It's a practice in monotony. Magic is hard. It's cultivating scenarios that will only happen once and never again. It's not predictable, it relies on things that shouldn't be occurring, manifesting in rapid succession. This ain't no finger tut, hand dance, bad slam poetry trickerism. This is magic for real. It requires blood, sweat, tears, cum, risk, sacrifice, and manners. Plus you got to know your history. This is my realm, Liminal, watch where you step. You've got the hard job."

"What's that?"

"You've got to talk to her."

Ethiopia, Denkali Depression
Taggert

"አክሱም , የኩሽ ልጅ, በአማራ እና ሶማሊዎች መካከል የኦሮም እና በትግራይ , ስለ ሌጅ የሕፃናት . Afars ኩራት, የሲዳማ የተወደደ . የጉራጌ ልጅ ልዕልት , ታደስ ታምራት , Astar ባሪያ , Mahrem , Biher አሳዳጊ ስለ ልጅ ሙሽራ , የተጠራችሁብትን !"

I have no idea what A.C. is screaming in Samantha's face, but it better work. He pushed her through his dimensional shift not a second before us, unconscious no less. But instead of arriving quelled, she managed to summon protectors out here. If the moon were hot as the sun, it would look like this massive valley filled with large rocks of salt, turmeric colored rocks, and large pools of foul smelling liquid I wouldn't call water. No one lives out here, yet armed gunmen picked her up in a jeep and were aiming toward civilization proper by the time we arrived. I just managed to deal with that set of shooters. A.C. shouted his bird song language in Samantha's face just before four more jeeps hit a salt dune and careen toward us about fifty yards out.

"Is it working?" I face a rabid Samantha kicking A.C. in the balls hard.

"Not yet," he squeaks.

"Stop fucking around, man!" I cause one of the drivers' legs in the jeeps to spasm. Narcolepsy take another driver. They crash into each other, but the others riding in the car all dismount and start shooting from a distance.

"Who is fucking around here?" A.C. shouts back. I'm thankful for the gust of wind he generates to catch a fleeing Samantha, but it won't do me much good. The heat here, along with the pressure and the ever presence of salt, is making body manipulation more than difficult. It's all I can do to keep standing, let alone avoid bullets.

The shelter I take behind a small salt shelf chips away quickly as the boys from the two standing jeeps come in hot and focus their fire on me. I could kill them all, easily. But we are in the same position; all of us fighting for a woman who we feel compelled to protect. Her power versus my love. I kill them, I'm killing an aspect of myself. And despite the pain, there are other options.

My pain is theirs. If I'm thirsty, so are they. But they're fighting through it to get to her. I thump their thyroids until they can't see because of the sweat pouring down their faces. The Denkali is often the hottest place on the planet and today is no exception. In under a minute they're holding their throats searching the jeep, begging for water. Whatever drives them to protect Samantha knows they need to be alive to save her.

I leap from my weak cover and kick one set of men from their jeep. It's only when I pick up A.C. wavering in the air on a flimsy wind that I realize how drained I am. The sandy orange-and-red bluffs are merging into one giant mush in my vision.

"Where is she?" I manage to ask, driving to him. "How the hell did she get away from you?"

"Shut up, man. This is her place. Ethiopia, all of ancient Abyssinia is her power spot. Plus it's hot!"

I open my Liminal senses to get a vector on Samantha, like an old scent obscured by a blanket sprayed with brine. I catch the angle but drive off what passes for a road and hit a cliff. There's a plain of more open rocky land fifty feet below us.

"Easy," A.C. says calmly and lets his winds catch the jeep and slow our descent to where I can hit the road again without crashing. "Stay with me, Taggert."

"There!" I point with my chin to the horizon. Not sure how she got there so fast on foot, but she's stopped moving and is breathing hard. I guess there's a limit to her power.

"Go!" I tell A.C. when I look in the rearview. The two jeeps that got by me free themselves from a ravine to the east of us. They're closing in fast on our tail. A.C. grimaces and takes to the air, struggling to fly faster than the jeep's forty miles an hour. Samantha reaches in my direction and for a second I think the spell has worked, but then I feel the wave of excitement rush over the two drivers behind me. She's calling to her people behind us. I yank the emergency brake and pull left on the steering wheel, hard.

My passenger side merges with the driver's side of the jeep trying to speed by me before we both flip into a shallow pool of bubbling mineral-rich liquid. Those passengers that don't break limbs getting thrown into salt pillars I knock out with my powers. Still, one jeep got by me. I find a rifle hanging off the back of the heavily concussed driver. Standing on our still smoking wreck, I hype my eyesight and take aim at the last jeep's tires as they speed toward Sam. I hit three out of four. Still, they don't crash.

"Mother fucker," I mumble. I dump the five-gallon red plastic container of water that I find in the back of the truck over my head.

I douse myself with half then swallow the rest, demanding my body process it in under forty seconds. Exchanging the rifle for a .45 off a twenty-two-year-old soldier boy who will get diabetes if he doesn't quit eating junk food, I prime my body for a long jump.

I'm running twenty miles an hour at my first leap. I sail through the sky, leaping like the old-school Hulk, but descending I draw a bead on three of the jeep men now running toward Sam and A.C. Thigh and arm shots might be enough to kill them out here. That's the most mercy I can offer. My landing is sloppy, made worse because I can't see A.C. Where the hell did Samantha go, for that matter? Before the soldiers can figure out how I managed to rain bullets from the sky on them, I leap again to the horizon. Over the ledge of what looks like an impact crater I see A.C. struggling with Samantha. She is summarily whipping his ass.

"Get her in the water!" he tells me as she lands an elbow to his throat, then a shin to his ribs. The leather pants aren't impeding her martial flow at all. From the lip of the crater I see no water, only a dark green-and-yellow bubbling pool this area is known for.

"You mean that?" I jump down to help him. A.C. has her in his wind, but even the breeze begins to submit to her will. He can't answer due to the wound to his throat, but he nods. A.C.'s wind ends a few feet shy of the giant pool. I ask forgiveness and tackle Sam like a football. I'm bigger, stronger, but it feels like tackling a refrigerator. She barely moves until I use leverage and lift. Once off the earth, I can feel her natural body weight return. But the African soil calls to her as though she were Antaeus. Arching her over my hip, I begin to crumble. She'd collapse on me if A.C. didn't come through. He jumps, pushing all three of us into the pool.

Lake Tana, Ethiopia
Taggert

"Where is she?" I wasn't asleep, but I wake up to A.C. asking the question, wet. Not with sulphuric water, but in cool lake water. A.C. and I bob in the cool water like lost lures. Around us small islands, some no bigger than a house, covered in dense foliage, stand sentry. Ready for problems. Ready for us.

"Where are we?" I ask.

"Lake Tana," he says like I'm supposed to know. "Second part of the spell has to be recited here." I'm thankful for the A.C. express, but his transportation magic is discombobulating.

"Did she drown?" I panic.

"Don't be an idiot. She's the spirit of this place. She can't drown in her own blood," he says

"I'm the idiot, how come you lost her?" The blame is just because I'm scared. We both know it.

He doesn't bother answering. Instead A.C. takes to the sky on a gust of wind to look. No need. I feel a mass of bodies moving on the west-most island in the lake. I turn to see a fleet of pontoon-shaped boats, piloted by men with rifles and machine guns, heading at me.

"Don't worry, I got you," A.C. says, lifting me out of the water on a gust of wind and circling to the back end of the closest island, away from the bullets.

"You're going the wrong way," I tell him.

"How's that?" he asks

"She's trying to get some breathing room. She sends that island's guys after us, meanwhile she's chilling the island to the right of us," I tell him.

"And you know this how?" he asks.

"I read bodies, remember? And I know her body better than most. Trust, she's over there." I point at the island.

Halfway to the island the wind cuts out below us and we careen headlong into the wake of its beach. No use in chastising A.C., he'll just tell me about Ley Lines or some such nonsense again. But when he doesn't attempt to get us out of the water, I follow his eye line. On the beach, I see old brown-skinned Ethiopians dressed in robes with golden staffs raised high above their heads. They shout in a language that sounds like pretty birds fighting.

"Was hoping to avoid these guys." A.C. wipes the water from his face.

"Ex-lovers?" I ask.

"Funny," he says. "Priests. Wizards, really. They're the guardians of the Gu'ez ancient texts written around here. With the Alters in control, they can use those old spells to . . ."

What hits us is a nausea born not of the body, trust I check, but of spirit. It's what alcoholics find when they hit their bottoms, it's dope-sick in a K hole chasing a dragon with a monkey on your back. It's the bends of reality, and it cripples the both of us.

"Stop them," I tell the Wind Boy during puke breaks. Each cramp threatens to take my legs from me. Doesn't help me stay above water.

"Sacred land for them equals unholy land for us," he says, trying to stay up while his soul is cramping. "My wind doesn't do anything over there. I can't stop them from chanting."

"Well, I can stop hearing them." Control over my body is almost instinctive. I shut down my hearing and instantly feel better. A.C. must be weak. I can actually feel his body, his eardrums in particular. I get his ears to produce enough wax to block his canal. He stops convulsing in mid-spasm. I start swimming toward the chanty priest to end the drama when I feel a splash behind me. A.C. is replaced with bubbles under the water. I dive to see a gray hippo holding the Wind Boy in its mouth.

It's murky and shallow so I almost miss the three other lake cows, despite their size. I increase my blood gas efficiency and apologize mentally to Prentis for what I'm about to do. I launch myself at the hippo with the entropy blade and stab deep into its right shoulder blade. It lets go of A.C. but barrel rolls on to me. The thousand pound animal pins me against the floor of a lake.

I change my blood chemistry and maximize for strength. It burns energy quicker, but I'll need all the muscle I can muster. I manage to shift my knees under me just as the other hippos come to join their bloody and wounded kin. I've never seen pissed off hippos before. I'll never make fun of these bastards again.

With a huge exhale, I kick the big hippo off me, sending it flying out of the river into the air. A slightly smaller one drives at me showing all of its teeth. It's all I can do to roll away. But all of a sudden I'm swimming toward the surface. Then I'm flying in the air, pushed through open space on air currents. A.C. Almost forgot about him.

I switch my skin to be super oxygen-absorbent and take in every gulp of air I can get while I sail through the sky. I land, blade out and somewhat ready to deal with the wizards. But they're all laid out on the beach. A.C. taps me on the shoulder and points to his ears. I clear both our ear canals.

"Hated doing that to those guys." Whatever he did, I can tell he didn't use his sword or the guns. The wizards are still breathing. "But even with the ear blockage, I couldn't feel you under water with them chanting."

"Hippos, man? Hippos?" I say, catching my breath for true.

"I told you this is sacred land. Lake Tana is connected to the Nile. And Taweret is strong in the water." Guess he's beginning to recognize my "What the hell?" look. "Taweret is the goddess of childbirth, protection of women, all that noise. Her form is the hippo. Wait, you didn't stab one, did you?"

He's running before I can answer. From halfway across the beach I see why. Five hippopotamuses, including the one I stabbed, are running toward us. I follow Mico's trail up into the dense thicket of trees, following the minuscule trail. At the top of the mountain, a multi-sided, multi-colored octagon of a yurt, the size of a small-town Baptist church, on stilts sits adorned by sacred images. Big-headed

Ethiopian looking men fighting dragons and demons and the like. I've seen approximations of such paintings a world away, in Samantha's Brixton home.

"She's in there." A.C. breaks stride just to grab a skin filled with water.

"What is that?" I ask, running more from the sound of oncoming hippos than to follow him.

"Oldest church in the lake. Come on!" he shouts. Not really sure why. As soon as we enter the first walls, there is another layer of walls. And these images move. Visions of St. George slaying a dragon, priests of old receiving gifts, and saints rebuking demons all begin to move and make noise.

"You know women aren't even supposed to be in the inner sanctum!" A.C. shouts. This is the first time I've heard him frustrated. "Enchanted damn walls."

"So ignore them. Where's the door?" I ask as one of the supports of the building is knocked by what could only be the largest of the hippos.

"It keeps shifting! That's the problem!" he shouts as the building is rocked from the other side.

"So we make our own," I tell him and pull my entropy blade. "It cuts what's not supposed to be there, right?"

"Indeed," he says, pulling his sword. "But same spot, same time, same intention, or who knows what we'll open." I'm about to agree when I see the smallest of the hippos, still about one thousand pounds, actually walk into the building behind him.

"Quick," I tell him. We strike the secondary wall just as the hippo begins to charge. I can't tell if he notices the thing, so I throw him into the inner sanctum before the beast can grab him. Not enough time to dive in myself so I run. I'm halfway around the building when his buddies outside succeed in knocking the church off its foundation. I get half a blessing. The building tips away from the hippo's gaping maw. I run on the middle wall, now turned horizontal, of the building until I fall into the hole A.C. and I created. I land on the alternate interior wall in time to see the Wind Boy spit a mouthful of water into a savage Samantha's face.

"ራስህን Taweret ልጅ አስታውስ . የእርስዎ ሰዎች ሆይ: ምድር ከአንተ ይፈልጋል ያስፈልገናል . እርስዎ ከማይወዱ ሰዎች ጥቅም ላይ እየዋለ ነው . የእርስዎ የምድር ጤዉ , ያንተ ምድር ውሃ , እኔ መንፈስ ይነቃሉ."

Her voice disappears first, then her body. A.C. drops his wind and falls to the ground by me, exhausted. Outside, I hear snorting beasts with far less passion than before.

"We done?" I ask.

"Halfway." A.C. begins to disappear in front of me as he says it, already pulling us to the next site.

Lalibela, Ethiopia
Taggert

"She has to eat honey in the air, while no part of her body touches the ground," A.C. tells me. I blinked, breathed, and now I'm in high altitude, standing over a cliff. I feel the melanin count around me and know I'm still in Ethiopia.

"Are you for real?" I squat, grabbing a handful of red soil in my hand. It's cooler here. We're higher in altitude than the salt pits of hell for sure, but even the lake. The air is as clean and cold. Behind us the remains of a six-story church—carved out of a mountain from the looks of things—is half caved in. Like a giant foot stepped on it but could only press down hard enough to destroy the top layers of it. Time is doing the rest.

"This is Lalibela," A.C. tells me.

"Never been to Ethiopia before, okay? Samantha kept talking about coming but we never had time. What makes this place so special?" My hackles are up. Something familiar and dangerous is nearby.

"Those churches!" Wind Boy points to the wrecked temples. I see them clearly now. They are mountains that are carved into the shape of crosses. When these Ethiopians took on Christianity, they didn't half step. "They were some of the first religious monuments the Alters took out when they gained ascendancy. They couldn't fully corrupt the Ethiopian Orthodox church without them."

"And this helps us how?" I ask.

"It's a dodge. The power we need isn't in the church, it's in the honey."

"What fucking honey, mate?" I grab him, and to my surprise he lets me. Or maybe he's just as tired as I am and can't just wind power himself away.

"The town was named after a holy king." A.C. twists quickly and I lose my grip on him. "He was anointed by bees at his birth. In one of the old tongues that's what Lalibela means . . ."

"Anointed by bees," I echo.

"Yup. And bees anoint with honey," he says like his point is made.

"Where is the honey and where is Samantha?" I demand.

"Honey is in a log up there." A.C. points to a nearby grove of trees. "Samantha is probably in there." He points in the opposite direction at the wreckage of the church.

"This spell better work," I tell him, walking into the ruins. "Get back here quick with that honey."

The church goes deeper than I thought it would. Large boulders still lie at the base of their wrecked mountain monuments, almost admiring their work. But they've also cracked the ground, opening long, wide stairs into a basement of the building. The whole building is precariously balanced, untouched and unexplored probably since when these stones first fell—or were thrown—however many decades ago. I make my way down the steps tending toward the light that shines through from the half ceiling overhead; rays of cloud-cloaked sun rain down as if coming from a skylight. While my senses stay open for Sam, I pick up something else from the shadow of the steps halfway down. I give my eyes extra cones so I can pick up the contours of the body in the corner. A girl. Young, black, skinny, but better fed than most in this world. I've seen her before, but for the life of me I can't remember where. I make sure my back isn't to the cracked precipice of the stairway before I address her.

"This isn't the safest place, little girl," I say.

"Then you should go home, little Liminal." Her voice is too calm as she stands. Still, nothing threatening. "What you're looking for isn't here."

"Who are you?" I ask.

"A friend of the Manna." She can't be taller than four foot, no more than fifty pounds, and still I'm wary of her as she angles around me and makes her way back up the stairs. "Come back to the light. That way leads to nothing but pain and darkness for you."

"I can't. Samantha is down there." I hear the girl mumble something but it's her footsteps I hear more as she ascends. I keep going down, even more freaked out than before. Seeing a hooded figure sitting in the middle of the cellar floor bathed in gray light doesn't do anything to calm my nerves. And neither does his voice.

"I will confess surprise." It's a slow and belabored voice, but it's Nordeen's. I want to run back up to the little girl; tell her she's right as I place my foot on the final step in the cellar, but it's no use. I never ran from him. I never could.

"She has a contract with me, your Samantha. I thought she forgot about it, or that she'd never call on it. But here I am. It was a simple contract, really. She could call on me one time to destroy one of her enemies. And that if she called, I would have to come. No matter where she was. Forgive me, Taggert, if I ask two questions. The first is where are we? Lalibela, I can guess. But in a broader sense, if you catch my meaning."

"The Alters have won," I tell him, trying to sound strong. "At least for now. This is their world."

"Ah." I hear the old master's smile. "And no doubt Samantha made her choice to join. But not you, little healer? Do you still rage against the inevitable? Is this what cost you the affections of Samantha?"

"A little more complicated than that, Nordeen." I wait for another boulder to drop on the building, on me, as I say his name, circling around to try to catch a glimpse of his cloaked face. "But basically yeah. I haven't stopped fighting."

"I raised you to be smarter. Even your woman chose better than you. And now she's chosen me to end you."

"This isn't your fight. This isn't even your reality . . ." I tell him, not sure if he's a ghost, a delusion, or worst, the real deal.

"Are you so sure? Or is this my native land, while I was just a tourist in yours?" I know that smirk in his voice. He only gets it when he know the truth hurts more than the lie. "I'm surprised you hadn't put that much together yet. Or did you think you and your fallen herald were the only ones who could travel across dimensions?"

"I saw you torn apart," I say to shut him up, to gain time to access the threat. "A thousand animals fighting over scraps of you in the backwaters of the American south."

"A haunted land," he says in disgust. "More spirits and souls there than healthy bodies. But even then, consumed by all manner of bird and beasts, did you truly imagine me dead?"

"Not dead but vulnerable," I say and unsheathe my blade. "My girl took you apart. And I took down the king of the Alters . . ."

"With considerable allies," he says, conceding nothing. "And a full belly. And forewarning. Here you are with your steak knives— oh, only one? How sad. No allies, starving from the fracas before, and full of surprise to see me. This combat is over before it's begun."

"So you say." He's right. I don't care. I pass my blade to my right hand and step forward favoring my left side. I'm balanced, calm, breathing. I know Nordeen. His attack won't come from straight ahead, from where he's standing. A bomb will explode in the shadows.

I'll look. It will be nothing. I look back. He'll be gone, and a trickle from my neck will let me know my jugular is severed. Ignore the distraction, stay flexible. That's the only way to survive this.

It's that thinking, plus the adjusted cones in my eyes which I've been too tired to switch back to normal sight, that allows me to see it all. He throws open his cloak and lets loose two twenty-foot-long constrictor snakes filled with some type of sparkling energy. They foment a reaction in my peripheral vision that's drawing, almost hypnotizing. But they are the distraction from the real threat, Nordeen. He's lunging, moving faster than any snake possibly could. But even that's not what I'm focusing on. A tremendous infrared buildup in the shadow behind Nordeen looks like a giant. Half the height of the basement, a body of fire, neutered and smooth all over, but built of heat, grabs Nordeen and yanks him back into the light. Nordeen turns, totally surprised, in time to get a colossal flaming fist to the face.

"The Manna said you wouldn't listen," the Colossus speaks in infrared waves of energy to me as it pins a snarling, animal-sounding Nordeen to the ground. "Run and clear the ayaana of the Manna's chosen one so that we all may live." It manages to vibrate toward me before Nordeen's two glowing snakes, now giant mutant pythons, leap at it.

"You dare manhandle me, you minor spirit?!" I've only seen Nordeen like this on the astral plane; his head alight with the same flicker as the snakes, but the form of a lion all around him. Sparks issue from his mouth whenever he speaks, another stolen power from a long deposed foe. But he's forgotten about me, focused instead fully on the fire spirit that's now recoiled in the corner thrashing violently against the sparking serpents. "I am a Liminal! I choose the destiny of worlds!"

A black death, a full absence of color, light, sound, and mass—a moving absence erupts from Nordeen's mouth just as the fire spirit turns both heads of the snakes into paste and throws their bodies at him. One of the tails flicks and breaks the steps above me, making an exit impossible. The darkness grabs the fire spirit. The little girl I passed earlier appears, manifests more accurately from the shadows and grabs Nordeen. He thrashes—burned by her touch—but she has the presence of mind to look and speak to me, even if it is with the fire spirit's voice.

"Go, Healer! Be worthy of our sacrifice." I remember the girl now. On a beach in Somalia, Mico and his crew found this girl and played music to form a treaty between this girl and that spirit. I never caught her name. I never will.

The gray light turns to shadows as I look overhead. From the cliff above the church, I see a boulder, larger than all the others that have fallen, moving toward the overhanging cliff. I move quick. I beef up my legs and leap to the remains of the first floor. In midair Nordeen grabs for my calves, but the fire spirit and the little girl hold him down for a second more. The heat from the creature singes my leg and my back but I ignore the pain; the boulder is falling. No room for mistakes. I spring off the pew to meet the boulder in midair, then push off of it to get high above the ruined church, to the cliff above where A.C. and I first stood. I feel like a billy goat. I ignore the sounds below me. I don't believe a mere boulder could kill Nordeen, if that was even him. But the girl who stepped in front of the bullet for me?

I land in front of an enraged and out-of-breath Samantha; behind me, the cliff that overlooks the mountain church. Her muscles tell me she pushed that boulder herself. I'm too weak to fight her. Luckily I don't have to.

"Die. You've already lost," she hisses.

"Then come kill me." I open my arms wide.

"Gladly." She shoves my chest, sending me backward over the cliff. That's fine. I take her with me, grabbing her arms at the last second.

"A.C!" I shout at the top of my lungs. He catches us with his winds, though she fights it. With a log filled with angry bees in one hand, he smears her face with the honey. Samantha fights him every step of the way. And of course, the shouting:

" ራስህን አምላከህ እግዚአብሔር ሳማንታ በረከቶች ማረጋገጫ . ይህ ቅዱስ ግር ጋር ለመመገብ የእርስዎን ማዕከል, ያግኙ , ዘላለም የተቀደሰ ብቻ ጣፋጭ ቃል ይናገሩ.

I fall, back to earth, with no hope of saving myself. I keep my eyes peeled on A.C. and Samantha but something flutters in my vision, and in a second they are gone and I have landed, hard.

Gamo Highlands, Ethiopia
Taggert

If it were rock that had broken my fall, I'm not sure I could've healed myself. But this is soft grass, pliable land. We're on farming land. And surprise, A.C. is cursing. We're in a small valley covered in brown grasses well trodden by horses and herds of goats.

"Where's the butter maidens?! There's supposed to be girls with butter in their hair setting up to get married. There's supposed to be a bunch of old men chanting, and guys dressed up to find wives!" A.C. shouts, stomping his feet.

"There's a church right there," I tell him, getting to my feet slowly. The western style protestant house of worship sits on the eastern ridge of a small incline.

"Fuck that church! It's sacrilegious. There's not supposed to be anything piercing this land." He turns to me, upset. "Don't you get it? This land has been sacred since Abraham was Abram. Fifty thousand people on the planet and these lands were holy. That grove of trees right there? There's supposed to be a fire down there. We anoint Samantha's head with ash from that sacred grove and sacred fire, and the spell is done! Do you smell any fire? You see any people?"

197

"Yup," I tell him and look at the horizon. A hundred men, all on horseback, all with rifles, look down on us from the same area as the small church.

"I don't know what to do," he tells me. "You're as tired as me, I can tell. I mean we can take them on but . . ."

"Can you hold them back?" Bad timing in asking as they start descending the hill into our little valley as soon as I speak.

"For how long?" he asks, already pulling his sword.

"As long as you can." To help him out I hit all the riders with a vicious case of diarrhea. It's gross and a distraction, but it'll help. I increase my lung capacity and funnel a nice echo chamber in my throat. My breathing sounds like I'm humming through a megaphone.

"Samantha! You win! I'm done! Come, claim your prize." To prove I'm serious I pull out the entropy blade and drop it at my feet. I make sure to keep it closed after what the Wind Boy said about piercing the land. From the sacred grove, Samantha walks triumphantly. I could speed this up, walk to her, but I don't want to spook her. A.C. does his best, shooting columns of wind at horses and dodging bullets while protecting himself from a hundred shitty riders. They've got numbers on their side; he's got experience. But both are tired and prone to mistakes.

"What strategy do you think will save your life now, poor healer?" This is not my lover's voice. This is what her hate sounds like. Samantha has never had enough hate on her face to make those types of grooves in her forehead. She stands shorter than me but looks down on me with a rage, a fight I've never seen.

"The wind spirit hasn't given up." I gesture over him and then slip my jacket off. "Once he told me about the sacred fire, that was it for me. If we can't rescue you, what hope do we have fighting for the rest of the world?"

"And what of your precious girls, Taggert? Will you recruit them to the Alter's cause as well?"

"I'm not here to be recruited, love," I tell her. "I'm here for you to end me." Her eyes query but her mouth smiles. That questioning is enough for me to stall my original plan.

"So this is sacrifice? For what boon?"

"This is a mercy killing. You guys win, and I don't want to see how this whole thing turns out. So take me out. But just do me the favor, let it be by your hand."

"You think I won't!"

"I know you will. That's why I'm asking. Getting taken out by a lover is always better than going by the hands of your enemy . . ."

". . . and suppose the person is both?"

"Don't matter. The Samantha I knew loved me. She would have died for me. Shit, she did. Makes a certain amount of sense that you'd take me out the game. No tricks, Samantha, just do it quick. And no one else. Not the Alters, not your humans, just you."

I'm barely done speaking when she grabs my throat with the strength of fifty men. The grab alone is enough to almost break my windpipe, but the squeeze. I'm on my knees in a second. It's not just the lack of oxygen, it's the pain of the crushed larynx . . . Still, I don't make a move to defend myself other than to keep looking in her eyes. The world is going quiet and gray, but somewhere I can hear A.C. screaming my name.

She adjusts her grip allowing me to gasp for one second, but it's only to get a firmer grip on my entire neck, flattening her palm on my Adam's apple and then pushing upward. But in that shift, I see it again, the questioning in her eyes. It could be a trick, I realize as my arm starts shaking, involuntarily clutching for the entropy blade, the heart of my original plan. But the wavering of her eyes has infected her brow, and the top half of her face looks like it's in absolute pain choking me while the bottom half is in near pornographic excitement. Not that my body cares. I feel something deep stirring.

It hasn't been this pronounced since the head of the Alters, Kothar, had me in a similar position. I was dead, or as close to it as I get, when the spirit, the Liminal thing inside of me, rose up and said no. Only it didn't speak, it burned. It scorched its will to live in my spirit and my actions. It's burning again, and I hear A.C. in my head talking about sacred fire. This is the only holy fire I know. I imagine that Liminal fire Samantha and I share catching at my throat and let it spread. I can't see it, only feel it. When she tries to pull away I pull her closer to me, grabbing her wrist with my free hand.

"Let go!" her mouth says but another part of her moves closer to the fire. Her Liminal self burns brighter now, a forgotten flame finally fed by a forest fire. It's exhausting, but it's the only solid progress I've seen, so I don't dare quit. I give her my everything, healing all those wounds I can't see, can't feel, only sense. I fill her with every ounce of my Liminal energy and invite her Liminal spirit into me. We consume each other, leaving only spiritual coal where our souls used to be. When I finally collapse, the ground has never felt so inviting.

A.C. stands over me. He's sweating and as undone as I've ever seen him. But he's alive and smiling.

"What did I do?" I say, not bothering to stand up.

"A smaller version of Mico's trick with the light from his soul. Only he opened up a keyhole, you threw open your soul wide, and allowed it to meet its kin in Samantha."

"Is she . . . ?" I ask, rolling to my side trying to slowly repair my broken larynx.

"She's back," he says, pointing to Sam tending the wounds of the riders who'd come to aid her out of instinct.

"That was dangerous what you did," she tells me when I muster enough strength to enter the remains of A.C's fray. It's the chastising in the voice that I love.

"No more dangerous than you sending messages to me across the dimensional ditch to save us from the Alters." She bristles at their name.

"I have had quite enough of those creatures. We all have." Sam sinks sharp-nailed fingers deep into the ground, and I instantly know what sacred ground means. Whatever language A.C. was speaking to cleanse her soul sounds as clear as English compared to what she speaks now. The whole earth quakes and anyone standing on the ground from here to all of Ethiopia—and beyond even, I can feel people in Djibouti, Eritrea, Somalia shake and fall. The land loves them all, loves them so much that it cleans them of the Decimation, of all desires for self-harm. A total psychic enema. The shaking of the land is the shaking of the people's souls.

"The horn of Africa is free from the Decimation," Sam tells us both before she passes out.

Heart of the Whirlwind
Prentis

"Found one!" tell Mico after I grab the glow in the dark thumb drive from the bottom of the red trunk that smells like the hide of an animal I've never met. It's the only activity I'm gonna attempt until the sun decides to chill out and give us some relief.

"I swear there will be a half an hour dedicated to my love for you in this set," Mico tells me, swiping it from my hand. There's no power generator in the tent, but he's plugging the flash drives into some gearhead playback machine. Like something from *Star Trek* but all he does with it is plug the random USB flash drives and SD cards we find in the doss he left behind the last time he was here. Lot nicer than I am, these desert folk. Would've thrown his kit out ages ago. Mico's contraption has a headphone jack in it, so he's been walking around listening to all songs on it, all the while talking to me.

"No need for secrets. What is it?"

"Syrian Orthodox church hymns," he says on beat.

"You are such a hippy," tell him. Send two mice behind the trunk, one with an image of a USB stick, the other with an SD card "And a slob. Stuff was so important, yeah? Why not take better care of it?"

"It wasn't important," Mico says, then sits down. "I mean it was, but it wasn't rare. Not like it is."

"Not end of the world important," say sitting to listen to him.

"Right. When I got here, I was just a DJ . . ." He slides off one headphone.

"Munji said you were already dealing hash with him and Fatty then," correct him.

"That was just my job. My life was the music, following the sound . . ." Mico says.

"What sound?" Brown spotted mouse comes out of a black sack in the corner of the trunk with three flash drives I never would have found. Mico didn't answer, just sat silent and waits for me to get it.

"It's like A.C. I keep forgetting he's there, but if I pay attention to him he's no different than anyone else. It's the same thing with this sound. There is the wind, the roll of the sand, the minor creaks and strains of the tents, the footsteps of the people outside the tent, the shuffle of my own clothing, the rustling of the mice, and beneath all of that, there is the song that the Bint al-nas are always singing. When they aren't talking to each other, they're humming it, breathing it. There are no lyrics in the traditional sense, because whatever you say fits into their tempo, their rhythm perfectly. To say it's unconscious is giving too much credit to the conscious; this shit is primal. It lulls then pops and fades into obscure meanderings, then comes up like a EDM tune when kids sing it, but nothing could be as soothing as one of the water men asking if you'd like some water, all on beat, all without trying."

"Feel like a sinner speaking English," tell him.

"Imagine living here?" He laughs back as I throw him the drives the brown mouse found. "It was misery and ecstasy."

"Ya sappy git!" tell him. "Could have stayed here, spoke the only language it takes a second to learn, and lived the life of strong women, easy songs, and mystical journeys. Shite, prepared for it, didn't ya? That's why ya packed all your old drives and gear away, yeah? What stopped ya?"

"The Manna." Fair longing in his voice for the first time when he says it.

"The motherfucking Manna," Before I'm done a old head peeks her head into the tent and wags her short spear at me from a distance. Throw my hands up in surrender and bow in deference at the same time. It's enough for her and she departs. "Fucking hear everything?"

"Secret to a good choir is the ability to hear each other." Mico nods as he plugs in one of the drives. "Nina Simone. Man, talk about a good ear. She could hear what a song wanted to be and make it her own. After she covered a track, it was nobody else's. I heard her version of 'Strange Fruit' before I heard Billie Holiday's. As far as I was concerned, Billie had no business singing that song."

The blank look on my face lets him know I've heard neither, so he passes his contraption my way. I hear a woman, obviously a black woman, sing about rags and old iron. Like a good tune, usually stuff to dance to, but I like music in general. This thing almost had me broken, yeah? Not just the singer, the miserable lyrics, or the general tapestry of the music, was how naturally that song fit into the rhythm of this place, of the song that the Bint al-nas sing all the time, with their lives.

"This lady been here?" I ask.

"Nina Simone? No! But she's heard this song. All the good ones, the musicians whose talent we can't deny. No matter the country, the time, the genre of music, hell, even the dimension, they've heard this song. It's powerful."

"Over here about to bawl like a baby."

"Not just emotionally powerful, Prentis. I used the disturbance in this song to track you when . . ."

"Wouldn't say that name around here unless you want a spear waved at you." Joke, but he knows how I feel about Nordeen. So he comes down to sit next to me on the floor.

"I could hear the disruption in this song that our enemies were making throughout time . . ."

"How does a song travel through time?"

"A song is just a relationship of sounds. The meaning is made by human minds. Human minds are just sets of relational information. Just as minds travel, so too can music. "Want to give him shit but I've seen too much to pretend I'm too dumb to get it now. Especially after my talk with the Manna."

"So you heard the disruption in the tune and you threw Taggert and Tam back in time to come fetch me?" I ask, letting the mice play on my lap.

"That was the plan. I thought I was so smart but I ended up burning myself and Tamara out on the first leg of the trip." The shame was still weighing on him.

"But these Bint al-nas, they do stuff like that all the time. Just sent Tag to Eel Pie Island, didn't they? And there's no Liminal powerhouses like those two to help out. Plus they sending people, yurts, goats, and all kinds of stuff through time. So how you fuck it up with just you three?"

"The manna told me not to, and I did it anyway." Could've swore he said Momma for a second. "Plus it's not about power, it's about skill and harmony. Relationship. You know how hard it is for those two to trust anyone that isn't you. So imagine having to sing together."

"Man, your atoms should be scattered across the universe." I laugh. Finally, he does too.

"I couldn't . . ." He starts rolling on the floor. "I swear I couldn't talk for like fifteen hours. Those two are so damn stubborn!"

"Getting them to take one step off of where they think they should go is mission impossible. You got them to go back in time, mate. Deserve a medal, ya do!" I stand up and look at the other two flash drives. Plug one in and I'm greeted with familiar tunes.

"Hey, this is Dizzie Rascal?" Mico turns his head from the ground and listens to the sound from my headphones.

"Yup, early demo. A friend got it for me."

"This is before him and Wiley fell out, right?"

"This was before it all." Mico says it and it's like he's there. "No stupid beefs, no awards. Just rapid-fire lyricists over old-school drum and bass licks. He spit twelve bars over one of my tracks and I felt anointed in this musical spirit."

"All of this is spiritual to you, ennit?" I ask him. "This music, it's your religion. You threw these drives into a trunk because they were all just arrows pointing to this spot you got to, yeah?"

"When you stop playing the dumb street kid, you're pretty insightful." He stands and swipes his gear back.

"Still can't understand why you took off from your personal Shangri-la . . . The Manna points you here, then tells you to leave and wipes your memory of it. For what?"

"Take a step back," he tells me, and I do. "Not literally, girl. Think about it in a different way. Remember, the Manna is older than the most ancient redwood. It took two hundred thousand years for human life to get to this point on this planet. And we barely have three thousand years of consistently recorded history throughout the entire species. The Manna is a singular entity that has existed for at least a hundred thousand years and has access to what can only be called memories of a million years before. There's not a step we can take it hasn't predicted and accounted for."

"So the fuck what?" I ask. "No offense, but it's old as shit, I get it. I don't get what that has to do . . ."

"It knew the Alters were coming. It fought them before. It knew you'd be taken . . ."

"What?" I go reptile cold.

"What's the other option?" he asks, not putting the headphones on. "That the Alters snuck past its alertness and punched a hole in time and kidnapped an unaligned Liminal? No, it had to know."

"And it stopped you from trying to save me . . ." My head's swimming.

"You're thinking too small . . ." Mico says it slowly.

"Says someone who doesn't have nightmares of what those fucks did to me! Made me fight my family! Made me pervert the animals! And the Manna not only allowed it to happen to me, it didn't want you to stop it?"

"Listen." He starts to hum the tune, to sing the song that the Bint al-nas live in. Trying to calm me down at first, but I see his focus as the heat of the day begins to gather above his eyebrows. His singing voice is different than his speaking voice, more assured and steady. It can do things, like sing two tones at the same time, and more. He can articulate different words at the same time, with two different voices from his throat. He harmonizes with himself. I'm listening as he does it, sing and chant in unison, but different words. They fit in perfectly with the Bint al-nas song that tolerates no disruption. Word he chants is mine. He chants Prentis.

"It's all the same to the Manna, kid," tells me in the singing language. "Our pleasure, our pain, it doesn't matter. We've got a job to do. We're all part of this universal song. You asked me about leaving? The Manna told me to leave paradise, so I left. I didn't understand why. It hurt like hell. And remembering being here hasn't been made any easier, but guess what's more important than my happiness?"

"The end goal of a conscious mushroom that's older than god's grandma?"

"Exactly." Still fuming a bit but then I get it. "Wait. This music. This universal music, this is what the Alters have cut the gray world off from?"

"Yes," he says slowly.

"But the songs on the USBs and whatnot, this music, it's not from the gray world. So these tunes they've got that . . . the relationship to this Bint al-nas beat or whatever. They've got the rainbow in them, don't they?"

"Indeed they do." Mico nods.

"So just by playing this music, in the gray world, you change the color balance, make it a bit brighter, yeah?" And then I get it for real. "Fuck to shit, the Manna had this planned out back when you first got here, didn't it?"

"Possibly. I've learned not to be too confident of anything when dealing with it. But it does always seem to have a back door, a way when no way seems possible," he tells me, getting up on the bed to spread the collected drives out.

"We could possibly save the world with a tight DJ set from Jah Puba?" Realizing and asking at the same time.

"It is possible." He smiles at me.

"I love this job!" I shout.

"It's not a job." The singer's hands are soft as he takes mine. "It's a life. A calling. If you serve the Manna truly, there's no room for anything else. You have to be willing to sacrifice everything for it, your sanity, your loves, even your family."

"Not gonna happen," tell him easy as pie, taking my hands from him. "That's your bag. Get it. Fatty is your lodestone to magical singing land where you drop off rainbow music for the dark dimensional whatever. But you, man, you're like Nina Simone. She's great but you can tell she's a diva. She never sang with other folks, right? That song you hear? I feel it. Only it's not just human voices, it's snakes and fish, birds and wolves. I know slug mating scents and elephant death moans. Mistaken the soloists for the choir, you have. You hear humans, I hear all animal life on this planet. And you know what binds us all? It's not sacrifice and it's not hurt. It's the love. I didn't always know that. Know who taught me?"

"Taggert." He nods.

"Exactly. Taught me what love was, he did. Yeah, it might require some pain, but that's not what it's built on. It's built on love. It'll make all that pain worth it. Give you the strength to fight the devil when you need it, make a loyal servant desert his god when necessary, even. So I'll fight the fight every step of the way, mate. I'll take on the cool allies and I'll square off against the bad men them. But only way you're dragging me from my fam is if I'm no longer breathing."

"Is it possible for you two not to make a mess of everything you touch?" Fatty asks, stepping into the tent. Mico breaks eye contact with me first and does his habitual stare/not stare, at her.

"Oh, relax, we were just finding the magical bullets to save Oz from the dark tower of the emperor, or some such," tell her, displaying the drives on the bed.

"When this is over, if we are still alive, you must read a book," she tells me as she hands me a deep red bandanna. "For your hair. Get ready, it's time to go."

Outside, families are singing goodbye to each other as Fatty leads us through the pathway of tents and yurts. Children, mostly boys, sing blessings and luck to us as they pat our legs. It's a tender gesture. Even if they aren't crying they touch their cheeks where tears would be and then rub them on our pants legs. "Keep some of us with you" is the translation.

Just past the tents, huts, and leather cabins, an assemblage of badass women makes me feel ashamed that I've never worked out a day in my life. All of them hold their short spears casually, the way Fatty lets her short rifles rest by her thighs. They tie their hair back, check backpacks, and work elements of the song I only heard in the heart of a windstorm. Camel-hearted woman stomps up to Mico and almost scuffs him as she pulls him to the group.

"You sing what I tell you to sing and nothing else, you hear me?" hear her shout to him. No soloist opportunities. To my right, Munji and Fatima hold each other's faces, crying. Mico is an idiot. Doesn't know what true power is. It's all about family.

"I give you this, girl." From behind me, Bingy offers his machete, hilt first, resting the blade against his bicep.

"You staying behind as well?" Put my hair up.

"I am no warrior by heart. I tend a garden, zene? Plus, da girl Tamara tell me a plan that work better if I man a stay ere." Take the machete before he gets the sense I don't want it.

"Man, I trust you to have my back. I don't know these chicks." Hug him hard. He's a Rasta, not used to girls embracing him. He's from the gray world, not comfortable next to the brightness of my world. But God bless Bingy, he doesn't squirm. Hugs me back and lets me break the hold.

"I know five last night. Three dis morning. Strong women." He smiles at me.

"Stronger man," I tell him. "The plan doesn't work without Bingy man. Stay ready," tell him as I walk toward the circle of women.

"Always, rainbow warrior. Always."

Women are all different ages, some as young as twelve, some as old as seventy. Two hundred total. Only women are born in this village but that's about all they have in common. Some are plump, some bone skinny; still, they're all fit. They are Asian looking, deep dark black African looking, Middle Eastern looking, South American looking. They smile and play with each other, almost all turning their backs on Mico, juvenile like. When Fatima comes to my side, she's just about done with her tears.

"He'll be fine," tell her about Munji.

"If anything happens to him while I'm gone, I will burn this whole place down using the flaming parts of Mico's rotting corpse." Fatty spits.

"Wouldn't go around announcing that, home girl," I say. It's hard to find a way to secure the machete without cutting myself.

"So how does this go?" Fatty demands of Othica. "I mean, I don't sing."

"Yes you do," The 6'4 woman says in her deep voice. "All parts of you sing. You breathe, you sing. You swallow, you sing. You move, you sing. You sing now. You hear it?"

"No." Othica looks like she's about to swing on her niece, so I step in the middle.

"Close your eyes," I tell Fatty. "Trust me enough to do that. Close your eyes. Ok, now breathe. Five deep breaths, in through your nose, out through your mouth." Wait until she does it. "Okay, that's a five count for you. Just listen to what happens in the next cycle, the next five counts of breathing. Just listen for repetition in anything, inside or out, zene?"

Fatty gets it after the third breath but has enough sense to listen for the next two breaths before opening her eyes. Othica sees the same, then sees something in me. She scuffs Mico over to me and Fatima.

"You will listen to the animal girl. You will match her. She will listen to me. Everyone will listen to me and match me. Sing as I sing. Animal girl, you are singing with everything, not just air. There will be times when it will feel like you cannot breathe, but you don't need to breathe to sing. This you understand, yes?"

"Wait, what now?" Fatty protests.

"I got it," I tell them both.

It starts with Othica's heart, it's a loud beat. More than audible. Can feel it. It's got an immediate drum quality. My body, like a baby matching its heartbeat with its mother's. Mine just goes to hers. Starts to hum in her belly. Doing something in her organs, almost like Taggert does, that's causing the hum. Don't think I can do it until hear the rest of the women humming alongside. Say what she will about Mico, he sings well. Me and Fatima are the last ones to match the sound, but once we start, it's easier to maintain.

When a group of seven women start hitting high clicking noises, I think it's breaking down before we even get officially started, like geese getting caught in a jet engine, but I realize that they're just a different part of the chorus. Othica doesn't match them, but as they work I can hear their effect; raising the level of our hum. Soon, two more subsections start alternating harmonies. Sounds like they're using instruments, but it's just their voices . . . and the wind. It's picking up, keeping pace with the song, but it's not a song yet, it's just a rhythm. Jesus, haven't even started the singing yet.

What do you call it when every voice is a chorus? That congregation of voices tuning? No one is trying to sound like anyone else, all the voices are just trying to find their places. And it's not regimented like. There is no one singer better than the others, they ebb and flow in and out of four lead vocal positions, no words, still just humming, maybe some do a master mumble—like that scatting things rappers do. But none use their language, so none of it makes sense. But I hear another language in it. A deeper one.

Want to smack Mico in the head when he gets carried away and tries to use volume and vibrato to take one of the lead vocal positions, but my body tone changes sharply, and it's enough to silence him. Through their song, the Bint al-nas all laugh. It's infectious. Couldn't stop humming with them and the wind and my body even if I wanted to. But the joy of the laughter reminds me to relax into what we're doing, like Taggert always tells me: Tension is the cancer of preparation. Panic, a prayer to chaos. So I let go of the tension of a new situation, strange magics, and distant family and try to enjoy the song.

They were all waiting for me. Soon as I let my shoulders go what sounds like tambourines all start shaking and rattling as everyone's voice gets louder and merges with the roaring wind. Something hits my eyelid and that's the only way I know my eyes are closed. On instinct, I open them. There is no town to be seen, no desert, no ground even, only a whirlwind of sand encircling us all. I'm about to look up when Othica's voice begins singing words.

"I could have been one of the most notorious . . ." Mico and I are stunned; we falter for a second but Fatima comes in on the second line for us without missing a beat. Want to ask how she knows that song, but it's not the time. And it doesn't matter. Soon, from one of the other groups, I hear "Darling Nikki" by Prince coming from another section of our troupe. An old Beastie Boys verse gets thrown in beside something a Bedouin girl played nine centuries ago if the collective memory of this amalgamation is to be believed. It's crazy. We are a network, we're joined, like a pod of dolphins, a wolf pack, or a herd of elephants. Been linked to animals this way, but never people. The sounds hold the memories, which hold the songs, which hold the ability to move.

Othica moans something hard, and even through my closed eyes I see thick white smoke come from her mouth. It's the same smoke that came from Mico back in Jamaica. The Manna. Soon others are doing the same, sign/coughing up this same white smoke. Permeates our circle, linking us biologically. Feel the pull of those connected by the Manna to go a certain way. Open my mouth, ready to take the Manna and the rest of the journey, but Mico somehow stops it. Open my eyes to look at him. His eyes are still closed but he's able to whisper at me, "Not yet."

The Manna doesn't take me, but it lets me ride. It doesn't take Fatima either, but it encircles her tighter than it does me. There's no chance for jealousy, and no need. The song is not one song, it's all songs, all good ones anyway. Hearing them all at the same time, and it's not a cacophony. It's a coordinated pitch-perfect medley, like when DJs do those mash-ups that fit together songs you never thought should be together but then you realize they're perfect in unison. Only those are only songs in a strict 4/4 mechanical rhythm, these are bodies . . . and now memories. Fit together, we are a system.

Open what's left of my eyes, which is really more like opening my perception, and feel the union descending, controlled falling in the same way we were all lifted up to the sky and spread across it like a thick paste. This is a coalescing, a controlled condensation, like cooling caramel, or the pell mell birth of a litter of kittens. We are the wind, moving through time and space pushed on by the Manna, spread out by the Manna, intangible, held together by mist, monotony, and the memory of a god. The focus of the Manna descends on an island, the middle of three. The old god knows it as Meno, but all I feel, all I see are the flames on the east side of it.

Sand under my feet, voices in my ears, breath in my lungs, and I know we've landed. Even I'm singing and I don't remember starting or stopping. But opening my eyes, I see we're no longer in whatever bliss land we were just in. Fatty's already got her rifle cocked, but she's not advancing. I look over my shoulder, where she's looking, and see why.

"Are those angels?" ask realizing how useless, flaccid, and pale language and my voice is.

"Yes," Mico says, still the song in his voice. It fights the sound of fire fighting against wood and fist in the near distance. He stands where the surf meets the shore, but he's invigorated. He needed that trip. His eyes shine against the early afternoon sun. "And they're attacking our friends."

"Then we fight angels," Othica says in her language. Her sisters don't hesitate. They walk alongside her into the fray. It takes me a second to realize I'm marching alongside them, but as the flames get hotter and birdlike human forms surrounded by fiery wings continue to divebomb toward the yacht docked not sixty meters from us, I hear the warrior woman sing again, and I know I have to be a part of it.

Gamo Highlands, Ethiopia
Taggert

"I'm surprised you're awake." Samantha can always tell when I wake. The Gamo highlanders that rode to Sam's defense were the same ones who led us to the civil administration building, which was already in the process of being taken over by the people. Apparently, Ethiopians are revolting all over. It's a small two-story building made of cement and the cheapest local materials money could buy. I passed out on the second floor supported by a small cot in some civil servant's office to the sounds of gunfire near and far.

"I'm surprised you're conscious," I say, moving slow. I'm more sore than I've ever been and my body is not making its usual efforts to heal itself. I'm taxed.

"I've been unconscious for far too long." There's no light in the room, the window being boarded up and the power to the building apparently a distant memory even before the shooting started. All I see is Sam's silhouette as light rushes around her thin frame from the morning sun in the hallway. She's holding a tray of what smells like a milky porridge. "I've brought food."

"I wish you hadn't," I tell her, sitting up fully. As usual, she ignores me and comes to the center of the room. Over her shoulder she has a gray-and-orange mat that she throws to the ground. I try to move to spread it out, but my whole body tells me to slow down, so she has it spread with her feet before I can even get over to the small feast she puts in front of me.

"Here is bula. Your body will appreciate it. Over here is some kinche made with goat milk. They found some bread and honey as well. I boiled a few eggs. I can make you some coffee . . ."

"Stop it," I say, almost shaking. "Please. You're talking to me like we're okay. Like I didn't . . ." It hurts to say the words but then I realize that's exactly why I have to say them. "I failed you."

"Yes, you did," she says calmly, still preparing a small bowl of porridge for me. "Eat now, so that I may chastise you later." I hadn't noticed the dark red pants tied with a cord she wore when she walked in, but as she stood quickly I heard the cloth straighten.

In dark silence, I eat until my body begins to slowly repair the damage the healing spell has done.

"Gamo means lion, did you know that?" Samantha says, sitting on a small cushioned stool in the middle of a foyer as she roasts fresh coffee beans over a Coleman outdoor stove.

"No," I confess, standing shakily, not knowing if or where to sit as I leave my room. "Where's A.C.?"

"Helping the Highlanders win another attack against the agents of the Alters. They are warriors high on their liberation. They feel no fatigue. And the wind does not need to sleep," she says, casually sifting the green beans with a hooked knife. "I am Halaka here, so they heeded my advice about working with him."

"Halaka?"

"An advisor. It's an annual position, at least it was in our place. A trusted elder of sorts. Do you plan on standing until you fall?"

There's something right about being on my knees in front of Samantha. Plus the morning is cold, so I get as close to her and the oven as possible without getting in the way of her vigorous sifting of the beans. When she doesn't speak for a while, I try.

"The Manna told us that you were key to ending the Alters' reign. I don't suppose that was all we needed to do?"

"If the world were the Horn of Africa, then yes." She almost smiles. "My people are free." She emphasizes the "my." "No doubt, in time, we could take back all of Africa. Even the Alter strongholds of Madagascar, Zanzibar, and the Canary Islands, no doubt thanks to Mico's pet Alter's influence over islands. But time is fleeting, no? And since when has the world cared for the psyche of Africa?"

215

"But you're free of their control, that counts for something, no?"

Sam risks her newly browned coffee beans going black by taking the time to look me in the eyes.

"That, to me, is everything." She enunciates every word.

"I should have come for you sooner," I tell her.

"Why didn't you?" Sam asks.

"I was afraid to tip our hand. It's only a matter of time before the Alters lead a frontal attack here, now." It's a truth I figure out as I say it.

"To the east, A.C. has already repelled two Terror Tomas. Do you have a plan?" She nods that beautiful head of hers, her hair rebraided. It's not as tight as it was when she was under the Alter's sway.

"Yes. I don't know if it will work," I admit.

"Do you ever?" Sam almost laughs.

"You're mad," I say.

"And conscious enough to be so, in part thanks to you." She finds a way to flip all the beans in her makeshift pan while still holding the coffee knife in her hands. It's a casual, almost unconscious movement. Even without my Liminal sight, I imagine I'd see the coordination and strength it takes for her to manipulate fire, knife, and the unruly weight of hundreds of coffee beans.

"How do you feel?" she asks me as I lie back on the cold cement floor.

"Like southern fried shit." My body warms itself instinctively. Good. My power might be coming back.

"Still?" she asks, genuinely confused. I take the moment to check in with my body. Something has shifted. The capillaries around my eyes are opening. My oxygen transfer rate is ramping up, my lungs are working better. Ruptured muscles in my back and around my ribs from where that damn hippo tried to molest me are knitting together.

"What was in that food?" I ask, sitting up.

"Food, you suspicious old man," she tells me. Sam rests the coffee tray down on the Coleman quickly and pulls her own plate of food, some stewed meat and injera. "Here, eat."

She shoves the spicy stew, thick with ginger and turmeric, into my mouth with her fingers. It's a rough intimacy, but it can't be faked. She won't take her fingers out until I suck them clear of food. In another second she's back to roasting the beans, now a dark brown.

"Have you tasted anything as good in this world?" she asks casually.

"The rainbow!" I say, finally getting it. "You've brought the color, the spice back into the world!"

"It was never here." She smiles at my stupidity, as usual. "I've introduced it. This is not our world, remember? Left to its own devices, the gray shift will reverse in this world. I bring a new light to Africa, one the Alters fear. It is as you say, now that the Alters have lost me and Yasmine . . ."

"That wasn't Yasmine," I start as she turns off the burner.

"That wasn't your Yasmine, Taggert," she says calmly, but the tension is clear. "She never was. But strange as it sounds, she had worth aside from what you could see."

"I didn't mean it like that . . ." I say

"Then what did you mean? Why was it okay to kill her but not me?" Samantha's heat matching the heat from the beans.

"There was nothing to liberate! Tam looked in her head. Whatever the Alters did to her was deeply rooted. There was nothing of my . . ." I try to say.

"Exactly!" she shouts and walks down the hall and disappears into another office. I stand, in part because I'm afraid she's going to come back with a rifle to blow my head off.

"It always goes back to what is yours, what you can control, what you know . . ." I relax slightly when I see it's only a small handheld coffee grinder in her hands. Only slightly.

. "Can I just say that I wasn't the one who took her out?" I offer.

"You've never flinched from your responsibilities before, Taggert. Don't start now. Those girls don't wipe themselves without permission from you." She squats, her ass near touching the ground as she pours a quarter of the coffee beans into the grinder.

"I'm fine to be the asshole for not coming for you sooner. But Yasmine, this Yasmine, was never part of the plan. She was too powerful. And just so we're clear, your god never made any mention of her either."

"Oh, you and the Manna had a conversation?" Sam says incredulously. I wait until the noise of her cranking the beans dies down before I try to speak.

"We found the Bint al-nas," I tell her. Apparently, A.C. had rushed off without briefing her. "They are with us. The Manna hasn't given my plan what passes for its blessing . . ."

"Do you have . . ." She stares intently at me, hungry.

"No, I didn't bring any of it with me. I didn't think it would be safe." Again, she hits me with silence as she puts a steel kettle on the Coleman stove. "Is it really Yasmine that has you upset?"

"I see worlds, Taggert," she tells me. "To travel, to take others to other worlds, one must be able to see those worlds. I look at people and see all they have been, all they could be, all that they are. It was that vision that allowed the Alters to trap me. Some visions, once seen, can freeze the sensitive in place. They trapped my soul like a bug in amber by showing me this world and all of its repressive gray. I couldn't escape its pull. Once locked in, all I could do was make the best of my situation. Yasmine, for all of her . . . issues, was my confidant, my friend in this world."

"I'm sorry," I say.

"You can't be. You didn't know her. She wasn't your ex-lover, the mother of your child. She was a woman orphaned as a child and born into a world of rape, murder, and struggle. And she survived. Not only that, she thrived. When the demons of her world proclaimed themselves gods and no one protested, she was one of the first to offer herself as a general leading the damned into the apocalypse." She speaks in something of a whisper but doesn't bother looking at me.

"And I'm supposed to like that?" I ask.

"Idiot, I don't care if you like it. But you will respect her." Pouring high in the air, Sam lets scalding hot water fall perfectly into her small octagon of a coffee grinder. Instantly, the smell of the crushed beans perfumes the air. "You will respect this dark gray world as part of existence, because even though it is not 'yours,' it is not as how you want it to be, it still matters. It is still home to human beings who matter."

"Yes, ma'am," I tell her as I follow her and the coffee into the office she grabbed the grinder from. It's a larger, more stately office than the one I slept in. She has a pallet, similar to the one I slept on, in here. A large gray-and-blue woven mat rests on a round table with three small hard-fired ceramic cups in front of standard third world governmental steel chairs. In the early days, right after Nordeen, it was always a comfort to wake up and find her next to me, whispering in my ear, "Everything is fine. Your girls are safe."

"Do not attempt to mock me, Taggert," she tells me, taking a seat.

"And risk the entire Horn of Africa descending on me? Even I'm not that stupid." I take a seat by the door. "Listen, I get what you're saying. The Manna made a similar point using a different line. I'm just wondering, and it's a true question, if the fire for this argument isn't based on any of my other failings."

Gracefully, Sam sits and pours two perfect cups of coffee with more skill than any Japanese tea ceremony master. Through it all, she finds a way to laugh at me while not looking in my direction. It's the face she gets when she's trying to find the words.

"You are imperfect, Taggert, as are we all. If we are lucky, the imperfections of our loved ones do not impact us. I was not lucky in this instance. But you came for me and risked everything to free me. Does that make everything okay? No. But I understand the decision you made and the choices we will both have to continue to make if this world is to be clear of the Alters. And now, more than perhaps anyone else, I understand why that is so important. They must be destroyed. If we have to lose each other to save the world, I'm okay with that trade."

"I'm not." I sip the coffee. It tastes more like coffee bean tea than the dark stank mirk I grew up with. It's perfect. More than perfect, it wakes up deep parts of me that I didn't know were sleeping. My healing responds in kind and instantly my aches and pains are gone.

"Your actions say otherwise. Given the same options, I might well have done the same thing. How you feel for your daughters, I feel for this land." I don't have that much caring in my body. But I can't tell her that. Not now.

"So we're done? You and I?" I'm surprised how much it hurts to even approach the idea. All Samantha can do is giggle into her coffee.

"I'd say yes, but I still need a date for prom." I feel like an idiot again. "You'd smack Prentis if she focused on heart games when so much was on the line. Hold yourself to the same standard, healer. If this planet survives, if we survive your vague outlines of a plan, and all our parts are still in place, then we can speak of romance. For now, give me details on how we save the world."

"You first," I tell her. Snapping back into business mode: "You've got the best intel on the Alters, as you've been closest to them."

"No," she says, pouring us each another cup of coffee. "They used your brother as an intermediary. They were afraid of my vision. They'd never say, but I think they were scared of me knowing too much about them."

I wait for a minute, taking in the feel of the early morning sun, the smell of gunfire and animal blood some five miles away, the clarity of the moment before I muddy the waters with his name. "Nordeen."

"Fuck." It sounds queer coming from her lips. "He's in play?"

"Is he? I saw him, thought I saw him, when we were bouncing all around Ethiopia to rescue you."

"It wasn't him," she tells me, relaxing back into her chair.

"How do you know?"

"If Nordeen saw you, you'd be dead." Her confidence is more disconcerting than the sentiment. "His hate for you, his sense of betrayal . . . Not only are you the prodigal son that never returned but your girl Prentis also tore him limb from limb with her animals. Don't imagine your reunion to be filled with love and kisses."

"There was a spirit, the one off the shores of Mogadishu, remember? It fought with him, protected me from him," I tell her.

"I'll show you how to honor the spirits of dead gods later. If there is a later. But for now, I wouldn't focus on Nordeen. In all of my time with the enemy, his name was never mentioned. He may be a minor presence in this world, or maybe he found a way to reach across the void from our world to attack you in the shadows. In any case, he doesn't seem to be a major player in the Alters game."

"What is?" I ask.

"The Decimation is the icing on the cake. Even now, they'll be scrambling to get more 'volunteers' to compensate for those of my people who've come to their senses. But that's all to block a critical mass going the other way."

"A critical mass of what? People not committing suicide?" I ask.

"Don't be simple, Taggert. It's all about aesthetics." Sam looks at me and once again I feel like an idiot.

"Who cares what people find attractive, Sam?" I try not to bark.

"Suppose you find the death of children appealing? Or the rape of nations erotic? Imagine toxic air is as enlightening to you as the most expensive perfume. That's the aesthetic control the Alters, Rice is looking for over humanity. And once they've locked that in, it's nothing to drive the entire population of the planet to ruin. The resistance has to be against what the Alters stand for."

"Babe, they don't stand for shit," I say.

"Exactly, and don't call me babe," she says with no affection. "They stand for absolutely nothing. We need a critical mass of people, humans from this world, born into the gray and dark to believe—no, that's too weak of a word. They've got to feel the power of possibility, the generativity of the universe . . ."

"All the while looking into the abyss and dismal future the Alters have all but guaranteed them," I say, realizing how right she is.

"Does your plan accomplish this?" She folds her arms.

"Give folks hope?" I laugh for a second. And then, "Wait, kind of. It's the islands, right? That's where the Decimated go for their Bacchanal before the end, right? Any islands, right?"

"Yes." She nods.

"Are the islands all connected? Internet, phones, the like?" I posit.

"They must be. The suicides must be coordinated for the infernal magic to work," she says.

"So we take one, then we can talk to them all?" I realize.

"And say what, Taggert?" Sam asks.

"I'm gonna leave that to Mico." Finally, I'm seeing the edges of my plan.

"He's still alive?" She stands, excited.

"Despite his best efforts to piss me off," I let her know.

"We've got to get to him. Now that I'm free, they're going to send everything they've got against him!"

Part Four

The east wind is weak in this place. The tobacco is weak and the breeze blows cold. Asthma is the pestilence that plagues most in this time. The east wind's mind is stuck here, giving no lift to the eagle, downing the hawk. And so change is near impossible.

The mice eat the coyote in the southern wind, in this place. Youth turns to seniority without the benefit of wisdom in these lands. Patience has turned to quick temper without the penitent southern air's arms to spur calm. Sweetgrass and sage are sour in their fields. And so change is catastrophic.

The great bear drowns in the water of the western winds' heart. The cedar smells of tar and all introspection is turned outward, making mocking performances of insight for one and all. The God of Connections holds on by its stray filaments to its children and its allies. But should it fail, none know what change may come.

Quelled as it is, the white buffalo freezes in the fields and the northern wind takes credit. No one is able to go home. There are no ancestors, no gods, all of them scattered across foreign globes. There is no night, only dark. The total absence of light and spirit. Change happens in the dark. That is our only hope.

One story leads to many, all told at once. The difference is the listener. What ears are ready for what stories? This is the story of the

Liminals but this is also the story of the Manna. It is the tale of the fall of Mico and the rise of the first Liminal vassal of the Manna. It is the tale of the rebirth of hope in a world born devoid of it. And it is the tale of my death.

No one will sing my memorial, no obituary will report my good deeds and who I left behind. No one will remember me. But I write this to let friend and family alike know, I regret nothing. I was born a Child of the Wind, even before I was taught its secrets. None of my siblings was more dedicated to this life. I fought for the rights of all things, ideas, peoples, gods, worlds, to move and be moved. With cursed weapons and dubious allies, I fought against the forever stillness and would have for a thousand more years been given the opportunity. I regret not a thing.

Except Chabi. I regret not having more time with Chabi.

Gili Meno, Indonesia
Prentis

Not what I thought angels look like. Screaming, flaming winged, naked, neutered flying giants, not one of them under seven feet tall. Wind Boy said something about them before, but who remembers what he says? And fresh bloody stumps where ears would be on a human? Nary a wang anywhere, though that'd probably be more scary, yeah? Angel wang? Half done as soon as we "arrive" at their screams alone. To come from such harmony to such chaotic sound—plus them dive-bombing like enraged carrion birds at the old pirate ship at dock, each time sending out blasts of heat to rival the sun. It's not a game to these angels.

Not alone. Othica chants some low-level reminiscence of our journey chant and all her warriors hoot, shout back as we all close the distance between the fiery dive bombing hell and us. As the warriors let their spears fly, Mico takes to the air, for the first time without being covered by his dead spirit Africans or whatever, and hits the circling flock of angels at their home. He shouts something in magick talk, and the well-choreographed air dance of the angels goes to shit. Some fall to the beach and the scorched sand begins to turn to glass as those warriors still with spears stab at the downed overgrown bird men. Other angels fall into the sea, and the rising vapor gives us all some much needed cover as flaming balls of angel hate come like rays from their mouths and eyes. Doing good at dodging the ones coming from the boat, but I miss one from a downed but not speared angel on the beach. Would be served well done, if Othica hadn't pushed me out of the way at the last minute.

"You who stupidly serve the void," she tells the angel who stands, wounded but even more dangerous for it. "Come see what a loyal daughter of the Manna has to offer." Do my best to scramble out of their fight radius, but Othica uses her hand to command me to stay still. The angel ruffles its wings. One truly catches fire. The other only smoulders. It wants to take off, attack from above. It's not used to being on its legs. Still, it's an angel.

Its wing covers the distance between it and Othica with a quickness, bringing with it an arc of flame. Limber for her size, Othica flips effortlessly in the air at the last minute, spear still in hand, laughing.

"I fly better than you, broken wing," she says right before it starts screaming rage. Chest forward, it charges. Othica buries her spear in its heart just before it's in strangling range. It stops shrieking. Shocked by its mortality, the angel falls on one knee. Othica walks behind it, reaches over its shoulder and pulls her spear up from its sternum, across its heart, and releases it at the right shoulder. As the angel falls, she extends the still smoking wing and chops it off at the back shoulder. Quickly she removes all the feathers and throws it at my feet.

"There's your angel killing weapon, Prentis. Now get to it. There's more where your boyfriend there came from."

I stay by Othica, watching her back through the carnage. We try not to get distracted by fallen Bint al-nas, though there are a lot, some of the younger ones. And two old women. Still, we're giving as good as we get. Overhead, Mico sings, punches, kicks, and throws angels as they come at him. He's even released some of the African souls. They confuse and annoy the angels, but neither can touch the other. This is a battle of flesh.

Wasn't sure why we were fighting to get to the ship, considering that's where the angels were attacking. But as soon as we make our way on deck, I see poetry. It's bloody and brutal, but poetic nonetheless. With a fully feathered broken angel wing, this dark-skinned girl half dances, full murders, any angel that enters her orbit of death. She grabs one who tries to dive-bomb for her with her left hand while swinging up and hitting another in the mouth that was just screaming for her death. Then switches hands, twists her hips, and drives the flying angel into the deck with neck-breaking force as she stabs a third angel in the trachea with the sharp end of its friend's wing. Despite the heat and effort, she's barely sweating.

"Othica, Prentis, meet Chabi," Mico says as he descends. He's out of breath.

"Tam told me about you," tell the dark girl. But she's got battle lust in her eyes so I give her space.

"That one would be useful right now," I hear her in my head.

"My people can handle our share," Othica boats.

"Do the math." Narayana, deep down and scary Narayana walks to us with two angels by the throat from below deck. As they thrash, he shakes them like disobedient fryers until whatever passes for life in their bodies is gone. He looks to the sky for a second then launches them at their companions like fastballs. "It takes five of your Bint al-nas to fell one of these angels . And our numbers are about equal. Attrition is on the enemies' side."

"Unclean thing," Othica shouts and takes an offensive pose against Narayana.

"No!" I get between Othica and Chabi, who looks to defend the Alter. "He's with us, switched over."

"You cannot trust . . ." Desert Lass starts.

"Trust I will murder every part of your face if you don't put that spear down," Chabi says in a voice that's totally convincing. "Now put it down."

Without will or control, Othica does.

"What the hell?" start to ask, but Mico pushes me down, forward rolls to Othica's spear and uses it to slice a mist-secreted angel across the neck who is aiming to barbeque all of us from behind with his flaming wings. Its head stays on the ship as the rest of its body keeps a stiff flying form and continues to fly over the ship and into the ocean.

"We don't have time for scrapping between us," Mico says, giving Othica her spear back. "Chabi, you can't use your voice against the angels?"

"For obvious reasons," Narayana says, picking up the earless head of the angel. "They savaged their own forms to be immune to my protégé." He launches the head into the overhead mist, but even through the cover I see one of the bright orange blurs of an angel's wing go dark.

"Don't sound so impressed," I tell him. "So what, it's fisticuffs? Angel by angel? Fighter by fighter?"

"Is it ever anything else, really?" Can't tell if Chabi is hyped or slagged by the fact, but don't have a long to study it. Set of six angels, all taller than the others with two sets of wings, land on the other side of the boat. Look at Chabi and Narayana, tight and ready to fight. Othica redoubles her grip on her spear but doesn't move. Mico sighs then moves his lips in some silent whisper to call for the strength of the black spirits in his arm. And then there's me, with a striped broken angel wing.

"The one in the middle is mine," Narayana says, walking forward. We're all about to follow him when a tidal wave of air shoves all the angels overboard and into the ocean.

"No way that was gonna be a fair fight." Barely recognize A.C. descending from the air, but right behind him, Taggert falls to the deck, his entropy blade drawn. Behind him, Samantha falls. Not sure if she's still evil or not. Don't care. Rush to him before he's fully landed. Hug him hard, trying not to cry. Taggert's here. We've got a chance.

"Talk to me, kid." Can feel him scan me for injuries. "What's the score?"

"Could be a lot fucking better," tell him.

"You pulling your weight?" The question confuses me. "I'm seeing angels and Bint al-nas going down by the dozens all over this bridge. I haven't even seen one wounded seagull."

"Can't . . ."

"This could all end right now, little girl," tells me, pulling my arms off of him. "Either we find a way to survive this beach or humanity dies. If you can't . . . then we're done." Pets my face then turns to the rest of the crew.

"We get off this boat now. It's too central a target for these flamin' crows. A.C, keep the mist covering us. See if you can get them to lower their altitude. And give that entropy sword to Chabi. Othica, keep Mico safe. He's the one they really want. Mico, let those spirits go. I don't care if they can't hurt the angels, they can confuse the hell out of them and we're losing too many warriors out there. We baffle these damn things and kill them in the confusion. No clumping, folks. Don't give them an easy target. Let's go."

A.C. pushes me, Taggert, and Samantha off the boat and onto the beach with a series of gusts. Samantha looks as panicked as the rest of the big hitters, but as soon as we hit the beach, a crew of Bint al-nas surrounds the two of us. Taggert frees himself from our crew, presenting a solo target. One of the larger angels from the boat sees him, hovering just out of reach, a barn owl surveying a rat. It breaks in its screaming long enough to shoot a blast of fire from its mouth. Taggert moves just enough to get away from the flame, keeping his eye locked on the angel. It disappears into the mist above but swoops behind Taggert and descends, its wings pinned to its back. I'm about to shout for him to move when Taggert notices the oncoming heat.

Just as the angel is about to grab him, Taggert jumps, spins, and lands his heel in the face of the angel. He extends the kick perfectly, breaking not only the thing's nose, but whatever passes for its back as well. Can all hear the multiple cracks, even through the din of bodies falling, screaming, and flames getting snuffed by water.

"I can't . . ." Taggert screams and I know he's talking to me. Scramble over to him, keeping my head low. "My powers don't work on it. I can't manipulate it." He's telling me as I realize his plan. He didn't want the angel dead, he wanted to see if his Liminal ability to could affect it. Its snuffed wings keep trying to light, evidence of some consciousness, but Taggert punches it in the face whenever the angel gets too fiery.

"You try," tells me. Reach out to the body, the soul of the thing. Not an animal any more than it's human. Barely flesh, more the shape of an idea, covered in force and desire. But there's something in it, something I remember. An intelligent design, disgustingly familiar. Don't know this angel but I've made something similar to it. About to tell Taggert, but I'm taken in the air.

Screaming, yelling as powerful rough hands grab first my hair, the scruff of my neck, and finally my side as it throws me against its shoulder violently. Uses velocity to keep me in place, like an old sack, as it flies away from all safety. Spirals in the air, dive-bombs, and loops, to lose those who chase it and to disorient me. Looking over the back of the angel and gain hope as Mico gives chase. But two other angels block his path. Pounding on my kidnapper's back to no effect. Only stall on its upward swoop is when a mangled corpse of one of its compatriots, no doubt abused by Narayana, flails in front of it. Grabs me by the skin of my back and looks in my face.

"You're on the wrong side of this fight, angel!" It doesn't say anything, but can feel its face growing hotter, focusing on mine. Going to burn my head off. That's not how the Manna said I'd die.

A parrot slams its body into the side of the angel. It's purple and orange and even more beautiful for the lack of color in this world. Didn't call it or any of its kin to rescue me. Didn't want them to die the way the herd of camels did in the desert. Little parrot knew, but he came to me anyway. Fought to free me. Now, I owe.

Bird's death is enough to distract the angel. Raise both my feet and springboard off its chest. When the move actually works, I recognize Taggert in me; boosting my strength, my calm, and reducing my need for air and attention to pain. Angel ripped pieces of flesh out of my back but I'm free . . . and free falling. Above, a swarm of tropical birds all interfering with the angel as it advances on me, all allies of the first bird, inspired by his sacrifice. In a second, they all burn. What I was afraid of. Name an animal that can stand against an angel.

Falling, get an overview of the battlefield. Not sure what humans can do against angels either. The angels still have the advantage on land and the air.

Still falling, the singed and burnt bodies of my bird friends sink back to the earth faster than me. If they only had armor, or scales like the dinosaurs they came from. Intelligent design of the angels comes back into view. If this is about the end of all things, if these are the last days, then I'll be forgiven for this last blasphemy. Long as I survive this fall.

Launched from below, Taggert's karambit embeds itself in the forehead of the angel on my tail. Just as I'm about to go splat, a strong gust of wind counters gravity. Land on my belly and face. But I land. Taggert lets his power over my body go. Feel the rush of panic he was saving me from.

"Damn it, girl!" Da yells, yanking me to my feet by the collar and hugging me with one arm at the same time, "Stay close!"

"Cover me," tell him with the same voice he asked me if I was carrying my weight with. He gets it. In a second, Othica, four of her warriors, and Chabi are surrounding me. With their backs out and eyes up to the sky, I close my eyes and reach out to the animals of the island. Humans of this world have been messed with as much as I have. But the surviving animals, such as they are, are relatively undisturbed. On my world, Komodo dragons only get to be around 150 pounds. But here, small ones can get as big as 200 pounds. Reach out and make them bigger, a lot bigger. Double in size, 500 pounds and twenty feet long. Make their hides thicker and grow a dead layer of non-pain-conducting skin between their hides and their internal organs.

Making them attracted to fire is easy. They're lizards. But I link fire with food and mating in their limbic system. That will get them running to the angels. But now the hard part.

Called dragons because folks didn't know what else to call them. People thought they might be related to dragons of old. Folks were right. Scaly buggers are some of the last survivors of the big animal period of the world when humans and human ideas were nothing more than bony gristle for them to grind their razor teeth against. The komodo dragon has a spirit, a god.

Connect with that god through the blood of the lizards and show it my face. The dragons of the island all hiss in unison. My name they hiss. And the god hisses back, blessing its children with its power.

They come from caves, from trees, from the water, from everywhere. They hiss at the Bint al-nas but only attack the angels. The angels' designer prepared them to be servants and messengers for men. They had no preparation for the children of a lizard god.

"Did what Nordeen taught me," I confess to Taggert. He looks at me confused as the lizards surround us, protecting us. "Taught them their true nature. And their true power."

I whisper in my Liminal voice and the beasts earn their names. They yell fire back at the angels. Not the divine-human fire the winged creatures have been doling out, but the dragon fire—the spirit of their species, older and more naturally noxious than anything a human could ever create. Acts like an acid on the angels' wings, faces, and hands. They fall mewling and gasping for relief. If they had words for prayers they'd be tumbling out of the messengers' mouths. All they can do is drop to their knees, stretch their arms upward, and plead for relief as they turn to ash.

"I will give offerings to the scaled spirits for the rest of my days," Othica tells me, patting me on the shoulder.

"You might want to offer quick," A.C. says, pointing to the east. Twenty of the flaming flying prickless, bigger than the ones on the ship, all with voices deeper than all their brethren combined, descend on us. Already I'm feeling the heat.

"Are they just going to keep coming?" Taggert asks, this time dropping his jacket. Don't have to ask the Komodos to turn to face the angels. Each one of them will die before they let me fall.

"Wait," Chabi asks, already running toward the ship. "Where's Narayana?"

When he did it on Pangkor, I was already on the plane. Saw it from above, the impossibly large water hand submerge the island in its grip. Saw when he did it with the two phoenixes, but everything was going crazy and it happened so fast. Swear it was smaller then. But this time, this water hand feels big enough to drown the world.

"The fuck is he doing?" Chabi screams at all of us as A.C. gets in her way. But she's pointing at Narayana. If the hand had a wrist, Narayana would be in it, fully submerged and in charge. He extends his arms and legs, and the fingers of the massive water hand flexs. Oncoming angels don't stop but they change formation, creating an arrow and aiming right at the old Alter.

"Stop them!" Taggert shouts at A.C. But I pass the order to the dragons. Thirty of them waddle quickly into the surf, raise their heads and shout their fire in the direction of the angels. The flames cause the angels to alter course, break form even, but they don't slow down.

"The wind will not abide you anymore, you fiery fucks!" A.C. shouts. He spins his arms and winds at his torso as though he were a top five times before letting his gyrations go in the direction of the angels. Nothing happens. Then there's a sandstorm on the beach. It's literally that quick. We're all blown off our feet. Othica and the Ethiopian girl that's riding close to Taggert almost take to the sky with the sandstorm, but Da catches them both. One of the Komodos offers Taggert his tail for grounding.

The wind is as big as Narayana's hand. It blows the flaming wings back, making their sustained flight near impossible. But they fight, flapping heat and elevation against us all, making glass shards out of the sand A.C. sends at them. Look at him and see the strain. Mystical or not, twenty against one isn't a battle most can win.

"I can't keep this up." A.C. confesses, aging with every second.

"Then stop, fool!" Narayana shouts from inside his water hand. "And watch how a true warrior meets his fate." The old Indian-looking Alter arches his back, stretches, and the water hand slaps all the angels backward. Mist and their screaming turn the skies into the rankest battleground ever. They dive at him again, severely weakened and with no coordination. Narayana curls into a ball, and the giant water hand becomes a fist. He punches them out of the sky.

"He killed one!" I shout. "Or extinguished one."

"Nineteen to go," Taggert says, trying not to sound nervous.

"What the fuck is the old man thinking?" Chabi can't hide her fear.

"He's doing it for us," A.C, nowhere near fighting form, tells her from his knees.

"Doing wha . . ." Then Chabi gets it. "Fuck, A.C. get me up there!"

"To do what?" He tries to reason but Chabi already has him in some murder death throat hold. "They'd roast the skin off your bones before you landed a single blow," he manages to choke out.

"Get down!" Othica shouts as three of the angels make it past the giant hand trying to rain fire on us. Even then Narayana slaps the water of the ocean, sending pool-sized deluges onto the beach which smother all remaining fires, including the ones on the angels' wings. It's nothing for the Komodos and the remaining Bint al-nas to make short work of the snuffed angels.

Sixteen other angels arch into the sky high above us where none of us can see. Don't have time to react as the heat builds. Can feel them bearing down on the beach from directly overhead. Taggert makes me feel like I'm on speed, prepping me for whatever death is about to happen. Angels move like dive-bombing missiles. If crew was waiting for me to figure out how to stop them, we'd be dead. Barely make out their strategy, they want to take out the island. These three are big enough to fly through the island and, I don't know, sink it? These are suicide-bombing angels, moving too fast for the Komodos to target. They're going to hit the island.

"Now, Taggert!" I hear Chabi shout, but it seems like Taggert was already throwing her his entropy blade. Impossible for anyone to move as quickly as she does. My head doesn't want to get how she does it, but in the time it takes me to exhale, Chabi jumps, slices the head off of one angel using Taggert's blade, launches that head into the other angel's body, knocking it off course, and then leaps from the dying angel body to the third angel with A.C's sword extended and drives it through his heart before any of them can reach land. Want to fucking applaud. But then the remaining angels scream.

"Get me up there!" Chabi shouts to A.C.

"He can't," I tell her. He's so weak he can barely stand.

"Somebody." Don't know her, never met her before. But she's not used to asking for help. She's begging for it as her mentor grips hard at fifteen-foot angels ready to kill us all. He's got them trapped between the fingers of his giant water hand but they're slipping.

"Chabi!" Narayana shouts, and water sprays. "You hold the Entropy of Bones. You are my child and you hold my curse. Remember me. Forgive me."

Chabi screams, but it's too late. Narayana slips into the ocean, dragging the remaining angels into the deep. As soon as they hit the water we're in a swamp of humidity and haze. They boil off hundreds of gallons of seawater. Their screams make even the dragons want to run away, but soon those noises are muffled. Then there's silence. Nothing but silence.

Chabi wades deep into the water between the islands as extinguished angelic bodies bob to the surface. She's in a panic. She screams for him.

"Narayana!" When he doesn't answer, she dives as deep as the landbar will allow her to go, then surfaces, almost catching air. Still screaming.

"Narayana!" What can any of us do? Us, half-dead, wounded, and barely breathing. Our miracle was surviving. Narayana knew what he was doing, what he was sacrificing.

"Narayana." Chabi says the sunken demon's name softly for the last time on the edge of the island.

Gili Air, Indonesia
Taggert

Gili Air flinched and shuddered at the death of its de facto god, Narayana. Then it shook itself free of the Decimation haze. Maybe the grief songs of the Bint al-nas cleared the air, and as they buried their dead, the decomposing bodies kicked the land free. They came with four hundred and lost twelve to the angels. Another fifty are wounded but should be game ready when the time comes, if Othica is to be believed. I tried to give her a pep talk. Twelve out of four hundred against angels is a win in most circles. She responded by singing the names of the twelve that fell. By the time she was done, all the Bint al-nas had started singing the names in a round. They haven't stopped for the past six hours.

Maybe the Wind Boy did something to break the Decimation grip and didn't tell anyone about it. That's his way. No doubt he's trying to compensate for not saving Narayana. I've got to break him of that guilt before the Alters come. I need heroes, sacrifice maybe. But not the recklessness of survivor's guilt. I'm not the one to talk to him, though. I'll sic Samantha on him. She has something to do with the Decimation fugue as well. She's been doing her version of counseling to the normal people on the island since just after the angel battle. Somehow, the whole idea of slaughtering themselves for the betterment of the world revealed itself to be the most idiotic idea ever. The natives from the high hills have come down to the beach to mingle with the formerly suicidal tourists and bathe in the waters that have drowned demonic angels and the kind of drowned things alike. Sam is leading the baptisms like she was never on the other side, Mico acting as her second.

I've been on homicide/suicide watch with Chabi.

"I gotta kill something soon," Chabi tells me as I come up behind her on the beach. She's doing her murder katas on the beach where Narayana fell. Everyone else has the common sense to give her space.

"Give it time." I know how weak it sounds.

"Or you could just send me off to the Alters and let me do my work. I've already taken one down with my bare hands," she tells me, whipping a hand a millimeter away from my ear. Would have shattered my eardrum beyond even my repair, had it landed.

"Big deal. They killed you one time." I'm barely done speaking when her heel starts sailing at my head. I don't move.

"That won't happen again." She twists her hips hard the instant before she would have broken my forehead with the blow. Her back is to me as she practices kicking invisible enemies in front of her while boxing intangible foes to her right. "I was distracted before. Never again."

"Suppose Rice comes by?" I forgot that A.C. was with me. As usual. He gives the murderer dancer an even wider berth than I do.

"Don't talk to me, you." She stops her katas to stare him down. "You're lucky I don't . . ."

"Kill that noise." I stand between them, regretting it immediately. "We just lost one important player, I'll be damned if I lose another before the real battle starts."

"I could have helped!" she screams and everyone on the island buckles a bit. Reminds me of Tam when we first met. All the power in the world and none of the discipline. At least when it comes to that psychic voice of hers.

"It wasn't worth the risk." Mico flies in—standing erect like he's riding on a magic carpet—from farther down the coast, and lands by my side. "You're too valuable to be wasted on anyone other than the Alters."

"That's my decision, Mico. That's not for you, or A.C, or even Narayana to choose. Do you get that? I decide how, when, and where I lose my life."

"You're wrong." Even Mico stiffens when I say that.

"Fuck you say to me, old man?" She is genuinely ready to fight.

"You don't get to call when you lose your life any more than anyone else on this island does. You owe a debt." I dense up my limbs, hoping it's enough to sustain a blow from a woman who's broken angel bones by looking at them too hard.

"Only creature on this planet I owe just died saving your punk asses," Chabi hisses at me.

"Dumb ain't a good look on you, so stop trying to wear it." I almost yawn. "You're grieving, I get it. But all of us, Narayana included, spent valuable time and energy to bring you back. Fuck how you feel woman, that's a debt. We're not asking you to do anything short of help us save the planet. Good news for you is you get to destroy those that murdered you. But this is not the time for personal squabbles."

"Damn a squabble!" she shouts back with death in her eyes. "I took down three of those angels in less time than it takes to tell. I could have done the others if I just had a damn boost!"

"You think you're here just for your fighting skills?" I ask. "You don't know your own worth. Suppose one of those angels got a wing free or shot another fire face blast or . . ."

"I would have handled it." She believes it.

"Or you could have been blown to kingdom come and then we'd all be done," I say.

"What exactly do you think I can do in this fight other than kill?" Finally, a genuine question.

"Narayana taught you the Entropy of Bones. I want you to train the Bint al-nas," I say.

"I can't just . . ." Chabi starts.

"You taught Tamara and all she knew was scraping from me. I'm good but you're magic. Plus these desert women are warriors born, all infused with the Manna. We lost too many people in the last fight. They need to know how to handle themselves against Alters."

"So that's it? I'm your drill sergeant for the chick army?" She laughs at me.

"You're of more use if you can figure out how to use your voice," A.C. says, finally speaking up when it looks like she won't kill me. "We can link to the other islands of the world. All of them. Your voice controls people. You can tell the willing Decimation victims to cut the shit."

"Who says they'll be listening?" Good. More questions, less killing posture.

"Cold calculus here," I tell her. "They don't all have to be listening. Just enough. The Alters' plan only works if a collective ten percent of the population kills itself. We stop one percent of that, the world is saved."

"No way your plan is going to work," Prentis says, riding one of her giant Komodo friends through the thick bush. "Not in its current form. That's what Tam says."

"Why not? And I thought I told you two to not head talk this far apart?" I remind her, stepping clear of the lizard as A.C. and Mico do. Of course, Chabi just looks at it, measuring the strikes she'll need to murder it dead.

"She said it was worth the risk, Tag." Prentis dismounts her lizard and slaps its ass to send it on its way. "And your plan won't work – her words now –because as usual, it's too straight ahead." She laughs. "Ram your head against a wall. That's a Taggert plan. Tam says we've got to keep Mico spinning, DJing, broadcasting everywhere while dealing with the Alters. She's out in the world. Alters are proper pissed and they're coming."

"Let the fuckers come then!" Chabi shouts. She's almost blood crazy. Prentis looks at me, asking if she can help. I take a step back.

"You'll take them all?" Prentis asks, her smile never disappearing.

"As many as I can," Chabi says, already feeling the set-up.

"And the ones that get by you?" Prentis asks.

"You guys aren't weak . . ."

"No, but we're tired. We've been running around in a world that isn't ours for a few months now with precious little to show for it. We'll fight, but honestly? Next fight's our last. If we can't get it done, we're done for."

"That's not my fault." Chabi tries to get mad at Prentis, but my girl isn't saying anything untrue.

"Fair play. But if you're not down for the fight with us, do me a favor? Take a boat and go to Bali proper, or Gili Meno. Tamara said Alters are rallying their troops on the mainland. Take as many as you can out over there so we don't have to deal with the grief of seeing your fallen body."

Chabi stiffens. A.C. makes a move toward her but I tell him to wait with a small flick of my wrist. No reason to stop Prentis now.

"We don't know each other. Why would you grieve . . ." Chabi starts with a foreign sound in her voice.

"Tamara told about you. Narayana trained you. Rice seduced you. Killed you. How you saved her in the middle of the forgotten sea from the ghost sharks. A.C. blabbed about you and the boat. Proper tragic, your life. Happy you've got a new body. New chance. Much of a chance as any of us have," Prentis offers, calm, the way you would talk to a skittish colt.

The tears are real, but strange as they fall down Chabi's round face. I don't think she's ever cried before in this body.

"I don't need your pity." Chabi tries to bark.

"Not offering. Asking for help." Prentis looks back at me, A.C, and Mico. "Proper shite, I know. You've earned proper mourning time. Can't see how your relationship with the drowned bad man was anything but complex, but still, he meant something to you. Thing is we're on a bit of a clock. Alters are coming and your boy Rice is taking the lead. Tam has a plan for some asymmetrical warfare type ish and you're key. If you can't be arsed, we've got to find an option Y cuz A through X options are spent."

"Rice is coming?" Chabi stiffens as she asks.

"He saw Narayana as his biggest threat," A.C. chimes in. "With him out the picture, Rice will want a front seat to the destruction of the Liminals."

"Anyone in your little committee here have a problem with me taking that sub-demon out personally?" We all shrug consent. "Good. DJ, play your shit tight. A.C, next time I tell you to put me somewhere, tired better not be in your vocabulary. You train your girls good, Taggert. Prentis, you're student number one after I work out the kinks in this body. Now all of you, fuck off my beach."

"Always was a charmer," A.C. tells me as we make our way back through the trees to the open-air hotel. Former Decimation Disciples, as Prentis has christened them—the locals—give us wide berth, as we make our way back to our makeshift headquarters.

"Be nice!" Prentis says, push-kicking A.C. in his ass. "She was the dead captain of a ghost ship."

"You'd think she'd be grateful." A.C. smirks.

"Think you wouldn't be butt hurt that she's not throwing herself on you," Prentis mocks. "Tam told me the story of you two. I know you want to see her ghost panties."

"How old are you exactly?" he asks, but then floats away quickly. She grins with satisfaction. Mico takes the left off the beach into the luxury resort. It's all white columns, thatched roofs, and high arches with a massive set of teak doors barring casual entrance. Two stories, with eight rooms on each floor, surrounded by a damn near useless pool given how close we are to the ocean. The type of architecture you'd expect from seafaring Indians. Given time, I'd probably appreciate it. But I'm getting the sense it won't stand much longer than us.

"Figured out the lizard trick pretty quick," I tell Prentis. Four Komodos stand sentry at the doors of the hotel. They're so still, except for their eye movements, they look like statues. Toward the back of the brown-and-beige building—I'm assuming the former staff quarters—I see three larger ones patrolling, dragging eighty-pound tails with ease.

"Wasn't like I didn't know how, Tag," she tells me, petting one, stalling entering the giant wooden doors. "Could always feel the animals' spirits talking to me, guiding me to make changes to them."

"Like the sharks and the praying mantises." I didn't mean to remind her that I had been on the receiving end of her animal attacks. She winces so hard the giant lizard looks at me like I hurt her on purpose. Lucky for both of us, it stays still.

"The sharks Narayana helped with in a way I still don't fully understand. They were more spirit than flesh. But the praying mantises, yes. Their—if I say spirit will you laugh at me?"

"Just talk."

"Spirit of them, thing they're based off, the god of them, yeah? Whispered the cheat codes to their bodies to me. Let me do to their bodies what I do to their minds." She rests her head against the shoulder of the lizard. It groans in satisfaction.

"Given everything we've been facing . . ." I start but already she's cutting me off.

"Nordeen whispered through animal voices. How he found me, how he trapped me." I nod. That's what he does. He finds that odd fucking angle you've got no defense for. "Keep being afraid. Every time I hear animal whisper, afraid it will be Nordeen's voice. And if he shouts . . . Taggert, if he does I don't know if I'm strong enough to . . ."

"You killed him back in nineteen . . ." I try to remind her.

"Not daft enough to believe that." She looks at me, taking her head off the dragon.

"I just stopped him again in Ethiopia." I smirk a bit.

"Wait, what?" Finally, my girl looks up.

"I don't know. Maybe it was him, a memory of him used against me by the Alters. A shadow of his power. I don't know. What I do know is that man doesn't have the same power over me that he used to. And he sure as hell doesn't have any power over you." She nods solemnly.

"You remember how you broke his hold over you?" I ask as we sit on the steps to the estate.

"He was coming hard and fast for you, Tam, and Mico. The Alters as well."

"And you said 'Fuck that noise.' You wouldn't let him hurt us. Wouldn't let him hurt me. Lil Prentis, you just took down a squad of angels . . ." I say.

"With help!" She slaps the toe of one of the closest lizards. It still doesn't move.

"Oh, you an individual now?" I steal one of Tamara's favorite lines. "Everything we do, every step we take, we take as a crew. Don't sell yourself short, kid. You've got the power. And we're going to need every bit of it if we're going to survive."

"Oh yeah," she says after hugging my neck hard, "Tam says your plan sucks."

"You've said."

"No, really sucks. She says better to be slick." Prentis touches her temple.

"Slick how?" I ask.

"You're gonna love it."

Gili Meno, Indonesia
Taggert

After Prentis mumbles of a murder party, in which the Alters are the main attraction, I make my way to the eastmost coast of the beach, far from Chabi. The sun pretends like it's about to set, but the hard reflection from the bay's water tells me we've got hours yet still of its hard gaze. Those who came to die, the Decimation dummies, keep flinching as giant Komodos run, fuck, and lounge in the sun, or as a band of Bint al-nas sin and run in unison. The normals don't realize they're the biggest threat to this reality; that their simplistic suicide pact added to the entropic rush, the end of all things. Luckily, Mico is bringing a bit more bright into their lives.

The island was apparently a floating party bus long before the Decimation, if the accouterments are to be believed. I find the crooner tweak scratching on one of them. A two level palm roof structure with packed hay walls and tied bamboo columns every nine feet running parallel to the beach for eighty feet. The cool concrete floor on the second floor is the only indication this thing was made after the eighteenth century, but crudely lashed to the top of each column is a high-quality speaker. They all link to a stage at the front of the structure on the second floor. There, the lonely DJ practices his craft with headphones and flash drives.

"You good?" I ask, already knowing the answer.

"Just figuring it out." He doesn't lie, but Mico's former trade, his heart really, rests in authenticity. He doesn't know how to obfuscate.

"Figuring what?" I pull one of his flash drives from his hands to get his attention. "And don't try to convince me watching Narayana go down didn't do your head in."

"I recruited him." Mico sighs but doesn't stop plugging the small flash drives into a contraption that looks half turntable, half computer. "When I met him he was broken and incomplete. He'd just gone through the Blighted Lands to try and save the soul of the only creature that had ever given him a chance. A djinn. The one that taught him the Entropy of Bones."

I nod, pretending I understand any of it.

"He failed and lay on the coast of the Astral Plane, shattered. Alters are closer to nonexistence than existence anyway. But where do they go when they want to die?"

"You're not waiting on an answer from me, are you?" I ask.

"I don't know the answer. Neither did he. I told him that there was some refuge in that. We, who'd seen what most of the created world couldn't imagine, still had gaps in our knowledge. I asked him to imagine a world where we could be friends, allies. Imagine what we could do as loyal comrades. He said it wasn't in his nature to join with the created world."

"What did you say?" I ask.

"Told him to fuck his nature. To go with what works. To go with me." Mico smiles at the memory.

"And he did," I say.

"And now he's dead. He's gone." His heart goes out of him a bit.

"Mission accomplished." Mico slides his headphones down, genuinely pissed.

"You wanted him dead?" He might actually throw a punch with his spirit arm.

"Don't be an idiot, man. We've got the assembled hordes of 'What the fuck?' coming our way. The last thing I need is to be a man down," I say, stepping off the stage and looking at what had been a dance floor. "Especially when my lucky charm and one of my strongest assets are off galavanting behind enemy lines. You never promised Narayana immortality. You told him he could choose his destiny. He wasn't bound to the material of his creation. And in the end, he sacrificed himself for the good of us all. He did what he didn't think he could do."

"And took out a few flaming angels while doing it." Mico smiles a bit, speaking into the microphone.

"Yeah, he did," I concur, then ask, "You hear the girl's plan?"

"Given that it relies on me sitting in the crosshairs of the Alters for as long as humanly possible, you're wondering if I'm willing to do it," he tells me, adjusting the levels on an instrumental version of "It Takes Two" by Rob Bass and DJ Easy Rock.

"And I'm wondering what the Manna thinks of the plan," I tell him. "You're still my most direct link to your god."

"For now." He smiles as he drops Tuareg voices in over the beat. He can't help but sway a bit, finding the groove. I can see the spirits on his arm wiggle a little in time with the music from the floor. "The Manna respects the plan. More than that, I can't articulate."

"Because you're keeping secrets, or there are no words in the human language?" I ask, trying not to be frustrated.

"We're way past secrets, Taggert. This is the final battlefield. We break the Decimation wave here or it takes over everywhere. I will stand here by your side. And if you ask, I will stand here by myself."

Gili Meno, Indonesia
Taggert

"The break is temporary," Samantha tells me, sitting across a bowl of fruit. Her hand is in Mico's. There's something she's feeding him that's allowing him to stay conscious. He's been on the turntable for the past two days. He sounds good and his powers must be working because he's drawing a crowd. It's mostly the reformed Decimation dummies, but this morning I saw some of the Bint al-nas on the dancefloor. Small sign indeed.

"What break?" I ask.

"From the Decimation," she says. "When the people who were affected listen to Mico's music they don't feel the pull anymore. When I work with them, it breaks as well. When I can get Chabi to stop training the Bint al-nas to murder and get her to talk to the Decimation folks, that breaks the hold the longest. But it's like a gravitational pull, a black hole . . ."

"The pull of the Alters is too strong," Mico says finally. I can see why she's holding his hand when he pulls away from her. He's shaking. "I'm doing my best to channel the Manna's effect. That's the only thing I know that can stop their mass suicidal tendency, but . . ."

"There's not enough of the Manna, the pure Manna, for him to work," Samantha tells me. I cut a piece of dragon fruit and feed it to Mico. I offer some to Samantha, doing my best to share no intimacy with her.

"Relax. The Alters have been spreading their brand of misery for a clear century uninterrupted. We've won a few battles, to be sure, but I wasn't expecting us to win the war on skirmishes," I tell them. But then I look like a simpleton because no part of them was looking for comfort. "What am I missing?"

"The Alters can feel their 'subjects.' They know where they are," Sam says, nibbling on the dragon fruit. "They feel us pulling against their influence. So they know where we are."

"I sent some of the spirits out last night just to make sure they weren't creeping up on us in the dark. One went as far out as Bali." Mico shows me his arm. That tattoo I made could never capture the movement that the spirits perform on his arm. I see it now. Mico isn't shaking because he's scared or tired. He's shaking with the agitation of the African spirits in his arm. "The Alters are amassing there, performing all manner of skullduggery to prepare to . . ." But he sees I'm not paying attention. Prentis comes running to our table fast and hard. Small spiders wrap around her body by the hundreds, spinning bright silver and red webs. But that's not what's concerning her.

"What, kid?" I stand.

"Tamara . . ." she says and points at a hybrid seaplane coming in from the eastern sky. I open my senses and feel Tamara's body on the plane. But her brain activity is sporadic and delayed, like she's having a stroke. Prentis looks like she's about to piss herself.

"Mico, in the air. Make sure they didn't grow a tail. Somebody find the guy . . . with the wind . . . whatever his name is," I say, running to the beach. Prentis's lizards run by her side trying to carry her as she bolts.

A.C. is already chilling the air for the pilot by the time I get to the beach. The plane's landed in the water between the islands, but it's farther out than I can walk in the water. So I have to wait until the door opens and A.C. flies the first body out. It's not Tamara.

"Othica!" I shout into the crowd that's formed up behind us. The giant comes forward. "That's Ahmadi. Keep him safe and secure. Damn it, A.C! Get Tamara out of there!"

I'm trying to heal her from a distance, but I can't figure out what's wrong with her. I need my hands on her. When A.C. drops her on the beach, Prentis is the first to her. Tamara can't stand, can barely speak. Dried blood cakes on her face.

"Talk to me, girl," I say, grabbing her face with both hands. "Who did this?"

"Self-inflicted dumb shit," she tries to joke. "But I got the growing boy. You see?"

"Good job," Prentis says, patting Tam's chest and trying to hold her own tears back with her hand over her mouth. "Just relax now, okay? Let the old man do his thing, okay?"

"You better leave me my scar, Tag," she tells me.

"What the fuck happened?" I scream at Pasha as A.C. drops him on the beach.

"We ran into Poppy. We didn't fight, but she had to push her abilities in the middle of Alter space . . ." The fucker is already apologizing.

"This is how you take care of her?" I shout at him.

"Hey!" Tamara's bloodshot eyes lock on mine as bloodstained teeth and tongue speak. "Lucky did his part. This is on me. Let him be."

I empty my powers into her, but she's like a vase with a hole in the bottom. Every bit of healing I give her I can feel fading as soon as I stop. I give up my breath energy then back off. Shit. I couldn't heal her scar now if I wanted to.

"She going to be okay?" Prentis asks.

"They both need rest." Samantha speaks for me. I feel like I just ran an ultramarathon on a dare. I can barely keep my eyes open.

Gili Air
Prentis

"Stay still!" tell Tam as sixty spiders to work on her web armor. Not the first time we've been alone since they dropped her bloodied and broken on the beach. First time conscious, mobile, and alone. Looking out to the other island, where the angels fell in nice beach chairs.

"Weirdest sensation ever!" Tam flinches every other second. "One of these things bites my nips, I'm blaming you."

"Don't bite them, they won't bite you," I tell her. "Doing what they love, spinning webs. Cross-hatching and lattice structures they've been laying will make it harder for sharp edges to get through."

Tam nods. Usually by now she'd have asked me about what I was thinking. Usually she's in control of conversation. My turn.

"Shag the lucky boy?"

"He likes the ladyboys."

"Fuck off. Think it's transgenders."

"Facts. He said its girls with boy penises he likes. So whatever that is. And no shade on him for it either. He's earned his keep."

"What's a girl penis?" Laugh. "Hear he took out the one that looked like your mom?"

"Fair lot more than that as well."

"Do tell, but after dishing on who else you brought back."

"Fuck was I to do, P? Once I peeked the scale of all of this." Her brain, still calculating. Good. Means I still have faith in her.

"You've been in the church or in the desert, or hanging with mystical warrior wenches this whole time. I've been feeling the people, the humans. I saw every billboard through their eyes, telling them it was okay to commit suicide. The rallying for depression, oppression, and misery. Fuck seeing it, I've been feeling it. When shite gets that bad, you've got to fight it with everything you've got."

"So what did you get?"

"Liminals, P. Almost everyone I could remember."

"No Rajesh." My rapist in another life. Definition of a bully. Deluded myself into thinking we were part of the same crew. Rapists only crew up with other rapists and bullies. I'm neither.

"No." She knows something is off in my reaction. "Not him. He was my first test case. Went to the curry shop to see if he was there."

"And?"

"He's not the same Rajesh. Literally. In this world he didn't even know Alia. They weren't running any part of the underground anything. He's a square, making deliveries for his parents' restaurant. I barely caught a whiff of his powers when I scanned him. He's not the same guy."

"You murder him for me?"

"We survive this clusterfuck, promise to my soul we murk the bastard dead."

"For crimes his otherworld doppelgänger did." I laugh. "Some fucking heroes."

"Fuck a hero. If time wasn't short, would've done him then and there."

"But had to get to Alia," I tell her. That fake crew that I was in, Alia was the ringleader. Master manipulator, insanely smart and vicious. Her Liminal power to make illusions that were as concrete as reality turned her into the most powerful Liminal I'd ever met, before Nordeen. Best friend before Tam. Family before Tag. Sister when I had none. The one that gave me to the rapist as a plaything.

"How . . . ?"

"G'wan, girl. And don't stroke out trying to get in here. Tell your tale."

"We both have reasons to hate the slag in our world, yeah? Swear to all I hold holy. She's more powerful, grown even. But all the psycho bunny stuff, it's not there. All she wanted was peace and quiet. Had a husband and had illusioned up some fake kids to go along with the whole thing."

"Domestic as sin in Peckham."

"Who's dishing details?"

"Show me yours first."

"Anyway! So's the lucky and I head over to her. Get her to agree to join up with Tag, can make those kids of hers real."

"How?"

"Not the imagined ones. Ever see Alia for real? Without an illusion?"

"How would I know?"

"Proper deformation, inside and out," tells me. Happy that there's something I don't know. "Webbed fingers, half hooves where feet should be, cleft palate, patches of hair growing in random spots, extra lobe of skin flapping over the right side of her face to accommodate an extra lobe of brain. Not too far off from those Terra Tomas. Turns out her fallopian tubes are all jacked or whatever."

"Easy fix for Tag," I put in.

"Right? Easy trade. Just had to convince her the Alters were beatable."

"Hit her with the psychic wap?"

"Couldn't risk it not working. Had to try something trickier."

"Wot?"

"Truth. Gave her the full plan. She was iffy but signed up."

"Okay. So how'd you get roughed up?"

"Back when you were . . . gone, Tag led us all to this Liminal. A Somali named Ahmadi. He could talk to plants the way you talk to animals. Make them grow, make them stronger, all of that. Given the state of Manna, figured he might be of use. I was right. Alters had him caged up proper. Took the Lucky, Alia, and every bit of me to get him out of there alive and in one piece. But that rat-toothed bitch Poppy took a chunk out of my psyche as we bopped out of Somalia. Was bleeding out my eyes, my ears, nose, all of it." Some might expect this one to say she was scared, hurt even. I know better. Fight's not over. When it's done, they'll be a puddle in a corner that'll respond to Tamara Bridgecombe. Not now. Too much work to get done. Don't even try to take that composition away from her now. That's how simps become sinned upon.

"Saw that. Safe now."

"You say. But for how long?"

"Safe is overrated anyway."

"Facts. Let's go break some shit."

"'K. But so Pasha doesn't want to ride the Bridgecombe express?"

"He's nice with the blades, and the backup is impeccable. But he's not in it for the romance or even the bump and grind, yeah? It's like he's never had a friend before, never been relied on and had someone trust on him. Gets off on it, he does."

"Right . . ."

"Perv, ewww. Not like that. He was good people in a world that celebrated the bad, so he compromised. Now he's got us, rainbow warriors in the gray world or whatever. So he's with us."

"Feel bad you and Tag made a suicide bomber meat puppet out of him? Cuz given his preferences, like a hate crime kind of." Tam tries to stand. Spiders ain't done so I push her back down with two fingers on her shoulder. She's too weak for what's coming. She sees it.

"Piss off! No!" then "A little. Finally. "Shut it! Who've you been talking to?"

"The Manna. More to tell. Sit and prep yourself."

"About what?" Tam gets curious.

"So much that I forget half of it whenever I try to remember," tell her honestly. "But she, it . . . reminded me that humans and Liminals are also animals."

"What are you seeing?" Kills her to have to ask. Stronger, she'd just read my mind.

"Taggert turned your blood into something like crayfish blood." Trapped in the sight of it.

"Fuck does that mean?"

"Your cells can turn into stem cells or neurons as needed." It's wondrous, I almost add.

"That's good, right?"

"Yes and . . ." I start. "Extending Alia's powers well strained your stem cells and neurons, both necessary for you to do all your psychic trickery. Proper naffed, your brain is."

"Tag and them said as much," she tells me, trying to sound hard. "Any hope for a girl?"

"Neuron factories in your brain are still there. The ways for you to do everything is still in place. You just need a massive infusion of energy, or time, luv. Just time." Sounds like a defeat when I tell her.

"All the Alters are in Bali. Did you know? A.C. told Pasha they infected the local belief system. They're manifesting themselves as Indian gods. Taking over local stone idols by infusing them with their Alter consciousnesses."

"Local Indians have a monkey god?" I ask her.

"Hanuman," Tam tells me. "Why?"

"A parrot said me there's an army of stone monkeys swimming and floating their way here now. Says the biggest stone creature it sees is all blue, looks like a man and is walking on the ocean floor and can almost reach the surface. The butterflies tell me more stone idols are on their way."

"I was thinking we'd be dealing with flesh when they came." Tam stands and lets the spiders fall on their last webs to the sand.

"Does it make that much of a difference, fam?" Stand with her, checking the web work for lazy spiders too confused by the project to make the effort. No holes, no gaps, no evidence of sloth in their work as Tam picks up a spear the Bint al-nas donated to her and spins it around her head. Arranged the spider's webs to be hard as coral, flexible as cloth, light as silk, and bulletproof. Bint al-nas all over getting the same webbing spit all over them. Only uniform we'll have.

"Guess not, luv," Tam says. "It's all about the DJ. You really think MC Jah Puba has what it takes?"

"If there's one thing Mico knows how to do,"—I smile—"it's move the crowd."

Gili Air, Indonesia
Taggert

I'm feeling half myself when Mico starts his set. Naturally, he sets a Gil Scott-Heron spoken word track over some Congolese drumming hitting at 140 beats per minute. It's loud enough to wake that sleeping thing in my chest, my Liminal skill. It's soulful enough to pull Samantha and a crew of followers she's managed to attract. That's enough rhythm in it for the Bint al-nas to hum, click their tongues, stomp, and dance to Gil's voice; has enough pain to even draw Chabi.

All of us, we Liminals, wind spirits, Manna worshippers, the lucky, and reborn death dealers shine clad in gossamer armor provided by my beastie girl. Looking out on the dance floor filled with wounded warriors armed with split spears, cursed pistols and swords, and jagged souls, I could feel sorry for any other enemy. But not the Alters.

"Long months ago, I stood on another shore with men and women not from this world," Mico tells the crowd with the same cadence and tempo as the Bint al-nas. He's always on beat. "We called ourselves the Clan of the Gray Rainbow and our goal was simple: to liberate this world from those that would drag it into the forever shadows." Othica starts a half war cry, half celebratory yodeling that the Bint al-nas take on en masse, then Prentis, Tamara, and Pasha. Soon the whole crowd of Decimation dummies howls with them.

"We've lost allies along the way." Without it sounding prefab, Mico is able to add a drawling electric blues to the soundscape. "I've lost friends. But I've regained a family I thought lost, allies I thought would be against me forever, and collaborators I'd never imagined."

Prentis sends a flock of birds and more butterflies than I've ever seen over the amphitheater to accent the message. The howling before can't match the stomping and cheering that overtakes us now. I feel it in my drawn-out soul.

"If you dance, if you sing, if you will allow yourself to love every-one here, now, I promise you, even if you fall, you will not fall alone!"

The Bint al-nas slam their spears down in unison, making me think "You will not fall alone" is a saying of theirs. It's in their stomp-ing, their streaked tears of joy I know these women will be there to the end. When Prentis and Tamara join in the cheering, an unbidden tightness grabs my groin and my stomach. But this is their fight, their world as much as it is mine. Moreso in fact.

I'm not so lost in my thoughts about the girls I don't notice Mico handing me the microphone. It's only when Tam mouths the words "Say something" that I realize all eyes are on me. Off guard and on point, I defer to honesty.

"We're not all going to make it." Nobody flinches. "We won't all get out of this alive. I won't be able to heal all of you. Hell, I may not be able to heal myself. The dark shadow of hell is bringing its full torturous weight down on this little island. And if we fail, if we lose, then humanity, as a concept, is over." I see the girls shaking their heads at me. But the rest of this crew, they aren't backing off. Their backs are still stiff. Even the lucky boy. It's enough to make me want to give them hope.

"DJ Jah Puba took out their head honcho. My daughter out there in the crowd turned one of them into a quivering mass. My other daughter took out their main Liminal support. Chabi, right there, she destroyed another. You know, now that I think of it, right here, we probably have more Alter Killers than have ever been assembled in one place." Everyone smiles at that one.

"The odds are stacked against us. But if we win. If just one of us is standing at the end of this battle, well, shit. Then that means that you were part of the crew that looked entropy in the face, took all it had to give and said fuck off!" The crowd goes nuts. The shouts of "Fuck off!" shake the foundation of the building.

"Tell the darkness, 'Fuck off!' Tell the despair, 'Fuck off!' Tell your fears, 'Fuck off!' They might beat us, but we'll never quit! Some of you don't know this, but what happens here is being broadcast across all the Decimation islands. Already people are turning away from that chaos and towards us. East Africa is already liberated. If you've ever wondered what your impact on the world would be, this is it, people." Mico echoes my last words with his equipment so you can hear "This is it" in my voice long after I leave the stage. You'd think the sentiment would be lost in the repetition, but that's Mico's skill, to infect every moment with meaning. Soon everyone is laughing, sweating, dancing, and crying all at the same time.

And that's how we all stay, dancing and feeling for four hours. Far from draining us, it builds us up. Along with Bint al-nas, Mico's beats replenish us in ways we didn't, I didn't, know, I was spent. Tam shuffles and rubs her backside all over Prentis and Pasha. Samantha spins, rocks, and sashays with the Bint al-nas and A.C. But it's Chabi that surprises everyone. What starts as a move-for-move dance/fight stance between her and Othica turns into the type of graceful leaping and arching that most ballerinas aim toward but never get. At the same time, Chabi remains predatory, decisive in her movements, lethal in her approach to the dance floor and to life. I'm glad she's on our side.

Mico's official set starts with slaves. From my college days, I remember the manufactured chain gang songs of Texas prisoners recorded by Alan Lomax. I don't know where the Bint al-nas heard them, but they hum along in perfect harmony, stomping their feet with every pickaxe strike. But Mico adds a deceptively funky acid jazz backing track on the song that gives the less rhythmically oriented something to dance to.

From there, a building grand piano track takes over the minor chords from the backing track as a Jay-Z, Tupac, Biggie, and Wiley vocal melange rides over the chain gang narratives. It's an energetic seventeen minutes of aggressive bass and minor chords. He gives me a head nod when he mixes in Ludacris's "My Chick Bad." He points to my girls dancing with his chin.

Mico brings in a lonely harmonic chord to breathe a small sonic break before laying down an old Outkast track. It's enough to keep people dancing but also provides a slower pace to give folks some breathing room. As the tale of friendship begins to fade on the track, I recognize the voice of Khaled. But it's not the typical Rai instrumentalism I'm used to. In fact, it's the same southerplayastic Dungeon family. Jah Puba mixes the vocalists so well it sounds like the Algerian lyrical legend is in direct conversation with Andre 3000 and Big Boi, despite speaking different languages. Halfway through the track, Mico hits the rewind and then restarts the track's vocals but this time it's all under a Rai instrumentalization.

I take a moment to look at Mico. Glowing, sweating, working, listening. Smiling. No one is more in the moment than him, but he's also thinking five steps ahead of the crowd. He knows when to bring a song in, to take it off, to slow it down or to speed it up, to ass treble, bass, echo, to pan. But these are just the tools.

The power is in the music. Seeing Mico in his element, I realize he's had an accurate assessment of what he does this whole time. Mico is merely a conduit. The music, not from this world, ripples across this dance floor of apocalypse warriors and feeds us all. It radiates through the speakers and the video and his every Decimation island inhabitant. Mico does what he can't help doing, he draws a crowd. The music does the psychic work—shaking folks from the Alters' hold—but Mico makes the people want it.

It's Beenie man, Jhadan Blackamore, Vybz Kartel, and Damian Marley over traditional Thai melodies for an hour before Jah Puba lets MC Solaar vocals play background to Ali Farka Toure guitar riffs. A glint in Mico's eye, and I know he's been struck with inspiration. With Jimi Hendrix's "If 6 Was 9" loaded on his second deck,

Mico lets the two master guitarists first duke it out, then collaborate, and finally build on each other's talent. Eventually, Mico layers the singing of two Tuareg female voices on top of that collaboration to balance out the masculine vibe.

Janis Joplin's "Mercedes Benz" functions as the vocal glue for the next collection of collaborators. Her opening lament to God is both the answer and the question to Nina Simone, Etta James, Sister Rosetta Tharpe, Umm Kulthum, Edith Piaf, Nancy Sinatra, Mary J. Blige, and Valerie June. Mico follows up with a twenty-five minute jimbei tribute to a forgotten god of fire, played by a Cubano master. I know who played it because I can hear it. The music contains its own metadata, transmitting not just meter, measure, rhythm, and tempo but also its origins. And the origins contain the gift of the gray rainbow; the memory of a world not dominated by the Alters.

Having a front row seat at the best concert one could ever imagine with four hundred of the best people I've ever met. But for those born and raised in this world, a world where Robert Johnson was never rediscovered and Bob Marley fell to a U.S. government assassin, where Jimi Hendrix vanished into obscurity between a methed out Little Richard and a rage-filled Ike Turner. Where DJ Kool Herc was arrested for throwing the block party that started hip-hop, where Chano Pozo wasn't saved by Santería and where Miles Davis was taken after that third album, to those born in such a world, what Mico spins isn't music, it's salvation.

And to Prentis and Tam as well. There's no discrimination in their choice of music or partners. So long as they can be close to each other, they sway, buckle their knees, throw their hands in the air, shimmy, step, slide, and jump with the type of abandon I wish I could have provided for them every day. The girls make sounds of their own, sometimes singing along, sometimes hooting in counterpoint to the music. Pasha does a good job trying to keep up, but born of this world, he doesn't know if he should move in the rigid form this reality has taught him is dance or fall on his knees before Mico and his speakers. When his arms go and I see the empty knife sheaths at his side, I check mine. For the first time since they were formed, the entropy blades are fully silent.

Samantha has that rare ability to fully dance and get other tasks done. When she taps my shoulder I pay attention to the monitor she's pointing at. The uplinks we provided to all the other Decimation islands are two-way audio-visual. Mico told us we wouldn't need the audio if he was doing his job right. The man deserves a raise. Those that aren't drenched in sweat in Jamaica, Fire Island, Catalina, the Caymans, the Canary islands, and Easter Island are literally on their knees crying before a video of Mico spinning. Sam points out three particular smaller screen divisions where local DJs seem to be tag teaming with Mico.

"People all over are sending in their death songs," Samantha semi-shouts in my ear. Her lips brush my lobe and I don't want it to end.

"What's a death song?" I ask, wrapping my hand around her waist gently.

"The last song people want to hear before they die. A lot of the initial ones were shit. But more and more are coming through—unsigned, unreleased, underground stuff filled with this world's music magic." She's surprised, happy.

"Four and three and two and one." The track starts, and I swear it's an old Beastie Boys track until I realize it's three women rapping in Spanglish over a stripped-down klezmer/polka beat. Mico dissolves some chord progressions on an organ behind it and it's an instant classic. Crowds everywhere lose it.

"See?" she tells me and kisses my lips. "It's working."

"They're coming," I tell her. She nods, then flicks her nose with her thumb like an old school boxer. The smile never fades even as the chants of "Taggert" get louder on the dance floor. I look down from the stage and see Othica pointing at me with her spear. Then she points to her shuffle-stepping feet.

"I think you've been invited to dance," Sam says. Before I have a chance to resist, she pushes me off the stage. The Bint al-nas continue to chant my name in perfect rhythm, with a Mos Def, J. Dilla, Chance the Rapper mashup I never thought I'd hear again until I'm face to face with the sweaty seven-foot camel-hearted leader of their clan. She cups the back of my neck and pulls my forehead to hers.

"This is your war party," she sings to me in her language. For them, war party means the celebration of life before death.

"Our war party," I say back in her language.

"No. We would not all be here if not for you. It is your daughters who provide the strategy. Our spears and voices serve the Manna and serve you. Win or lose, this is your war party. And it is a good one." Her breath smells of sage, lemongrass . . . and Manna. It makes me wonder who I'm speaking to.

"The enemy hasn't shown up yet," I tell her.

"They're here." It's the Manna speaking through her. It's giving me the last bit of help it can until we win or die.

I wait for the quarter of a second when Mico's hands aren't on any piece of equipment then body ping everyone, according to plan. Immediately, Mico shifts the music to a spare snare hand-clap version of some Beach Party song, giving it more bounce and soul than the original ever intended.

"Good war, everyone. Fight hard," Tam thinks back to the same set of people. She sounds strong. She is strong. Tam takes Prentis by the hand and leads her across the dance floor to Mico. Like all of us, he's sweating. But he's also focused and in charge. A microphone waits at the side of his decks for my girls. I'm scanning all horizons trying not to get caught unaware.

"I could have been one of the most notorious . . ." Tam and Prentis start. Suddenly a section of the bamboo wall shatters. Shards sever the cords connecting the monitor to the decks, then continue on to threaten all on the dance floor. Five Bint al-nas move quickly to deflect and shatter the debris. For the first time in four hours, the music stops.

"Enough of this Hare Krishna shit," Baron says, floating in and fuming from the opposite side of the dance floor. "Where's Taggert?"

"Right here," I tell him, stepping in the clear path everyone has made between us. "But I'm not your problem."

"For once we agree." He starts levitating toward me. All I can feel is his hate. "You won't be my problem much longer."

"Sorry, brother," I tell him, as the wind begins to push against his telekinetic advance with such force that he can't move forward.

"Hey, Alter ball licker," A.C. says, standing behind Baron. "Let's wrassle." Once Baron identifies A.C. as the obstruction in his path to me, his rage shifts. Baron flies quickly toward A.C.

I hear the shots before I see the guns in A.C.'s hands. Six shots apiece from each revolver cluster around Baron's third eye, neck, and heart, but none of them make contact. Baron's strain is clear as he stops floating even as he suspends the white-hot bullets in midair. He's strong in his telekinesis, refusing to let anything but the smallest purchase of space be gained by each bullet every second. Those cursed bullets will never stop coming for him. All Baron is doing is delaying the inevitable.

"I'm impressed." A.C. says like he's watching Little League practice. He holsters his pistols.

"Is that . . . all . . . you've got?" My brother's fake confidence doesn't crack.

"Unfortunately for you," A.C., says pulling out his sword, "no."

"You're a coward, Taggert!" arc his last words. A.C. slices through Baron's trunk like it's butter. With first contact, Baron's power fails him, and the cursed bullets find their home. He's doubly dead in less time than it takes to tell.

"Another man done gone . . ." comes from the same speakers Baron tried to destroy. How Mico managed to connect them, I'll never know.

"I could've been one of the most notorious," Tam and Prentis go back to their solo. But now I hear something more tragic in Tam's voice. She walks toward her uncle's broken and bullet-ridden body repeating the same line in response to Mico's loop of "Another man done gone." When she gets to his body, Tam repeats the verse to herself but looks at Mico.

"Don't stop dancing!" Mico shouts the crowd into motion, echoing with no equipment. Mico lets loose a jump-up Ragga tune with Tam's vocals, freshly recorded over it. The crowd loses it. It's a merge of a mosh pit and a group hug. I clear the space between Tam, A.C., and Baron's dead body in a second.

"One down," A.C. says, cleaning off his blade.

"Foot soldier." I nod.

"Should've probably done that earlier," Tam quips.

"I was actually hoping we might find a way to turn him," I confess.

"You're sounding more like Mico every day," A.C. says. He turns his back; an eighteen-foot stone arrow shatters our makeshift dance-hall's southern roof and lands its point directly into A.C.'s back. Tam pushes me clear before the splayed stone feathers clip either of us. The momentum of the arrow drives A.C. through the dance floor and into the earth below.

"A.C.!' she shouts. The crowd threatens to panic.

"Don't stop dancing! That's what they want." Mico shouts over the speakers. I feel his crowd-summoning powers working in overdrive as he cranks an Old Dirty Bastard tune.

"If anyone can survive it, kid," I tell her as I navigate around the enormous arrow and pull Tamara to her feet. "Game face, Tam!"

She nods, and we run to the window to see what shot that damn missile. Should've known. Rama.

"Ray Harryhausen should sue." I laugh. Scores of stone Indian Ramas, Shivas, Hanumans and his monkey disciples, Ganesha, Indras, and Vishnus, along with stone tigers, wild boars, eions, and elephants stomp out of the ocean. All of them sculpted from devoted hands, perverted into housing for the Alters. From the ocean, not even bothering to come to land, a giant Rama draws another monstrous arrow and aims at us.

"Who?" Othica asks, attracted to the same window as us.

"Don't worry about it. Get some of your people to the pillars that hold this place up. Mico is the priority. We've got to keep broadcasting. But only take who you need. We also need to keep the focus on the dance floor." She's gone without a word.

"What about big boy?" Tam asks as the stone Rama aims.

"You said you were ready." I look at her.

"I can't catch that arrow!"

"So don't let him release it." Then she smiles. At the Rama's anchor point, just below its chin, Tam breaks the stone drawstring with her power. The resulting backlash knocks the giant statue off its feet. The splash makes everyone not already fighting cheer.

"Good job!" I smile. Below us, Bint al-nas fight alongside Prentis's fire-breathing lizards. But she's also morphed her silver spitting spiders from tiny weavers to wolf-sized eight-legged defenders of us all. Number-wise we're good.

"Still no big Alters," I tell Samantha. Tam tails me, old feelings of frustration and resentment toward Sam building in her, as French Cuban twins harmonize a complicated love letter to the Goddess Oya on Mico's turntable.

"What are you talking about?" she yells at me over the battle sounds and Mico. Before I can explain, she takes us down a flight of stairs to the ground floor of the battle, the beach. A stone four-armed Shiva lobs a skull at me just as I hit terra firma. I stay in its linear attack angle and kick the skull back, opting not to pivot into its trident's wide sweep. The entropy blades are thankful for my call. It feels good to have them back in my hands.

Before the fake god can take a step, I slice two of its hands at the wrist. The stone snake around its neck almost catches me, but I slant wide and circle to the ground with both blades in front of me, taking out what fake tendons it has. The snake gets decapitated just before the stone Shiva.

Closer to the ocean, Tamara has hurled two small stone monkeys into a human-sized Ganesh with her power. Before it can react to the hole in its chest, she sends it clear across the beach into the leg of a larger stone Indra, crippling it. She's sweating but still in it.

"There," Samantha says, coming from cover. "You just finished two Alters," she tells us as we pant.

"Why would they take stone forms?" Tam asks.

"Not stone. Objects of worship for a millennium. They've collected the psychic energy of devotion in these divine forms and are using them to end humanity. Can you think of a greater perversion?" Sam's disgust is haptic.

"Traitor!" a blue, washed-stone Sita says behind Samantha, sword drawn. In the chaos of the stone Hanumen children and Ganesh's fighting the desert women, I miss this Alter. Tam and I move to intercept, but Sam cups her hands and points her palms in our direction. A clear signal for us to stay back.

"I could never betray you because I was never yours." Arms still out to her side, Samantha advances on the fake god. She ignores its stone blade and the chaos around us. "I was never part of this world. Come and see mine."

Revivalist preachers of old have nothing on Sam as she grips the side of the stone Alter's head and begins to chant in the language of the Bint al-nas.

"I am the child of gods so old the mountains have forgotten their names. I am the chosen of the Manna. I am the Liminal woman of the Habesha. You could never hold me. See what I contain." As soon as both of her lips touch the stone Sita's forehead, it crumbles to dust.

"Told you she had diseases." Tam almost laughs. Above us, Cypress Hill's "Born to Get Busy" sounds appropriate. Before I can move, one of Prentis's giant scaly beasts tumbles into me. I'm as compassionate as I can be stopping its tumbles. I have to boost my biceps and thigh muscles to stop its momentum, the beast weighs as much as a baby elephant. It sighs thanks as I right it back on its feet.

"You made a friend." Tam smiles, petting the lizard. I scan its trajectory. Three Bint al-nas and fire lizards are going hard against a two-story-tall Sita with an attitude.

"Go back upstairs," I tell my daughter, and grab a split, discarded spear before jumping on the lizard's back. He gets the idea. But before we can take off, the biggest stone Alter, the one Tam knocked flat on its back, stands again. This time he floods the beach. Tam keeps the land around the dance hall dry.

"Fat chance, Tag," she says, walking to meet her challenge. Before I can insult her, I slap my lizard mount. It spits a stream of fire at the groin of the Sita Alter, then does its quick gallop toward the walking apostasy. The stone giant, too busy with the Bint al-nas stabbing at its feet with spears and song along with the three giant lizards on it's back, does little more than flinch.

I hurl the spear at its solar plexus. When I hear it sink into the stone chest, I jump from the reptile's back before it gets into striking range. I grab the spear and swing up to put my feet on the shaft. It's hard because the Sita is rocking and turning. But I only need a second of balance. I leap off the spear just as the Sita arches its back At eye level, I hear Mico drop Protoje's "Criminal" and think he's playing it just for me. I pull the entropy blades and slice across the critter's eyes. Its fake eyes go blind. Too quickly, it pivots to swat at me. I catch its thumb, swinging around it, and backflip off the backhand. My landing behind the affront to Indian gods everywhere isn't pretty, but I don't break anything.

Othica runs over from up the beach with a larger than normal spear. She swings at the beast's legs, knocking out boulder-sized bits and driving shards of shale everywhere. When she's done, the blind giant can't stand. Casually she walks to its neck, jumps high in the air, and severs the two-ton head from the rest of its body. The Bint al-nas sing and howl for their leader. She barely has time for their praise.

"This is taking too long." The giantess pulls me to my feet.

"That works to our advantage." I try to believe it. Othica is already distracted by the growing shadow covering the island. The Stone Archer with impossible aim advances on us. And at the beachhead, only Tamara. I can feel her summoning her power. But Prentis beats her to it.

"What are those?" Othica asks once we get close to Tamara.

"I believe those are phoenixes," I say. The giant peacock looking birds beat their wings in perfect time to A Tribe Called Quest song Mico spins as they descend on the giant. A massive flock of birds of paradise and prey precede the mythological birds. It's a glorious assault. As the phoenixes tear the stone Alter apart, it does it's best to scream with rocks for lungs. Plus the Rza beat Mico throws over the sound almost drowns out Prentis's panicked shout. I look to the dance floor above us and see her, frightened.

"Pitch me now!" I tell Tam. She doesn't hesitate. A second later I'm careening through the hole the stone arrow made. But Tam isn't at full strength. She barely gets me the lift I need. I end up rolling in on the ground like a thrown sack of potatoes.

'They're here!" Prentis shouts, pointing at the other end of the dance floor. Flooded as it is with female desert soldiers scrapping with the stone monkey Alters, it's hard to see the two flesh-made Alters in the far doorway.

"Is this your soundtrack to the end of all things, Vassal?" Rice, in a waist trimming cream white suit, sounds like every privileged white prick I've ever wanted to slap. "I'll be honest. I hate it."

"I don't take requests," Mico shouts from his station as he throws on an E-40 track called "Yay Area." I know it's been hard for Chabi to hold back but she's done a great job hiding on the dance floor until Rice showed his face. I knew he wouldn't be able to resist making a personal appearance. Poppy, standing next to him in her black silk pajamas, is the surprise.

"S'up, Rice?" Chabi says, already making her way past crippled and broken stone monkeys.

"Chabi, I can explain," he says. I've only seen that level of fear in one other Alter's eyes. Rice's father. Right before we turned him inside out.

"Explain why you killed me, fuckboy? Come on! Explain it!" she barks. He runs out the door. Chabi gets smart, turns, and jumps out the same hole Tamara threw me through. Before she goes, a finger pointed at Poppy and a command, "End that bitch."

"Ah, Nordeen's little wounded healer." This black silk pajama Becky's voice sounds like a syphilis serenade. "You sired that child who stole from me, didn't you? I can't abide your continued breath, I'm afraid."

"Bet my breath smells better than whatever fetid gas passes your lips," I tell her, pulling my blades. "But who am I to judge?" We meet in the middle of the dance floor, but I've missed a lot of her friends. Rats, deformed with overgrown teeth—and no chill—surround her like a fallen cloak, snapping and biting.

"Prentis," is all I can get out. Poppy lands a bone-breaking kick on my side just as Sly and the Family Stone's "Family Affair" fades out and "Trouble on My Mind" by Tyler the Creator and Pusha T comes in. An instant later, I'm across the room desperate to heal a rack of compound fractures in my ribs while fighting off her twisted rats.

"Prentis!" It hurts to yell.

"Aren't real rats!" she shouts back standing over me, trying to control the plague monsters. I watch two Bint al-nas fall in front of Poppy's whispered hateful power. But Mico doesn't stop spinning. His beats are protecting the rest of us from succumbing to her madness.

"Those birds outside real?" I suggest. The healing is awkward for the same reason I couldn't heal Tam properly; Alters hurt at weird angles. But as I gasp, Prentis's air force of a thousand birds flies by us as they flood in and make meals of the Alter rats. They barely pause Poppy's progress toward Mico.

"Don't stop dancing!" the DJ shouts as he transitions from a Sha-bazz Palaces track to a polyphonic Rashad Roland Kirk rendition of a John Coltrane song. Poppy reaches out slowly to touch him, but Mico is no punk. He screams his Manna-powered scream in her face. I've seen it break lesser Alters. She smiles and moves with cornered rat speed and strength, grabbing his throat. His howl is cut short.

"Off him!" Prentis swings on Poppy and it feel like the world goes quiet. Gone are the sounds of the battles outside, the ocean, the song of the Bint al-nas. All I can hear is Mico's heartbeat. I'm spitting blood but I'm standing, walking to the stage, when Poppy uses one hand to slap Prentis across the stage. My girl collapses like a rag doll.

"Sing now, Manna boy!" The human-shaped disease laughs, choking Mico out. What Bint al-nas that can throw spears and songs at the stage do, but it equals nothing.

"Where's your god?" the witch mocks. "The God of Connections? Your patron? Where is your cloak against the eternal cold and dark now, Mico? Does it exist? Did it ever?" I hear a crack in his neck just before I get to the stage.

"Fuck off, ya tired slag!" Tam slams the Alter into the ceiling with her telekinesis. The force breaks Poppy's grip on Mico's neck. It staggers Poppy. Barely. The Alter lands on her feet. But she hasn't seen me. So I sink both entropy blades into her back and drags down to the ground. It's like cutting through hide; the smell of what passes for Alter blood fouls the air. Poppy shrieks, but doesn't fall.

"The next island over." We all turn to see Prentis, standing slowly.

"What?" Poppy shakes and staggers, realizing how wounded she is.

"You asked where his god is. The answer is 'The next island over.' We sent all the humans along with Bingy man, Pasha, Fatty, and Ahmadi before you deformed evil wankers showed up. Bingy and

Ahmadi coaxed the Manna into growing there, and everyone over there has been smoking the pure stuff for a good hour now. If the plan held out, then they also coaxed it into growing under this island as well. That means you're standing on his god right now."

"It doesn't matter! The Decimation is still our—"

"Shut your face!" Tam slams the Alter to the ground with less force but more effect now that it's weakened. "Don't you get it? Africa is liberated. We broadcasted from Gili Meno so all the other Decimation islands see liberation is possible. You've been fighting us, but the real war was for the people of this reality. And they've freed themselves."

"What about these souls?" Poppy points to the dance floor.

"Drop it," Tam says to the air. Somewhere in the psychic ether, Alia hears and lets the massive dance floor illusion fall. What the Alter assumed were souls debating the Decimation on the dance floor were the long-dead African souls that usually lived in Mico's arm.

"Well, at least I killed your prophet." Before I can get my hands to move, Tam rips what passes for a heart out of Poppy's chest. She collapses as the Alter does. But I see my girl breathing.

"What you got wrong with you?" I ask Mico as I crawl to him, cradling his head in my lap.

"Fix him?" Prentis asks what all the Bint al-nas, what the spirits' silence, demand. He can't talk, can't swallow, he can't breathe, the weight of his head is crushing his esophagus and spine. Alters hurt everything they touch.

"Too weak," I whisper. The African spirits hear it. They swirl, brawl, and rage with enough fury to scare the Bint al-nas.

"There are still Alters on this island," Prentis reminds me. "We need them." I follow her eye line and realize she's talking about the spirits.

"Tag, give me the tattoo," Tamara says, shoving her arm in my face. Mico, coughing on his own sputum, offers his arm into my other hand. He nods. The vassal of connection's last request. So I spent myself, not duplicating, but putting the exact diagram from Mico's arm and putting it into my girl's. I do this instead of what my instinct is, which is to heal him. That's not what he wants. It's not what will save us.

Gili Air, Indonesia
Prentis

Everything the Manna said would happen has happened. As the Black spirits flood into Tam's arm I know they'll find a space and comfort in her even Mico couldn't provide. They'll feed her, giving her all the strength she can handle. Now there's only my choice.

Poor Tag. Sit next to him as he tries to find some way to control what's happening to any of us. But we don't control our lives. None of us. The best we can do is make the best choices at any given moment.

"Mico." Crouch to speak into his ear. What passes for breath sounds is more and more like fluid passing through broken rocks. "The Manna told you about this moment, didn't it? It told me as well. You are vassal for the God of Connections in the world of flesh. No one could have done a better job. Rest now. I take your burden. Animals are flesh, see? I will hold your memory as a guide. Your legacy will be treasured in the Manna forever."

With his final breath, a large cloud of Manna eases from Mico's mouth. Larger than his body should be able to carry. Bigger than the smoke he gave to Bingy. Size of an overhead cloud. His portion of the Manna, held and grown in his body, carried through space and back in time. I stand. All the Bint al-nas recognize it and begin their sacred hum. Open my mouth and invite it into me. It feels like an old friend. Instantly, I am infinite.

"You good, Tam?" say, with the god making room for itself in me.
"Oh, fuck yeah!" she almost shouts, charged by the rageful spirits.
"Cool. Let's go Alter bashing then!"

When I accepted the Manna, so too did every animal I ever touched. Gives them a critical advantage over the remaining Alters, already reeling from a lack of leadership and the fact that no one had killed themselves. The African spirits, hungry for vengeance, and the Bint al-nas, girls that like to sing songs of power and throw spears, we're all owed some stone bashing. Between us, we take down the remaining Alters in under twenty minutes. All save one.

Tam and I catch up with Chabi at the east end of the island, staring off into the distance at a high-speed boat.

"That Rice?"

"That it is," Chabi hisses. "Slipped away."

"The fuck he did." Tam smiles. "I can fly."

"I want to kill him with my own hands," she tells us.

"I've got a phoenix you can ride on."

Mico's African spirits, guess they're Tam's now, disable Rice's cigar boat before the phoenix can drop me and Chabi off. The last Alter steals the joy of his panic from us. Acts like he stopped his boat, like flaming birds drop badass chicks on his deck all the time. He's shaking a damn cocktail. His calm demeanor drives Chabi's rage. Still, she holds her ass-kicking until Tam lands on the back deck of the speedboat.

"Cocktail, anyone?" He offers the steel tumbler. Tam, near vibrating with the power and rage of the spirits, snatches it out of his hands and throws the container into the ocean with a telekinetic gesture. "Rude."

"Oh, you have no idea," Tam tells him.

"No, it's you and yours that are the clueless ones." He sits on white leather cushions. "I bet you think you've won some great victory. Destroyed the evil and saved humanity from total annihilation."

"Pretty much." Tam laughs.

"Maybe this concept is too hard for you ladies," he sneers. "But understand that me and mine are creatures of entropy. The eternal cold is no more interested or concerned in human affairs than it is in the affairs of a match after it's been struck. At some point, the flaw that is existence will die out and it will never reignite. The lack of ignition, that stillness, that is my cellular makeup. Destroy this body, this consciousness, all you're doing is returning me home. And eventually, you will join me."

Manna pushes its voice through my mouth and I don't resist.

"Rice Montague raised you," it says.

"And your agents destroyed him," Rice replies calmly, unfazed by the fact that he's talking to a god.

"And yet you never questioned why an agent of entropy would raise a child," the Manna says. "During your kind's last tantrum, I infected you with the idea of child rearing."

"You lie!" Finally, some shock in the bastard.

"Why would I? The battle is over. You lost. This time, I introduced forgiveness to your kind. My previous vassal took one of your kind in. As a result, Narayana—one of the most powerful Alters—supported your opposite number, a Liminal. He loved her. Sacrificed himself for her. The child rearing project is complete, that path of annihilation for your kind is over. When next you try to advance the end of all things, you will have to find another way."

"Then you acknowledge that this is not the end," Rice calls out for some semblance of victory.

"Between your kind and my children, there will never be an end. I grow, you shrink. But between us, dynamic life will always exist. And that is my victory. So know that I forgive you," the Manna says through my lips.

"I don't," Chabi says.

"Yeah, she don't," I say, the Manna retreating back into my subconscious.

Never seen the Entropy of Bones done fully on a body before.

Gross.

Epilogue

Gili Air, Indonesia
Taggert

We cremated my brother on a set of craggy rocks at night. Just me and Tamara. Neither one of us said a word. What was there to say? On the way back, I almost ran into Othica, who stood in near total darkness on the beach, looking out into God knows what.

"They told me he was your brother," she said.

"Not him. But something like him." I told her the truth.

"He was fortunate to have someone to bury him." She put her massive hand on my shoulder.

"And we're fortunate not to need burying," I told her, lightly hitting her ribs.

A few days later, the Bint al-nas sang a huge hole in the middle of the air. Hadn't seen it done so elegantly before. Imagine a sliver of glass, splitting light into a prism, then collapsing that light onto itself to make a kaleidoscope of rainbows. Fully spectrumed and dazzling rainbows right above the bay.

The Bint al-nas dragged all their dead, including Mico, back to their peaceful desert in the middle of nowhere. Can't imagine what they'll have to explain to their people. Fatima looked on through tear-drenched eyes as Bingy, Ahmadi, and her father went with them.

"They are your people as much as anyone's," I said, watching as they hummed and rowed boats through the portal. "They'd make a place for you."

"I don't want a place in their world," she hissed. "I don't want the singing, the spears, the mid-desert heat. And I don't want that fucking god anywhere near me."

It was good to know I wasn't alone in that sentiment. A week and a half later, after the Decimation dummies started clearing the beaches of wrecked stone statues, smashed frozen in impossible positions, Samantha told me she was leaving. I had just come from a swim around the island as the sun was beginning to hide behind the horizon. She met me on a beach by the westernmost part of the island, the part closest to where Narayana murked the angels.

"You look better." She was one to talk. Someone needs to explain how she can be wearing a simple gray sarong and wrap, wet no less, and still look like something out of a fashion magazine.

"Feel better." I smiled.

"It's time." She offered me a towel. "The Habesha need me."

"Makes sense." I took the towel and dried off thoroughly before walking with her toward her hotel. Commerce was an illusion by that time already. There were no authorities to come check on the Gili islands. In some ways, we were more disconnected from the rest of this world than we were from our own. "How are you getting home?"

"It depends on how many people are traveling with me," she said slyly.

"You know every norm here will go anywhere you say . . ." I joked.

"I was thinking more about your girls," she said.

"Oh trust, they don't need a plane ticket anywhere. Those two can get to Mars if they want, no doubt." I laughed, reveling in my fully functioning body. The Alter-infused pains weren't easy to escape. But with time, I was able to fully knit myself together.

"And their father? Will he be joining me on my return?" She stopped walking at that point and looked at me dead on.

"To be what?" I asked, holding her hands and feeling her power once more. She'd smoked the Manna. I could feel it listening as we spoke. "Number one manservant to the Chieftess of the Manna?"

"Can I tell you how many people would kill for that position?" she said, nodding at me.

"No doubt . . ." I started.

"No, listen Taggert. Everything is different now. Remember, this is a whole new world. East Africa broke first from the Alters' grip. However this reality makes sense of what happened, it will privilege that part of the world, my part of the world. Our reality never allowed Africa to truly shine. Now it can. Indeed it must. Colonialism can't survive there anymore. The rampant consumption of all resources can't continue. Things have to change. We don't have to lose."

"And all it took was the death of Mico L'overture," I said quietly.

"Many Bint al-nas died as well," she told me.

"I didn't know those women. But trust I'm pissed for them as well," I say.

"Is that the only emotion you know how to have, Taggert? Anger? It was war. Everyone knew that they might . . ."

"But only one creature knew who would die. The Manna. The die was cast before any of us stepped on the killing floor," I said

"You can't hold the Manna to the same standards as . . ." she started.

"Samantha, I will always love you. You call me and I'll always come. I owe you that. But don't ask me to forgive the god you worship. And for sure don't ask me to serve it. Far as I can tell, it's taken enough from me." I said it slowly, so she got it.

Bless her, Sam didn't say any more about it. That night we all sat around a beach fire, told Mico stories, drank, and smoked freshly picked island weed from a smashed Rama flute. I let myself get drunk and high. At three in the morning, Sam and I disappeared from everyone else's view and made our way up a dark beach to my room. We took a shower together and I climbed in bed. I swear she kissed me first.

When I woke the next afternoon she was gone, along with ten recent converts to . . . whatever the hell she'd end up calling her religion or government. I put on a pair of khaki shorts and a large sleeveless T-shirt with the face of an elephant on it and made my way to the dance floor. Prentis had been camping out there, taking meals and meetings on the salvation stage, making it her base of operations. I could always find her there. It didn't escape my notice that she was often sitting or standing exactly where Mico went down.

"Hey, Tag," Tamara shouted as I approached. "Was there like a ghosty dude with a sword and guns that was in the scrap as well?"

I wanted to say no, but the outlines of the concept seemed so familiar I just shrugged my shoulders.

She waved me up, shouting. "Come figure this out because I think Chabi is going to go on a murder spree . . . another murder spree, if we don't get this sorted."

On the second floor, Chabi marched up and down the dance floor pointing at the giant arrow in the middle, shouting. I was thankful she was just using her vocal cords. Prentis sat on stage engaged but staying quiet as Tamara spoke with their warrior.

"He was here. I know he was here. And he was in my world. He was my friend," Chabi shouted.

"Okay. Not saying I don't believe you. Saying I don't who you're talking about," Tamara said.

"Taggert." The death dealer almost grabbed me. "Come on. You remember, what was his name?"

"Who?" I asked.

"I can't remember, but come on. This is what he did. Everybody forgot him and that's why he could . . . He was everywhere and nowhere all the time . . . Like air . . ." She sunk her bony sharp fingers into her thick mat of hair, angrily pulling at it.

"I don't know," I told her while I ravaged my memory for an inkling, a hint of him. Tamara looked at me, wondering if we'd all gone nuts or if it was just Chabi. And if it was just her, what would we do?

"Please." Her light brown hand stroked the massive arrow in absent-minded frustration. "I can't lose him too . . ." She wouldn't cry. She couldn't cry. But the wetness in her eye made me turn away from her. She was the type of warrior who couldn't abide her allies seeing her weakness. So I looked up, up at the giant arrow. It made no sense that it could fire. That it could hit whatever it struck. Even the feathers on its ends were stone. Feathers to catch the wind. It struck wind.

"A.C.," I said it softly, confused. But that was all he needed.

"I kill your brother and you can't even remember my name?!" we all heard on the wind.

When he came, A.C. came as a ghost. At least, as incorporeal. You can't kill wind, apparently. But in this new world, you can make a representative of the wind have to make new alliances to maintain itself in the world of humans. That's what the Alter arrow did. Chabi didn't care if she could touch him so long as she knew him and he knew her. Of course, once his ghostly ass appeared, intangible as it was, we all remembered him.

"Everything's different now," A.C. told us as we ate breakfast. "With the Alters beat back, Liminals will be on the come-up. Lots of you people."

"What do you mean, you people?" Tam laughed at him. "You mean people that can do this?" And she bit a piece of pineapple.

"Jokes from the bearer of the Sankofa souls," he said. "There's hope for us all. And don't worry about me. I get my sword and my guns back and I'll be as solid as any of you."

"Different how?" Pasha stayed on course. "What will be different now?"

"You can ask Taggert what wild Liminals running around can look like. Each choice you people make, I swear . . . Plus, and not to speak for the vassal of the Manna, but, well, humanity lost."

"Hold up, what now?" Pasha stood, trying to look at both the ghostly A.C. and the too calm Prentis at the same time. "We beat the Alters, they're all gone . . ."

"And in the process, they took out the vassal of connections in the world of flesh," A.C. said. "Mico connected humans through music. But the new vassal over there connects animals. So the God of Connections will now connect the animal kingdom first, and humans, if possible. Later. Maybe."

"Connect animals to what?" Pasha asked.

"Everything," Prentis said. "That's the project. Connect animal, vegetable, mineral, mite, microbe, mammoth, man, and immortal to one another. It will happen. Over time, it will happen. It's just a question of how and when."

"Any other changes to sanity you want to let us know about?" Fatima asked.

"Did I mention the ascension of the gods?" He smiled.

"Not in detail," Tam snapped at him.

"Well, aside from being the God of Connections, the Manna is also the food of the gods. It's what gods eat. Even more than worship. With a new vassal, and, hell, two islands already to call its own, the growth of the Manna will be huge. Gods will be springing up everywhere. And not like in the shape of the former gods like the Alters did, but genuine real live gods gods. Expect a pretty crowded astral plane as all these consciousnesses vie for their pieces of the infinite cosmology."

"I can't . . ." Pasha started. "Are you still speaking English?"

——

When the voices started to rise, I got up to leave. Most didn't even notice.

"It's like they've forgotten about Mico already," Fatima said as she lit a cigarette. She leaned against the post on the first floor. From a distance, I watched her lungs dealing with the smoke the way I used to watch Yasmine's. My Yasmine's.

"I'm surprised you remember him," I said. "How much time did you actually have with him?"

"None. Less than none. He looked at me and saw someone else. It was pathetic. I'm not pissed because he's gone." For a smuggler, Fatima was bad at lying.

"Then what?"

"That thing, the Manna. It used him. It used him and it used me like a beacon for him to find, to lead him to a home he never had, to retrieve junk. Literal junk. It was the junk, the music on forgotten flash drives that saved the world. And it knew that. It used his love of music and people . . . me to get him to do what it wanted him to do."

"And we won," I said softly.

"But what happens when it fights again? You think we left people in those rooms up there? Those are tools to that thing. What did the ghost guy call your girl, Sankofa souls? That sounds like a pretty powerful weapon to me. I've seen them in action. Took down a pack of ice djinn. And don't get me started on the animal girl. Fuck, I don't know where my dad is. Leverage? A hostage? And how can I trust the word of anyone that willingly associates with this super fungus?!"

"You're not wrong," I told her.

"I'm not happy either."

The next day Chabi and A.C. took off for the States. According to the ghost boy, the guns were somewhere in the United States and the sword was in Afghanistan. It's what happened whenever he died, he lost his tools. Chabi was going to be his hands for a while. I didn't see them off or wish them good luck. I'd like to think they understood why.

I caught up with the lucky boy while he was helping some locals build their house back up. It was a small two-room brick and cement-floor home a good mile away from the beach. He was pitching in, like everyone else. The villagers never understood why work went easier when he was around, but they were happy for it. I stayed in the cut, away from the norms, and gave him enough of a dead leg with my power for the kid to realize it wasn't natural. When he started coming my way, I whistled the pain away.

"You'd think by now, I'd earn a bit of respect," he complained, pushing past a fallen palm tree to me.

"Nothing but, little man," I told him. Before he could snip anymore I produced both entropy blades. Folded.

"What am I supposed to do with these?" Pasha asked.

"Keep them safe. Take them off my hands. Use them to protect my girl, if she needs protecting."

"I don't think you understand me and her . . ."

"Don't care. I need these things off me now. Can't think of a better person to hand them off to," I said.

"Um, Tamara? Prentis? They're the bigwigs now. Why not give the blades to them?" I thought about it for a second then started to walk back toward the beach.

"Because honestly, they're not as lucky as you."

That night I let my Liminal senses drift across to the other island. Alia's body was familiar, if bigger than I imagined. I wasn't interested in looking at this dimension's version of her. Mine had been enough. But Tamara told me what she put on the line, how much she risked. We had been the bright shiny football for the Alters to kick, but without Alia's illusions covering the African souls, we all would have lost. I owed her.

Back in the day, I healed her in under five minutes and it near wiped me out. So I took the whole night, making sure she stayed asleep. It's like repurposing a spaceship to be a family caravan, working on her body. She's fit for more than the simple life she wants, but who am I to tell someone where to find their happiness? I cleared the fallopian tubes and made sure her ovaries were well stocked before stopping. She did her work well. I could provide a just reward. Someone deserved it.

Fatima and I took off together. Lord knows where she got the fifty-foot yacht, but it was quiet and powerful and just enough space for us to have time apart. That first night, I would've swore that Prentis or Tam were going to drop in on me at any moment. But nothing. The same the next night. It took a week of me waiting to realize they weren't coming for me.

With two fully furnished, small bedrooms, Fatima could've laid out whenever she wanted. But it took her four full days before she made sure I knew how to pilot the ship. Even then, she pretty much just collapsed on the salon floor when she wasn't navigating. GPS satellites were shit thanks to the global chaos we caused by stopping the Decimation, so we navigated by compass and star. We would've gotten to our destination faster if we knew where the hell we were going.

In Langkawi, we saw the recently liberated but confused collective consciousness stumble into bits of action. Not only was the main aesthetic of this world broken, but nothing had stepped in to take its place. No one knew what to appreciate, how to behave toward one another. It wasn't as though savagery and skullduggery became the default. Rather everyone was sniffing at one another like new puppies in the pound. We resupplied and left quickly.

In Da Nang, we heard news. It was old news and garbled, but it was an attempt to make sense of what had happened. Already the Decimation was being referred to as a mass psychosis the world had never experienced before. A sophisticated set of rich sociopaths had promoted it through a global conspiracy somehow involving the underground drug trade, music producers, and unscrupulous government officials around the world. It was only through the efforts of small pockets of revolutionaries—primarily in East Africa—apparently psychosocially resistant to the cult of personality that the efforts were rebuffed. All around the world, repressive regimes that were either in cahoots with or silent about the Decimation were succumbing to political, social, and armed pressure. If Fatima heard, she acted like she didn't care.

I had to almost double her ration orders as I was still healing, but other than that she took care of the needs of her ship. Every now and then in a port, I'd catch a whiff of that almost cinnamon-like Manna. I'd look and see an old Vietnamese sailor and wonder who was looking back at me. Nothing ever came of it, except my paranoia.

Fifteen days later we were trying to find a decent harbor in New Zealand. Auckland was shut down due to the world economy going into freefall. Seemed like everyone all came to the realization that gold was just a shiny metal good for fuck all. No one was interested in mining for it, or for diamonds, copper, zinc, silver, or the rare earth material necessary to keep tech giants in place. The slaves freed themselves. Nobody knew the price of anything anymore. Luckily, Fatima knew a Maori family in Cape Saunders that owed her a favor.

"Where we headed, Captain?" I finally asked her after two days sitting in dock.

"Where's the farthest we can get away from the Manna and all of it?" she asked me, in her captain's chair, looking out on the South Pacific.

"You're carrying it with you," I told her. I pointed to her head. "Right there, lady. As long as you hold on to it, it'll follow us wherever we go."

——

When I woke up the next morning we were out of sight of land. I had the feeling we were east, but I couldn't be sure until she let me steer the ship. She started doing that more regularly. Started sleeping more as well. And crying. But only in her sleep. The last time I'd been out to that much sea, Mico was weaving some spell and Tamara was keeping me floating. Something about having my hands wrapped around a giant brass wheel and a constantly moving compass was comforting. I only imagined the ghost sharks coming to get me as I slept once.

"Why did you leave with me?" Fatima finally asked me when we were a day or two outside of Panama. The worst weather we'd experienced was rain. A massive typhoon hit the Philippines just as we left New Zealand, but other than that it's been only the occasional heavy wind. So despite spotty GPS, Fatty sat with her feet up on the helm, pulling swigs from a bottle. I'd made burgers. She finally started eating. I was getting worried. She didn't have that much more weight to lose.

"I needed a ride," I told her.

"I'm not one of your little girls, I don't need you." She needed the booze to speak her truth.

"That's funny. You think those girls need me."

There was a slacker dawdling at the Panama Canal. The main through-way of products from the U.S. to Asia and vice versa was at a near standstill. Fatima kicked me off the ship's wheel as soon as we spotted the enormous tankers filled with shipping containers anchored by the entrance of the port. Fatima got on the radio and started speaking in a Spanish too quick for even me to understand. I went out to the bow and let my eyes focus on the distance. Chinese and Indian deckhands were eating and dancing to Bhangra music. I went back in and told Fatima after she got off the CB.

"There's absolutely no world agreement on global prices, so no one wants to move any product anywhere," she told me with a half smile.

"None of the ships' captains know if they're going to get paid, and if they do, they don't know how much that payment will be worth. So they're letting deckhands get into some of the containers. Same with the canal. It costs money to get through, but no one knows how much it should cost, and digital transfers of currency are a bit iffy right now."

"So we're stuck?" I asked.

"Fuck that noise. I know a guy. Plus I've got ten uncut diamonds in the hold. He's on his way."

"Pretty expensive hall pass. Where we headed, Captain?" I asked.

"He's only getting one. And you'll know when we get there. Now shut up and don't embarrass me in front of my people."

Fatima's guy fueled us up as well as got us through the canal. I was able to barter my doctoring skills for supplies on the other side of the Canal. I cleared up everything from dysentery to broken limbs. It felt good to do simple healings again. Nothing had been simple for so long. In return, we got enough to eat and drink for another three weeks. Turns out we only needed supplies for about ten hours.

"We're here," Fatima told me as soon as the island came into view.

"And here is . . . ?"

"Grenada." Finally, a smile on her face.

"Okay. And how did you pick Grenada?"

"Never been." She looked at me. I nodded. Then she cried for a good long time. You'd never be able to tell when she spoke again. Her voice was as flat as ever.

"I didn't love him. I couldn't have. I didn't know him. But I miss him. I miss what he could've been to me. What I was to him. I know it doesn't make sense. But it's not fair either. It's not fair that this stranger can come into your life, tell you that you're meant to be together, and then just die on you."

"Amen."

"Fuck your god talk." Not a hint of malice.

"Fair enough."

"How do you deal with it, Taggert? How do you take the power-lessness?" she asked.

"Power is overrated, lady." It's all I can give her. I head below deck to pack up what limited gear I'd scrounged.

Grenada was immune to the Decimation. Apparently, it would have happened during something called J'ouvert, a daybreak masquerade that starts carnival. Not one Grenadian was willing to do anything during J'ouvert except party, and somehow that kept the Alters away. I guess it wasn't the only site of resistance either. All around the Caribbean and the world, small pockets of people didn't fight the Alters but they damn sure didn't go along with them. The Grenadians took the end of the Decimation as a sign that they needed to turn every weekend into J'ouvert. Cut off from the demands of external commerce and fully able to produce enough food and rum for those on the island, Grenada turned into a nonstop weekend party.

Five days into port and somehow Fatima secured a converted light-house for her home. She offered me a bedroom, but I asked her for the ship instead. She couldn't say no. She didn't say much about it until I was lowering her into the away boat.

"It's quicker to fly to Ethiopia, you know?" she told me. Took me a second to get it.

"I'm not trying to leave. I'll stay around here, in the bay. Maybe see some of the other islands. But I like the rum here."

"There's enough room at my spot. Or you can get another. What? You afraid I'm going to molest you or something?" I should've been so lucky.

"The sway of the ocean beneath my feet feels more honest than solid land," I finally confessed to her. "There's nothing solid. You know that. On solid land, I'm tempted to believe I have some control, some sense of what's happening. But on this ship, out in the sea? We're all powerless. I don't mind being powerless. I just hate thinking I've got some control."

So I stayed on the ship. Not pathologically. I came off for supplies. Fatima helped out. I fished, cruised around, met folks. Good people. Helped when I could. But I slept on the boat, lived on the boat, traveled on the boat. For a year.

Then my girls came.

"Don't you dare run, old man," I heard in my head as I smoked a joint on deck and listened to the short wave. The world was knitting itself together, making sure some parts stayed torn. Global leaders had to figure out what to do with the fact that no one would tolerate slavery anymore, of any kind. On top of that, domesticated animals, chickens, pigs, cows, sheep, were also rebelling. It was impossible to ranch and wholesale slaughter the way it had been done for a century and a half. If you wanted meat, you had to track it down and kill it yourself.

"Where am I going to run where you can't find me?" I sighed deeply. A week earlier I'd helped some locals track a few wild boar that were tearing up the cane fields. I pulled five boar steaks from my cooler and heated up the grill. Right after I set slices of pineapple to soak in the overproof rum, I heard Fatima's outboard racing toward me.

"I know," I told her as soon as she got on deck. It'd taken a few months, but recently Fatima had stopped wearing her rifle on her hip all the time. But now it was back and fully loaded under a beautiful yellow summer dress.

"You call them? You tell them I was here?" Fatima asked, breathing hard.

"I didn't have to call them or tell them anything. They knew. They always knew. We weren't hiding. They were just leaving us alone."

I felt the wind as Tamara landed on the deck behind me, but I didn't feel her body. I turned and saw why. Fatima looked so shocked. Tam was cloaked head to toe in the all-black faceless shine of the Sankofa spirits.

"Tam?" I asked.

"Oh shit," she said and instantly absorbed the spirit back into her arm. "Sorry, Fatima, for real. Didn't even think about what that would remind you of, luv. Swear." She wore a mechanic's jumper that had never seen a spot of grease but more than its share of blood. Not hers.

"Why would you?" Fatima sounded almost defeated as she threw herself into one my lounge chairs. Me and Tam hugged hard.

"Look good, kid," I told her, resisting the urge to scan her with my powers. "Still got the scar, I see."

"Keeps me humble, you know? Look at you, Mr. Island Living. And fuck off for not saying goodbye. Not taking me with you."

"I'd just slow you down these days, kid."

"You always slowed me down, Tag." She smiled, refusing to let me go. "That's why I needed you."

"You got it backward, Tamara. I needed you. But I'm grown up now. Come on, let's get some food in you."

Fatima didn't speak until the meat, the pineapple, and the rum were all half consumed. When she did, I had a hard time figuring out if she was ally or enemy. Fatima had never been around Tamara all that much. They didn't know each other. And Fatima barely trusted me, let alone the bearer of her former love's brand.

"You here to take him away?" Fatima asked.

"Wot? No! I came to see my da. That's it. He wants to stay here, he's more than earned it," she said to Fatima. Then she turned to me. "But if you want to be out in the world, there's things that need fixing."

"Global domination not enough for your plant god?" Fatima shouted and stood.

"Fatima," I said softly. "Why don't you head back to shore? It's just Tamara. I'm okay."

"I . . . I can . . ." She seemed at a loss. She even pulled her short rifle, but pointed it at the deck. "I can protect you if you want me to . . ."

"I'm okay," I told her, going over to her and rubbing her shoulders. I hadn't reached out to her with my powers ever, and this wasn't the time to start, but I read her and felt the despair and the tension in her body. "Tamara would never hurt me. I'm good." She walked like a zombie back to her small dingy and piloted back to land.

"What the fuck happened to her?" Tam asked after I sat.

"Her love was used as a signaling collar by a god more concerned with its plans than those that actualize them." I couldn't help it. Spite crept into my voice. "And what the hell with those spirits?"

"I'm sorry, I'm sorry . . ."

"Haven't you ditched them yet?"

"Ditched them? Island sun hit your brain, Tag? I can't ditch these spirits. You were there. They bond for life."

"Whose life?" I asked and took a bite of pig. Tam took a shot of rum in order not to fight.

"Do they just squeeze a sugar cane until it turns alcoholic?" she asked, shaking off the overproof rum.

"Pretty much." She looked good. Strong, confident. No battle scars. No fatigue. Whatever she was doing, it wasn't taxing her. "What's up with lucky boy?"

"Says thanks for the blades. They've been more useful than he'd have imagined. Turns out . . ."

"Jesus, kid. Don't make me be the asshole here. I don't want to know what you guys are all into, okay? I just want to know if Pasha is okay? Alive? Happy? Safe?"

"Okay, Tag. Okay. Sorry. Yeah. He's good." We stayed quiet for a while as the sun beat down on us. "This a mistake? Me coming here?"

"You're okay," I told her. "We're okay. I'm glad to see you. You look good."

"Thanks. I'm taking care of myself. No sewer living. No getting into . . . trouble just for the sake of it. Hey, I even ran into Samantha not too long ago. Didn't call her a skank or anything."

"I knew that maturity would kick in one day." We both laughed. "She look good?"

"Busy. You listen to the radio, so I'm not telling you anything new. But all that stuff with the African Union? That's her doing. And the world is paying attention."

"Good for her." I meant it.

"She told me you could have been number one concubine or something."

"Or something."

"She wanted me to tell you the offer still stands."

"I like my boat." I poured more rum and passion fruit juice for both of us. After a while I couldn't hold back anymore. "Where's Prentis?"

"She . . . She's not sure if you wanted to see her."

"Prentis isn't sure or the Manna isn't sure?"

"Package deal now, Tag."

"Don't I fucking know it."

"Prentis misses you something crazy. But she knows how you feel about the Manna, so she . . ."

"Sent you here to feel me out." I nodded, getting it.

"Can you blame her?"

"Nope. Smarter play than I would've done. Tell her to come."

"You sure?"

"Yeah. It's going to happen sooner or later. Might as well get it over with."

"It'll take her a few hours to get here."

"Good. I want to show you something. I found this hole in the ocean floor. You go through it, and on the other side there's this underground cave with air trapped in it. It's pressurized."

All day Tam and I swam and explored. We ate and talked. We laughed and remembered. We cried and remembered. She held it well, but Mico's death hit her as hard as anyone. I'm happy for that. She's still human, for now at least.

That night, I went back into the bay with the boat. Tam changed into a white skirt and gray tank top I had downstairs.

"And whose clothes are these?" she asked.

"I meet people. Sometimes they spend the night."

"If you let your daughter wear some random skank's clothes . . ." she started.

"Don't worry. No skanks allowed." I smiled, but then I caught her distraction. It was just a second, but I knew what it meant.

"She's on her way," Tam said. I nodded. "I'll take off in a minute so you two can be alone."

"Smart. You leaving the island?"

"You want me to?" she asked. Genuinely. So I grabbed her and squeezed her tight, like I'd never done before. Like she never let me before. Like I should've done from the second I first met her. I wrapped her in my arms and I hugged her like I was the father I always should've been. And I told her.

"I don't want you to take off ever. I want to be the wall the world has to break on before it can touch you, to shield you from any and every thing that could ever hurt you. I want you by my side every second of every minute of your life." And then I let her go. I looked in her eyes and I looked at the scar she chose. And through her tears I saw the strength of her mother.

"But you're a grown woman. You can make your own choices, yeah?"

"I'll stay for a bit, if you don't mind," she told me, wiping the moisture from her face. "Want to make sure you and Fatty over there are properly taken care of. Heroes of the unknown world that you are."

"Ask nice and maybe she'll let you stay in her house," I yelled out to Tamara as she levitated over the water and onto the shore.

"Yes, Just have to dodge the buckshot," Tam thought back to me. It'd been awhile since I'd been in concert with her. There'd never been a need to yell. She always knew what I'm thinking.

Two dolphins escorted Prentis to the side of the ship. Somehow she was barely wet. She didn't ask for help climbing the anchor chain to get on deck, but I still offered my hand. I didn't know how to differentiate who was running her body, so I stayed silent and watched until she spoke.

"Hey, Da," I don't know why I cried but I did. I held her in my arms gently. We both sobbed a little. "Mad at me?"

"What did you do for me to be mad at? You never had a chance, kid. From day one, the bigger and badder than me had their eye on you. Are you mad at me?"

"What for?" she asked but didn't move from our embrace.

"I couldn't keep them off of you. First Nordeen and by extension the Alters. And now the Manna. I told you I'd keep you safe . . ."

"But Tag." She pulled back then. She took a few steps back on the deck to look at me and to show herself off a bit, I think. "Did it to keep you safe. Haven't you put it together yet?"

"Lay it out for me, kid." I wiped my eyes a bit more. The reflection of the half moon off the bay was particularly bright.

"How the Manna works. Choices have to be made. It compensates around that. Choices poor Mico made, choosing to help us, meant he had to die . . ."

"I don't accept that!" I shouted.

"Doesn't matter. That's what the Manna thought. So another choice had to be made. Another Liminal to be selected."

"And if not you, then it would have been Tamara," I said, thinking I understood.

"No, ya daft idjit. You."

"Never! I'd never have . . ."

"We're talking a god in the shape of an infinitely long-lived sentient tuber, Taggert. Wouldn't be so quick to decide what you would and wouldn't have done. Hell, I'll give you the option to make you say yes right now. Become the Vassal for the God of Connections or watch me and Tam die in front of you. Know what you'd choose because that's the choice that was given to me."

"So why didn't it offer me the option?" I said, sitting in my chair and pulling out a large joint.

"Ask it in a second. Want to tell you something first, though." She took my lighter and held it steady for me. I never felt so old in my life. I was shaking. "I knew what it would mean to be a servant of the Manna. I can handle it. Hear me good, Taggert. I can handle everything the Manna throws at me. But can't handle you not in my life. It's killing me, Tag. You and Tamara are my only family. Without you around, I'm in half." She's bawled so hard I wanted to hold her again. But just before I tried, she stopped. And it spoke.

"Taggert," it said with a neutrality Fatima could only point to with her voice.

"Why didn't you give me the offer?" I asked, looking down. I couldn't see Prentis and hear the Manna.

"You would have said yes then spent every imagined moment alone trying to figure out how to resist." I heard it sit in a chair across from me.

"Does she know that you're using her? That you want me to work for you and so you're making her suffer without me?" I asked, fuming.

"I am not that cruel. She suffers because she loves you and is loved by you and you disappeared. I want my vassal to be happy and so I want you two reunited. But you have also earned a reprieve from my work. No Liminal who hasn't taken me into them has done more for my cause than you, Taggert."

"Then give up Prentis!"

"I can't. We have chosen each other. This is the fate that will play out. But there's no need for animosity between us, healer."

"State your terms," I said.

"I will retreat as far as I can in my vassal until such time as she is needed. When I call she must come. But I can leave her to you until then. She deserves as much peace as she can find."

"Does this end?" I asked. "Between you and I? We've crossed time, realities. Every love I've had, every child, every good and bad thing I've done, traces of the Manna have been on it. Do I get to have a life without you?"

It walked to me in Prentis's body at that point. It put its hand on my chin and made me look at her face. The disconnect between its ancient voice and her still baby face almost drove me mad.

"The life you would have without me would shatter you much more than I ever could, young healer. You name me jailer, pimp, prosecutor. When I free, liberate, and defend everything you are and could hope to be. You have earned so much of my respect that I even allow you to suffer because you choose to suffer, even though I know I could heal you of that pain. Even though your pain causes my vassal to suffer, I allow you the gift of choice. I am not your enemy, Taggert. I would think that by now, you would have understood that."

"You will recede from Prentis?"

"When she is with you and when she is not needed. Yes."

Prentis
Grenada

Could tell Tag about Nordeen still being out there. About the new threats coming to Sam, queen of Africa or some such. How there's rumors spreading all around the world about the power of the "Rain-bow Liminals"; the ones from another dimension came to rout the ill and kick ass of any wanker dumb enough to cause mischief. But that'd just raise his temperature. Between me, Tam, Chabi, Wind Boy, the Lucky and some others we've picked up along the way we're fine. Don't need him. Pity the fool that interrupts his naptime. I'm bad, Tag still the baddest road man there is. Bare facts.

About the Author

Ayize Jama-Everett (ayizejamaeverett.com) was born in Harlem, New York. He has traveled extensively in Northern Africa, Northern California, and Oaxaca, Mexico. He holds three Master's degrees (Divinity, Psychology, and Creative Writing), and has worked as a bookseller, professor, and therapist. He has a firm desire to create stories that people want to read. He believes the narratives of our times dictate future realities; he's invested in working subversive notions like family of choice, striving when not chosen to survive, and irrational optimism into his creations. His four-book Liminal series has been published by Small Beer Press. His graphic novel, *The Box of Bones,* with noted artist John Jennings was published by Rosarium Publishing. He has a graphic novel adaptation of *The Count of Monte Cristo* forthcoming from Abrams Press. Shorter works can be found in *The Believer, Los Angeles Review of Books,* and *Racebaitr.*